THE FIRST
TO DIE

The First to Die is a work of fiction. Names, characters, places, and incidents are the product of the author's imagination or are used fictitiously. Any resemblance to actual events, locales, or persons, living or dead, is coincidental.

Willow River Press is an imprint of Between the Lines Publishing. The Willow River Press name and logo are trademarks of Between the Lines Publishing.

Copyright © 2025 by Suzanne Trauth

Cover design by Morgan Bliadd

Between the Lines Publishing and its imprints supports the right to free expression and the value of copyright. The scanning, uploading, and distribution of this book without permission is a theft of the author's intellectual property. If you would like permission to use material from the book (other than for review purposes), please contact info@btwnthelines.com.

Between the Lines Publishing
1769 Lexington Ave N, Ste 286
Roseville MN 55113
btwnthelines.com

First Published: November 2025

ISBN: (Paperback) 978-1-965059-65-4

ISBN: (Ebook) 978-1-965059-66-1

Library of Congress Control Number: 2025944472

No artificial intelligence was used in the creation of this novel.

The publisher is not responsible for websites (or their content) that are not owned by the publisher.

THE FIRST TO DIE

Suzanne Trauth

Also by Suzanne Trauth

What Remains of Love

The Dodie O'Dell Mysteries:

Show Time
Time Out
Running Out of Time
Just in Time
No More Time
Killing Time

*For my mother Martha, who instilled in me a
love of books at a very young age.*

Home is a name, a word, it is a strong one; stronger than magician ever spoke, or spirit ever answered to, in the strongest conjuration.

--Charles Dickens
Martin Chuzzlewit

Chapter 1

Now

"They found Mom. You need to come home."

Her older sister Gaby wasn't one to waste words.

Connie should have been relieved, comforted, something. Unfortunately, it was fifteen years too late for that. And anguish she had buried deep in her body, and mind, erupted with a vengeance.

She cooled her heels in San Diego until the last possible moment to return for the funeral. The less time spent there, the better. New Jersey triggered chilling images tethered to that night. To the last time she saw her mother.

The plane thumped to earth, delivering Connie Tucker to the past with a bounce. Everything about this state was a rude wake-up call. She couldn't wait to board the return flight to California. At fifteen, she left New Jersey in a rage, thrown out of the only home she'd known, dumped thousands of miles away on a relative she'd never met. Nerves twitching, her insides were a stew of anxiety and bitterness, wondering how people here would react to seeing her. Connie shook her head to tamp down the unruly thoughts and scold herself. They were the ones

1

who should be nervous.

Down the parkway in the rental car, exit onto Lenox, right onto Mercer, left onto Third Street. Past Antonio's Pizza where she and Gaby bought slices on their way home from school because who knew what their mother would cook for dinner. Past the playground attached to St. Gabriel's. At the corner of Mercer and Third, a few patrons ambled in and out of a bodega. The street was mostly empty. Her heart bounced in her chest.

42 Third Street. She lowered the car window, her breathing shallow at the sight of the ancient Lincoln in the driveway. The blue paint polished and gleaming. "Buy American" was her father's motto when Connie was a kid. The same automobile she and her best friend Brigid had "borrowed" until Gaby blew the whistle on her. Grounding was followed by exile two months later. She swallowed raging emotions—love, hate, sadness. If Connie closed her eyes, her parents magically materialized on the porch swing, creaking steadily back and forth on warm summer nights. Sometimes Uncle Charlie sat on the steps and the three of them drank beer, Charlie telling stories and her father laughing. But that was before.

Connie stepped out of the car and surveyed the neighborhood. Much had changed and much had remained the same. Down the block, Porter's Bar and Grill still boasted the neon signs out front advertising beer, wine, and food. After his stint on the police force, and her mother's disappearance, her father found employment at the bar—back then a hangout for current and former cops, a nerve center for law enforcement chatter. Old Man Porter was fond of her father, of the whole Tucker family.

Despite the sun shining in a brilliant blue sky, the area was tinged with gray. Sunny in San Diego and sunny in Hallison, New Jersey were two different animals. But even worn out as it was, her Jersey home beckoned, a magnet luring Connie into a tangle of sensations and history. Part of her, she hated to admit, yearned to be here again, but before nostalgia could overwhelm her, she stiffened her resolve: do her duty to her mother and then back to the other coast.

The day was already sweltering, humid air like a wet sheet clinging to Connie, her bangs plastered to her forehead, her shirt dotted with damp patches. Urban smells permeated the neighborhood—exhaust, heat shimmering off the pavement, cooking odors. Third Street radiated a kind of shabby warmth despite reopening sharp wounds. As she climbed the steps to her family's front door, a voice boomed behind her.

"Connie Tucker!"

She whirled to her left. "Rosa!" she sputtered. Rosa Delano. Standing on her front porch. Daughter of the next-door neighbor, Mrs. Delano, whose front yard featured neat flower beds and trimmed bushes. The woman who'd been a kind of second mother after Connie's first one disappeared.

"Yeah, that's me." A cigarette dangled from between bloodless lips, graying hair a tangle of frizz, her expression sullen.

She'd aged. And not well.

Rosa smirked. "Came home 'cause they found your old lady, huh? Si-mone." Hands stuffed in jeans pockets, she extended the second syllable to mock the dead woman. "Bunch a bones by now, I guess."

Connie's stomach lurched, her fingers forming a fist. Attack mode. *Breathe*, she told herself. *Stay in control*. She'd forgotten how mean Rosa could be. In and out of the Delano house when Connie was growing up. Sometimes gone for months, once even for a whole year. Neighborhood gossip churned out tales of Rosa's arrests for petty, and not-so-petty, crimes, their father warning Gaby and Connie to stay clear of her. That was easy to do since she was away for much of their pre-teen years.

"Wonder who buried her? Si-mone."

Connie refused to take the bait. The hell with her. "Tell your mother I'll stop by later."

"Fat chance. You keep away from her." Rosa opened her screen door. "Guess you figured Si-mone was still alive all these years, huh?"

The question split the air like the crack of a whip, jerking Connie's head backwards. "How dare you talk about my—"

Rosa laughed in triumph. "Ha! Listen to you. 'How *dare* you?' Always did act like you were better than everybody else. Always had to have your own way." She slouched into the Delano house and let the screen door slap shut behind her.

Heart hammering, Connie was left to wonder probably for the thousandth time how sweet, generous Mrs. Delano could live with someone as nasty as Rosa. According to Connie's mother, she was already a troublemaker when her parents were killed in a car crash and she was adopted by Mrs. Delano at thirteen. Connie was only two or three when Rosa rolled in next door like a storm front that never budged. Now, twenty-seven years later, her words hung around Connie in the ether, burning through a tangle of jumbled ideas and leaving the charred truth—Connie *had* figured her mother was alive somewhere.

Needing a minute, she stepped back from the front door and confronted the Tucker residence, which exhibited contrasts identical to most of the other homes on the street: window frames in need of scraping and painting, and her mother's favorite old-fashioned glider— and slightly rusty matching metal chairs—crowding the porch, hinting at benign neglect. Yet, two flower baskets hung from hooks on the porch pillars with cascading red, yellow, and blue blooms. Someone tended to those plants. Gaby, no doubt.

Connie steeled herself, donning emotional armor. Knocking brought no response, neither did pressing the bell, broken years ago and apparently never repaired. She'd kept a key to the house—from spite—and jiggled the lock a fraction, the way she'd done as a teenager breaking the curfew her father had tried to establish.

The door swung open.

With the windows shut tight, primal odors hung in the air like church incense. Lingering smells of baking, fresh laundry, furniture polish. Connie pulled a carry-on suitcase into the house. "I'm here." Where were her sister and father? The car was in the driveway. She'd texted her arrival time and expected someone to be in the house to meet her. Instead, she was greeted by silence. Perfect.

A chair in the hallway held a stack of mail. Circumventing the living room to her right, Connie moved straight ahead to the kitchen. A used coffee mug and bowl sat in the sink. Otherwise, the room was orderly, a table in the breakfast nook had placemats, *The Star-Ledger*, and a vase of flowers. The sweet scents of lilacs and roses filled the air.

Back to the hallway she stopped in the arched entrance to the living room. Taking it all in. A new couch and the worn leather of the old recliner, her father's favorite piece of furniture, and a flat screen television. The coffee table was the same. Also, the rug she and Gaby had danced on with their mother to ABBA all those afternoons. *Their beautiful French mother.*

A rush of memories confronting her on all sides, blocking progress, keeping her captive, nowhere to go but back into that night.

Chapter 2

Then

Thirteen and fourteen, Connie and Gaby sprawled on the sofa, the television blaring a syndicated quiz show, their mother running down the stairs, her heels clicking on the wooden floor, her favorite maroon and gold scarf wound fashionably around her neck above a black sweater. Her blond hair in waves, 1940s style. On her way to rehearse Stella in *A Streetcar Named Desire*, her first major role in New Jersey theatre.

She adjusted an earring. "Dinner is in a pot on the stove. Do your homework. In bed by ten." She kissed each of them on the top of their heads. "You are growing girls and need your sleep." She lifted Connie's chin, gazing into adoring eyes. "Someday we will share the stage, *ma chérie!*"

Connie bounded off the sofa, grabbing her mother's hand. "You promised I could see a dress rehearsal."

"You went last week," Gaby said. "Mom has to go sometimes without you." She brushed her brown curls off her face, inched her glasses up her nose, and raised the volume on the remote.

"You're jealous." Connie stuck out her tongue.

Simone raised a hand to stop her daughters. "Not tonight. It will be too crazy."

"Then when?" Connie protested. "The show opens in three days. I have to go or I'll just die!" And she might. "What if something happens and this is the last chance to see you on stage?"

"Like what?" Gaby asked. "You're so dramatic. Stop whining. You sound like a baby." She tossed a pillow at Connie.

"Shut up!" She threw the pillow back.

Their mother glanced at her watch, fidgeted with her car keys. "You might be in the way. I need some peace and quiet before the rehearsal starts."

"Mom." Connie grasped her mother's hand.

"I'm going to be late."

She played with the gold band on her mother's finger. Mom seemed nervous.

"Why should you get to go?" Gaby pouted, though she had never expressed any desire to tag along to the theatre. No interest in it.

Connie ignored her, flashing her hard-to-resist smile, dimples and all. "Please?" Her voice sliding up the scale. She'd been wrapping her mother around her little finger since she was a toddler. Sometimes with laughter, sometimes with tears, always cute.

Their mother sighed, touched her blond waves, and surrendered. "Bring your homework for the *entr'acte*."

Connie snatched her backpack off the floor where she'd thrown it. The *entr'acte*. She loved how her mother sprinkled French words into ordinary conversations.

"Tell your father Connie is with me," their mother flung over her shoulder to Gaby as she swung a blue tote bag onto her arm.

Gaby shook her head, frowning at her younger sister's triumphant grin. "It was your turn to do dishes."

Connie laughed as she followed her mother to the door, thrilled as always to be with the sophisticated woman who reminded her of a model on television or a movie star like Marilyn Monroe in her mother's old movie magazines. She slammed the door behind them and hurried into the chilly September evening for the drive to the Flint Theatre in Colmar.

Climbing into the front of her mother's used, red Ford Tempo, sliding gingerly onto the vinyl seat with a repair patch of gaffer's tape covering a rip in the plastic. Her mother deserved a new car. This one was embarrassing. Connie inhaled the smell of gasoline, ever-present because the fuel pump leaked on and off, that clashed with her mother's perfume. Coco Chanel. Her father was a whiz under a car's hood—he kept his Lincoln in excellent condition. Inside and out. He should fix the fuel pump.

Rain began to splatter the windshield, intermittent drops at first, then a downpour attacking the glass, the worn-out wiper blades struggling to keep pace with the water.

"I'm hungry."

"Didn't you get a snack after school? I left Mrs. Delano's oatmeal raisin cookies and apples on the counter."

"I need, like, real food. There's a McDonald's." Connie pointed to the golden arches up ahead.

"We don't have time. You can get a sandwich at the café."

Next door to the theatre. Connie hunkered down in her seat. Pouting. McDonald's was a drive thru. How long could it take? Simone tapped a staccato beat on the steering wheel as she drove. Connie stole a glance sideways. She couldn't bear it if Mom was upset with her.

Fifteen minutes later they parked in the lot adjacent to the Flint Theatre and huddled under an umbrella as they rushed through the lobby and onto the stage.

The stage manager tapped her watch. "Your call was ten minutes ago." She eyed Connie and scowled. "Stay in the house during the run, please."

"Sorry." Simone darted into the women's dressing room.

Connie turned to follow her and bumped into BJ, the lighting technician, in his work uniform: overalls, work shirt, and a red baseball cap. He was cute—his chin had a dimple like hers—and smelled good. Old Spice, one of the actors said. How did he keep himself so clean working in the scene shop?

"Hey short stuff. Hanging out tonight?" He ruffled her hair.

During the past year, BJ had allowed her to scramble around the stage while he taught her about Fresnels and ellipsoidals, when and how to use top hats and barn doors on lighting instruments. They had bonded over Connie's desire to learn anything and everything about theatre and BJ's willingness to guide her education.

But tonight, she only had eyes for her mother. "Uh-huh. See you later."

Connie perched on a folding chair in the women's dressing room to observe actors applying makeup. Inhaling the smell of greasepaint. When the cast was given the fifteen-minutes-til-curtain call, her mother patted her cheek and smiled. "Sit in the house out of the way. Yes?"

"Yep."

A knock on the dressing room door, then it opened a crack.

"Everybody decent?" BJ asked.

"Enter at your own risk," someone said and the female cast members laughed and continued to chatter and finish dressing.

BJ walked in, winked at Connie, and met her mother's eyes in the mirror as he changed a light bulb. "That'll do it." He removed his cap, swiped at his forehead with a white handkerchief, and leaned down to speak to her mother so softly Connie couldn't hear what was said. But her mother frowned, turned away, brushing him off. BJ slapped his cap back on his head, mouth shut tightly, and strode out of the dressing room.

"Mom?" Connie asked.

"Stay away from him tonight," her mother said, her expression unusually stern.

"Okay."

In the backstage rush to start the rehearsal, Connie ignored the stage manager's instruction to sit in the house and managed to slip behind the set and into the wings on stage right. Actors made entrances here, but it wasn't as busy as stage left. The theatre was full of nooks and crannies—a Grandma Tucker saying—and last week she'd discovered a cubbyhole formed by two black velvet curtain legs that blocked the audience's view of off-stage activity. If she rubbed her cheek against the scruff of one curtain, she placed herself in a perfect location to see actors onstage through a slight opening where the legs met. The action was more exciting from her hiding place. This close to the stage, Connie could see sweat and damp faces. When Stanley yelled "Stella" to her mother, spit flew out of his mouth.

It was wonderful seeing her mother as Stella, sexy and beautiful, strolling onto the set. Pride rippled through Connie's body. She closed her eyes. This was where she wanted to be, next to her mother on the stage, surrounded by the musty odor of old curtains and the sharp tang of fresh paint. Forget studying during the *entr'acte*.

At the act break Connie ran to the dressing room while the women in the cast changed into second act costumes, dabbing at foundations, reapplying lipstick, chattering.

"Did you see the leak? They gotta get the roof repaired."

"I dunno, but I heard thunder. Some storm."

"Where's the breakaway bottle?"

"I left it on the prop table."

"Can I borrow your powder?"

"Will somebody tell BJ we need a light bulb in here? Another one blew."

Her mother watched Connie in the mirror, a gentle smile on her lips, until the stage manager stuck her head in the dressing room and called places for act two. Then her mother pointed at an unopened book on the counter. "Don't forget homework."

The second act started late because a door onstage was stuck, and the director yelled at the crew. Connie crept back to her cubbyhole by the curtains.

Dress rehearsal had reached the midpoint of act two when suddenly the theatre went dark. The director yelled again, demanding to know what was going on. Connie halted, alarmed in the pitch black.

"Power outage!" BJ bellowed from somewhere nearby.

Chaos.

"Actors stay on stage," shouted the stage manager.

"Connie? Stay in the house," her mother called out.

But Connie was scared in the dark and not where her mother thought she would be. *Go back to the dressing room,* she told herself. Her mother would go there, despite the stage manager's instruction, once she realized Connie was not out front. She slipped between the curtains, bumping into a prop table and offstage scenery, pressing against the wall of concrete blocks. *Breathe and count to ten,* like she did when Gaby made her so angry she'd almost pop.

"Hey kid! Where you going?" The prop master, a chubby guy with a clipboard and a head-set, waved his flashlight back and forth onto Connie, the prop table, the wall, and the curtains. "You're not supposed to be back here. You're supposed to be in the house."

Connie swallowed hard, her eyes wide. "I'm looking for my—"

"Sit." He pointed to a pile of coiled cables in the corner. "Stay here until we get the lights on." His tone softened. "Don't want you to get hurt in this craziness."

She collapsed onto the heap of rubber loops. How long would it be until the lights came back on? Her mother had no idea she was backstage, and unless the prop guy ran into her, she would worry. Tears sprang to Connie's eyes. She couldn't make her mother worry. Impatient and determined, she waited a few minutes, then rose, careful to stay against the back wall again. Best to avoid anyone else wanting to be helpful by forcing her to remain where she was.

She reached the hallway that led backstage. Connie knew from previous exploration that there were two extra doors back here—one that opened into a utility closet and the other a storage space.

A voice barreled down the hallway. "BJ? Where are you? Get the emergency generator going. Forget about the rain. Just do it."

Hide! Connie turned the handle of the utility closet and slipped inside. The dark in here even blacker than the dark backstage. Within seconds, drops of sweat were rolling down her face. In the airless space, her lungs filled with dust and the odors of cleaning supplies. Stifling a sneeze, she sneaked out of the closet and crossed the hall to the dressing room. Her mother had to be there by now. A trace of pale light leaked from beneath the door while voices rose and fell, one her mother's, the other deeper. Like a man's.

"Simone...why not? We can—" Pleading.

"No!" Her mother, resisting. "I never...I told you...Let go. Leave me alone!"

The dressing room door banged open—

Chapter 3

Now

Connie jumped at the knock on the front door. Neither Gaby nor her father would need to knock. She yanked it open to a whoosh of fresh air.

"Hey," a woman murmured.

Connie blinked, gawking. "Brigid." Fifteen years older than the last time they met on the porch, Brigid Maloney had to be at least seven months pregnant, a purple spandex top stretched to the point of transparency over her bulging belly. Her brown hair pulled into a ponytail atop her head, she had tiny aging lines around her mouth, a few sprinkled across her forehead. Life had taken a toll on her one-time best friend and high school partner in crime.

Brigid stared at Connie, then raised her arms, hesitated, then wrapped her friend in a bear hug and the two rocked back and forth, Brigid's body warm. A familiar dance to Connie, though her gut clenched.

Connie pulled away after what felt like an awkwardly long time and stepped aside to widen the entrance. "Come in," she said. "How did you—?"

Brigid jerked her thumb over one shoulder. "Mom lives down the street."

"How is she?"

"Fine. She saw you and called me." Making no move to enter the house, Brigid pressed a hand into the small of her back and leaned to one side. "Something about your mom, huh?"

"Yeah."

"After all these years. What's going to happen now?"

Connie rubbed her thumb against the peeling paint of the doorjamb. "Not sure. I haven't talked to Gaby yet. Or Dad."

Brigid twisted her torso and squinted into the sun. "The neighborhood's been buzzing ever since they found her. You know Hallison."

"I can imagine." Connie stepped out onto the porch and closed the screen door behind her. Not sure where to go with this conversation, she dropped into the metal glider and patted the seat beside her.

"Been a long time. Some changes around here." Brigid eased into the seat and rubbed her abdomen.

"I see. Congratulations."

"Uh-huh. Number four."

"You've been busy." Her banter felt forced with Brigid, her first Hallison contact. Besides Rosa. Her neighbor's sardonic laugh still rang in her ears.

"Nine, seven, three, and now this little monster." Brigid peered at Connie and swept moisture off her forehead. "You look fantastic. Must be California livin'."

"Thanks." Blond hair courtesy of genes and sunny days and a blue silk blouse that had placed her credit card on a precipice last month. Connie smoothed the top over her midsection, then crossed her arms.

"I never heard from you." That was Brigid: get right down to it. Her sharp eyes had softened.

She was hurt. Connie would have been, if the tables had been turned. Her rage at being sent away resulted in no desire to communicate with anyone in New Jersey, including Brigid.

"How come you never came home? Except for that one visit?"

The shit show Christmas. Connie shrugged. "Hallison didn't feel like home. I was pretty pissed off, but Dad insisted I visit that first year."

More than pretty pissed off. Slamming things, accusations, tears—lots of tears, from both Connie and Gaby and, Connie was certain at one point, even filling her father's eyes. Regret and guilt, on all sides. "It was hard. I couldn't talk to anyone. Even Gaby."

"We had a nice time, though, yeah?" Connie heard hope in her friend's voice.

She smiled. "Sure did. Playing Monopoly with your sister. It was the high point of the holiday for me. That and Christmas Eve, when Uncle Charlie and his wife came by with presents. Things were always better when he was around." Charlie gave her a chance to breathe, to let down her defenses for a bit. "Otherwise, everything else was really tense. Kind of unbearable."

"I remember Charlie. Your dad's partner, when they were both cops."

She nodded. "Like they were married, they'd say. Until Dad resigned."

"After your mom disappeared."

Connie nodded again. Then they rocked on the glider for a while, until Brigid looked at her out of the corner of her eye. "I never really understood why he sent you away to live with your aunt."

"'Living with your Aunt Marie is best for you now,' he said."

Brigid shifted in her seat. "How is she?"

"She's been ill. Cancer."

"Sorry."

"Anyway, she said she couldn't handle coming back for the funeral after all these years." Connie stared into Third Street, the neighbor across the way—unfamiliar to her—sweeping off the porch, watering her lawn. Common household chores. The kind she and Gaby were charged with when they were kids. Fighting over who had to sweep and who got to water until one parent or the other warned them that they could find them additional work if necessary.

Brigid massaged her back, then reverted to Connie's sassy high school friend. "I'd like to get me some of that West Coast sparkle you got going."

Connie smiled. "Would you like something to drink? Not sure what Gaby has in the fridge, but—"

Brigid wagged her arm. "Nah. I'm on my way to Porter's for lunch." She grimaced. "I get an hour off for good behavior. Then I gotta pick up the baby at Mom's." Turning serious, she rested a hand on Connie's arm. "Come with, why don't you? We could…catch up."

Connie wrestled with the decision. Gaby and Dad weren't home, and she had no idea when they would be. She'd text her sister. Lunch with an old friend was more appealing than hanging around an empty house. "In a few minutes. I'll meet you there."

"Sure." Brigid's touch on Connie's arm seared a hole in her protective shell. "You always figured your mom would come home."

"Yeah. Just not in a box."

Her friend nodded as though she wanted to say more but couldn't find the words, then waddled off—there was no other word for her gait. How their lives had diverged. Connie speculated on the babies' papa…

She found her father's stash of liquor, same kitchen cupboard as in the old days, and swallowed a shot of whiskey, the alcohol burning her throat. Taking the edge off. No way could she waltz into her past without backup. She texted Gaby to say she was having lunch with Brigid, reapplied lipstick, ran a brush through her hair, and counted to ten.

Three minutes down Ferry Street to Porter's Bar and Grill, which had always been a safe, stable haven in an ever-changing world. At least that's how Connie imagined its regulars felt. In a parallel universe she'd be sitting on a stool in there, swapping yarns of her job or kids or husband. Instead, fate in the form of her father had whisked her away to a life in California—so different from Hallison. And here she was, dipping her toes back into her past, living, for the moment, in that parallel universe.

Front entrance open, sounds of clinking and chatting and merriment meeting her on the sidewalk before she crossed the threshold and the day transitioned from bright sunlight to a dark, cooler interior. Pausing inside the door to get her bearings, she slammed into her childhood history. It was all there; nothing had changed. Scarred, mutilated wooden tables along one wall. The long antique bar on the opposite. Straight ahead a direct path to the kitchen and restrooms. And that smell—stale beer mixed with a tinge of cooking grease and sweat. A comfortable aroma. Like home.

For lunchtime, Porter's was busy, almost every stool at the bar occupied, patrons tilting into each other or working their way through their lunches or waiting to place their orders. Behind her sunglasses, Connie scanned the room to see if she recognized anyone, if anyone seemed to recognize her. Brigid waved manically from the last table in the back. Connie glanced at the bartender and did a double-take. Roddick McBride. Dack. The kid she'd had a crush on freshman year, the guy who'd showed off on the ten-foot diving board at the local swimming pool, and by sophomore year, the boy who kissed her in the front seat of his dad's pickup truck. Rubbing her breasts. Her nipples swelling inside her padded bra. They swore they'd meet up again when Connie was eighteen. But by that time, she'd surrendered to life in California. Texts and emails dwindled to nothing. Each moved on.

Without table service at this time of day—that hadn't changed—Connie elbowed her way to the bar to order a drink. No sooner had she put an arm on its glossy surface than Old Man Porter—that's all anyone ever called him, Connie had no idea what his first name was—planted his slim, bony frame in front of her. Her eyes filled. She loved the old guy.

"The other Tucker girl, by God!" He reached for her, landing a kiss somewhere between her mouth and her ear, and motioned to a customer to shove his stool over to make room. Now they were face-to-face, noses nearly touching. "Good to see you, toots. Figured you'd be back in town. How 'ya doing? California treating you okay?"

"Fine. Hard to take it all in….Mom…"

Porter pressed his lips together, brushed a hand across his cheek, the creases around his eyes crinkling. "If there's anything you or your dad or Gaby need, you come to me." He chucked Connie under the chin. Like when she was a kid, when he allowed her and Gaby to sit at the bar and drink free Cokes. He was Old Man Porter back then, too.

"Thanks. I appreciate that."

Porter dismissed her gratitude with a flap of his hand. "You're like family."

According to her sister, when their father resigned from the Newark police force after their mother disappeared, he spiraled down into a black hole of depression before he landed on various jobs as a night watchman and security guard and bartender. Gaby claimed Porter's saved him, offered her father a place to reclaim his dignity. At the time, Connie couldn't have cared less about his dignity. It was her mother she desperately needed. She figured Old Man Porter knew what he was doing by hiring her father. "Dad still work here?"

"He's taking a few days off. Go sit with Brigid. We'll bring your drink over. What'll you have?"

Connie, tempted to order a beer to chase the shot of whiskey, settled on a seltzer instead and spotted Dack smiling at her. Still hot, if a little heavy. His face fuller, with a neatly clipped beard and a small gold earring in his lobe. Hairline receding a bit.

At her approach, Brigid nudged a chair away from the table with her foot. "Take a load off. Did you say hi to Dack?"

"Didn't have a chance to talk. He's pretty busy."

Brigid rubbed her belly. "Busy, all right. He needs a hobby."

Connie laughed, "Uh-huh," then noticed Brigid's sly expression, her meaning landing with a thud. "So Dack...?"

"Yep. My baby daddy."

Connie's shock tickled her friend. "You didn't think he was gonna wait until you came home, did you?" The old, mocking Brigid.

"Course not," Connie stuttered. The oldest child was nine. They didn't waste much time after graduating high school. "I'm happy for you. Really. Happy."

"Hey."

Connie whipped her head around and met Dack's deep brown eyes. "Hi!"

He planted her seltzer on the table. "Welcome back. Sorry about the reason." He gave her a brief, clumsy hug. She accepted it.

"Thanks. Well...congratulations. You have quite the family."

He slipped a casual arm around Brigid and plopped onto a chair. "They're killing me. Costing me a fortune," he complained with a proud smile. "How's the old neighborhood looking?"

"Pretty much the same. Lots of memories."

"Swiping beer from your dad's stash in the fridge," Brigid said.

Connie burst out laughing. "After he told me to keep my hands off it. Right." The taste so bitter she gagged but drank the beer anyway.

"The night we climbed out your bedroom window onto the roof—"

"It's a wonder we didn't kill ourselves."

"Where was I?" Dack asked.

Brigid grinned. "Probably cruising chicks downtown."

"In that old pickup," Connie said. Dack's embarrassed grin told her he also hadn't forgotten those nights in the front seat. Reminiscing released pent-up tension. She settled into the curved back of the bentwood chair.

"Anyway," Brigid said, "we had to get to my house 'cause I had a curfew." She glared at Connie.

"I had a curfew too."

"As if you paid any attention to it. We ate at McDonald's to sober up with money you lifted from your dad's dresser—"

"Borrowed," Connie said, defensive. There was no way she would let her father be the victim.

"Yeah right. It wasn't the first time. Boy, were you good with lies. That story you made up about missing my curfew because we had to stop and help some lady who'd been mugged." She shook her head. "Mom bought it hook, line, and sinker."

Dack laughed. "You two were juvie ds. It's a wonder you didn't end up in jail."

Connie froze, her smile a thin line. She *had* been sent to jail, after a fashion. Exiled to California. The shoplifting from the bodega was her father's last straw.

As if Brigid read Connie's mind, she coughed, then sucked the rest of her soda at the bottom of the glass. "So. Tell us about San Diego. Didn't hear much from you after that Christmas."

Connie shredded the napkin under her drink into damp strips. "What's to tell? Sunny days, palm trees, sandy beaches all year round. Laid back life."

"Uh-huh. Are you doing theatre? You loved being on stage in high school."

"Not really." Connie couldn't expect anyone to understand. How her mother's disappearance at the theatre destroyed her dream of performing. The one thing that had been Connie's passion. It had been her mom's passion too.

"If we ever get to California," Brigid said, "I'd like to see that sidewalk where the stars put their hands and feet into cement. And that huge Hollywood sign."

"Los Angeles."

Dack flipped a towel over his shoulder. "I'd settle for Malibu."

"Yeah right," Brigid said. "We ever get out there, you're taking the kids to Disneyland while I soak up the sun." She grinned, then turned back to Connie. "So, what are you doing in San Diego? Got a guy on a string?"

"No guy." Connie finished her seltzer. "I tend bar at a beach joint."

Brigid's features formed a question mark. "You go to college? You were near the top of our class even though you skipped school and never studied. I figured you had a photographic memory. Like you could open a book, glance at a page, and memorize it."

Connie shrugged. "I lasted two years at San Diego State. Didn't do it for me."

"You've been bartending for, what, how long?"

"Almost ten years."

Brigid's eyes narrowed, absorbing the fact that Connie had spent a third of her life doling out drinks at a bar. "I don't get it. Why—"

Dack cut her off. "You miss all this?"

"Some of the people." She gestured to her friends, then frowned. "What?"

"I bumped into Rosa Delano. It was not pretty."

Brigid chewed on an ice cube, shaking her head. "She's a nasty piece of work."

"She wasn't around that much when we were in high school. Am I right?"

"She was around enough to get us in trouble. Calling up our mothers…ratting us out. Well, my mother," Brigid hastily corrected. "The rest of the time she spent in jail."

"Jail? Really?"

"She's a regular there."

"You mean still?"

Dack's head bobbed. "Out on bail for a drug charge."

Connie sat forward in her chair. *What a nightmare life.* Then she remembered their scene moments ago and her sympathy evaporated. "She said some mean things about my mother."

Dack leaned across the table. "Everybody in the neighborhood always saw how much Rosa hated your mother."

"What in the hell was that all about? She was a pain in the ass the whole time Gaby and I were growing up." Connie locked her arms over her chest, scowling. "I hope the police questioned her."

Dack and Brigid shared a quick, too-soon-for-this-conversation glance and shrugged.

"Here we are." The Old Man swept in and set two plates on the table before the women. "Took the liberty of choosing your lunch. First time back at Porter's." Burgers topped with cheddar cheese, tomatoes, bacon, and onions with a side order of crispy, shoestring fries. Heaven.

Brigid dumped ketchup on her French fries, then took a big bite of her sandwich. "I'm eating for two."

Connie smiled at Porter. "God, I miss these. Haven't had anything to compare to a Porter's burger in years. Probably since I left home."

Meat juice ran down Brigid's chin and she swiped at it with a paper napkin. "Get used to this, kiddo. Basic staple of the Hallison, New Jersey diet, remember?"

"I do."

Old Man Porter frankly stared at Connie as she poured ketchup on her burger. His gaze bored through her. He shook his head, his aged rheumy eyes misting over. "Can't get over it. How much you look like Simone. Only a few years older than you are now when she…"

Laughter and bar babble reverberated off the walls, surrounding the bubble of silence at the table, Porter's unfinished comment hanging in the air. The lump in Connie's throat stopped her cold—she couldn't take a bite of food. Instead, she set the ketchup bottle on the table and grabbed Porter's hand. He turned hers over and took it in both of his.

"You see your dad yet?" he asked, his calloused palms a life saver.

"Not yet. Nobody's home."

He sighed. "At the funeral parlor. Charlie was taking them."

Old Man Porter had thrust the reality of Connie's presence in New Jersey front and center—she wasn't here on a lark to revisit school days. She was here to see her mother's remains interred in the ground.

A "bunch of bones," Rosa had said.

A sob caught in Connie's throat. She hadn't cried after receiving Gaby's message; in fact, she hadn't cried much after her mother disappeared. She'd refused to be comforted.

She pushed the plate of food away, grabbed her bag, and rose. "I have to go." She delivered a quick hug to Brigid, Rosa's words ringing in her ears: *Guess you figured she was still alive all these years.*

Chapter 4

Now

"Can't get over how much you remind me of your mother." Connie's father slumped against the back of the glider next to her, looking away, twisting his wedding band, running a hand through thinning, curly gray hair. His dress shirt frayed around the collar; cuffs turned back from his wrists. Pale, sagging features that sported days of stubble hard to read. He'd lost weight over the years. Liam Tucker—the Little Irishman, as he was known—was even littler. Appearing older than his fifty-something years. Underneath the deterioration, though, there were telltale signs of the handsome rogue he used to be, notably his piercing blue eyes, the same eyes Connie had inherited. "Thanks for coming home."

"She was my mother. Of course I'd come home," Connie whispered, the old hostility rising up like bile. Staring straight ahead as though fascinated by the kids playing hopscotch in the afternoon heat. The atmosphere heavy.

"How's your aunt?"

"Up and down. Another round of chemo." Connie kept her head averted.

"I guess traveling's hard for her now. She sent me an email." His hand inched across the metal seat toward his daughter's, revealing a heart tattoo with her parents' initials on his lower arm. "Connie…"

Traveling. Fifteen years ago. Her father was standing outside the TSA security line at Newark airport. Hands jammed in his pockets, eyes red-rimmed. "You'll understand this someday" is what he said. Connie heard "You're not wanted." Even now, sitting next to him, she wondered why. *Forget it.* This visit wasn't a father/daughter catch-up, either.

She moved her hand, avoiding his eyes. "Where's Gaby?"

"Work. The library."

One of her sister's birthday cards—Gaby hadn't missed a single one; Connie stopped sending them after she left her aunt's house—mentioned she'd gotten a job at a library after college. Six, seven years ago? "In Newark?"

"No. Here. Hallison."

Connie broke eye contact with a robin that had perched on the porch railing. "She works down the street? In the neighborhood?" It was an accusation.

He fidgeted, one knee springing up and down. "She wanted to stay close to home."

The words seared Connie's brain like a branding iron. "*I* wasn't given the choice to stay close to home."

The air between them, already chilly, now turned to ice. Her father stumbled: "Hallison offered her…a better opportunity." He massaged knuckles on his right hand. "We should talk about…I'm sorry. I can't change the past."

She swallowed, her mouth dry. His apology too little, too late. "It's over. I've moved on." Brigid was right. She *was* a good liar.

Her father sighed from deep in his belly, closing his eyes and resting his head on the back of the glider. "I held out hope all these years. As long as your mother's body never turned up."

She had no stomach for her father's litany of laments. "I'm going to unpack." She stood and took hold of the screen door handle, her pulse quickening at the essential question. "Where did they find her? Gaby never said."

He hesitated. "A construction site on the outskirts of Colmar. A new development being built."

"Colmar? Right next door to Hallison, for God's sake? All this time she was lying in the ground a few miles from here." Not out of state, or in another country, as swirling rumors suggested in the weeks after her disappearance.

"Yes."

Connie turned to her father, counting to herself. Like she did whenever some emotion risked swamping her sanity. She made it to six. "How did they identify her?"

Her father coughed, the words unspooling slowly. "Her wedding ring. The date. Our initials."

Connie braced herself, heart thrumming, breath on hold. "How did she die?"

He shifted in his seat and met Connie's eyes, his lips quivering as if to force the statement out of his body. "Fractured skull. Then strangled...with her own scarf."

Connie sagged against the door frame, his words knocking her backward. The scarf her mother had worn that night to the dress rehearsal. Maroon and gold. Some kind of sound escaped her because her father jumped up, grasping her shoulders to prevent her from sliding to the ground. She shook him off and ran into the house.

Upstairs in the hallway, Connie leaned into the railing, forcing air in and out of her lungs. *Oh Mom.* She closed her eyes. Beaten. Strangled. These next days would be sheer hell. She ducked into Gaby's room, at the front right of the upstairs. Same bureau, desk, and chair, the paint now sunshine yellow, a change from the mousy beige that Connie recalled.

To distract herself, she focused on the bureau covered with family photos—she and Gaby sitting in the wading pool in the backyard; she and Gaby in coats and hats and gloves, building a snowman; the family of four posed on the front steps of St. Gabriel's. Easter. Connie picked up the photo and brought it close to her face. The sisters possibly five and six, her father chipper in a new suit, and…her mother. Connie's eyes filled for the second time that day. She hadn't prepared herself for this—seeing her mother as a young, happy woman. Shoulder length, wavy blond hair, full, curving lips, eyes bright and alive. Stunning. Only a crazed animal could hurt such a beautiful being.

Chapter 5

Then

Connie adored her mother, imitating her hair style, borrowing fancy silk scarves that came from France to play dress up. On days when the sisters squabbled, Gaby called Connie a copycat.

Her mother would whirl around the living room, spinning and swaying to her favorite music. Eyes closed, blond hair flying, the rhythms of ABBA sweeping her girls into their mother's orbit. The lyrics of "Dancing Queen" reverberating off the walls of the Hallison house. The faded furnishings came alive whenever her mother cranked the music up as loud as she could. Connie's father was at work, or he would have lowered the volume, and the neighbors were accustomed to Simone's late afternoon post-school ritual with her daughters.

If Connie happened to glance out their living room window, she'd often see Mrs. Delano looking out hers, smiling across at the family dancing, happy. Unless Rosa came barging into the house—then she'd frown, close the window, and draw the curtains.

Connie could have twirled with her mother all night, her body thumping to the beat of the music, her bare feet slapping the braided gray and beige area rug.

On one afternoon Connie liked to replay, Gaby had spun away from them and plopped onto the sofa, legs tucked under her, arms crossed, expression blank. "When are we eating?"

Connie could have cared less about dinner. She and her mother were "two peas in a pod," Mrs. Delano said. Always dancing. And laughing. Connie sucked in air, breathing rapidly to keep up with her mother.

"Someday, we will travel, *mes petites—*"

"To the South of France!" Connie leapt into these daydreaming sessions, planning a future where she and her idolized mother jetted off to another world. Away from their mundane New Jersey neighborhood. Even as a grade-schooler she dreamed of the day she could travel to her mom's birthplace.

At last, the two of them collapsed, out of breath, eyes shining, onto the sofa next to Gaby who scooted over to make room. Their mother flicked off the cassette tape recorder on the old wooden coffee table.

"Now, *mes chéries*, let's tell a story about two beautiful girls and their silly mama." She put an arm around each daughter, pulling them tightly to her. French words and the smell of perspiration mingled with notes of jasmine, patchouli, and orange blossom in the perfume wafting off her warm body. She kissed the tops of her daughters' heads. "Who wants to start?"

Connie loved this storytelling time. Spinning creative plots, inventing fantasies, her mom urging them to fill in the gaps. The action growing ever more bizarre. Like trips to the moon, or entering a time machine, or becoming characters in a Harry Potter universe.

"I'm hungry," Gaby complained, resisting the make-believe. "What's for dinner?"

There were no aromas drifting out of the kitchen. Her mother wasn't generally interested in cooking. Probably she would open a can of something like Chef Boyardee or stick frozen TV dinners into the microwave. Her father complained that he could eat better in the bus station, and her mother said, "Well, then go ahead and eat there." Connie had giggled at the vision of her cop father eating his dinner sitting on a bench in the Newark bus terminal.

Who cared about dinner when they could fly off to the South of France?

Gaby gave in, as they all knew she would.

"I'll go first," Connie said.

"What else is new?" Gaby sighed while their mother laughed.

It was true: She always did go first. But Gaby and her mother always ended up following her lead. That afternoon, she was already halfway there.

Those were happier times.

Chapter 6

Now

Connie slammed the door on any more memories and escaped into the hallway. She covered the short distance to her old bedroom to find the bed and desk and nightstand shoved to one wall and boxes stacked against another. Dusty.

Her room on hold. Waiting for something to happen. Like everything else in her life.

The sight of the four bare walls prompted a wave of despair, followed by irritation. No one had prepared for her homecoming. She'd left in a rush fifteen years ago, leaving behind books and clothes and high school stuff. Mementoes of a previous time. All stashed within those boxes, she imagined.

Connie rolled her luggage into a corner of the room that would be her home for the next few days. A hotel would have been a better option. Of course, a hotel costs money and her credit card was already on life support—

"I intended to clean up in here. I thought you were coming in tonight."

Gaby stood in the doorway. Connie hadn't heard her creep up the stairs and down the hall.

"Took a red-eye. Cheaper."

She stared at her older sister and found her, like everything in New Jersey, the same and not the same. Same brown curly hair, blue eyes, square chin, glasses. But her pale complexion and visible frown lines made her look older than her thirty-one years.

"Let me—" Gaby darted into the room and shoved a box into the corner opposite Connie's bag.

"Leave it. I can move things myself."

Gaby rubbed her hands on her denim skirt and regarded the single bed as though surprised to find it there. "Sheets are in—"

"I remember where the linen closet is." Connie's voice tight, her body aching from shouldering the past and the present sorrow, never mind the overnight flight and jet lag.

She and her sister had been joined at the hip—Irish twins, Gaby only ten months older than her—until Connie turned fourteen, when their paths diverged due to her partying, her scrapes with the law, and her visits to the principal's office. Distraught over their mother's disappearance, her father was AWOL. No one in the house to control her. So, when Connie started acting out, according to the therapist, Gaby withdrew and drifted off to a safe place: the library. That therapist would never know how much Connie loved and missed her sister.

But when she was hauled into the Hallison police station for shoplifting, it was the beginning of the end. Her cop father couldn't handle his daughter's juvenile delinquency, and encouraged by the therapist, school administrators, and most of his relatives, he sent her to live with her aunt.

Gaby fiddled with a key ring. "I'm glad you're home."

Despite Gaby's quick, self-conscious hug, and despite inhaling her sister's clean, lavender scent, Connie's hackles rose, her face hot. "She was my mother, too. I wouldn't miss…this."

"I wasn't suggesting you would." Her sister swept a strand of hair off her forehead. "There'll be a service at St. Gabriel's, and a gravesite ceremony and then a repast."

"Where?"

"Oak Park. Most of Dad's family are buried there."

"I meant the repast. Where are people gathering afterwards?"

Gaby blinked, then produced a full smile. "Where else? Porter's."

If Connie hadn't been so exhausted or so wary of dropping her defenses, she would have smiled too. Where else, indeed.

Gaby's expression changed, her mouth turned downward. "Charlie offered to pay for the funeral. Dad said no, he had it covered."

Connie wondered about this. Uncle Charlie was so close to her parents that his offer made sense. Charlie O'Shaughnessy, the Big Irishman, they called him, as opposed to their father. Charlie, like a big, light-on-his-feet bear, riding with their father when they were Newark policemen.

"Then he offered to host the repast. Some upscale, fancy restaurant. Dad said no again. Firm. Any celebration of Mom's life had to be in the place both he and she loved."

Questionable whether the neighborhood bar was her mother's favorite watering hole, but whatever.

"The Old Man plans to close the grill to the public for the afternoon."

"Nice of him."

The funeral mass at St. Gabriel's was crowded with Tucker relatives who were scattered around the state, friends and neighbors from the old days in Newark and Hallison, Gaby's co-workers from the library, folks from Porter's, Brigid and her family, Mrs. Delano with Rosa, a perpetual smirk plastered on her face. Who were those people in the back? Why were they ogling her? Creepy. Of course, the whole thing felt creepy. Connie wouldn't be surprised if total strangers sat in the church, people curious about the case of the woman who'd disappeared fifteen years ago.

She stared straight ahead at the altar backed by a rose window, bits of red and blue stained glass lit by pale light and flanked by statues of St. Joseph and the archangel Gabriel. Patron saint of messengers, according to the nuns who'd taught her in grade school. Could there be a message for her in all of this today? For Gaby? For their father?

Father Pete—a "cool guy," as per Brigid—celebrated the service and did an admirable job of eulogizing her mother, though he didn't know her. Gaby asked Connie if she wanted to speak. No way. It was too much. For Gaby too.

Outside the church, and at the gravesite of the Tucker family, where Connie's grandmother, great aunts, and uncles were buried, the overcast day matched the mood of the occasion, a gunmetal gray sky threatening a cloudburst at any moment. Distant thunder rumbled.

The three of them stood opposite the casket, on the spot where a headstone with "Simone Tucker" engraved on its marble surface would eventually be placed. After prayers and the placement of roses on her mother's coffin, Connie trailed her father and sister to the waiting limousine.

"She can rest now," said her father.

Gaby hooked her arm in his and turned her head to check on Connie. Found her staring at an elderly, heavyset man with a full head of white hair and warm, dark eyes that disappeared in his puffy cheeks when he smiled at her. Earlier she'd spotted him wheezing his way up the graded lawn to the burial site, leaning against a tree in the background.

"Who is he?" Connie tilted her head in the man's direction.

Her father paused, half in the limo, to follow his daughter's line of sight. "Detective Nardone. You don't remember him? He was the lead investigator on the case. Retired now."

The "case" being her mother's disappearance.

"He's a good guy," her father said. "Did everything he could, left no stone unturned. I had no beef with his investigation."

Says one cop about another.

"I guess the missing person's case is closed," Connie said.

"Yeah." Liam climbed onto the back seat of the limo, followed by Gaby.

Connie gazed at the old detective moving slowly to his car up the road. "So who's investigating the murder case?"

Chapter 7

Now

It was a relief to enter the brightly lit interior of Porter's Bar and Grill. Uncle Charlie had compromised with her father: the repast at Porter's, the food and drinks on him. The buffet was catered, a little upmarket for the bar, but the assembly appreciated the various hors d'oeuvres, salads, finger sandwiches, and pastries. They dug in.

Connie studied the spread, debating between a cucumber and dill sandwich or a cheddar and tomato chutney, when a booming laugh exploded behind her.

"Well, well!" Uncle Charlie had her in his arms, a crushing embrace. "My prodigal goddaughter returns." Holding her out at arms' length, shaking his head. Connie knew what he was thinking. The likeness to her mother was uncanny.

Only Charlie could laugh at Connie's fifteen-year ejection from the Tucker family and call her the prodigal daughter. She laughed too. Only for him. They always got along much better than Charlie and Gaby. Her sister resisted his bonhomie.

Charlie was around the Tucker family a lot when they were kids. Cop partners from the Newark police department coming to the house in Hallison after work. Those were fun nights because Charlie often bought dinner, better than any meal her parents wrangled, and brought surprise gifts for her and Gaby. Candy, toys, even a bicycle once that their father refused to accept. "Too much," he'd said. Charlie had laughed and winked at Connie as if to say, "I'll get around your father." He always did. Like a second father to Connie. Hence, the Uncle Charlie.

By the muscular, strapping looks of him, her actual father hadn't fared as well as his old partner.

"Good to see you, Uncle Charlie." Though about the same age as her dad, he could have passed for ten years younger. Wearing a crisp, pale blue dress shirt, his brown hair combed back sleekly from his forehead, Charlie's skin was a deep tan. A Rolex dangled from his wrist. The sly grin and penetrating eyes were exactly as Connie remembered. No longer a plumpish bear. "What have you been doing all these years?"

Charlie smirked as if mocking himself, hands in his pants pockets, jiggling coins. "Security for a New York City banking conglomerate."

"Wow. Nice." It no doubt paid more than walking a beat on the mean streets of New Jersey.

Charlie surveyed the crowd. "Couldn't convince your old man to hold this in Uptown."

"Colmar?"

"I live there now, in Jackie's family home. Her parents have passed, so we inherited it last year."

He'd married into his wife's fortune. Connie followed Charlie's gaze. At the far end of the bar, two tables had been joined to accommodate a group. His wife Jackie was seated at one end surrounded by a group of women—a few neighbors, Brigid's mother, and Mrs. Delano.

Thankfully out-on-bail Rosa had left half an hour ago after downing several drinks, a large plate of food, and injecting some poison into Connie's ear as she exited. "Guess now you'll never find out what happened to your mother," she'd stage-whispered, then cackled and planted her hands on her skinny hips. "You'll leave *my* mother alone if you know what's good for you. She's done with you Tuckers." Then Rosa had marched out of Porter's, leaving Connie open-mouthed in shock and rage.

If they weren't at her mother's repast, Connie would've gone after her.

Right. And done...what? She'd never even slapped anybody. Rosa had been fighting all her life.

Again, pitying thoughts of Mrs. Delano rose up in her.

"I heard you'd come home," the sweet woman had said to Connie last night across the fence separating the two backyards. The facial lines were deeper, the hair white, overall a little more frail. Yet the same kind eyes and warm smile that had prompted a catch in Connie's throat.

Before Connie could even reply, headlights from a vehicle had sliced down Third Street and swung into the Delano driveway. Rosa's SUV. The older woman froze, then blurted out, "I'm glad you're here," and hurried inside.

Connie put thoughts of the Delano house behind her. Surely her own family had enough troubles on a day like this. Shifting her attention back to Charlie and his wife's table across the bar, her gaze stopped on one arresting figure. "That elderly woman," she said to Charlie. "Is that...?"

"Yeah. My mother. Deirdre." Charlie sighed and rolled his eyes. "She lives with us now."

Deirdre O'Shaughnessy, the matriarch of Charlie's family. Imperious, haughty, overbearing. Connie had only one memory of the woman. Gaby's seventh birthday party. Connie's mother had decorated the house with streamers, invited the neighborhood, and spent a ton of money, blowing the Tucker weekly budget on party prizes, sandwiches, sodas, and a beautiful cake. Everybody sang "Happy Birthday" and Gaby stood close to the cake to blow out the candles. Except that some kid bumped her, she tipped sideways, and, in an effort to avoid falling, reached out for something to grasp and accidentally found the cake. It was a total mess. Icing everywhere. Gaby cried, the kids went wild, her mom tried to clean up, the neighbors sympathized. Only Deirdre lit into Gaby. How could she be so careless? After all the trouble her mother went to. Blah, blah, blah. Gaby cried harder.

First Rosa. Now Deirdre. More hard feelings to tamp down. *Great to be home.*

Connie scanned the bar. "We came here when Gaby and I were little kids. If Mom wasn't around, Dad would plop us on barstools and hold court with his cop buddies."

"Mm, long time ago." Charlie waved to a man at the bar and patted Connie's hand. "Talk to you later."

Brigid appeared at Connie's side and handed her a glass of white wine. "Think you could use this."

"Thanks."

"It was a nice service."

"Yeah. Sad." Connie took a gulp of her wine, tart and chilled, and glanced at the table where Mrs. Delano sat. A tall, thin man, the sleeves of his white shirt rolled to his elbows, his tie loosened, a flop of hair over his forehead, bent down to distribute several small plates with cannoli, sfogliatelle, and miniature fruit pastries to the women. Connie gazed harder at the group. "Is that guy...?"

"Yep. Finn."

"He was in the..."

"Seminary when we were in high school."

"He's a priest now?"

"Nope. He's been out five years. Went back to school. Lives in Clifton." Brigid groaned. "We have a therapist in the family."

"I saw him talking to Father Pete earlier."

"They're buds from seminary days." Brigid smiled. "Actually, it's nice to have a big brother around."

"He never snitched on us."

As if he overheard the two of them sharing notes, Finn straightened and walked over.

"Hi. I hear you're a therapist now." Connie smiled.

"I am. If there's anything I can do…if you need to talk…" He nudged a shock of light brown hair off his forehead.

Connie nodded and he smiled back. "Be good, little sister," he said to Brigid and walked to the bar.

Brigid sighed and looked around. "Big turnout. Lots of people loved your mom."

"Someone didn't," Connie murmured.

An hour later, half-filled glasses and half-empty plates littered the table where Mrs. Delano, Brigid's mother, Charlie's wife Jackie, and a few others sat. A spirited discussion was underway about a family who lived in Newark, then moved out of state and finally moved back, the whys and wherefores debated by the group of women, all former neighbors in Newark.

Connie sat down next to Jackie who drank a martini, pretending to listen to the conversation about people she didn't know, while checking her phone and searching the packed grill, no doubt for Charlie. She reeked of sophistication—jet black hair pulled into a severe bun, bright red lips, gold dangling earrings with matching necklace. And a diamond ring that covered a substantial portion of one finger. Connie remembered her from the theatre, always striking, sometimes with Charlie in tow.

Jackie turned to her and Connie felt herself blush. She'd been staring at her.

"I met your mother a few times at the Flint Theatre," Jackie said, her voice warm and engaging. "She was a beautiful person, a gifted actor."

Connie thanked her, grateful someone had mentioned her mother's acting talent. It hadn't mattered all that much to her sister, but to Connie, her mom's life in the theatre had stoked her own ambition. Never mind that she wanted no part of that life anymore.

The ladies at the table moved on from talk of old neighbors to memories of her mother. Mrs. Delano took the empty chair next to Connie and put an arm around her. "Your mother would be so happy you're here. It's wonderful to see you."

She leaned into the warmth of the older woman's side. Comforting.

Mrs. Delano squeezed her arm. "If you remember a person, they're not really gone from you."

Someone across the table raised her glass. "To Simone."

"To Simone," the rest echoed.

Deirdre guzzled a glass of Irish whiskey and squinted at Connie. "So like your mother," she said, slurring her words a bit, touching her gray, perfectly coiffed hair, fingering a strand of pearls. No evidence of her humble Newark past.

Jackie put a hand on Deirdre's arm, her smile tight. "Why don't you slow down?"

Charlie's mother took no notice and fixated on Connie. "Anybody ever tell you that?"

"That I resemble Mom? All the time. From when I was little." Relatives, strangers on the street, everyone commented on it. *So like Simone.*

"She was so pretty," Deirdre said. "They were always together. Charlie and Liam and Simone. I called them the Three Musketeers." A few chuckles followed her pronouncement.

Charlie, phone in hand, approached the table and stood beside his wife. "Where've you been?" Jackie muttered. He dismissed the question and finished off his drink.

"They grew up together on the streets," Deirdre said. "Didn't you Charlie? Getting into trouble six ways to Sunday. You and Liam."

"Mom," he said with a boatload of patience, "We weren't that bad."

"What about the nights you came home with bloody lips? Huh?" She nodded, victorious. "Bloody knuckles, bloody everything. Who got those stains out? And that time you saved Liam's caboose in that alleyway? You said those boys had it coming, so you gave it to 'em." Her Irish brogue thickening.

"It was nothing. A neighborhood skirmish. Some guy jumped your father," he said to Connie.

No surprise there. Charlie had his partner's back even as a teenager.

Gaby approached the group, and Mrs. Delano scooted her chair closer to Connie to make room for her.

"The police academy. Now *that* was a story." Deirdre picked up her whiskey. "Nearly got thrown out, the two of them."

"Now Mom, we didn't do—"

"There was that fight with another cadet you said Liam started."

"Dad started a fight?" Gaby pressed her.

"They used to fight all the time," Deirdre proclaimed and nodded her head, vehement.

"Our neighborhood was pretty rough and tumble. Old news." Charlie stuffed his cell in a coat pocket. "We need to head out. I have an early day tomorrow."

"The three of them...they had secrets. Mark my word." Deirdre grinned, cunning.

Jackie plucked Deirdre's jacket off the back of her chair, helping her mother-in-law to her feet. A tinkling at the bar halted their progress. Old Man Porter tapped a glass in one hand, then draped the other around Liam's shoulder. "Let's raise a cup to Simone." He surveyed the silent room, then his gaze settled on Connie. "A loving wife, mother, friend." Choked up, Porter lifted his glass, and the crowd followed suit.

"To Simone!"

Connie's father, tears streaming down his cheeks, raised his glass. The toast was greeted with a gentle echo, the bar respectful as though eavesdropping on a private moment. Somewhere in the back, a tenor voice began to sing "When Irish Eyes Are Smiling." Despite her mother being French, the Tuckers were one-hundred percent Irish as far as his family and friends were concerned. Others joined in the singing, the swelling tune building to a soft crescendo as the final notes faded...*sure they steal your heart away*. Gaby crying outright, her father wiping his face, Connie dipping her head to avoid the eyes of the room. Someone blew his nose, then a quietness settled over the gathering.

Until a crash of broken glass. "Oh, shit!" Deirdre's drink had slipped from her hands. The remainder of the whiskey in her glass formed a thin layer on the table and left spots on Deirdre's pale pink blouse.

As if her cursing had broken a spell, folks laughed, uneasy. Jackie mortified, Charlie exasperated.

"That's it," Charlie said. "Let's go, Mom. Jackie?"

Deirdre tilted sideways, yanking her purse off the back of the chair. She waved goodbye to the table, defying her daughter-in-law's best efforts to keep her moving, while she played the role of the Queen Mother. When she homed in on Connie, she blinked, thrust her head forward and repeated, "Exactly like Simone." She fumbled with her hands, fingers groping in the air as she formed some shape. They walked her out the door.

The bar settled down, the hum of voices softening, as more folks took their leave. "Charlie has his hands full with Deirdre," said Brigid's mother. She mimicked tipping a glass to her mouth.

Brigid put an arm around Connie. "Mom, are you gossiping again?"

"Simply repeating what I heard."

"Where? The Ladies Sodality? The beauty parlor?" Brigid shook her head. "I have to get going. Hope the babysitter's still alive."

Connie kissed her friend's cheek. "I'll call you."

Soon, it was Mrs. Delano and the Tucker sisters left at the table. Mrs. Delano pulled them each into her. "Your mother made me promise if anything ever happened to her that I'd take care of you two."

Connie eyed Gaby over their neighbor's head. This was a new one for her, Gaby too, by her expression.

"I tried for a while. Your father did the best he could. And the two of you. Such beautiful, lovely women. Your mother would be proud." Mrs. Delano hugged them.

Never mind that one of the "beautiful, lovely women" was sent away to finish her growing up across the country.

"We want to extend our condolences."

Connie and her sister glanced up.

The group from the back of the church. Up close, she recognized some of them—folks who'd worked with her mother at the Flint Theatre in Colmar. Older, some bodies reshaped: The paunchy, mid-fifties bald guy was her mother's director on *Streetcar*. The classy actress who played Blanche to Simone's Stella, in a chic, black ensemble, dark hair hanging loose to her shoulders. They had tolerated the pre-teen Connie hanging around backstage and in the dressing room, watching rehearsals from the house. One called her a mascot, another their lucky charm. Now, all of them appeared uncomfortable, as though they were responsible for her mother's death because she disappeared from their theatre. "We're so sorry," the director said.

Gaby found her voice first. "Thank you for coming. Mom loved working at the theatre. It was like her second home."

Connie had a flash of her sister throwing a fit as mother and daughter took off for the Flint that last night.

"Connie, right?" the actress said. "You look—"

"Yes. Thanks," Connie said, pleased but weary of the comparison.

In the tense silence, the director coughed. "Our sympathies," he said as they moved off.

The storm clouds had shifted to the east, replaced with a weak, white-yellow early evening glow. Old Man Porter deposited glasses in soapy water.

"Let me help you load the dishwasher," Connie said.

The Old Man shook his head, sorrowful. "I like to do 'em myself. Keeps me busy. Your mom was like a daughter to me."

A lovely notion. "Some story about Charlie saving Dad's 'caboose,' according to Charlie's mother. That was one I'd never heard as a kid."

"The way your dad told me, they were young, teenagers, street punks. Running around Newark, getting into trouble." Porter placed rinsed glasses on a drain board, then wiped his hands on a bar towel. "And it was your dad saved Charlie's ass." The Old Man smiled sheepishly at his language. "Sorry."

"No problem." Connie tried to visualize her father and Uncle Charlie as violent teenagers.

"Good man, your old dad. Tough. He'll get through it. 'Ya know, he was a hero back in the day." Porter shared a story about her father as a young cop, risking his life by saving a kid in a burning building. "Earned a medal for it."

Wait, what? "That's another story I've never heard."

"Bet there's a lotta things about your dad you never heard." The Old Man smiled and chucked Connie under the chin.

Maybe. "If you're sure you don't need my help with the dishes?"

Porter waved her away and she glanced around the bar at the few stragglers left. Standing up front was the detective she'd seen earlier at the gravesite, not realizing he'd been at Porter's all afternoon, hidden in the crowd. He was shoving his arms into a suit jacket when Connie approached him.

"Detective Nardone."

He looked up, nodded. "Louis." He tugged the coat around his expansive middle. "My sympathies." He gasped a little on the last words.

"You investigated my mother's disappearance."

"Yes."

"This is a little bit of closure for you."

"For you too, I imagine."

"Not as much as you might think. For years I figured she might...she would..." Words stuck in Connie's throat.

"Come back? It's a normal response when someone goes missing. Your mind doesn't want to let go. And if the person is never found, well, hope—"

"Springs eternal."

"Yes." Smile lines appeared on his cheeks, then he said, almost as an apology, "You must hear this a lot, but—"

"I do. Hear it."

"You're about the same age…"

"As my mother was when she disappeared." Connie closed her eyes and inhaled, allowing the thought to surface, then move into sound, vocalized. "Although I should say murdered, now, right? No one's even hinted at the crime all day."

Detective Nardone coughed, wiped his mouth with a white linen handkerchief. "I won't say something glib to make you feel better. So, yes…murder."

Connie exhaled sharply. "Finally, someone is acknowledging it. What happens next?"

Nardone cocked his head, appraising her. "What do you mean?"

"Who investigates her murder? Will you do it?"

He stared down the bar at Connie's father in conversation with Old Man Porter. "I'm retired now. Anyway, I'm moving out west soon. The cold case unit will take over."

Connie had watched enough Netflix to recognize that task force. "On TV the detectives are always successful. What about in real life? What are the odds someone will actually be arrested for my mother's death?"

Nardone shook his head. "I can't say at this point." He turned to the door.

"I've read funerals are great locations to pick up clues on murder cases," Connie persisted. "Did you see anyone here who struck you as suspicious?"

The brash question stopped him. "I understand your impatience—"

"Why is everyone so indifferent? Lots of sympathy for her death. But what about how that death happened?"

Louis Nardone raised a hand as if to settle her. "It'll all be investigated. Again. I'm sorry we never found the perpetrator." He paused. "If we'd only had a witness from that night."

"What?"

"At the theatre that night. If we'd only had a witness. She was onstage, that we know, and then she disappeared. Of course, with the power failure there was a lot of confusion."

Connie froze, a wave of nausea roiling the pit of her stomach.

"Anybody could have slipped in or out of the theatre without being noticed," he went on. "If we'd had more information, we might have been able to identify suspects. Everyone in the theatre that night was connected to her somehow. We questioned all of them but…" He spread his hands as though helpless. "Your mother's case was the single biggest regret of my law enforcement career." He patted Connie's arm. "I'm not sure what the future holds with an investigation, but my advice? Get on with your life. Your mother wouldn't have wanted any of you"—he looked at her father and Gaby, who were making their way toward them and to the door—"to let her death run your lives."

Behind a neutral mask, she seethed. Hands balled into fists. "How do any of us know what my mother would have wanted?"

Detective Nardone regarded Connie for a brief moment. "You take care." He turned for the door.

At her elbow, Gaby said, "Ready?"

Chapter 8

Now

Connie lay on the twin bed in a tee shirt, the window open, the filmy curtains flat against the sill, no air stirring in the late summer sultry night. Acclimated to the weather paradise of San Diego, she found the temperature and humidity overpowering. The Tucker house had room air conditioners in her father's and Gaby's bedrooms; no point installing one in Connie's old room.

Outside brakes screeched, a man swore loudly, someone yelled back. In the distance a siren blared, grew stronger, then faded. A dog howled.

So many nights Connie had lain here listening to neighborhood noises outside—and, during that last year, to the family arguments inside. The sporadic clashes between her parents were spirited, usually short, and ended with banging doors. After her mother disappeared, the battles were one-sided, her father battling with himself. Neither she nor Gaby got in his way, steering clear of him and his moods. Connie ran wild during those days. Underage drinking, driving without a license—who had a license at fourteen?—shoplifting, rage crashing through her system like waves pounding the coast. Uncontrollable, unvoiced.

Detective Nardone's words at the repast played on a never-ending loop. "If we'd had more information we might have been able to identify suspects."

Unwilling to go there, she drove her attention back to the conversation with Dack and Brigid in Porter's—the neighborhood's knowing how much Rosa had hated Connie's mother. Could Rosa have been involved? But she had no reason to be at the theatre. Unless she met her mother somewhere else that night. That seemed unlikely. Still, the police should have followed up. Maybe her father knew something about Rosa, one way or the other. He was so hesitant to mention her mother's murder. It was almost like he was hiding something, like he had more knowledge about the night she died but was keeping it to himself.

Sound sleep was a distant goal.

The next morning, Connie drove the manicured toe of her flip flop into the floorboards of the front porch, sending the creaking glider back and forth, the air close and stifling. Lingering jet lag, coupled with last night's uneasy sleep, left her cranky, unwilling to engage with her father and sister at the uncomfortable breakfast table. She'd brought her mug of coffee outside.

"If we'd had more information we might have been able to identify suspects," Nardone had said.

Connie pushed the detective's excuse out of her head. She'd long ago steeled herself to close the door of that night in the theatre. What sense was there in reopening it now? She couldn't go back and unsee what she'd seen, ignore what she'd heard, reveal the promise she'd made to her mother that night. She'd been loyal, kept her secret. Revealing that promise would make no difference at this point, anyway.

Exhausted but tense, stir-crazy, she had to get out of New Jersey, return to her life in San Diego. Bartending at The Shack, balmy days, pretend-carefree nights. Mindless. Limbo.

"Hey." Gaby positioned herself inside the screen door. "Dad wants to talk with us."

Connie placed her feet flat on the ground, halting the glider. She could refuse to have a conversation with him. He couldn't coerce her into—

"In the kitchen." Gaby withdrew into the house.

A line of lightning zigzagged across the sky to the east. Connie cringed. Though she wouldn't admit to her fear, ever since the night her mother disappeared, she dreaded horrific rainstorms and everything they brought with them. Wind. Thunder. Lightning. Darkness. One of the many saving graces of San Diego—fewer extreme weather events. With a single clap of thunder, sheets of rain burst from clouds that had been gathering all morning, lifting the humidity momentarily. Typical New Jersey. It would be back later, leaving the atmosphere heavier and stickier than before.

With a sigh, Connie pushed herself to her feet and trailed Gaby to the kitchen table where her father sat, his hands lost among papers and small bags on its top. He glanced up and nodded to the chairs in front of them. "Please." He withdrew his hands from the pile before him, gingerly, as though a sudden move could damage the documents, resting one palm on top of the heart tattoo on his left arm.

He sniffed, then wiped his eyes, brushed a hand over his unshaven face. "Things of your mother's. She put this all together the week she…"

A formal-looking sheaf lay among the papers. "Is that her will?" Connie asked.

He unfolded the papers, scanned the sheets. "She left her share of the estate to me."

She couldn't believe her mother had much to leave them. She'd probably saved little from her part-time job as a receptionist in a pediatrician's office. Something her parents quarreled about over the years—her mother's money habits. Her father called her a spendthrift. She called him a tightwad.

Common in marriages, leaving the estate to the surviving spouse. Such as it was.

"You girls…" Her father winced, gathered the packages into a mound in front of him and lifted first one, weighed it, passed it to Gaby, then lifted another, repeated the ritual for Connie.

Gaby studied her name written on the manila envelope in her mother's neat hand. "What are these?"

He shrugged. "She sealed them up, didn't want anyone to see them until she passed. I couldn't…before. But now…"

Now it was safe to distribute their mother's bequest.

"Go ahead," he said. "Open up."

Connie let Gaby go first. Her sister slipped a thumbnail under the envelope's flap and pulled out a small jewelry box. She flipped open the lid. A pair of their mother's favorite earrings: tiny emeralds, her birthstone, embedded in gold, heart-shaped settings. "Mom." The word wobbled, vulnerable. Gaby shook her head, as though she couldn't accept such a valuable gift.

Too late. The giver was in no position to honor a giveback.

Connie opened her package. A similar little box but with a ring, a plain, thin, gold band with another chip of an emerald. She smiled to herself, sad as Gaby. The ring had memories attached to it. Playing dress-up, her mother letting her wear it for a short time before she tucked it safely away. Connie slipped it on her finger. A perfect fit. Gaby inserted the earrings' posts into her ears.

"There's a few other things," their father said.

He handed them each another package—poetry for Gaby, a play script for Connie, both with their mother's personal notations—and an envelope with photos.

Gaby said ruefully, "I look like the Tucker cousins. Brown curly hair and glasses."

"You do," Connie agreed.

"And we know who *you* look like, don't we?" Gaby asked, only half-joking.

Connie gathered the jewelry, the script, and her photos. She needed air, to take a break from this post-death activity and confirm her flight for tomorrow.

"Wait a minute. There's something else." Their father rubbed the edges of a last packet. "She told me the day before…that she had something else for you two, but that I wasn't to open them. Not that I would. Why would I? I didn't open anything else," he grumbled. "Said it was stuff from France. To give them to you after…her show closed."

Gaby's remembrance was a yellowed, lacy, hand-embroidered handkerchief wrapped in tissue paper with a note saying it had belonged to their mother's grandmother. Gaby lifted it to her nose and inhaled. "Lavender."

Connie eagerly opened her last gift. Two sheets of paper. No relic from the past. She unfolded the first to confront foreign words.

"What is it?" Gaby asked.

"Frère Jacques." The French lullaby their mother sang to them when they were little. "And something else. A story?"

She extended the second piece of paper to Gaby, who glanced at it and shrugged. Touching her handkerchief with reverence, no doubt glad she'd gotten a piece of their mother's history instead of a French story.

"You should get it translated," Gaby said.

"I will." Connie refolded both papers, placing them in the envelope. Her mother's handwriting was the most precious gift. But something bothered her, niggling at the back of her mind. The timing of the treasures. "You said she put these away for us the week before she disappeared? Even the day before?"

Their father sighed. "Yeah."

"Isn't that strange?"

"What?" he said.

Gaby poured herself a cup of coffee, holding the pot out to Connie.

"No thanks. I mean, it's like…she knew something. That she wouldn't be here to give them to us."

"It is strange," Gaby said slowly.

The kitchen fell silent except for her sister sipping coffee and her father drumming his fingers on the table. It was a habit Connie remembered from childhood whenever he was anxious, frustrated—or, according to her mother, hiding something.

"Dad?" Connie pressed.

"What?" He stared out the window into the backyard at the old elm tree that had supported a rickety treehouse years ago.

"Was there something about her disappearance that we never learned?"

"What are you talking about?"

"It feels funny to me. Like a loose end. Detective Nardone said she'll be a cold case. Will you get involved?"

"Involved?" His voice shrill. "I was involved enough when she disappeared. Day and night. I resigned from all that. I don't want any part of it."

The words exploded out of Connie: "You don't want to find out who murdered Mom?"

Chapter 9

Now

Murdered. The word they'd been avoiding. Gaby coughed, swallowing a mouthful of coffee.

Their father shoved his chair away from the table and crossed to the kitchen counter. "It's in the past. I don't want any part of it," he repeated, stomping out of the room, calling over his shoulder. "Going to Porter's."

"It's a little early for that!" Gaby yelled after him as she emptied her mug in the sink. "At least change out of that ratty tee shirt."

The screen door slammed shut and Gaby followed Connie back to the porch.

"How could he not want to know about Mom's death?" Connie snapped, dropping onto the glider, exhaling her anger. "What's wrong with him? Bad enough he discarded me. Is he doing it to her, too?"

The rain had stopped as abruptly as it began. Blanketed by midday humidity, the air was cleaner, an earthy smell of new cut grass replacing leftover factory fumes and car exhaust. Thick and moist. Comforting.

"You had more trouble than I did with Mom's disappearance." Gaby plucked dead blooms off the flowers in the hanging pots.

"Meaning?" A note of belligerence crept into Connie's voice.

"Somehow it was harder on you. I was destroyed, yeah, but you...couldn't get over it. It was like she abandoned you."

Connie twisted in her seat to glare at her. "I was supposed to forget my mother was no longer here and 'get over it'?"

"You know what I mean."

"No, I don't. Tell me," the child in her ready for a fight.

"The acting out. Getting in trouble—"

"That again. Yeah, I got picked up for shoplifting, but I was a kid and—"

"The nightmares."

Connie shivered from a chill though the day was in the mid-eighties. "What nightmares?" she murmured.

Gaby turned to face her sister. "The ones that woke you and me and Dad up every night. You screaming. Walking in your sleep sometimes. Sorry Connie, but by day you were unpredictable, out of control. At night you were a holy terror. Dad had no choice after…"

"After what? The solution was to dump me in California. No offense to Aunt Marie, but she wasn't exactly warm and fuzzy. She didn't want me there any more than I wanted to be there."

"He couldn't control you. You stopped seeing the therapist who said a change in location might be the only thing to save you."

"Save me from what?" The blood rushing to her ears so loud Gaby's voice seemed far away.

Her sister hesitated, crossing her arms. "From yourself."

Connie stiffened, closed her eyes trying to avoid the memory. She'd buried the episode deep within, even deeper than that last night at the theatre. The bottle of pills, her mother's headache medication, left in the medicine cabinet. An overnight stay in the hospital. Smells. Disinfectant. Shoes squeaking on tile. Somber voices. And then, a few weeks later, the trip out west. She thrust out her chin to fight her stinging eyes, the looming tears.

"I'm sorry," Gaby said, "but I have to get to work. I took this morning off—"

Connie rose. "I'll change my flight. See if there is one tonight."

"You don't need to do that. Please. I want you here. Dad does too." She reached for her sister, who backed away.

"It's better for everybody if I go." Connie forced a thin smile. "I think Dad has secrets. Something about Mom."

"Secrets? Seriously? Who doesn't?"

Even her. Especially her. Connie headed for the house, her back to Gaby.

"Connie, wait."

"What?" She turned to her sister.

"Brigid told me at the repast you stopped acting in California. Why? You loved it. Being on a stage. You were a star freshman year."

Again, that question. How to explain to someone else what she couldn't understand herself? Connie had tried to regain her theatrical footing but when her mother was no longer around to encourage her, to paint a picture of them sharing a stage in the future, acting felt empty, hollow. She lost her grounding. "I grew up."

"I don't think you did. I think you're still the child whose mother deserted her, whose father punished her by sending her away."

Connie opened her mouth, about to let loose a tirade.

Gaby held up a hand to cut her off. "You *do* need to grow up."

Connie said her tough goodbyes later that night, throat constricted. Her father and a tearful Gaby assuming that was the last they'd see of her for years. Stung by Gaby's earlier comments about growing up, she flopped on the bed on top of a pile of dirty clothes. Fighting the urge to pack. Needing to feel Hallison one last time. The humid air on her skin, the leftover smells of the day—damp earth and car emissions—wafting in the window. The curtains still, the night quiet for once. It was two a.m. Her flight left in less than eight hours. She had a life to return to, even if it was only bartending at The Shack.

And yet she was unsettled, her heart heavy, mulling over the last forty-eight hours. Despair at the memory of seeing her mother's casket displayed in the cemetery mingled with confusion. Her mother was murdered, and her father appeared disinterested in learning who was responsible. The retired detective had apparently done all he could during the investigation and in any case was no longer involved, moving out of state soon. A cold case squad would take over, but her former cop father wasn't curious about the initiation of that investigation. He was so vague about the whole business. Like something was going on.

Connie rolled over onto her stomach, heedless of the clothing underneath her. She hadn't had a restful eight hours of sleep since Gaby's phone call plucking her from California to New Jersey. Her eyes came to rest upon her inheritance from her mother, photos and an envelope on the nightstand, the ring on her finger. She retrieved the treasures and propped herself up against pillows. Setting aside the family pictures, she picked up the papers written in French. The lyrics to "Frère Jacques" were understandable. In fact, she had learned them by heart. But the other sheet was a mystery.

Connie searched on her phone for a way to decipher the message. Google Translate. She slowly typed in the foreign words and their English counterparts appeared.

I want to tell you a story. Once upon a time there was a silly mama and her two beautiful girls and they danced, happy. But their mama wasn't happy, not really. And if she had to go away someday, she wanted her girls to know how much she loved them and would always miss them.

Connie's hands shook. What was her mother trying to tell her? She was going away? The final sentence: *Don't forget me and maybe someday we will share the stage.* It was signed "Mama" with a row of Xs and Os.

She had burned with excitement at the prospect of fulfilling their joint fantasy. Then her mother disappeared. Not only had they never shared the stage, they'd never shared anything. Ever again.

She read and reread the message, her clammy hands leaving damp patches on the paper. It was a dispatch from the grave. Connie wrestled with her next decision. To tuck the paper in her bag, get on that plane in a few hours, and pick up where she'd left off in San Diego. Or...

Adrenaline kicked in, her pulse racing. Connie paced in the small bedroom, weighing what she was willing to do. If she stayed and pursued answers to questions, sought to understand why her mother left such a cryptic communication, she'd have to return to that night at the theatre, to open the door she'd kept closed for more than fifteen years. To confront the promise she'd made to her mother.

Detective Nardone's words challenged her: "If we'd only had a witness."

Chapter 10

Then

In the theatre's dark hallway, Connie pressed against the rough brick of the wall. She held her breath, drawn to the dressing room by voices that rose and fell, one her mother's, the other deeper. A man. Pleading.

"...Simone...why not? We can..."

"No!" Her mother resisting. "I never...I told you...Let go. Leave me alone!"

A thump against the dressing room door as it flew open and her mother stumbled out. Costume askew, hair messy. Sweat shining on her face in the dim light spilling from the dressing room. She collided with Connie, each shocked to see the other. She pushed her daughter deeper into the shadows a few feet away, blocking Connie as a figure followed her mother into the hallway.

BJ, brandishing a flashlight, watching the two of them huddled together. Then his hand was on her mother's arm. "You can't run from me."

"Get away from us!" Her mother cried, hugging Connie, wrenching them away from his touch.

BJ's face twisted in a grimace and pointed his flashlight at Connie. "Short stuff. Too bad you had to see this. Your mother—"

"Shut up BJ! You don't know what you're talking about," her mother whispered, frantic.

"I know enough." He grasped her mother again and forced her to face him. "You love *me*. Not—"

"No! Stop or I'll tell Ted your little secret!" Suddenly her mother stopped struggling, her features harsh, frightening. "You'll be out of the Flint Theatre. You'll never work in a theatre again," she growled.

Connie had never seen her mother's beautiful face so hard.

He rocked backwards as if struck. "You wouldn't, because I saw what *you* did."

Connie pulled at the strap of his overalls, crying. Distraught. "Let her go!" Why would her friend do this to her mother?

"BJ! Where the hell have you been?" The director shouted from the end of the hallway.

All three of them froze.

"What's with the backup generator?"

"I'll find you," BJ said to her mother, his voice hoarse and low, sounding desperate. "Remember. I know what I saw."

He shuffled off. Her mother pulled Connie into her arms, her body heaving, gasping for breath. "Forget all this. Please. For me. Promise," she pleaded.

Connie, scared, buried her wet cheeks in her mother's chest, leaving a damp spot on her dress. "Why was BJ so angry? What did he see?"

"Sh, baby," her mother murmured soothing sounds.

Emergency lights sputtered on, then off, then on again. Watery and dim.

"It's nothing. Promise me?"

"What secret? He said you loved him. What did he mean?"

"Nothing. He's...confused."

"Are you okay?"

"Of course, *ma chérie*. Your mama almost made a terrible mistake is all. Now promise me. Never tell anyone what you saw tonight."

"I promise." Connie cried, sniffling, fat tears rolling down her cheeks.

"Never." Her mother hugged her so fiercely Connie could barely breathe. She kissed Connie's cheek and smiled. At least her mouth smiled. Her eyes told a different story.

Chapter 11

Now

Tears blurred her vision. She *had* been a witness in the backstage hallway the night of the storm. The fight with BJ had been so traumatic for her mother that she made Connie promise to forget what she'd seen and heard. For fifteen years Connie had forgotten. Had kept her promise, even though she didn't understand the meaning of what was said between BJ and her mother.

But now she had to make a decision. Time was running out if she was going to stay. Louis Nardone was leaving town shortly and she had to begin with him. Begin *what?* Exotic beach drinks were in her wheelhouse. A murder investigation when no one else in her orbit seemed as disturbed as she was? Alien territory.

Connie twisted her mother's gold band that she'd placed on her finger earlier that night. With a deep breath, she tapped numbers on her cell phone and waited. Then, "I need to change my reservation."

Connie craved fresh air.

When she'd awoken in yesterday's rumpled clothing, the house on Third Street had been quiet. Her father might've been at his job—he still did some security work part-time and Porter's wasn't open yet—and Gaby was no doubt at the library. After a long, hot shower, clean clothes, and two cups of black coffee, fortified by her decision to remain in New Jersey, Connie felt more focused than she had in years.

On the street, gulping in the mid-morning air as the sun burned her bare arms, a trickle of sweat rolled down the inside of her shirt. Almost fifteen years since she wandered this neighborhood. What was mostly an Irish and Italian area when she was a little girl had transitioned into a multi-ethnic, working-class melting pot. Back then, smoke spewed from factories, sending pollutants skyward. When waste management plants and trash incinerators released a toxic stew into the air, her father used to say, "Stinks like shit." Newark, minutes away, was home to several Superfund sites. Connie read somewhere that one's income level dictated how close one lived to pollution. True here; not so much in Los Angeles, where smog blanketed the city without regard for socio-economic status. Another reason she was happy to live in San Diego.

A military surplus store and a hamburger joint on her left, she turned right down Ferry Street where a group of young kids bounced a ball off a wall of an apartment building. Where a handful of women gathered on its stoop. They smiled at her. Friendly. She missed that. In the middle of the block, a red brick monolith rose three stories. The Hallison Public Library. A small patch of lawn and red oak trees out front were neatly trimmed, its windows sparkling. The library was still a welcome oasis in the neighborhood, a beacon of possibility. A respite for the area residents. No one dared tag graffiti on its walls or throw trash on the steps. No wonder Gaby loved it.

Outside the library Connie paused, removing her sunglasses, torn by her rash decision to stay in New Jersey. Wanting, needing her sister to understand the decision.

Her sweaty palms left an imprint on the glass door.

It wasn't the best idea to interrupt Gaby's work day.

Too bad. She was here now.

In the lobby, a place she hadn't entered since she was fourteen, a lot had changed. A modern circulation desk, colorful wall murals, posted listings of community events. On the left, rooms with signs indicated a computer lab, audiovisual and digital materials, a meeting room.

When Connie approached the young man behind the desk—shaved head, nose ring, a world away from the older librarians she'd grown up with—and asked where to find Gaby Tucker, he pointed in the direction of the stacks. "Half an hour ago, she was headed that way."

She circled computer terminals. The last time she was here, alphabetical rows of drawers contained cards that had to be manually searched for the correct volume. There was a time when Connie liked the smell of the library, the dusty books. The atmosphere had a fragrance. Calm. Welcoming. Then she stopped going. And then she'd left for—was banished to—California.

Up and down aisles she cruised until she saw Gaby with another staff member, deep in discussion, scrutinizing the cover of a book. When her sister first hung out here, she told Connie that she loved to run her fingers over the titles of books. To flip through pages. That the books seemed alive to her. To Connie, as a teenager, her sister's love of this place seemed eccentric.

Images of the day she left home sprang to mind. On the porch. Crashing out of the house, slamming a carryon bag over one shoulder. Heading to the airport. Gaby fidgeting, her hands stuffed into her pockets, her eyes clouded with worry. Then hugging. Rigid resistance from Connie, though she could feel Gaby's heart pounding against her own chest.

"Maybe you can come home at Christmas," Gaby had said. "I'll call you."

As Connie and her father backed down the driveway in the Town Car, Gaby had waved goodbye, her whole demeanor deflated, features downcast, shoulders slumped.

Connie was beside herself leaving her sister. But she'd already donned the outward shell of fury that would serve as her protection in the years to come. Gaby tried to reach her for weeks, then gave up. That was the way of the world. You lose people. You leave people. You move on. Until now.

Connie waited until the co-worker stepped away from her sister, but before she could approach Gaby, a security guard buttonholed her. Connie slipped down the aisle next to theirs, peered through the shelves. *Skulked there*, she had to admit to herself. *Eavesdropped*. She had a good view of both of them. They could see her, too, if they wanted. But each seemed aware only of the other, though they barely made eye contact.

The guard rubbed his eyes and yawned, his blue uniform shirt covering a slight bulge at his middle. "Hey."

"Hi," Gaby answered, her attention on the book she was holding.

He shuffled his heavy black shoes. "Sorry about your mother. How was the funeral?"

"Thanks. Difficult. As you can imagine."

"Yeah."

"But my sister came home. That was a bright spot." She smiled.

She'd given Gaby such a hard time, and yet her sister was happy to see her.

"Nice," the guard said. "Hey, I'm going to try the diner on Boynton Street for dinner tonight. Wanna come with?"

"I don't think so, but thanks for asking. I need to be with my father. You understand."

He did. Checked his watch and moved away.

Gaby adjusted her glasses, brown curls popping out of the scrunchy that held her thick, unruly curls together, and rolled the cart before her to the holding area by the Emergency Exit where others were parked.

Connie eased down the aisle, following her sister into the women's room, where Gaby removed her glasses and rubbed a wet paper towel over her eyes.

"Hi," Connie murmured.

Startled, like a kid caught with her hand in the cookie jar, Gaby's head popped up. Glimpsing the space to her right, then left, the sisters' eyes met in the restroom mirror. "You're still here?"

Connie handed her a dry paper towel. "Can you take a coffee break?"

Behind the library was a plaza where patrons could sit and read or simply enjoy the shade of the trees that surrounded the seating area. Only two other people across the way occupied the space. A light breeze lifted bangs off Connie's forehead.

Worry lines creased Gaby's forehead. "Is something the matter?"

Connie scooted forward in her chair. "Yes. I think something's very much the matter." From her bag she withdrew the paper with the translation of their mother's brief communication and handed it to her sister.

Gaby's lines deepened as she read. "What does this mean?"

"I think Mom was trying to tell us something. Do you remember anything she said or did around that time that would suggest she was leaving?"

"Leaving? To go where? Why?" Gaby's voice rose, and the couple on the opposite end of the patio twisted in their seats, curious. She flushed. This was her domain, and she most likely didn't appreciate being ambushed.

"I don't know, but I'm going to find out. I want you to help me." Connie refolded the paper and returned it to her bag.

Gaby studied her. "Is this why you didn't go home today?"

Home. Right. "Why did Mom die? Who was responsible?"

Gaby checked her phone. "You're not Miss Marple."

"What?"

Gaby sighed. "You're not a trained investigator."

"I have been trained in loyalty, though. I'm going to ask questions. Detective Nardone, Uncle Charlie. People at the theatre."

"The cold case detectives are investigating now."

"I'll contact them too." Connie retrieved her sunglasses from a small side table. "I have to do *something*. After reading her note, it's like she's speaking to me. Asking me to…"

"What?"

"Do what she can't. Find her killer."

Gaby's eyes widened. "Connie, that's….You're not a cop. Dad would have a fit if he heard what you were planning. What you're suggesting is dangerous."

"Then let's not tell him." When Gaby checked her phone again, signaling the conversation was over, Connie touched her sister's hand. "Maybe you're right. I need to grow up, get over some things." She paused. "I can't do that in San Diego."

Gaby stood. "I have to get back to work. Please don't do anything else until we talk tonight. Promise me?"

Another promise. The first one, to her mother fifteen years ago, now this one to Gaby. Connie's throat tightened, a burning behind her eyelids. It was a familiar plea. As kids, her sister would elicit Connie's pledge to do this or not do that, usually something that would keep them out of trouble.

"I promise." She crossed her heart, another youthful gesture that summoned the past. "If you go with me tonight."

Gaby was already walking to the entrance into the library. "Where?" She stopped and looked back at her.

"Yesterday Charlie invited all of us for dinner. Dad might not want to go but—"

"You already accepted the invitation?"

"Yes. I called Jackie when I decided to stay." Connie rose, moved to her. "She was glad to hear it, said to be sure to include you and Dad."

"I don't feel comfortable around Charlie. He's so full of himself."

"Tonight can be a new beginning. Let's find out." Connie reached past Gaby and opened the door. "I'll see you at home."

"I didn't agree to go." Gaby brushed past her.

"Can you be ready by seven?"

Chapter 12

Now

"So, Uncle Charlie lives in Colmar." Her dad's old partner had certainly come up in the world. Connie steered the rental car onto the parkway as the sun descended lower in the Jersey sky. "Like another planet when we were kids."

Seeing Colmar was a glimpse of a lifestyle that she assumed she'd never experience. Nothing like Hallison. Colmar equaled oasis to Connie—tranquil, classy, and safe. A trip there was a passport to an idyllic, pastoral setting. Entertaining herself by fantasizing about the people who lived in Colmar's mansions, she could tick off things you'd never see there: garbage cans at the curb, chain link fencing, empty lots, graffiti, cop cars blaring sirens, loud radios. Colmar seemed fresher than Hallison—green, floral, perfumed.

Connie's spirits had lifted when Gaby left her bedroom at seven, dressed for the evening. Her father, however, wary when he found out Connie was remaining in Hallison for a while, had begged off. Too tired. Connie hated to think he was eager to see her go.

"I haven't been here for"—Gaby calculated—"two years."

"That long?"

Gaby shrugged. "Had no reason to be in Colmar."

Connie glanced sideways. "You look nice." The first compliment she'd paid Gaby since they were teenagers. The words flowed more easily than Connie would have imagined.

Her sister had donned a beige summer sweater and a bit of makeup. Her curly hair was tamed into a French twist. "Thanks," Gaby said. "But Connie…"

"Yeah?"

"Nothing." Gaby lapsed into silence.

Uptown Colmar—two square miles of multi-million-dollar homes and a green plaza, surrounded by boutiques, cafés, and antique shops. A gated community without the actual gates. Many of its residents commuted to New York City, a short train ride away. Their kids attended a private academy in town. Nothing like the public schools in Hallison.

Downtown Colmar possessed its own distinct flavor: first-rate restaurants, art galleries, and the Flint Theatre—where their mother was last seen.

The early evening, end-of-summer sun sent shafts of golden light across the sky lending a halo effect to the shops and houses Connie drove past.

"Uncle Charlie lives on Chappelle Road," Connie said.

Dozens of mansions in Colmar, but Chappelle Road had the largest, most stately homes. Brick Georgians, Tudors, modern midcentury masterpieces, sitting on anywhere from half an acre to three plus acres. Like a fairyland to Connie. Outdoor lights, illuminating the landscapes, sparkled in the dusk.

Her favorite mansion had been an English gray stone manor, with three floors of windows, a sloping lawn landscaped with trees and shrubs, and a circular driveway. She checked the address Charlie's wife Jackie had texted, then slowed down, checking the house addresses.

"No way!" Connie said.

"What?"

"The English manor! They live in the gray stone manor." Her voice shook with excitement.

"So?"

"As a kid I used to wonder who lived in this place."

Connie flicked on the turn signal and drove up the circular driveway to a parking area in the back of the house. She shot Gaby a look. "Living the high life tonight."

"I prefer Hallison. Burgers at Porter's. Or pizza and beer."

"Hey, come on." Connie smiled at her sister. "It's not every night we eat in luxury."

She swung her bag over her shoulder as they walked to the front of the house.

Chimes reverberated inside and the heavy wooden front door opened. Jackie, in cashmere lounge pants and matching top, her dark hair hanging freely, was a less severe, more relaxed presence than at the repast. "Come on in you two," she said, smiling.

Connie stepped in and offered a bottle of wine. "Thanks for the invitation." At the repast, she hadn't noticed how tall Jackie was. Tall as Charlie.

"You're very welcome. It's a disturbing time for your family and I'm glad Charlie and I are here for you." She kissed first Connie on the cheek, then Gaby.

They followed Jackie into a parlor past the foyer's dark wood and marble floor. The subtle aroma of lemon oil mingled with the fragrance of fresh flowers on a reception table. A grand winding staircase led to upper floors and a chandelier of hundreds of pieces of crystal sparkled in the evening light.

"Dinner's going to be a bit. We can have drinks in here first. Charlie should be off the phone soon." Jackie gestured to seats and crossed to a liquor cart on an opposite wall. "What can I get you?"

"White wine is fine," Connie said.

"Gaby?"

"The same. Thanks."

Jackie handed around glasses, then took a seat opposite the Tuckers and sipped a martini, tucking her legs under her as she got comfortable in an armchair.

"Are you still acting?" Connie asked her. Jackie had also been an actress at the Flint Theatre, though in small roles. "It was nice to see some folks from the theatre at the repast."

Jackie laughed lightly, brushing her hair behind one ear. "I'm afraid my acting days are over. I was never in the same league as your mother. Simone was so talented."

Connie and Gaby swallowed their drinks in silence.

"Here we are." Charlie entered and squeezed his wife's shoulder as he made his way to the liquor cart. "Sorry I got tied up. Business." He gestured as if to say "what can you do?"

"I need to check on dinner." Jackie slid an arm around Charlie's waist in a brief hug and glided out of the room.

Charlie studied the sisters over the rim of his glass, lingering on Connie. "How are you two doing? And your old dad?" He directed both questions to Connie, but Gaby jumped in.

"Hanging in there, I guess."

"Tragic as hell what happened to your mother but I'm glad for all your sakes that it's over."

Over? Connie thought. It wasn't over by a long shot.

75

She bided her time, waiting for the best moment to introduce her questions. Meantime… "When I rode through Colmar's neighborhoods as a kid, I'd fantasize about what life was like in the mansions. This one was my favorite."

"Plotting your escape from Hallison?" he asked.

"Well," Gaby said to her, "you don't need to imagine this place anymore."

"So, what do you think?" Charlie said, refilling his glass. "Reality live up to the fantasy?"

Connie smiled and glanced around the parlor. "Oh, yeah. More than."

They moved into a formal dining room where a bar was set up at one end, a sideboard with dishes at the other. This estate raised posh to a new level, the table massive by Tucker standards.

Jackie had rejoined them. "Connie?" She motioned to a chair, then indicated one for Gaby.

Charlie had slipped out of the room, then re-entered a minute later with his mother Deirdre on his arm. Same coiffed hair, same pearls as at the repast. She spread a snowy, linen napkin on her lap, a quick glimpse cut across the table at them the only acknowledgment of the Tucker sisters.

Jackie supervised the housekeeper serving course after course—soup, salad, coq au vin, risotto—and, demonstrating her expert social skills, kept the conversational ball in the air, asking questions about Connie's life in San Diego and Gaby's work at the library. Charlie listened, polite, and Deirdre devoured her meal with gusto, keeping one eye on her plate and one on Connie.

"When do you leave?" Charlie asked Connie. "I'll bet you're eager to get back to the sun and sand." He chuckled.

Connie set her fork on the edge of her plate. "I'm going to stay around a little while."

"Lovely," Jackie said. "I'm sure your father and sister will appreciate your company." She smiled at Gaby and motioned to Deirdre to wipe her mouth where a piece of food clung to her lower lip.

Deirdre paid no attention to her.

"Actually, I hope to do a little digging," Connie said, ignoring Gaby's frown. "Ask a few questions about Mom's death." One hand beneath her napkin squeezed her nervous, twitching leg. Thinking about her plans was one thing, it turned out; saying them out loud to anyone but Gaby was another matter. Still, Uncle Charlie was a former cop, Dad's former partner. He'd understand her need for answers.

"What kind of questions?" Charlie refilled his wine glass, offered to refill Connie's.

"No thanks. I'm good. At the repast I spoke to the detective who led the investigation of her disappearance—"

"Nardone."

"He said the cold case unit will take over."

"Sounds right," Charlie said.

"He also said he interviewed everyone who was at the theatre that night. That he was sorry there wasn't a witness to her disappearing from backstage."

"Nardone's a very thorough guy. The department was sorry to see him retire."

Connie's heart clanged in her chest. Stepping off a cliff into an abyss. "He didn't interview me, though. And I was there that night."

Deirdre's clinking rings against her wine glass sliced through the silence.

"Connie?" Gaby stared at her sister, bewildered. "What are you saying?"

Jackie looked surprised and glanced from Gaby to Connie.

Charlie finished off his drink. "Did you see something you neglected to mention?"

She hesitated. "I want to talk with Detective Nardone, and I have to do it soon. He's leaving town any day now."

The arrival of dessert covered an awkward pause. Jackie asked, "How long do you plan to stay in New Jersey?"

"Long enough to get some answers."

Charlie laughed. "So, you want to play detective?"

"I'm just curious. I've always had an active imagination, and I guess I fantasized that Mom would walk back into our lives one day." There. Out in the open. "Gaby always said I had a strange relationship with reality."

Gaby kept her head down, her focus on her crème brûlée. "Maybe that's why you liked to act."

Connie glanced at her sister. No need to bring that up.

"You perform out in California?" Jackie asked, eyes bright with curiosity.

"I did a lot of theatre as a kid. Mostly high school."

"Got the theatre gene from Simone," Charlie said.

Jackie folded her napkin. "It was a beautiful service. I didn't know your mother well. We only worked on a couple of shows together, but she was much loved."

"Thank you." Gaby took a sip of coffee. "Dad is taking it all really hard. Losing her the first time was devastating, but to lose her again? To see her buried? Overwhelming for him."

Connie shifted toward her sister. Gaby hadn't offered any comment on their parents since her arrival in New Jersey until now. In the company of a family friend she didn't particularly care for. Interesting.

Charlie sighed. "Your father did everything he could to find her. Missing person's report, posters around Hallison and Newark, checking hospitals, police stations in the tri-state area, questioning relatives in Newark. Nagging Nardone for updates. It went on for over a year." He shook his head. "It was like she got in her car and drove off."

Her mother had loved that bright red Ford with the gaffer's tape patch on the front seat. "If she did, she probably didn't leave the theatre alone," Connie said.

Charlie fiddled with the handle of his coffee cup. Jackie coughed lightly. Gaby dabbed at her mouth.

Then Connie blurted, "Mom left us some personal things. Jewelry, books, photos. Also, a French message where she implied she wasn't happy and might be going away. Would you have any idea why she would write that?"

Gaby's face reddened.

Charlie spread his hands. "No idea. Except that your parents"—he glanced at Jackie, who frowned—"had a rough patch about then. There was talk of a divorce."

"A divorce?" This was news to Gaby, too, from her expression. Neither parent had hinted at this. Though, they were fighting more than usual.

"I hate to get into all of this," Charlie said, "but you two were young. You don't remember details. Like the trouble your parents were having. The jealous fights. Accusations of an affair. It wasn't pretty. He did some stuff he wasn't proud of."

Jackie touched his arm. "Let's let this go."

Storm clouds hovered around Gaby. Connie could imagine what she was thinking: Charlie suggesting that their father somehow played a role in their mother's disappearance.

The tension now a shroud enveloping the dining room, Jackie made an effort to save the evening. "Let's have an after-dinner drink in the parlor and—"

"Was Rosa Delano ever mentioned during the investigation?" Connie persisted.

"Rosa Delano?" Charlie asked.

"Our next-door neighbor. She and Mom had some huge battles. Everyone in the neighborhood knew she hated Mom."

"How do you know that?" Gaby placed her napkin next to the empty dessert dish.

"Gaby, she resented Mom."

"I don't recall." Charlie cut in, nodding at Jackie.

Jackie helped Deirdre to her feet.

"Jealousy," the old lady announced. She shook her finger at Connie. "A green monster. A triangle."

The sisters exchanged glances. What was that about?

Chapter 13

Now

"So much for backing off playing detective." Gaby yanked the seatbelt and jammed the plug into its socket. "You had to share Mom's note with them?"

"I never said I was backing off. You were quick to tell them about Dad." Connie swung the car out of its parking space, steered them down the driveway, and started through town.

"Not the same thing."

"Anyway, forget about the note. Divorce? Did you ever get that idea?"

"No, and I don't believe Charlie. Such a big mouth. Like he knows it all. Asshole."

"Wow. What do you really think?" Connie pulled onto the parkway and noticed Gaby's grim face in its lighting. Charlie had never been Gaby's favorite person, but this hostility from her sister was unexpected. Undeserved. "Charlie has our best interests at heart. He probably feels we need to hear this."

81

"That Dad and Mom were having problems? She's dead and buried. Why lay that on us now? If even a particle of his story is true and Dad didn't divulge it, maybe he wanted to keep it from us."

"Is there a reason he needed to keep it from us?" Had he kept it from Detective Nardone? After a few minutes, she switched gears. "What about the green monster outburst from Deirdre? The triangle. Who was she talking about?"

Gaby tossed her head. "She's another O'Shaughnessy I can do without."

It was surprisingly easy to find Detective Louis Nardone, the only one in Hallison, and his home number was listed with Information. Thank God some folks still used landlines. Between bites of cold toast and gulps of coffee, Connie's call to him reaped an instant reward. The retired detective was gracious, asked how she and Gaby and her father were doing, offered his condolences again. And ignored her somewhat rude, dogged questioning at the repast.

Connie blurted out the point of her call. "Would you mind talking again? I have a few questions."

A beat of silence. "Can't let it go, can you?" Confirming the obvious.

"Sorry."

He wheezed asthmatically. "Can't say how much help I'll be."

Don't beg. That would sound pathetic. "I'd really appreciate it."

"If it was my parent, I'd be feeling the same as you. You were how old when Simone disappeared?"

"Thirteen. Almost fourteen."

"Gotta granddaughter that age." He coughed, catching his breath. "Can you come by later today?"

The hope that she might pry loose some answers lightened Connie's spirits as she drove to the other end of town from Third Street. Nardone's house on Palmer Avenue sat on the boundary between Hallison and the north end of Newark, not far from where several Tucker relatives used to live. The detective's address was a three-story brownstone with a wrought iron fence and two trees out front. The sidewalk clean, no one loitering on the front steps.

He welcomed Connie into his apartment, gestured toward a wraparound sofa in the small, cramped living room, and offered her something to drink. She declined, tracked his slow progress from the door to the end of the sofa. Boxes were stacked against a wall, and a table and chairs were turned on end, as if impatient for someone to carry them away.

"Asthma's acting up today," he said by way of apology. "Sorry about the mess. Moving is not for the faint of heart." His laugh was soft and warm as he examined the room. "I was living down the shore until my mother passed awhile back. I inherited her apartment."

"It's lovely."

"If my wife was around…"

"I'm sorry—"

"No need. We divorced a long time ago. Collateral damage of a law enforcement career."

Recollecting what Charlie said about her parents last night, assuming it was true, her father's work could have been one source of their troubles.

"My wife, she'd have hated living in the city. My daughter and grandkids are in Seattle, so the timing was right to move on. Gonna miss Jersey."

Connie missed Jersey too, though wasn't eager to admit it. Lots of conflicted feelings.

Louis Nardone had prepared for the visit. On the floor at his feet lay a manila file folder. The dog-eared edges hinting that its owner had opened and closed the dossier numerous times. "It was one case I couldn't get out of my mind. Kept going back to it." He stared out a window behind Connie that offered a view of Palmer Avenue. "Forty-year career, and some of 'em stick with you. Others…" He shrugged. "But this one. Beautiful woman, two nice kids, cop husband." He grunted and scooted forward, grabbing the folder. "So. What do you want to know? What's in your mother's missing person's file?"

"I want to understand what happened to her. Why she died. Who was responsible."

"I can't answer those questions, but I kept a copy of the file when I retired." He shook his head. "Not a lot to tell. Circumstances, interviews." He flipped through pages that Connie hungered to read. "Like I said, we questioned everyone who was at the theatre that night along with neighbors, family, friends."

Connie closed her eyes and breathed. "Except me."

Nardone looked up. "Excuse me?"

"I was at the theatre that night. No one questioned me."

He frowned, checked his file again. "You weren't on the list."

"Because I was only thirteen, probably. No one thought I was important enough to question."

He placed his finger at a spot in the file to hold his place. "Did you see something?" he asked softly.

Same question Uncle Charlie had asked. Connie clasped her hands in her lap. She explained sitting on the stage in the dark, feeling her way along the wall till she reached the utility closet before seeing her mother in the hallway. Where she was told to get her things and wait in the lobby for her father. That was all.

She didn't mention overhearing her mother and BJ in the dressing room. Arguing. No mention of the hallway scene—him threatening her, getting physical. Her mother's menacing expression as she referred to BJ's secret. No mention of her promise to her mother that night to forget what she had seen and heard. Why couldn't she tell this detective all about it? Now was the moment to come clean. *No!* She'd made a promise. Reason battled emotion. Her mother was dead. What would it matter now?

Not yet. Keeping silent was about more than a promise. It was also about understanding *why* there had to be a promise. What were her mother and BJ hiding? At thirteen, in Connie's frantic state, their dialogue barely registered. Now, fifteen years later, dredging up that night, she wanted to know what it meant.

What if BJ found her again later that night, as he said he would?

Nardone studied her, as if he wanted to read her mind. "You're sure that's it?"

She nodded.

"Okay," he said.

"No one you questioned saw anything?"

He shook his head. "Nothing useful from the actors or those behind-the-scene folks. Stage crew. People saw her onstage and then backstage, like you, after the lights went out. Then she disappeared. Like I said, with the blackout it must have been total chaos. I wasn't on the case until twenty-four hours later. When she didn't show up at home that night, or the next night at the theatre, folks got worried." Nardone frowned and scanned sheet after sheet as if for the first time instead of possibly the hundredth. "Everyone seemed to love your mother. No problems with people at the theatre. No conflicts."

Except with BJ that night. She wrapped her arms tight over her stomach. "What about our neighbors? Everyone on Third Street knew my mother."

"Nothing there. Although they were adamant about helping to search. Good group of people."

She hesitated. "There's a woman who lived, lives, next door to us. Rosa Delano. She and my mother didn't get along. Was she questioned?"

"Rosa Delano?" He checked several sheets again. "No interview with her. We did speak with a Mrs. T. Delano."

"Rosa's mother."

"This Rosa, did she threaten Simone?"

"I don't know. They fought a lot when I was a kid."

"Was she connected to the theatre?"

"Not that I know of."

The detective paused. "As I said, no witnesses to her leaving, either alone or in the company of someone else. Unfortunately, no persons of interest. Of course, we posted flyers and her photo and put it out over the wire, which produced a ton of tips. None checked out. As usual, some were pretty crazy." He paused. "Guy claimed he spotted her in the Florida Everglades. Somebody else swore she was in a farming community in Iowa. Smattering of nuts calling about aliens." He smiled ruefully, then sighed. "Dead ends everywhere."

Connie clenched her hands, the knuckles turning white. "Was my father questioned?"

"Oh sure. Spouse is the first one we go to." He ran the tip of a finger along Liam's story and summarized as he went. "He came to the theatre to pick you up. Simone had called him when the lights went out, the weather turned ugly, and she wanted to get you safely home, he said. Went to the theatre, got you, returned to Hallison. That was about ten p.m. or so. Stayed there the rest of the evening. His car was in Hallison until the next morning." He looked up at her. "I'll say one thing for your father. He made himself a darn nuisance for over a year. Searching on his own, pestering the Hallison PD, and me, for updates." Nardone released his body into the back of the sofa. "He was persistent. Unfortunately…" He spread his arms wide.

All of their efforts had come to nothing. A wave of despair broke over her. She fought it: "Detective Nardone, what do you think happened to her that night?"

He coughed and wiped his mouth. "I don't know what I think, other than she didn't end up in those woods by herself. She either left the theatre and met someone or someone who was in the theatre took her with them. We don't know the circumstances of her exit. Was she coerced? Willing? When and how did it turn deadly?"

"Hard to believe she was willing. Given how it ended."

"We don't know," the detective said.

"And then it turns out, after all these years, she was so close to home. Right on the outskirts of Colmar."

"Luckily, the construction crew was alert and the heavy earthmovers weren't on the scene yet." The detective closed the file. "She was in a shallow grave. Not more than a couple of feet underground. Whoever buried her was in a hurry and didn't count on that forest being turned into condos." He gently ran a hand over the thick folder, as if saying goodbye. "The cold case unit in the county prosecutor's office will take it from here."

"What will they do?"

"Standard cold case procedures. Examine the case file, review interviews, the police report, evidence."

"Do they ever get anywhere? Ever solve any crimes?"

"Sometimes, eventually. They have over a hundred cases on their roster, so it could take time. Months."

"Years?"

"Possibly."

Connie didn't want to wait years or even months.

"Is there anything else?" he asked gently.

"I've taken up enough of your time." Though she had the distinct impression Louis Nardone appreciated her company, a gift for a lonely older man about to leave his home. "When's the moving day?"

"Next Tuesday." He sighed. "Life moves on."

As he opened his door, he studied Connie and shook his head. "Remarkable. The resemblance. Of course, I've only seen photos."

Connie accepted the observation, as always. "That's what I've been told."

"Sorry I couldn't be more help but hang on to the wonderful memories."

As if that would satisfy her.

On the street, Connie's brain buzzed, a tingling that wouldn't let go. She walked swiftly to her car, slid into the front seat, switched on the ignition and the air conditioning, and sat. Something didn't add up, but she wasn't sure what it was. She shut her eyes and followed Nardone's instructions—though it wasn't to wonderful memories that she returned, but the night her mother disappeared.

She had wanted to tell Detective Nardone what she witnessed in the hallway outside the dressing room that night. But something else bothered her. What was it?

Chapter 14

Then

"Get your backpack and wait in the lobby," her mother said after the horrible scene with BJ. "I'll call your father to pick you up. I might be late tonight."

Connie was shaken by what she'd seen and heard between her theatre friend BJ and her mother. The threats and the crying. Her insides were all jumbled up. But she did as she was told, hands trembling as she wiped her face on the sleeve of her shirt. She retrieved her backpack from the counter in the dressing room where she'd deposited it before creeping into the wings to watch the rehearsal.

The backstage hallway was busier now. With the dim emergency lighting, cast and crew were free to move about, into and out of the dressing rooms. Fewer blinding flashlights and shouted orders. But where was her mother? In the hallway one minute, gone the next. Desperate to escape the backstage, Connie put her head down and practically ran to the lobby.

The lobby's emergency lights cast harsh shadows. Outside, the night was pitch black except for taillights from a few drivers who braved the storm. Her father should be here soon. The minutes felt like forever, Connie both anxious to leave and anxious to stay. To find out how her mother was doing. To learn what was going on with her and with BJ. Connie shuddered and zipped her jacket.

Her father's Lincoln pulled up at last to the front of the theatre. Connie tugged her hood over her head and dashed for the car, wind whipping, rain pelting and drenching her jacket. She slammed the passenger door and wrenched the seat belt, struggling with the incident backstage involving her mother. "Dad, I'm afraid—"

"Nothing to worry about. The parkway's safer than backroads."

Driving in the rainstorm was nothing compared to what she'd witnessed inside the theatre. "No. I mean Mom—"

"Your mother will be home in a while."

Connie looked at her father for the first time, at his distorted, grimacing face. She could tell he'd been drinking. "What's the matter?" She shrunk at a clap of thunder and a flash of lightning.

He stepped on the accelerator, zooming into the middle lane of the highway. Weaving in and out of the light traffic, splashing through water lying in puddles.

"Dad! You're driving crazy! What's wrong with you?"

What was wrong with both her parents?

Her father flipped on the radio, turned the volume up. No way to talk with him now. She slumped down in her seat, irritation replacing worry. She'd have to rely on Gaby as a sounding board.

He slowed down, a little, when they entered Third Street, coming to a rocking stop in the Tucker driveway.

"Go inside. Go to bed."

Connie didn't need to be told twice to leave her father alone. He could have his bad mood. She tramped up the walk onto the porch.

Pausing at the door, she turned to find him just sitting there in the glow of the dashboard, gripping the steering wheel. She cupped her hands and yelled, "Are you coming in?"

He didn't answer. Or if he did, the wind and rain drowned him out.

Chapter 15

Now

"Come with me. Please," Connie begged her sister across the reception desk. Begging was a new experience for her, but it appeared she'd have to get used to it if she wanted to get any answers about her mother's death. First Detective Nardone, now Gaby.

Her sister raised her hand to silence Connie and picked up the phone. "Hallison Library." She listened, patient, while Connie tapped her foot, impatient. "Let me connect you with the Reference Department. They'll be able to help you. That's right. You're welcome." Gaby punched a button, replaced the receiver, and turned to her. "Why?" she whispered. "Why would you want to go there?" She was staring into Connie's eyes. "I don't think I could face it. Seeing the ground, the hole…"

Connie ran a finger along the edge of the reception desk. The old wooden counter had been exchanged for a sleek, laminated surface. *Probably a waste of time*, she'd thought, the minute she'd crossed the threshold of the library and observed Gaby at work. Hunkered down in her hidey hole, digging in.

"Gaby," she said. "Listen. It's been two weeks. Surely by now the crime scene people have turned the site back over to the construction company. There's probably not much to see. Still, I'd like to...honor her. Satisfy my curiosity."

"We can honor her at the cemetery. As for your curiosity..." She frowned.

"I didn't say that right. It's not the same thing," she said with vehemence. "Dumping Mom's warm body in a hole in the ground in a dense forest is definitely not the same thing as lowering her remains in a polished mahogany casket."

Gaby's eyes opened wide. "Connie, that's so...harsh."

"Sorry, but I need to *see* where it happened, and I would rather not go there alone."

Gaby hesitated. The last time Connie had urged her to accompany her—to Charlie and Jackie's for dinner—had not ended well. But Gaby surprised her. "I get off work at three today," she sighed. "Come by and pick me up."

"Perfect. The crew should be on site if I need to talk with anyone."

"Why would you need to talk to them?" Gaby shifted her attention to a stack of mail.

She wanted to say more, but her sister's focus was library work and the ringing phone. "See you later."

Connie slumped over the kitchen table, chewing a bite of pepperoni pizza, the tangy sauce and stringy cheese triggering involuntary memories, like Proust's "petite madeleines." In a college English class, the only one she'd taken, her professor had assigned sections from *Remembrance of Things Past*, explaining how the French cake was a symbol of the past surfacing unconsciously, accumulating energy, sorting and arranging memories prompted by smell and taste. Like Antonio's pies. Like all of Hallison.

The only sound the ticking wall clock, her mind skipped back decades to meals in the kitchen, the red-and-white-checked oilcloth covering the table, along with mismatched plates and glasses. Her father telling stories, her mother laughing, the two of them dancing on one occasion, until a year or so before her disappearance, the arguments began and the atmosphere at home cooled noticeably. Her mother's acting interests took her out of the house, most often to Colmar and the Flint Theatre. Connie got the feeling her father resented the time she spent in the theatre, away from Hallison. But he worked double shifts, occasionally moonlighting as a security guard, and was barely around that last year. So, who was to blame for deserting the family? Which had come first, the theatre or the double shifts?

Connie dropped the crust of her slice onto a plate, feeling bloated. It was more than the food weighing her down. She'd worn a mantle of trauma since she'd arrived in New Jersey. Eating from the three basic Hallison food groups—burgers, fries, and pizza—in the span of a few days didn't help. Tasty, but damn, so heavy. The West Coast equaled green foods. Even the pizza there was more veggie friendly. The last dinner date she'd had in San Diego had featured farm-to-table salad, sautéed green beans, and curried goat, for God's sake. Which reminded Connie that her love life was another hot mess. Bouncing from guy to guy, the longest relationship she'd had in the past eight years lasted ten months.

The kitchen wall clock read two forty-five. She emptied her plate into the garbage, grabbed her bag, and hurried out the front door.

The road to the site of the future Windmill Luxury Condominiums ran along the edge of Colmar into a forested area that had, until recently, been uninhabited green space. Unknown territory for Connie. Her time in Colmar as a kid had been limited to trips to the Flint Theatre with her mother. Then, in the feral months following Simone's disappearance, this isolated part of northern New Jersey had been too far removed from the pizza joints and the bodegas that sold beer to underage kids to be of interest to her or her friends.

"I had no idea this was even part of Colmar, did you?"

Gaby was in no mood for chitchat. Connie glanced sideways at her staring out the passenger side window. Being dragged to the site of the crime. A week ago, they'd been out of touch for almost fifteen years. Though the hurt lodged in Connie's nervous system was still alive and well, blood *was* thicker than water. Resentment embedded in her core melted a bit when the two of them were together.

"I don't get what you hope to achieve with this," Gaby said to the side window. "I wouldn't mention it to Dad."

Another thing the sisters would keep from their father. Fine with Connie. "Where is he today?" She slowed as they neared the entrance to the site.

"He spends Thursdays at Porter's. Lunch and dinner."

A sprawling construction zone sprang up before their eyes. Gaby leaned forward to gaze out the windshield. "Man. It's going to be some kind of complex."

"I checked it out online. Three separate buildings with two and three-bedroom condos. Six floors plus the penthouse level."

"Crazy."

Connie drove up to a chain link fence prominently displaying red, black, and white signage: *Danger. Construction Site. Unauthorized Persons Keep Out.*

"I guess that means us," said Gaby.

Beyond the fence, workers in yellow hard hats and orange safety vests scrambled around cranes, steel girders, and bulldozers, but Connie couldn't hear any machinery. Since it was near quitting time, she guessed they were packing up for the day. She unclicked her seat belt.

"What are you doing?" Gaby asked. "The sign says, 'Keep Out.'"

An old groove for them, Gaby shocked or frustrated or infuriated—or all three—by her behavior. Well, she wasn't a teenager anymore. "What do you think I'm doing? I'm going in there and ask where they found Mom." She opened the car door, got out, and slammed it shut. Though sounding and acting bold, her pulse was racing like a kid's. Who was she fooling?

Gaby, maybe, for after wavering, Connie heard her push open her door. "Wait for me. They're not going to let us in, anyway."

Connie walked to the gap in the chain link where one of the signs swung on rusty hinges. She ducked under the sign. Yesterday's rain had turned the dirt into a slick of mud that spread from one end of the site to the other.

Gaby ventured beyond the fence as well and hesitated, seeming to weigh the consequences of going any farther in her dress shoes. "I should have brought sneakers—"

"Hey! Whadya think you're doing?" A big, bulky guy, maybe thirty yards away, clipboard and walkie-talkie in hand, waved and yelled at them. "Read the signs!"

"Told you." Gaby turned away.

"No. Wait." Connie waved back at the man—the foreman judging by the clipboard and bullish manner—and stepped over a puddle toward him.

He shook his head and chugged forward to meet her halfway, arms flailing, all signs indicating Connie and Gaby were trespassing and needed to leave. *Now.* Connie kept going as though she didn't understand his warnings. Head down, inspecting where she stepped, bypassing the messiest areas.

Now only half a dozen yards from them, he shouted, "Stop! I said stop! You're in a dangerous construction zone. You wanna get killed?"

Killed. A blow to her system. She shook it off, kept it light. "That'd make two of us."

"What? What the hell you talking about?" He removed his hard hat and slapped it against his leg. "Hate to be rude, but you two have got to—"

"Let's go." Gaby tugged her sister's arm.

"We're not going anywhere," she shouted. The old combative Connie rearing her head.

"Oh yeah? I'm calling security." He tapped his walkie-talkie.

"Go ahead and call them. You'll be embarrassed when they get here."

"Connie. Come on."

The foreman looked up. "What?"

"I'm Connie Tucker. This is my sister Gaby. Our mother was Simone Tucker. Her remains were discovered by your crew." Her voice ratcheted up, her breathing shallow.

The man's forehead creased. He backed up and replaced his hard hat. "Sorry about that. Really. But I can't let you wander around the site. It's not safe."

"Point out the location. We'll find it. My sister and I want to see where she was…" Her eyes stung.

He winced as though she'd socked him in the gut. "God. Okay. Wait here. I'll get someone to take you." He started to walk away, then pivoted back to them. "I hope they catch the bastard."

Connie and Gaby stood shoulder to shoulder before a heap of dirt that had been methodically sifted and mounded next to a shallow hole in the ground. Detective Nardone had described their mother's first grave accurately: only a few feet deep. Yellow crime scene tape, half-buried in the mud, encircled the area, surrounded by land that had been cleared and chewed up by machinery. Trees dispatched, the ground leveled.

Connie dropped to her knees. Pent-up tears started as a trickle and became a cascade. Child-like whimpers, buried so deep she wasn't even aware of them, escaped.

Gaby touched her sister's shoulder, then joined her on the ground, disregarding the damp patches on her trousers. The workman who'd been charged with accompanying them, at first edgy, checking his watch, now tugged his hard hat down over his forehead at the naked show of emotion. If Connie had any doubts about remaining in New Jersey to pursue the truth about her mother's killer, they vanished in the sobs that wracked her body.

Someone had to catch the bastard.

Chapter 16

Now

The light clatter of silverware tapping dishes filled the kitchen—the first meal the Tuckers had eaten together since Connie's return. Otherwise, it had been Connie and Gaby or Connie eating alone.

"Pass the pepper," Gaby said, and her father obliged.

Talk was sparse. Each family member focused on their meal.

In an effort to be a gracious houseguest—despite the fact that this was her home, too—Connie rose early to make breakfast after a run to the corner grocery store. Fresh fruit, bacon, eggs, coffee, and biscuits. The kitchen smelled delicious and inviting, the table set for three, a small vase of flowers for decoration. Even the weather had turned pleasant, the humidity lifting, the temperature in the low eighties, and a breeze through the open windows ruffled the curtains.

Connie's spirits had plummeted after yesterday's visit to the construction site. Sadness like a millstone on her shoulders. She hadn't slept well. Her father gazed off into space, a mostly full plate in front of him. Heavy lids, curly, thinning, bedhead hair. Drumming his fingers.

Gaby topped off their coffees.

Last night her father announced that he was going to meet with the detective who supervised cold cases for the county. He had a connection with him from shared days at the Newark police department. Hearing this, Connie made a decision. Talking with Detective Nardone and Uncle Charlie had been first steps that had yielded significant information: there had been no persons of interest in her mother's disappearance, and around the same time, her parents were discussing a divorce. The cold case detective was next on her list.

She brushed a napkin across her mouth. "I'm going with you to the county prosecutor's office."

Her father shifted his attention back to his daughters and the uneaten bacon and eggs on his plate. "No need. Thanks for breakfast."

"You're welcome. I'm coming." Her teenage aggressiveness emerged.

Her father raised a hand as though he intended to argue, but instead he lifted his head and nodded, surrendering to Connie's determination.

Gaby had no intention of joining them. "I have to get to the library." She cleared her dishes and left the kitchen.

Connie offered to drive and to her surprise, her father agreed. It was the first time she'd driven him anywhere and, despite his quiet sorrow, he insisted on providing constant directions. Like she'd never lived in this part of the state. Her arms tensed, squeezing the steering wheel, teeth clenched. In the past, she might have lashed out at his commands, the only conversation between them. She counted to ten. Exhaling through open lips.

In the months after her mother's disappearance, Connie's frenzied fury had caused her to fling allegations at him. "You were a cop…so why couldn't you find Mom? That's how bad a cop you were. You couldn't even find your own wife. Guess that's why they fired you."

Though she knew the last charge wasn't true. Her father wasn't fired; he'd resigned a year after her mother's disappearance. Too broken up, too depressed.

Light traffic meant a much quicker drive into Newark than Connie anticipated, and they arrived at the parking lot close by the prosecutor's office with time to spare. Her father insisted on waiting in the lobby. Connie said she'd be right in, that she wanted to check emails, make a phone call. Truth be told, she needed a breath of fresh air—even if it was city exhaust—to face whatever they'd encounter. A new investigation that had to be better than the original one.

Approaching the glass front entrance of the white stone building, Connie braced herself, then joined her father to be checked out by security personnel and rode the elevator to the third floor. At reception he requested Detective Rutherford. The woman behind the desk punched buttons on her intercom and suggested they have a seat. The floor was hushed, almost tranquil. Gray carpeting, framed photos of historic Newark. Not what Connie expected from a county prosecutor's office.

"Liam! Long time." The detective, tall, trim, and stylishly attired in a charcoal pinstriped suit, strode into the waiting area and thrust out his hand. He shook her father's warmly, then turned to Connie. "And you must be…"

"My daughter, Connie. In from San Diego."

Connie gritted her teeth and smiled, wondering about her father's qualifier. Like she wasn't really from New Jersey. "Hi."

"Tom Rutherford. Call me Tom." He pumped Connie's hand, his enthusiasm traveling from his voice, down his arm, and into his palm.

They followed the detective down a newly remodeled hallway. Additional glass and the odor of fresh paint. He paused by a door with a gold nameplate, and gestured for them to enter, settling into a leather desk chair in an equally spare and neutral office, while they occupied seats across from him. He offered coffee, water, etc. They declined.

"This is more comfortable than a conference room," he told them.

Her father and Detective Rutherford—Tom—chewed the fat, as her father used to say, about the old days at the Newark PD, guys they remembered, the detective's shift in career. With the central air conditioning chilling the room to an uncomfortable degree, Connie regretted refusing a cup of coffee and allowed her attention to veer from the drone of their reminiscing to a watercolor on the wall behind him. A house on an empty stretch of beach, its boards weather-beaten. Off to the side lapped a turquoise sea. It reminded her of California. The Shack. Altogether seductive and inviting. She wished she could be there. Anywhere but in this office, discussing her mother's murder investigation.

"Sorry as hell to hear about Simone," Tom said. "Now we take over."

There was a glint in his eye, a slight verbal swagger. A hint that local law enforcement hadn't done a sufficient job investigating the disappearance and now the big guns were on the job.

"What's next?" Both her father and the detective swiveled their attention in her direction.

She'd been silent long enough. "What's the procedure from here?" Connie visualized the copious collection of papers in Nardone's thick fingers.

Tom's smile lost some wattage. "My office will review the case file," he said.

Her father sat forward. "Good. I appreciate all—"

"What does that mean, exactly?" Connie asked.

Speaking slowly as if to a child, Rutherford said, "We start at the beginning and review all materials. Interviews, records, evidence. Our team does research, sifting through the facts of the case."

Connie ignored his condescending tone. "What evidence was there, if no one saw her leave?"

"We don't know that—"

"The first investigation didn't turn up any witnesses." According to Louis Nardone. "Why do you think you'll find any now?"

"Connie." Her father's tone suggested a gentle warning.

Fuck that. New Jersey and her mother required the old Connie. So different from the mellow one she'd replaced her with, who shuttled drinks on the beach beside rolling waves and warm sand. "Will you investigate why she was buried at the construction site?"

Again, all patience, he said, "Of course. Back in the early 2000s that area was a woods. Uninhabited. Supposedly Green Acres. Wasn't planned for development. That changed three years ago. So, it was a perfect spot for this type of thing."

Jaw tightening, Connie squeezed the armrests. Her mother's death was a "type of thing."

When he offered reassurances to them that no stone would be left unturned, Connie tuned out. His smoother-than-silk manner didn't inspire confidence.

After another fifteen minutes of cop shop talk, they were escorted to the elevator, provided with additional promises that his office would keep the family informed and encouraged them to "trust us."

She didn't.

Her father was silent as they left Newark. Either he was assured Connie didn't need his assistance with directions or meeting with Detective Rutherford had subdued him. On the other hand, Connie's mind bounced like a rubber ball. As she had with Detective Nardone, she'd have to tell Rutherford that she was at the theatre and required an interview. Like baring her soul to a pompous ass.

Yet, something wasn't right…something had crawled up her spine and lodged itself at the base of her skull. She replayed the events of that night fifteen years ago—her mother coming down the stairs, ready for her moment on the stage, kissing them goodbye. Then her reminding Gaby and Connie about dinner on the stove, homework, and Connie whining to go along before the two of them rushed out. So far so good. Then the theatre blackout and standing outside the dressing room and hearing her mother and BJ and the ensuing fight in the hallway. Her father coming to take her home. Her mother still at the theatre. Once at home, Connie woke Gaby to tell her about the events at the theatre, but her sister just rolled over, muttered to Connie to shut the door on her way out.

Despite her best efforts to stay awake until her mother returned, Connie had drifted off, waking with a start when a door downstairs opened and closed, jumping out of bed to greet her mom. Relieved but stunned when she glanced at the alarm clock. Five a.m. She'd been out all night. Slipping into the upstairs hallway, Connie had stooped down to peer through the posts on the railing.

It wasn't her mother but her father coming home. Alone.

A few hours later when the sisters descended the stairs, dressed for school, expecting to see their mother fixing breakfast, the kitchen was empty. When asked where she was, her father said, "Visiting her cousin."

Even then, that hadn't felt right. Her mother wouldn't leave the house so early to visit her cousin, someone she barely saw, an hour away in upstate New York. The morning after a dress rehearsal. Everything was topsy-turvy. Cold cereal, no kiss goodbye, no one saying she loved them. By the time they returned from school—their father hadn't gone to work, hadn't shaved, was in last night's clothes—they'd known something was wrong.

Then there was talk of a "missing person," Mrs. Delano cooking dinner for them, and their father with Uncle Charlie and other cop friends in the house. Days, then weeks went by, the family settling back into routines—getting ready for school, having dinner, going to bed. Mrs. Delano and some neighbors continued to provide meals, and Connie spent more time with Brigid after school. When their father came home from work, mute and moody, she and Gaby avoided him and ate dinner alone. He often changed out of his uniform and left the house without saying a word. She and Gaby cleaned up after themselves and went to their rooms to do homework. Their father never really talked with his daughters about their mother being gone.

Within months, the sisters had gotten used to being motherless, if one ever gets used to that. Gaby referred to her in the past tense; Connie the present, anticipating her return. Something broke in her, the rage and pain and desperation of feeling abandoned were overwhelming. The gnawing guilt about hiding the scene she'd witnessed outside the dressing room between her mother and BJ tore at her soul. She turned away from her family and toward the behavior that sent her to California.

The problem now, fifteen years later, was this: Detective Nardone said her father was home by ten p.m. That wasn't completely true. It was morning when he finally returned the second time. Where had her father been from the time he dropped her off and his return at five a.m.? He wouldn't have lied to the detective investigating—as a cop, he understood the consequences. Unless he figured he could game the law enforcement system.

Connie felt certain her father was hiding something. Something about that night? Something about her mother's death? Oh God, what would that mean? Couldn't be. Her father guilty—?

"He's a good guy. Tom." Her father's voice jerked Connie out of her reverie, tightened her grip on the wheel. He was looking at her strangely. "You were a little hard on him."

"Rutherford's a cold case detective investigating a family member's murder. We need to be hard on him."

He sighed.

Connie backed off a tad. "You knew him back when you were a beat cop?"

"He was my partner for a couple of years."

She shot a glance at him. "Uncle Charlie was your partner."

"He was, after Tom." He barked a small laugh. "Tom got promoted. Charlie got demoted. He was on a fast track to a gold shield, then got in trouble with excessive force complaints. Derailed his progress."

"Demoted?"

"Happened when you were a little kid."

"Was he guilty?" Connie flashed on Deirdre's comments at the repast about "roughhousing" on the streets of Newark and getting into trouble at the police academy. Both Charlie and her father had a history of violence. Before they were police officers. "Of excessive force?"

"Most cops have complaints against them. Comes with the job."

"You?" Connie thrust the word at her father.

He avoided the question and closed his eyes, naked pain marking his features. "Don't know if I can go through this all again."

She focused on the parkway traffic, shrugging off his vulnerability. His plea for sympathy.

"The interviews," he said, "Sifting through our lives, talking about your mother."

Connie kept her voice steady and steeled herself to react calmly. "You don't have a choice. You want her killer to be found."

"Of course. Anyway, Tom'll do right by me. He'll take care of us."

What did that mean?

Chapter 17

Now

"Don't make me come in there!" Brigid yelled into the living room, moving her three-year-old son from her lap to the floor, patting his butt as he toddled off. "God, I sound like my mother. Like, twenty times a day. How did that happen?" She sighed and pulled out a fresh beer for Connie, another Coke for herself from the fridge. "Dack says we need his second job to make ends meet. I think he has the second job to give him an excuse to stay out of the house."

Connie laughed and chugged her drink. Her cheeks hurt from giggling for the past hour, reliving high school hijinks. Who got grounded for staying out all night, who cheated on who with whom, who got pregnant before graduation. And their own brushes with the law. A reprieve from dealing with her mother's death and the Tucker house on Third Street. It felt good to laugh.

"Sue Ann Simpson?" Brigid said. "She went to India to live in an ashram."

"Wow. That's…"

"So unlike Sue Ann?" Brigid grinned. "Remember, she was voted most likely to open her own beauty shop? Wanted to be a cosmetologist.

I was voted most likely to have six kids." Brigid regarded her belly. "I told Dack this is *it*. Either he gets a vasectomy or moves into the garage. I swear, someday I'm going to walk away and let him handle his offspring."

Brigid stirred a hamburger helper mixture of tomato sauce, ground beef, and cheesy pasta in a skillet while Connie chopped veggies for a salad.

"Saw the county prosecutor today. He's in charge of Mom's cold case."

"And?"

"And nothing. They start the investigation all over again."

"You don't sound very optimistic."

"The guy's full of himself. An asshole." Her description reminded Connie that Gaby had labeled Uncle Charlie that way. Both had been their father's partners. Was he an asshole too? She didn't think so, but who knew, out on the street. Sounded like he had been a "roughhouser" right along with Charlie when they were young.

Brigid stared at her, waiting for her to say something. Answer the question. Hell. What had the question been? Oh. No question. Wondering why she didn't seem to hold much hope for the new investigation. "We'll see," she said. "Whatever you're doing over there smells good." She focused on tossing the salad.

"Oh, I can make magic with a couple pounds of chop meat. These monsters devour it like nobody's bus—"

A crash from the living room.

Brigid dropped her head back, closed her eyes. "I'm gonna kill 'em."

Connie wiped down the table, mopping up spilled milk and the remnants of hamburger and salad while Brigid loaded the dishwasher.

The table had been a war zone, although she had to admit it was fun to listen to the boys argue and bait and poke fun at each other. Brigid complained about her life, but it was clear she was as happy as a pig in shit, Connie's dad would have said.

The kids ran to the living room, jumping off the sofa onto the carpet. "Get upstairs and put on your pajamas. Darryl, have you finished your homework?"

Five minutes of cajoling and browbeating were followed by two grumpy boys climbing the stairs and one grinning toddler smothered in Mama's kisses. "Give me some of that lovin.'" Brigid smelled the baby's diaper. "Ugh. We're only halfway to complete toilet training."

She disappeared to change her son and Connie finished up the kitchen, then went outside and sat on the porch steps. A blanket of stars in a clear sky stretched across the Hallison night. She inhaled deeply. East Coast air. Heavier, damper, comforting, like having arms around your shoulders.

A figure loping down the sidewalk paused at the bottom of the steps that lead up to the house. Unrecognizable in the shadows, until he stepped into the oval of light thrown by the porch lamp. "Hi Finn."

Brigid's brother, in shorts and a tee shirt, lowered himself next to her. "How you holding up?"

Connie shrugged. "They're still investigating."

"Between her disappearance then and the funeral now, it's like losing her twice, right?"

Connie, startled, mumbled agreement. Gaby had said the same thing days ago at Charlie and Jackie's. "I'll bet you're a good therapist."

Brigid appeared and handed Connie a mug of coffee. "At a hundred fifty an hour," she said.

Finn rolled his eyes.

"Kidding, bro." Then to Connie. "I hear he's great with patients."

"Been there, done that, back in the day." Connie blew on the steaming mug. "Everybody insisted I see a psychiatrist."

"Did it help?" Finn asked.

Again, she was surprised by his comment. No one had ever bothered to inquire about her opinion of the therapy sessions. "Apparently not. That's why I got shipped off."

Brigid patted Connie's knee.

"For the longest time I asked myself 'What if she's alive? Afraid or unable to come back?'"

"Like a character on TV." Brigid sipped her coffee.

Connie set her mug on the step below. "Mom wouldn't have abandoned us, but what if she had an accident and suffered from amnesia all those years? It's been known to happen."

"Yeah. Mostly in movies. I guess that's why acting is such a good fit for you. *Was*," Brigid corrected herself.

"Gaby says sometimes I can't face reality."

"Says the woman who sort of lives in a book shelter."

They listened to a medley of night sounds: televisions, crickets, automobile engines, neighbors' voices, waxing and waning.

"Finn, did you get the decorations?" Brigid asked.

"No, but I will," he said.

"Don't forget," Brigid commanded. "That's your one job for the anniversary party." She turned to Connie, excited. "Mom and Dad know about it but it's still going to surprise the hell out of them. You're coming, right? You're not leaving town anytime soon?"

"I can't leave until I have some answers." A car backfired and Connie flinched. "Or they find the murderer. But Detective Nardone said it can be months, even years of work. Frustrating. Going over the old file one more time. What are they going to find that's new?"

Brigid put an arm around her.

Finn shifted on the step and looked at her. "So maybe somebody needs to think outside the box. Like they do on those television shows."

"Meaning?"

"Isn't there always one cop who finds clues at the scene of the crime that everybody else ignored? Or mistakes in the timeline of the murder? Or—"

"We get the picture, Finn," Brigid said.

Her father's timeline. Something was wrong with it.

"Connie, remember my offer," Finn said.

"Thanks." But no thanks. Connie hated the therapist's waiting room when she was a teenager. To her, it smelled of raw emotion that she couldn't escape, like walking into a paper bag she couldn't punch her way out of.

As if he could read her mind, he said, "We don't need to meet at my office." He smiled, dug into his wallet, and handed her a card.

Think outside the box.

Connie wanted another perspective on Detective Rutherford. Her father was close to him and something about their coziness bothered her. Especially since his actions that night didn't seem to add up—the problematic seven hours from ten p.m. until five a.m. that didn't seem to be accounted for. Gaby was out of the picture: not having met the head of cold cases, she would only defend their father. The call was obvious. She deposited lunch dishes in the sink and tapped her contacts.

"Hi Jackie," she said after several rings.

They exchanged a few pleasantries and Connie apologized for the strained end to their recent dinner. Mention of the divorce, questions about Rosa, and Deirdre yelling about jealousy and green monsters.

"Don't worry about it. This is a stressful time for you and your sister."

"I wanted to speak with Charlie, but I got his voicemail. Any idea where I could reach him?"

"Is it urgent? He's at work."

To Connie it was urgent. "It's about the guy supervising Mom's cold case. I'd like his opinion on things."

"So, you *are* playing detective."

She sensed Jackie's lips curving upward in a smile. "I guess I am. Some things have come up that I'd like to run by him."

"Sounds like you won't rest easy until you get answers, so let me see if I can find him."

"Thanks."

Connie collected her bag and car keys, ignoring the dread that spread from head to toe. The next stop, after meeting with two detectives, was inevitable. She had no idea what she'd find at the Flint Theatre. Her mother's ghost? She shivered. Weaving in and out of parkway traffic, she confronted her motivation for visiting the theatre. Not that she thought she'd walk in the door and instantaneously have the answers she sought. Still, she felt driven to return to the place she last saw her mother. A place she hadn't been back to since that night, leaving her terrified to walk in the entrance.

The Flint Theatre website indicated that a show opened in two weeks directed by the artistic director and featuring the Flint's leading actress. Two of the theatre people she'd seen at her mother's funeral. This late in the afternoon, rehearsal might be nearly over; a good time to say hello and...what else? Connie wasn't sure. She'd improvise. After all, she'd be in a theatre.

She parked in a lot adjacent to the same upscale café she remembered from years ago. Connie walked slowly to the entrance, willing her feet to move, step by step. The empty lobby—renovated with sitting areas, potted plants, and a refreshment stand since the last time she was here—sent time reeling backward. She was a young girl waiting in the emergency lighting for her father to pick her up. Scared stiff about her mother. Shocked by BJ's disturbing behavior. Wondering what the hell was going on between them.

Shouting inside the theatre yanked her into the present. Counting to five, she opened the door to the dark house and witnessed the director and cast onstage, working through a moment. Slap. Scream. Faint. A woman ended up on the floor. Connie closed her eyes and inhaled the recognizable smells of drying paint and fresh lumber.

"Excuse me, but you can't be in here." A woman, fortyish, in jeans and a tee shirt, whispered. She'd materialized at Connie's elbow. "It's a closed rehearsal." She glanced at the stage, then back at Connie.

"I'm sorry. I—"

The stage manager gawked. Then did a double-take. "Connie? Connie Tucker? Hold on a minute, okay? We're due for a break." She hustled up the aisle, sliding into a seat a few rows from the stage.

Connie scrunched down in the back row, her heart fluttering like a bird's wings, and the scene onstage unfolded again. The actress repeating the action, the director correcting the staging, the male actor observing. Trying to get it right. She'd spent many hours here, also observing, trying to absorb the lessons doled out during her mother's rehearsals.

Connie pictured her mother waltzing into the casting call for her first Flint production, her beauty seductive, a model's figure, that million-dollar smile. The casting director bowled over. Her mother, hypnotic, standing center stage, thrilled to be in the theatre. It was her dream, she'd told her daughters often enough, how she took classes in New York for a year when she was seventeen, auditioning every chance she had. Working to master an American dialect and eliminate her

French accent. The dream might have been suspended when she married and had two kids. Until the siren call of the Flint Theatre.

Connie shut her eyes, summoning her mother in costume that last night, playing Stella. Perfect as the sensuous, indolent, pregnant wife of the brutish Stanley. Mesmerizing both her stage husband and the rest of the cast. Connie had been desperate to watch her play the role. That's why she insisted on coming to the dress rehearsal.

"Take ten," the stage manager called out, crossed to the director, and motioned toward Connie.

Ted. That was his name. He strode up the aisle, extended his condolences again. "If you can wait until rehearsal ends"—he glanced at his watch—"in thirty minutes, we could talk. In fact, join us for a drink. We usually go out for happy hour." He smiled.

"Sure. That would be nice." She had no dinner plans with Gaby, and her father had gone to Porter's. Connie settled in for the last part of rehearsal. Ted finished notes, actors gathered their belongings and mingled in the first row of the house.

Then she saw him. *BJ.*

The technician stared at her from the other side of the house. Dressed as she remembered him—overalls, work shirt, red baseball cap pulled low over his forehead—with a length of cable coiled around his shoulder. But the old BJ was sweet-looking, tidy, clean despite his work in the scene shop. Not this guy.

Goosebumps rose on her neck. Seeing him triggered a ripple of dread, sweaty palms. Tightening in her lungs. His piercing eyes bored into her, the intensity of his expression unnerving. As if he was asking her a question, as if he wanted something. She stared back. Plenty of questions for him.

Connie searched her memory: That night in the hallway he claimed her mother loved him, not someone else. Who was the someone else?

He said he saw what she did. What did she do? What was BJ's secret and why would her mother threaten to tell it to Ted? "You'll be out of the Flint Theatre," she'd said. Was it that damaging?

"Hey BJ, could you check the lumber order?" The artistic director called to him. "Due in tomorrow."

BJ nodded wordlessly and limped down the aisle toward the scene shop. He didn't have a limp fifteen years ago.

"I think the lamp on an instrument house left needs changing," Ted added, then smiled at Connie.

Bendel was Colmar's version of down and dirty. Glass, chrome, everything sleek and modern, minus the aroma of stale beer. Porter's was seedy by comparison.

Connie studied the others at the table, nursing her glass of wine: Ted, the leading lady, a couple of other younger actors, the stage manager.

"I think we'll have a fabulous show." Diana, the Flint Theatre leading lady, who'd played Blanche in her mother's *Streetcar*, lifted her glass and everyone joined the toast.

An actor signaled for another round.

Connie declined a second drink, digging in her bag for money as she listened to production discussion—rehearsal schedules, scenery issues, box office revenue.

"I noticed you talking with Jackie Flint at the repast," Ted said. "How is she? Hasn't been around the theatre lately."

"Jackie *Flint*?" Connie wasn't aware of Jackie's last name back then. And now, apparently. She was Uncle Charlie's wife. His rich wife. Hanging on to her family name. "Her husband is a family friend."

"The former cop," someone said. "He's on the board now."

"It's a heavy burden to bear. Having Flint as a last name," the stage manager said and everyone laughed.

"Jackie's family...?"

"...paid for the founding of the theatre thirty years ago," Ted said. "Grandfather Flint was the original angel. The role passed to Jackie's father, who underwrote a portion of the theatre's budget every year and sat on the board until his death. The philanthropic legacy was handed down to his daughter."

And Charlie, now that they were married.

"So, what do you do in California?" asked Diana, sipping a Cosmopolitan.

For the first time ever, Connie struggled to explain her life. What was that about? She'd never been embarrassed to announce that she tended bar on the beach in San Diego. That revelation often garnered envious reactions; it sounded idyllic and carefree. Bohemian and laid-back. But in the presence of hardworking actors, in this town of strivers and emblems of success, Connie grappled with an answer, finally landing on the truth.

An actor sighed. "Awesome. I could be a beach bum, keep surfer hours."

Connie colored, resisting the urge to correct him—many surfers weren't beach bums and kept to a strict schedule.

"Ted said you used to come to the theatre with your mother," the stage manager said. "Nice memories, I bet."

Grateful for the change in subject, Connie smiled. "Everyone was so tolerant. Letting me hang around in the dressing room, backstage, in the house for rehearsals."

"Simone said you wanted a career in the theatre. That you acted in school," Diana said.

"I did." The table waited. "I moved west to live with my aunt. Got interested in other things. High school." She shrugged, as though rejecting acting had been an inevitable result of growing up. Another lie.

"You sat in the dressing room watching me put on makeup," Diana said. "So intent, like you were memorizing my every move. Then your mother bought you a little kit and you made up your face along with the rest of us." She patted Connie's arm.

Connie flashed on streaks of pancake across her cheekbones, highlight and shadow on her eyelids.

"One night I found you sound asleep in the back of the house, with your homework on your lap," Ted said, grinning. "The rehearsal had run late. Past your bedtime."

Diana and Ted entertained the rest of the folks with stories from those days, with and without the pre-teen Connie in them. Some about her mother. Arguments when she didn't agree with a director's notes—yes, that would have been her mother—bragging about her two girls, the actress and the bookworm.

"Your mother was always the life of the party."

No surprise there.

"There was a cast party at a house on a hill," Connie said. "Somewhere in Colmar. You could see the New York City skyline. Lot of wild dancing...Mom in the middle of things. Champagne flowing. I even had a few sips."

Diana nodded. "Angela Westerman's home up on Rock View. Magnificent views. Glass windows on three sides of the house." She finished her drink. "Haven't been there in a while."

"Angela was something else," Ted said. "Fun. Thick as thieves with your mother. She quit the theatre after Simone disappeared."

One of Mom's friends. Someone worth pursuing.

Then, Diana, frowning, said, "Sometimes during the rehearsal for *Streetcar* your mom would get phone calls and be agitated, really upset. I asked her what was wrong, but she'd smile and shrug. Almost sad."

Sad didn't sound like her mother. But the phone calls?

Talk turned to the remainder of the Flint Theatre season, board issues, and the needed repair to the stage lighting grid which was dangerous due to several damaged pipes and a loose, rusted guardrail on the catwalk. According to Ted, the whole system needed to be replaced. The Colmar Fire Department recently gave the theatre a warning and BJ was working on an estimate for the cost of the fix. Connie remembered the thrill of walking on the catwalk over the stage and stooping down to peek below the system of pipes from which hung the complex maze of instruments. Thrilled as she leaned a tad too far over the guardrail, caught when her mother noticed her daughter in the air, and BJ at the opposite end of the catwalk. Her mother scolded him royally for letting Connie follow him to the grid. It was the first and last time she went up there, but she was safe. BJ had insisted she wear a safety belt that hooked her to the rail. Back then, obviously safer than it was presently.

Laying a few bills on the table, Connie assumed nonchalance. "I saw BJ at the theatre. He taught me all there was to learn about lighting instruments. How is he?"

The table went quiet. "He's had a tough time through the years," the director said. "Ever since that night."

"Did something happen? Besides the blackout?" Connie breathed the words softly, afraid of what she'd hear in reply.

"When the lights blacked out, he went immediately to fiddle with the emergency generator outside on the loading dock. He must have grabbed some sharp tool because he showed up the next day with his hand bandaged. Then later that day, he slipped and fell off the grid. Broke his leg." He shook his head.

Connie clasped her hands to keep them from trembling. Before BJ fiddled with the generator, he'd been in the dressing room with her mother, arguing, then in the hallway fighting with her.

"Hence the limp," Diana concluded.

"Everyone was rattled. I thought he might give up the theatre for a while after that. Take off a few months. But no…The Flint is BJ's life. After two weeks he's back. Broken leg and all." Ted finished off his drink. "Then there was some other stuff." He left the thought dangling, and no one followed up.

"It was a horrifying time. No lights, the storm, Simone, and BJ." Diana cringed, reliving it. "Then the police crawling all over the theatre. And interviewing us."

"Sounds like a TV series," quipped an actor.

She put an arm around Connie. "It was a very dramatic night with terrible consequences."

"Your father came to the theatre a couple weeks after to pick up Simone's…personal effects," Ted said. "Her script. Some other things. He was really broken up."

Wait, what? Connie had no idea that her father was at the theatre after her mother disappeared.

"I don't remember your father," Diana said, "only uniforms. Cops in uniform around here. Even before that night."

Dad must have come to the theatre to see Mom. Didn't sound like a couple heading for a divorce. "Did *Streetcar* ever open?"

Ted shook his head. "We postponed it for a week, but by then Simone's disappearance was too disheartening. We couldn't go forward. I wanted to remount it the following spring but the board said no. Haven't touched the play since."

The hour grew later. Connie stayed longer than she'd intended and when the group walked out of Bendel, dispersing to head home, Ted walked her back to the parking lot. "You're welcome to stop by any time. Sit in on rehearsals again."

"That's so generous of you. I might do it."

"It's the least we can do for Simone. Might rekindle your acting genes."

As she drove home, one thing was certain. Despite her fears, the Flint Theatre allowed her to feel close to her mother, to learn things she never knew about—her mother's friend Angela Westerman, upsetting phone calls the week before the show opened. It was also the place that created her nightmares, a magnet drawing her back to the scene of the disappearance. To the promise she'd made to her mother to never reveal what she'd witnessed in the hallway between her and BJ.

The confrontation made no sense to the younger Connie. It confused her even today. What secret did each of them have on the other? Her mother's threat that night was real—the Flint was BJ's life, Ted had said. If revealing BJ's secret would end his time with it, what would he do to prevent that from happening? Would that make BJ a person of interest?

Chapter 18

Now

"Did you get my text?"

Her sister stirred a pot on the stove.

"Yep." She took a taste of whatever the pan held.

"What is that?"

"Garbage soup. Don't freak out." Before Connie could react, Gaby added, "Leftovers, plus some vegetables plus some spices."

"Is it any good?"

Gaby bent her head over the steaming pot. "Mm." She ladled a bowl full.

Connie dipped a spoon into the soup and tasted. "Not bad. In fact, pretty good." She filled her own bowl and sat opposite Gaby at the table, adding a dash more salt to what was essentially a vegetable-beef-noodle concoction. She was hungrier than she realized.

"You went to the Flint Theatre."

"I saw a bit of rehearsal."

"Like the old days," Gaby said.

"Not exactly like the old days…at least, not like the last day."

Gaby nodded, scooped up a spoonful of soup.

"I went for a drink with the director and some actors. They talked about Mom."

The sisters ate for a bit in silence, the only sound the clanking of spoons into china. "They were at the funeral, right?" Gaby asked.

"Some of them. Did Mom ever mention a woman named Angela Westerman? Ted, the director, said they were close friends."

"Doesn't ring any bells." Gaby gathered their dishes and placed them in the sink. "I was hoping we could take Dad away for a few days before you leave. Give him a change of scenery. A break from Porter's. And everything. What do you think?"

The shattering of glass ripped through the house. Connie vaulted to her feet, running into the living room and then skidding to a stop, Gaby almost bumping into her from behind. Banging into each other like a circus clown act. Except this wasn't funny. Someone had thrown a rock through their front windowpane, shards of glass clinging at odd angles to the frame, the rest of the splintered window scattered on the recliner and the floor.

"Oh my God, what the…? Who…?" Connie's arms hung limp at her sides.

Gaby retrieved the rock. Attached was a note, clear and to the point in screaming block letters: GO HOME.

The sisters stared at each other. Connie ran outside onto the porch, scanning the sidewalk. No one and nothing out of the ordinary. Lights in living rooms, a car or two racing far off down the street. A kernel of fury battled with fear in the pit of her stomach. Who was responsible for damaging the Tucker property and sending the message?

In short order—before their father returned, since he didn't need any more conflict in his life, asserted Gaby—they cleared the broken glass from the living room and Connie arranged for an emergency repair early the next morning. They broke down a cardboard box and created a makeshift cover for the window.

"We have to file a complaint," said Connie.

"Hold on. Maybe it was neighborhood kids misbehaving. I don't want to stir up trouble."

"Huh? Raining glass in our living room isn't trouble?"

Against her better judgment, Connie acquiesced. Though she kept her views to herself, she knew who was to blame. Had to be Rosa Delano. Gaby refrained from offering an opinion on the guilty party and they agreed to tell their father the "neighborhood kid" story. To keep the rock hidden from him. Though she and her sister didn't discuss the rock's message, Connie was sure it was meant for her.

By nine a.m. the next morning, the window replacement guys were on site, sweating in the above normal heat, the temperature already skyrocketing into the high eighties. Gaby had gone to the library. Their father slept in, having stayed at Porter's until closing and ending the night with a few drinks. He wasn't overly upset about the window and as long as his daughters took care of the problem, he was content to ignore it.

Connie joined Brigid for a non-alcoholic happy hour at Porter's. The cheerful, boisterous crowd was well into the second hour of discount drinks, and the noise level surged as the alcohol flowed.

"A rock? What the...?" Brigid registered her shock at the window incident, sucking the life out of the ice at the bottom of her glass of soda. They sat shoulder to shoulder at the bar, leaning in tight to hear each other.

"I'm sure it was Rosa."

"Call the cops?" Brigid asked.

"I wanted to. Gaby said no. So, I went along with it. But I swear, any more little tricks like this and her ass is grass."

Brigid hooted at that. "Her ass is *grass*, man," she said, milking it, and they both laughed. "Now you're sounding like a Hallison gal. Proud of you."

"It was scary when it happened. I mean, how angry do you have to be to shatter somebody's window?"

Brigid crunched an ice cube. "Angry or threatened. What's Rosa's motivation?"

Connie hesitated. "Not sure. She hates us? I keep thinking she's connected to Mom's death."

"How?"

"Again, not sure. She especially hated Mom."

"If Rosa is guilty of something, maybe you're putting her on the defensive."

"What do you mean?"

"She could sense you're sniffing out the past and the rock was telling you to back off," Brigid finished with a meaningful look.

Connie weighed the observation. "Yeah. She's guilty of something. I can feel it."

"Another round?" Dack cleared glasses, swiping a wet rag over the bar's veneer.

"I have to go." Brigid pointed at her husband. "You, my friend, are on duty tomorrow. I need a night off and so does Mom."

"It's my night off, too. Poker—"

"Nope." Brigid chopped off his explanation, and Dack turned away, muttering.

Connie laughed at them. Quite the couple. When her phone rang, she checked the caller ID. "Gotta take this."

125

Brigid mouthed "call me" and Connie moved to the back of the bar to hear better. "Hi Charlie. Sorry for the racket."

"I can hear you fine. Jackie said you tried to reach me. What's up?"

"What's your opinion of Tom Rutherford? He's running the cold case investigation on Mom. Dad likes him, but I found out they were partners. I don't know. He turned me off."

"Old Tommy R. He got assigned desk duty for some questionable tactics when he rode with your dad. Gradually worked his way back in and up. He'll do an okay job."

"Just okay? Dad said he was promoted, not demoted."

"Your old man sometimes forgets how things happened back then. Tommy R was demoted before he was promoted."

"How could Dad forget something like that? Early senility?" Connie knew that was a cruel comment, but it earned a chuckle from her Uncle Charlie.

"Now, now."

"So…another thing. I wasn't going to say anything about this, but someone tossed a rock through our living room window last night. There was a note attached. 'Go home.'"

Charlie was quiet a moment. "Were you hurt? Did you call the police?"

"No and no. Gaby didn't want to stir up any trouble." She hesitated. "It might have been our neighbor. Remember when I asked you if Rosa Delano had been interviewed at the time Mom disappeared? She really did not like Mom and I'm no favorite of hers, either. If she's guilty of…something…the rock might be a warning of some kind."

"Two pieces of advice, honey. One, go to the police station and report this. Even a misdemeanor needs a paper trail."

"And the other?"

"Let Tommy R do his job."

Cop shops still made her pulse bounce. Her first trip to the Hallison Police Department occurred after the shoplifting incident in the neighborhood bodega. Connie, fifteen, and a girl a year older had taken candy, sodas, and chips, and stuffed them in a backpack. They hadn't gotten to the street corner when the owner caught up with them. All she remembered from that visit were the green walls, one of which was covered with glass cases filled with announcements and newspaper clippings concerning newsworthy town information. To this day, Connie couldn't explain why she'd joined the other girl on the pinching spree.

The green walls of the waiting area hadn't changed. Gray plastic seats attached together formed single units. Florescent lights glared from the ceiling and a dispatch window was manned by a brusque woman behind bullet-proof glass. Security doors separated the outer area from the inner station. She submitted her name and chose a chair opposite Dispatch to keep the woman aware of her presence. The outer station wasn't built for comfort, the solitary concession being a vending machine that produced coffee, tea, or hot chocolate. No soda.

To Connie's right, three generations of a family waited—an older man, younger woman, and two little kids who knelt on the floor using the seats as desks while they crayoned in a coloring book. To her left, a middle-aged woman sat alone, eyes closed, lips moving.

The steel door clanged open, and a man slouched out escorted by a policeman. The woman on the left sprang to her feet and crossed to them. The man waved her off, bent his head, and marched out of the station. She followed.

When her name was called, Connie jumped, startled out of her musing, and opened the door to the inner offices when a buzzer sounded. Greeted by a uniformed cop, she was led through the squad room to a chair and requested to take a seat opposite Detective Keogh, as indicated by the nameplate on his cluttered desk. He tapped a pencil against a sheet of paper, chewed fiercely, yanking at his loosened tie.

"So, you want to report vandalism? That occurred two days ago?" He cracked his gum.

This wasn't the best idea—Gaby was right. It was a misdemeanor and could have been a neighborhood prank. Except that it wasn't.

"Someone threw a rock through our living room window."

"Uh-huh. And you waited because…?"

"We didn't think it was serious enough, but a good friend, a former cop, suggested that even minor incidents should be reported."

He picked up a piece of paper. "Uh-huh. You could've filled this out online."

"Sorry. My first time reporting vandalism."

"Damage?" He wrote on the form.

"Three-hundred-fifty dollars."

"Misdemeanor." He wrote some more.

"I figured that, but it was frightening. I mean, the damage was bad enough, but there was a note attached to the rock."

He cocked his head and stopped chewing. "I'm listening."

"It said 'Go home.'"

"You got the rock and the note?"

Connie's heart sank. She'd been so rattled, she'd let Gaby dispose of them because "they didn't want any trouble in the neighborhood." As Gaby had pointed out, Connie could go back to San Diego, but she had to live in Hallison.

She shook her head. "Sorry. My sister…we don't have them anymore."

He pointed his pencil at Connie. "Who's supposed to go home? You?"

"Yes. I live in California."

"You an actor?"

Connie sighed. Typical. "No."

"Why would someone want you to go home?"

"Not sure. Maybe I threatened someone?"

"Threatened? You look familiar. Name?"

"Connie Tucker."

"Tucker...? Are you related to...?"

"My mother."

His manner softened, Keogh expressed his condolences, she summarized her feelings about her mother's murder—that she wanted to understand why someone would do such a thing—and included her suspicions about Rosa.

He removed the gum, wrapped it in a piece of paper, and lobbed it into the wastebasket.

"And you're not convinced the cold case unit will get the job done?" To his credit, Detective Keogh wasn't mocking her.

"I feel like I need to do something."

"Not uncommon." He pushed his chair away from the desk. "Again, sorry about your mother." He tapped the police report. "I'll follow through with this. I suggest you stop annoying your neighbors and leave the detection to the pros." He smiled for the first time.

Stop playing detective. She smiled back.

"I was a beat cop in Hallison when the Simone Tucker case made the news. I remember because of the storm that week and the APB that went out. A car meeting the description of your mother's car was spotted on the parkway a day later."

"What?" Sweat broke out under Connie's summer top, the station suddenly hot and stifling. "Was this part of the official record?"

"I assume so."

So preoccupied with Detective Keogh's revelation, Connie almost missed the Tucker house. She lurched back to reality in time to witness Rosa Delano withdraw her head from under the hood of her SUV, a hulking vehicle that looked as belligerent as its driver, and toss tools into the back seat.

Connie slammed the brakes, pulled to the curb, piled out of the car and ran to Rosa. "Guess you thought that little stunt with the rock was funny."

Rosa paused, her hand on the driver's side door. Oversize sunglasses shielded part of her face, her speech anything but intimidated. "I swear, you Tuckers think you run the world. Well, you don't, and somebody's gotta teach you a lesson."

Connie raised her voice. "I reported it to the police."

Gaby stepped out of the house, still in her work clothes.

Rosa perked up at the word "police," then she grinned. "Well, good for you. You think I'm afraid of cops? Lived next door to one all these years." She jerked her head in the direction of the Tucker house. "Your old man tried to threaten me. Never worked," she growled, her voice deep and hideous. "Time you went home, dontcha' think?" She climbed into the SUV and revved the engine, then leaned across the seat bench and called out the window. "Can't get over Simone's murder, that it?"

To hell with her hateful neighbor.

"Your mother was no angel. She did stuff that summer."

Connie stuttered. "Wha—?"

Rosa rammed the SUV out of her driveway and onto Third Street.

"What's going on?" Gaby waited for her sister on the porch.

Connie marched up the steps. "She as much as admitted she threw the rock."

Gaby opened the screen door. "Get inside." Gaby followed her sister into the living room, then shut the door. "You want the whole neighborhood to see you fighting with her?"

"We have to talk. Let's get some dinner."

Gaby seemed to weigh her options, then surrendered. While Connie flew around the kitchen warming up leftover kung pao chicken and vegetable fried rice, Gaby sat at the table, a beer in hand. She listened, immobile, as her sister described her misgivings about Detective Rutherford and the sighting of an automobile that matched Simone's red Ford Tempo.

Gaby, silent when Connie finished, took a swallow of her beer, and ran fingers through her curly locks. "You've been busy. Thought we agreed we weren't going to the Hallison police."

"Charlie said we need a paper trail in case anything else happens."

"Charlie? What's he got to do with this?" Gaby, as usual, dismissed their father's old partner out of hand.

Connie had never understood her aversion to Charlie. When they were kids, he treated them the same, though on one occasion she claimed he liked her better and Gaby had a fit, resulting in her throwing a deck of cards at Connie. Surely it couldn't all be traced back to that one snit.

"He was trying to help us," Connie said, "and for the record I think he was right." She took a forkful of chicken and chewed. "We don't agree on this, but I don't think it was a neighborhood prank. And did you see the way Rosa reacted?"

A note of irritation crept into Gaby's voice. "Rosa's always been annoying. Let it go, okay?"

"Annoying? She's a lot worse than that." Connie had no intention of letting anything go. "She said Mom was no angel. That she saw her do stuff that last summer."

Gaby's head snapped up. "What does that mean?"

"I have no idea, but Rosa knows something, or at least is pretending she does. She's always been a troublemaker." She sighed and sat back. "Gaby, you do want to know who murdered, Mom, right?"

Her sister winced at the point-blank question. "Of course I do. But…can't you let the cold case unit figure it out?"

They finished their meal in silence, the atmosphere glum. Immediately after dinner she intended to call Detective Nardone and ask about the sighting of a red Ford Tempo the day after her mother disappeared.

Chapter 19

Now

The next day when Gaby suggested a break in everyone's routine, a weekend away in order to relax and chill, their father said no way was he staying in a hotel for a weekend. Porter's needed him. Debatable. Connie didn't want to leave town overnight either. Since she couldn't afford to waste time. Too much on her detection plate. Louis Nardone was leaving for Seattle next week and she had yet to hear back from him about Detective Keogh's statement on the red Ford. Then there was the cryptic message her mother had left in French, and her father's timeline the night of the storm. And BJ. She had to go back to the Flint Theatre and confront him. What was she waiting for? Finally, she hated to give Rosa any credibility, but her comments about their mother were disturbing: "no angel" and "doing stuff."

The sisters struck a bargain. Gaby took a personal day off work and Connie agreed, reluctantly, to join her sister and father on a day trip. The compromise plan was lunch at a restaurant, situated in an outdoor museum, in central New Jersey.

"We can have a nice meal and meander among the sculptures," Gaby said.

133

"Why do we need to walk around statues?" their father asked, after consenting to go, also reluctantly.

Crass, but the same question Connie had.

Gaby banged out of the room in frustration, yelling back, "Because we could bond as a family."

Again, debatable.

In exchange for Connie's cooperation, Gaby agreed to join her in the attic to sort through their mother's things. Maybe her belongings had a story to tell, further revelations about her mother, something, anything that might shed light on her death. Maybe clues to deciphering the note she'd left to Connie that she wasn't happy and might be going away.

The next day was sunny and warm, humid but not unbearably so. Connie offered to drive her rental car—easier to avoid conversation if she was driving—and by eleven a.m. the Tucker family headed down the parkway to Garland, GPS leading them to the restaurant an hour away. Dialogue between Connie and her father was limited, he riding shotgun, and overriding the GPS on occasion. Gaby sat in the back seat, a slight, contented smile on her face. She'd managed to get them all together for this road trip. A victory. Connie kept her eyes glued to the road, hands clamped to the wheel.

The fashionable French Bistro had received great reviews, Gaby told them. It was the kind of place neither she nor their father had eaten at in years. Her treat, she said. Good thing. Connie's credit card had reached a tipping point. Seated at a cozy table in the window, already set with sparkling glassware and crisp linens, Connie had a view of the L-shaped marble slab bar stretched out opposite them. A gentle breeze circulated around the room.

"Let's have some wine," Connie suggested. A little alcohol would take the edge off her discomfort at sitting in the restaurant with her father, now that she questioned his timeline the night her mother disappeared. His alibi depended on accepting his claim that he was home at ten p.m. for the rest of the night. Connie knew different. He returned to the house at five a.m.

"At noon?" her father said.

"Pretend you're at Porter's," she said.

Everything on the menu was pricey, but Connie ordered a bottle of chardonnay and chose a beet salad and shrimp scampi. Their father stuck to known entities—French onion soup and the Bistro burger. Gaby scrutinized all the restaurant had to offer, then opted for Connie's selections.

The sisters sipped their wine, their father taking a drink to be social, but gently nudging the glass away from his place setting, absorbing the atmosphere. The bistro filled up, the customers a varied sort—men in suits, women in jeans, a family in nice casual clothing.

Their father dressed in his everyday uniform: khakis, a polo shirt, and well-worn sneakers.

"This is great, right?" Gaby said.

"Yes. Far cry from Porter's," Connie said.

"Porter's is fine," their father said, defensive.

"Gotta admit, the burger there is to die for," Connie said.

"We kind of grew up on them," Gaby added.

"You two had your share," their father agreed.

"On nights when you and Mom were busy," Connie said. Both before the disappearance and after. She ran her finger over a crease in the white tablecloth. "You're glad Detective Rutherford is on the cold case unit? Since you used to be partners?"

He blinked, shifted his gaze, and Gaby frowned, sending Connie a signal as she picked up her wineglass: Let it go for today.

No way.

135

He drummed his fingers on the table, his heart tattoo on full display. "Like I said before. Tom's a good guy."

"Uncle Charlie said Rutherford got demoted, then promoted. You said the opposite."

Her father looked flustered. "Charlie?"

"We were chatting, and I happened to mention our visit to the county prosecutor's office."

Her father slathered butter on a chunk of warm bread and bit off a mouthful. "Long time ago," he mumbled.

Really. "I went to the Flint Theatre yesterday. To visit, thank folks for coming to Mom's funeral."

"It was nice of them to come," Gaby said, careful, her glance begging her sister to stop with the talk of their mom.

Connie persisted. "Do you remember a woman named Angela Westerman? The director said she was a good friend of Mom's. Said she quit the theatre. Gaby and I don't recall her."

Could have been her imagination, now on overdrive, that detected a spark in his eyes before being doused by grief. "I didn't know those people. Never went to the theatre except for the nights your mother was in a show."

"And the night of the storm," Connie said. "You picked me up."

Her father recoiled as though mentioning that night produced an electrical shock.

"The crazy rain and wind, and you driving so fast through the pools of water in the roads. Like you were angry about something. Then you sat in the car for a while."

He lifted his head and leveled his gaze on hers. His blue eyes like steel. "Why bring all this up now?"

"The cold case investigators will ask us about that night, right?"

Father and daughter stared hard at each other, he blinking first. "I can't remember stuff from then."

"That's strange. Every minute of that night is seared onto my brain."

Gaby, almost panicking as she gauged the tension at the table, announced the arrival of lunch. "Here we are."

The three of them focused on their meals, Gaby adroitly shifting the conversation to neutral ground: what was happening in the library, goings on in the neighborhood, asking her father about Porter's. Connie remained silent, though she admired her sister's skill in handling the two of them. A talent she hadn't witnessed before. She supposed there were many things she had yet to learn about her sister.

"Isn't this nice?" Gaby scanned the restaurant at the end of their meal, all of them so full they passed on dessert.

When the bill arrived, Gaby withdrew a credit card—resisting Connie's weak attempt to share the expense—while their father gaped at the total. It certainly wasn't Porter's.

On the street, before heading into the sculpture garden, the Tuckers strolled around town to wear off the calories, past high-end clothing stores, home goods shops, boutiques that featured everything from kids' toys and games to bath and beauty products, all housed in quaint buildings dating from the eighteenth and nineteenth centuries. Galleries, a movie theatre, cobblestone alleyways.

"Imagine living here," Gaby said.

"Kind of reminds me of Colmar," said Connie. All mental roads led back to that town for her. "Downtown area around the Flint Theatre. Did you know Jackie's family founded the theatre?"

Gaby shook her head and their father, sucking on a homemade butterscotch candy he bought at the Chocolate Shoppe, either didn't hear her, or pretended not to. Two steps behind the two of them, Connie gazed at the back of her father's head, his thinning, gray curly hair trickling into his shirt collar. What would he think if he knew his daughter was suspicious of his actions the night his wife was murdered? Could Connie even go there? Only in a horrendous universe would her father be a person of interest in a crime against her mother. It was unthinkable…and yet…

"Now we're going to see the sculptures," Gaby said. "I read that they're amazing. Some are life-size, many based on the Impressionist painters like Monet." It all came out in a rush.

"I've had enough fresh air for one day," her father said. "Let's head home."

"Nope." Gaby was not to be deterred. "We came here to see the sculptures." She marched off.

He shot a glance at Connie. "Guess we're going to the outdoor museum."

They trailed Gaby, into the landscaped gardens with a myriad of flower beds and shrubbery. A gravel path led them past bronze sculptures, large and small, sitting on benches, hidden in trees, lying on the ground, appearing to laugh and drink and chat.

"Smile." Gaby snapped photos. "Pose with the sculptures."

"What?"

"Come on. It'll be funny. Put your arm around the guy."

Connie, reluctant, did as she was told on a platform next to a life-size statue. Then she snapped a picture of her sister and father sitting side-by-side at a table with a sculpture of a young couple enjoying an intimate tête-à-tête. Gaby laughing, her father smiling. The two of them seemingly oblivious to Connie's agitated state. They'd moved beyond the lunch cross-examination. Suddenly, her father glanced up, all traces of a smile gone as he glared at Connie, as if he could read her mind.

She felt wary being near him. Almost afraid. A new sensation.

As they walked to Connie's car, Gaby murmured, "It was a lovely day."

Connie's heart plummeted. It wasn't. Not really, what with her interrogating her father and him sidestepping questions. Anyway, old resentments died hard. But all it took for Gaby to enjoy herself was the three of them together. A pang of guilt caught Connie off-guard.

The late afternoon traffic was heavy as Connie cruised down the state route to the parkway. Streaks of receding sunlight slashed across her windshield and momentarily blinded her as she swung onto the parkway, a BMW on her tail.

"Get in the slow lane." Her father glanced out the passenger side window.

The BMW followed suit.

"Well, go around me, why don't you?" Irritated at the driver and the day, Connie stepped on the accelerator. "I hate these luxury car drivers who think they own the road." She moved to the center lane and increased her speed, ten miles above the limit, though in keeping with the flow of other vehicles.

The BMW whipped around another car and sneaked in behind her. Frustrated at what was becoming a cat-and-mouse game, Connie slowed and craned her neck. "Get his license plate number."

As if the driver heard her, the BMW slammed into the far-left passing lane with a blast of its engine and zoomed off. Connie's breath released in choppy puffs, and she reduced her speed, pumping her breaks a bit, noticing more play than she had previously. She should call the car rental and see about switching models. "What was that about?"

"Damn parkway drivers," her father said, offhanded, as he released his rigid grip on the dashboard.

As they traveled north, everything slowed, the parkway bumper-to-bumper for a mile. It was possible to drive to their end of Hallison on city streets and backroads—you could get anywhere in New Jersey via backroads.

"I'm getting off."

"The parkway is the fastest route."

Connie had no desire to argue about traffic with her father. Especially since the flow of cars sped up, easing into a consistent stream, allowing her to relax as she approached her exit. Tomorrow she would leave another message for Louis Nardone, make plans to head back to the Flint Theatre, tackle the attic with Gaby, and, if she could stand it, challenge Rosa about her nasty comments. Make her explain. Connie's mother *was* an angel and nothing her neighbor said could change that fact. Still…

In the rearview mirror, Connie saw a pickup truck barreling down on them. A screech of brakes.

"Oh my God! There's—"

"Connie!" Gaby yelled.

Behind them traffic collapsed, compressed vehicles like a bumper car mash-up filling her rearview mirror. In front of the Tuckers, the brake lights of the next car flashed a warning. Connie jammed on her brakes, pumping as hard as she could. Nothing happened. She swung her car to the right to drive down an exit ramp, but the pickup still charging toward her couldn't stop in time, hitting her bumper, hard, pushing her to the edge of the access road, headed for a steep drop-off to a wide grassy area.

Her father grabbed the dashboard again.

"Brake!" Gaby screamed.

"I am!" Connie screamed back.

She swerved to the left, bounced off a guardrail, yanking on the emergency brake, skidding to a brutal stop. Connie and her father were thrown sideways, then forward, the car coming to rest on the side of the exit ramp. Above them on the parkway, the sounds of scraping metal as other cars banged into one another.

A police vehicle pulled up opposite their car. A young officer got out. "You okay?" she asked.

First responders on the parkway sorted through the chain-reaction pileup. Tow trucks disentangled damaged automobiles and removed them from the scene. Fortunately for the Tuckers, Connie had swung them off the highway to an accessible area bordering the exit ramp.

All of them shook up.

The cop offered to call an ambulance, but the Tuckers declined, their father claiming it was a minor fender-bender. No airbags deployed.

While he bent the young officer's ear, Connie assessed the car's damage: the driver's side scraped and dented; the front bumper rammed into the front left tire. At any rate, the rental was not drivable.

"You did well getting us off the parkway." Gaby put her arms around her sister's wobbly body.

"I didn't see the pickup in time. Or the car in front." She started to shake.

"It's okay." Gaby rubbed Connie's back, taking charge, calling a tow truck, then a ride service. "We'll get home and you'll calm down."

As they climbed into the back seat of the Uber, their father up front, Connie murmured, "I pumped the brakes. Again and again. Hard. Something's wrong with them."

Gaby reassured her. "We'll get them checked out."

Connie shook her head. "The brakes were fine a few days ago. What could have happened? I haven't driven far enough to wear them down that quickly."

Something caused them to stop working.

Chapter 20

Now

On the way home, Charlie called to see if Connie had reported the rock incident but instead got an earful about the parkway incident.

"I'll stop by later," he said. "Call me when you get home."

Their father had a headache and a sore neck and promptly went to bed, too stressed to eat dinner. Connie and Gaby grabbed odds and ends and sat at the kitchen table, Connie picking at a salad of wilted greens and veggies, Gaby trying her best with a bowl of chicken noodle soup.

"His head hit the side window. I hope he doesn't have a concussion. Or whiplash," Connie said, her arms and legs limp as the accident-adrenaline that had pumped through her body dissipated.

"People get concussions all the time. If the headache's still here tomorrow, I'll take him to the doctor to get checked out," Gaby said. "I had one as a kid."

Connie frowned. "You did?"

"Fell out of that makeshift treehouse in the backyard. Disaster waiting to happen."

The treehouse. Connie's refuge. When anger threatened to engulf her as a kid, she hid among the branches of the old elm. "I think your memory is better than mine. For example, what do you remember from the days after Mom disappeared?" Connie dropped a napkin into her salad and pushed it away.

"What brought that on? This part of your investigation thing?" Gaby asked softly.

"I'd like to see if we remember the same things."

Gaby arched an eyebrow. "Besides you getting in trouble?"

Connie had to laugh. "Yeah, besides that."

"Well..." Gaby leaned back and studied a crack in the ceiling as if it held the answer. "I cried a lot. You didn't. Mrs. Delano brought us casseroles. You refused to eat. I spent time in my room. You spent time at Brigid's. Dad worked double shifts, hardly ever home. And one day we went to the Flint Theatre because Dad said he had to pick up Mom's stuff."

"Oh yeah?" The director said their father had stopped by to retrieve their mother's personal effects. She had no idea Gaby was with him. "Without me?"

"Because you weren't home. Off running around, getting into—"

"Trouble."

Gaby collected dishes from their half-eaten meals and placed them in the sink. "I kept the memory because this nice woman put her arms around me and let me cry on her shoulder while Dad went backstage to the dressing room."

"Where are they now?"

"What?"

"Mom's things he brought back. Her script from the show..."

"...and one of Dad's old shirts that I guess she wore in the dressing room," Gaby added. "Dunno. Thrown out?"

Attic dust covered the floor, Connie's footprints leaving a trail from the top of the steps to an ancient rocking chair. She surveyed the accumulated junk. "Gaby?"

"Coming!" Her sister appeared, kerchief tied around her head to corral her curls, a portable vacuum in her hand. "If we're going to dig through stuff, I'm cleaning as well."

"Last time I was up here was Christmas before California." That year they rummaged around for tree ornaments, settling for a couple of strings of lights, some glass balls, and worn-out tinsel. Their father avoided the holiday that year, but Connie and Gaby hiked to a lot on Ferry Street to purchase the cheapest leftover tree they could find. They decorated it and waited for their father to come home after an evening at Porter's. They opened a few gifts, mostly from his family. Christmases were different when their mother was in the house—once-a-year aromas of roasting turkey and pumpkin pies in the kitchen and toys. Come Christmas, she assured them Santa had a copy of their lists. Connie had no idea where she found the money, assuming she saved funds from her weekly budget and part-time job. Their father made a decent salary as a Newark police officer; still, she often complained about having to pinch pennies.

"Where's Dad?"

"Taking a nap. I think the accident yesterday freaked him out."

"Is he going to Porter's today?"

"He called in sick." Gaby sneezed. "Where do we start?"

"There?" Connie pointed to a corner. "And work our way out to here."

Blindly sorting through stuff when she didn't know what she was searching for could be a dead end. Had to be done, though. No other way to be sure she didn't miss some clue to her mother's death.

Gaby wiped sweat off her forehead. "It's ten degrees hotter up here than downstairs, with no ventilation."

Connie gazed upward at the rafters whose beams arced to form Vs, creating the steep, sloped roof of the nearly hundred-year-old house. "Wasn't there an old fan?"

"No idea." The single bare bulb offered limited vision. "Let's do it," Gaby said.

They bypassed tattered suitcases and yearbooks from high school, setting the photo albums aside, and waded through cartons, unearthing rusty kitchenware, broken toys, and a worn, grimy quilt. Connie held it to the dim light to view the red, blue, and green triangles intricately arranged in geometric shapes. Usable if cleaned, unless it fell apart.

"That's from Mom's family in France," Gaby said. "She told me it brought her comfort in a bad time in her life."

"She never said anything about the quilt to me."

"I was home more. You were always out running around the neighborhood. I listened to her, and not only when she was dreaming up vacations."

A twinge of jealousy—her mother had shared things with her sister. Hard to accept that Gaby knew more on the subject of their mother than she did.

"It was before she was married to Dad, she said."

Connie found coats that she and Gaby had outgrown years ago, along with tops, shorts, jeans, and jackets. Their father's old boots and trousers. A battered Monopoly game with the money missing, a five-hundred-piece jigsaw puzzle with possibly half the pieces gone. Memories. Forming a throw-out pile and a questionable pile, Connie and Gaby made progress for an hour, with Gaby vacuuming the floor as each area was emptied.

"What's in that?" Connie pointed to a brown bag stuffed behind a broken bicycle.

Gaby shrugged. "Open it."

She wiped a layer of dust off the bag and looked inside. "Oh…"

"What?"

Connie withdrew their mother's copy of *Streetcar*, a worn makeup bag full of pancake and powder and lipsticks, and a man's stained, white dress shirt, frayed at collar and cuffs. "Mom's things from the theatre weren't thrown out."

The sisters stared at the bag's contents. Like pieces of their mother. Gaby picked up the makeup kit, Connie held the shirt to her face, inhaling whatever scent remained.

"I don't remember putting it up here," Gaby said. "Maybe Dad did? Anything else in there?"

Connie stuck her hand in the brown bag and pulled out a bunch of papers. Loose pages of character notes written in their mother's careful hand, a takeout menu from a Colmar deli, rehearsal schedules. A small card from Broad Street Florists that read: *Let's have a great opening! XOXO*

She handed it to Gaby. "Flowers for Mom. From who? Sounds like someone at the theatre. Maybe another cast member?"

Gaby frowned. "Nice thought, whoever it was."

Connie replaced the items in the bag—they'd keep them up here for now—except for the florist card. She stuffed it into her pants pocket.

"I'm getting some coffee." Gaby sneezed again and wiped her eyes with the bandanna. "Want some?"

Connie shook her head and gazed around the attic. One last box they had yet to open. She ripped off tape and lifted the lid. A packet of notes addressed to SB, Simone Bernard, and signed simply LT, Liam

Tucker, tied together with a blue ribbon. Very brief, some a line or two. No dates on them. Probably before they were married.

Connie skimmed a few of the messages. Nothing extraordinarily romantic, but a different picture of her parents' relationship. Normal, simple, sweet. Nothing complicated or argumentative.

Beneath the notes were envelopes postmarked from several cities in southern France: Marseille, Arles, Nice. The postmarks were dated nineteen-ninety, ninety-one, ninety-two. Deeper in the box she found her parents' marriage license. April 1, 1990. Come to think of it, her parents never celebrated their wedding anniversary. Connie studied the document. Her older sister Gaby was born in October. That meant…a shotgun marriage! She laughed out loud. Her good Catholic father got his French girlfriend pregnant and had to marry her. Quickly. Did her father feel forced to make the union legal and Gaby "legitimate?" She was eighteen when they married, he was twenty-four.

"Charlie's here to see Dad. Find anything interesting?" Gaby entered holding a coffee cup and a fistful of black garbage bags. "We can fill these."

"A box that belonged to Mom."

"What's in it?"

"Letters from France. Notes from Dad that she kept."

"Let me see." Connie handed over the box and Gaby flipped through the contents.

"Did you know you were conceived before their wedding?" Connie asked slyly.

"Of course. They were married in April, my birthday's October." Gaby shrugged and smiled. "I'm 'illegitimate.'"

Connie tapped the stack of photo albums with her toe. "Let's take these downstairs."

"Once, Mom said no matter what anyone ever told me, I was a wonderful wedding present."

"What did that mean?" Connie asked.

"That they wanted me?"

Laughter greeted the sisters as they descended stairs from the attic to the first floor. When was the last time Connie heard her dad laugh like that? Not since she returned to New Jersey. Never mind surviving a pileup on the parkway.

Gaby opened the screen door. "You're perky, Dad," she said. "Better than this morning."

Both Charlie and their father sat on the front porch glider. Like the old days. Both of them relaxed.

"That's me. Perky," he said, wryly.

"Hi Charlie," Connie said, her eyes lighting up. "What's so funny? We could hear you two cackling from the hallway."

"Reliving the good old days at the academy," Charlie said.

"Not sure they were all so 'good.'" Their father sipped from a water glass.

"Sure they were. I used to cover for you when you were late for roll call."

"You covered for me? What're you talking about? I covered for you!"

They both chuckled.

"You never talked about your days at the academy, Dad," Gaby said.

Charlie leaned back and grinned, his muscular arms crossed in front of him. "How about the time you almost got caught with a cheat sheet on the Arrest, Search, and Seizure unit? Peabrain Peabody…" He turned to the sisters. "That's what we called the instructor. Your dad had trouble memorizing legal statutes and—"

"You're full of shit, Charlie. It wasn't me with the cheat sheet, it was Eddie Morgan." He crossed his own arms like Charlie's, but tighter. "And he did get caught. Unlike you."

Charlie grinned. "I could play the system, unlike the rest of you chumps."

"Chumps?" Gaby frowned.

"Just teasing your old dad. Liam did everything by the book. He was an outstanding recruit."

"What about you, Charlie?" Connie asked.

"Me? I was top of the class." He winked at her.

"Until the use of force complaint the first week on the street," her father said, guarded.

Their father's accusation didn't make a dent in Charlie's good-humor shield. "A little tussle with a homeless guy." He shrugged. "Nature of the job." He uncrossed his arms, popped up off the glider. "I gotta go. Early day tomorrow."

"On a Saturday? The corporate world running you ragged?" Connie teased.

"Sold his soul to the devil," their father announced with a trace of sarcasm. Connie guessed he would give his right arm to be where Charlie was now, making big bucks in high-end white-collar security.

"Hey, hey," Charlie said. "Cut that out or I'll have to clap you in cuffs."

Chapter 21

Now

Charlie said his goodbyes, their father went inside to cool off in his air-conditioned bedroom. Connie braved the humidity and settled into the glider with three photo albums. She opened one. The two sisters. First as newborns, then at regular intervals until they were six? Seven? Gaby, frowning, with brown hair sticking up in all directions; Connie laughing, blond curls a halo around her face. They'd entered this world looking and behaving so differently.

The screen door whooshed open. "Here." Gaby extended a bottle of beer. "Whew. I'm dripping wet."

Connie accepted it and took a sip. "Have a seat." She scooted over to make room on the swing. "I was going through this old album." She started over on the first page, pointing at the pictorial history of the two sisters. Lying on a blanket in the living room, sitting in a playpen, waving from a stroller. Running under a sprinkler in the backyard, dressed up in Halloween costumes. Connie was always a princess or ballerina, Gaby a cowgirl or ghost.

"You liked to dress up like Mom," Gaby said, tapping a photo. "Her scarves, jewelry, even her perfume. You were a little mini-me. Kind of obsessed. On the other hand, I generally had my nose in a book."

Connie touched one picture. "Mrs. Delano. She babysat for us a lot."

"Mm."

"It's been hard to speak with her. Except at the repast. Rosa's running interference." Connie gazed at the house next door, dark except for a single light in the living room. No point in resurrecting the rock-through-the-window incident. A sore point with Gaby.

They drank in silence, the only sound the creaking of the ancient glider and a dog barking somewhere up Third Street. "Did you know Dad was a hero cop when he was young?" Connie asked. "He saved a kid in a burning building. Old Man Porter told me about it."

Gaby had turned her head, her beer halfway to her mouth. "Really?"

A door slammed and someone shouted. A car backfired. Third Street noise. "By the way, congratulations on your college degree. Belated."

Gaby rested her head on the back of the swing. "I started a couple of years after high school. Part-time, then picked up more classes. Took me six years."

"It's wonderful. I'm proud of you." She swallowed a lump in her throat, Gaby blushing.

"You?" Gaby eyed her sister as she lifted the bottle.

"College, you mean?" Connie stared off. "I tried it for two years. Couldn't hack it. Wasn't for me."

"I figured you'd major in theatre. Acting. Whatever."

"Nope."

Heat shimmered off the pavement. "How was it...living with Aunt Marie?"

Connie bit back her immediate response. Like being the prisoner of a benevolent dictator who made sure you were fed, clothed, and sheltered, but never kissed good night. Like their mother did. "She tried her best. I didn't want for anything at least." *Except affection.*

"Do you have good friends out there?"

"Some. A few at The Shack." Connie picked at the bottle's label, tearing off strips.

"I don't mean to pry, but do you have your own apartment?"

Connie closed her eyes and saw the three story, rambling beach house where she rented a room and shared a bath. "Sort of."

"So...what's next? I mean, when you go back?"

"Next? Bartending at The Shack. What else?"

"Okay." After a beat, Gaby added, "I'm applying for a new position. Director of Special Collections at the main library in Newark. Haven't told anyone yet."

"Wow. Good luck."

Gaby rubbed a finger along the edge of the album. "It might be a reach, but shoot for the moon, right? That's what Mom always said."

"She did say that."

Gaby shifted sideways on the glider. "Connie, do you dream about...someday...?"

"Someday what? Not much to dream about in my line of work. That's the difference between us. Between Jersey and California. Out there I don't have to dream about anything. I can forget about the future and ignore the past. At least I could until I got your call." She avoided Gaby's eyes. "Speaking of the past, I've seen Brigid a few times."

Gaby's grin was wide. "First to get in trouble, after you. First to get pregnant. She jumped on Dack the minute you were gone. Heard she has three at home."

"Plus the one on the way."

"Still jumping on him," Gaby cracked.

"Guess I dodged a bullet." Connie laughed. The upside of being sent away.

Connie flipped pages of another album and pointed to photos of their mother and father and Charlie in their twenties, at a dress-up event. "The three of them looking pretty hot," she said.

Gaby pointed to another picture of their father and Charlie in dress uniforms. "This must be their graduation day from the police academy."

"All spiffed up. Handsome guys." Connie said. "What do you make of Deirdre's talk of a triangle? Do you think she meant the three of them? At the repast she said Dad and Charlie fought over Mom. And that outburst about jealousy?"

"Charlie's mother was a little crazy. My—"

"Birthday party. Yeah."

Gaby finished her beer and stretched. "I'll see about dinner."

Connie closed her eyes, swinging gently, her body softening in the Hallison evening air, the sun descending, the sky a blaze of orange and purple, the day's heat receding. She eased off the glider and grabbed the albums to follow Gaby into the house. As she realigned a few loose pages at the back of one of them, something dropped out, and when she stooped to pick it up, her heart beat a little faster. It was a playbill. *A Streetcar Named Desire*. Connie flipped through the pages until she came to the cast of characters, brushing fingertips over the name of her mother. *STELLA.......Simone Tucker*. The glossy programs were expensive for the theatre to print and unavailable to the public until the

153

show opened. She had begged her mother on several occasions to let her have one, but her mother always said, "After opening. Until then, only actors get them."

In the dressing room that night, the stage manager had handed one of the playbills to her mother, who stuffed it into her blue tote bag. Which was never found, or at least no one connected to the investigation of her disappearance mentioned it.

The blue carryall with the playbill probably left the theatre with her. If her father didn't see her mother that night after he'd dropped Connie off at home, when did he get the program?

Connie loaded the dishwasher. She hung the damp dish towel over the drain board and returned to the front porch. Restless, she weighed swinging on the glider versus going for a stroll. To think. She stuck her head in the house and yelled, "Going for a walk. See you later."

Down Third Street to the corner, over Ferry, around the block passing the library, its windows dark at this hour. Connie power-walked to keep up with her pounding brain and the endless loop of images. Her mother's message to her in French; the red Ford Tempo spotted on the parkway the day after she disappeared; the rock through the window; her father's troublesome timeline; Rosa's comment that her mother "did stuff" that last summer. And now the program and blue tote. Not to mention that night in the hallway with her mother and BJ and the promise she made never to tell what she'd seen and heard. BJ grabbing her mother. The things they said to each other. Threats.

She slowed her pace on the third revolution of the neighborhood and stopped in front of Porter's. With the door open, Connie could see the place was hopping. Might have been the full moon or the pleasant evening's air that triggered the crowd's raucous laughter, clinking of glass against glass, and the occasional roar when the Yankees scored a run. She stepped inside and worked her way to the bar, two deep as folks waited for service. They must miss Dad tonight. Dack ran from one end of the bar to the other, taking drink orders for the table service as well as from people juggling for space to lean in and get his attention. The Old Man handled the cash register, placed food orders, and lugged cases of beer from the back room. The lone waitress shuttled from the kitchen to tables. The place so loud one could hardly think or talk.

Connie caught Dack's eye and smiled sympathetically. He signaled, "What can you do?"

She'd been there at The Shack. Crazy busy nights. Then she was moving. "Excuse me. Sorry." In seconds she had jostled past patrons and popped behind the bar.

"What are you doing?" Dack opened bottles of Bud Light, and the waitress whisked them away.

"Going to work. I do this for a living, remember?" Connie turned to customers. "What'll we have?"

The Old Man watched her drawing beer, pouring wine, mixing drinks. Of course, it was all there in her, waiting to be set in motion. Like shuffling a deck of cards. Her hands knew what to do. When the Old Man brushed past her grabbing credit cards and cash, she bellowed, "Taking Dad's place." He grunted. The neighborhood hangout had mutated into a rocking joint.

For the next couple of hours, working in rhythm and backed up by the Old Man, Connie and Dack cut through the standing-room-only clientele. Reducing the throng of impatient drinkers to a manageable trickle.

"The natives have calmed down." Connie sipped a seltzer, dunking a slice of lemon with a straw.

"Thanks to you," Dack said. "Can't imagine what hit us tonight. Talk about slammed. And without Liam. How is he?"

"He's fine. Just needed a night off." She picked up a towel and automatically wiped glasses that the Old Man had dunked in suds, then in rinse water.

"We miss him," Porter said. "You saved our heinies tonight."

Connie laughed. "Happy to. Makes me think of home."

Home... Where was that, exactly? Now New Jersey, soon to be California again.

"Tucker girls. Smart." The Old Man headed to the kitchen and left Dack and Connie and the waitress to fend for themselves.

After another half hour, the bar emptied out. Clean up underway, the kitchen got ready to close. Connie collapsed on a barstool, tired, feet aching. She'd forgotten in the brief time she'd been in Hallison how physical bartending was.

Dack propped a hip against the bar. "Brigid said you had your car towed to Ricky's Auto Body. Much damage?" Dack asked.

"Surprisingly, no. The bumper and side door will need work. Getting off the parkway and onto the access ramp saved it." Connie massaged the instep of her right foot. "You used to mess around with cars when we were in high school."

"I rebuilt a complete engine in shop class," he said with pride.

She nodded. "What would've made the brakes fail? They were fine when I picked up the rental at the airport, but the last day or so, something felt off."

"Could be overheated or worn brake pads. Most common issue is low brake fluid. Like a leak."

"Wouldn't the rental agency check something like that? Top off fluids before renting the car?"

Dack shrugged. "You'd think. But these days?"

He launched into a story about taking his car to a mechanic for an oil change and having to redo the work when he got it home. How you couldn't trust auto shops and drivers were better off doing maintenance themselves. Connie bobbed her head, but her mind drifted elsewhere. Leaking brake fluid. And what would cause that?

Chapter 22

Now

Ricky's Auto Body was only a mile away from Third Street, a nice walk in the cooler air. Later would be another weather story, with worsening humidity predicted. Connie needed to check on the condition of her car before she blasted the rental company for giving her a defective—and life-threatening—automobile. Once she got the estimate, she'd give corporate a call.

She strolled through Hallison, passing more iconic locales from her childhood: a bowling alley where she and Brigid had spent Friday nights; Hallison High, with its playing fields stretching off into the distance and the building housing the auditorium that served as her first real theatre.

Her stint at Porter's Bar and Grill last night was fun. Her father was skeptical at breakfast—couldn't imagine his daughter picking up the slack at the neighborhood watering hole. That was his job. Gaby, on the other hand, beamed. "Glad to see you made yourself useful."

Connie stuck her tongue out and Gaby returned the favor. Both of them laughed.

The garage reeked of the sickly-sweet smell of gasoline. The mechanic, with oil-stained hands and a stubbly beard, didn't bat an eye when she explained how the damage had occurred during the pileup on the parkway. That she banged into the guardrail on the exit ramp. She guessed he'd seen it all.

"I gave it a once-over to see about engine damage. Looks good. But not the brakes." He handed Connie a written estimate. She glanced at the paper.

"They failed," she said.

"Sure."

"Why?"

"No brake fluid. By the time she got towed here, dry as a bone."

Dack was correct. Leaky fluid. "Can you tell how it happened? I have to call the rental company."

The man wiped his forehead with a bright red handkerchief. "Not sure. Could be a slow leak in the brake line. Like it had been damaged."

"Damaged?"

The mechanic shrugged. "Could have been an accident, like somebody nicked the line when they were under the hood."

Connie's stomach lurched, sweat forming on her forehead. If it wasn't an accident, it could have been deliberate tampering. Like someone messing around with her brakes, knowing what the result would be. Her mind immediately ran through the short list of who had access to her car and landed on Rosa. Even for Connie, it was hard to believe her neighbor was involved. Throwing a rock was one thing; cutting a brake line a whole different story.

The loaner was clean, with a whiff of stale cigarette smoke. It would do for a few days. The real problem? She had opted out of paying for collision damage on the rental contract—cheaper that way and she'd never expected to be in this position. Though the price of the repairs wasn't exorbitant, it maxed out her primary credit card. Good she had a second card for emergencies. This entire trip was an emergency.

Connie had to make some decisions, confront the hard facts. Talk it out…but with whom? There had been no news from the cold case unit, despite her leaving two messages for Detective Rutherford, and Detective Nardone hadn't responded after she left the question about the sighting of her mother's Ford Tempo on the parkway the day after she went missing. There was only one person she was comfortable sharing everything with. As usual. She tapped numbers on her phone and waited. "Hi Charlie."

Charlie and Jackie arranged for Connie to come to the Colmar house the next night for dinner. But before that happened, she had to return to the Flint Theatre. She'd made a decision: Events were coming to a head for her and she had to talk with BJ. To tell him what she planned to do. Go to the police and break her promise to her mother. Tell them everything she witnessed in the hallway outside the dressing room the night her mother disappeared. Even if she didn't understand what she'd witnessed. They would come to him for further details. Now, both she and BJ had to tell the truth. Whatever the cost.

She parked in the lot next door and hesitated when she glanced in the window of the café—Ted and the stage manager ordering from the barista. Connie hoped she wouldn't wear out her welcome at the theatre.

"Hi Ted."

He turned away from the counter. "Connie. Nice to see you again." Friendly enough.

"I hope it's not an intrusion, but could I sit in today?"

Ted looked to his stage manager, who said, "Of course. We're on a lunch break, so give us another fifteen minutes or so."

She sat at a tiny table in a corner facing the front window and scanned the coffee shop. On this particular afternoon the café was half empty, the patrons engaged with computers, iPads, and cell phones, some reading newspapers or books. Clouds scudded across an otherwise bright blue sky, the day beautiful, cheerful. Yet the morning visit to the body shop had tilted it on edge, doused Connie's spirits, and frightened her.

Thirty minutes later, she slipped into a seat in the back of the theatre, the house dimmed, stage lights at max. Rehearsal was in full swing, four actors on stage, Ted in the first row.

"Diana? Your line," the stage manager called out to the leading lady.

"Sorry. Got lost."

"From the top," Ted said.

Diana and a young actor that Connie met at the Bendel's happy hour went at it, screaming, throwing things. The actor threatened to kill Diana, who collapsed on a settee. This was some violent play.

Her eye caught offstage movement. BJ stood in the far aisle, gawking at her, like before, his look so penetrating it could shatter her resolve. *No.* She needed to talk to him. That thought sent a shot of anxiety coursing through her system. But it had to be done. That's why she came to the theatre today. She had to confront him about the night her mother disappeared. About what he said and did.

BJ moved off as Ted jumped on stage, traveling around the makeshift set, motioning Diana's scene partner aside. When they began the scene again, she crossed in back of a sofa and turned to her left, expecting the actor. In his place stood Ted. Without warning, he grabbed her roughly. Connie gasped and Diana screamed, thrashing, twisting. She pushed the director away. "What was that?"

Connie's pulse raced. Cast and crew stood, immobile.

"What were you doing? That wasn't the blocking!" Diana panted, her eyes wild.

"Let's calm down. Sorry. I didn't mean to startle you. I wanted to improvise the scene, see what we could get out of it."

Connie breathed deeply to steady herself. Diana could have been hurt. The actress stormed off the stage, waved her hand dismissing the director's apology as the stage manager called, "Take ten."

Connie followed her to the ladies' room. Paused to take a beat before entering, then pushed open the door. The actress stood at a sink, dabbing at her makeup, brushing her hair. She glanced up, seeing Connie in the mirror. "You're in the house today."

"Yes. I wanted to speak with BJ."

"He's around." She tucked her bag under her arm. "See that little scene?"

"It was upsetting." Connie's hands shook as she dampened a paper towel and patted her forehead.

Diana watched her. "It made you think about your mother."

Connie nodded. "I'm sorry. I don't mean to interrupt your rehearsal. I wanted to thank you for your kindness. My sister said she visited here with my dad after Mom was gone, and you were so nice. She said you let her cry on your shoulder."

Diana touched Connie's hand. "It wasn't me, but I'm glad someone from the theatre offered comfort." She opened the door. "Shall we?"

An hour later, the house lights popped on, the stage manager closing the theatre to call it an early day. BJ had headed backstage ten minutes before and now that the cast had vacated the area, Connie intended to find him.

She stepped deeper into the offstage area, past coils of cable, stacks of curtains, and leftover construction debris. Just steps away from the set, this section was shadowy, unsettling. Images hammered her—the power out, pitch black back here, people shouting and running past her, Connie searching for her mother.

She shuddered.

There was no sign of BJ. Scanning the area, her eyes settled on a long wooden table where the crew had placed rehearsal props. Glasses, Coke bottles, dishes, tablecloths, articles of clothing, a broom and dustpan. And a small piece of luggage.

She recognized that suitcase. Beige with contrasting brown leather strips on the edges and tarnished gold fasteners. Well-worn and badly scratched. Fifteen years ago, during *Streetcar* rehearsal, this was Blanche's traveling bag for her entrance into act one. If Connie opened it, the interior would smell like one of her mother's lavender sachets. Memories saturated her senses. Playing dress-up in her mother's high heels with an old skirt bunched up around her waist held in place with a fancy scarf, using that same piece of luggage to imagine one of their fantastical vacations.

Connie stepped over to the table and opened the suitcase with care, as though it might shatter, and inhaled its fragrance. Yes, lavender. And dust. She shoved her hand into a side pocket and withdrew a few cold pennies, placed there by the Tuckers playing make-believe. Her fingers closed around the copper coins.

"Simone let us borrow it." An overhead fluorescent flashed on.

Connie wheeled to her right as BJ moved into the wash of light a few feet away from her. His stare was still intense, but now, when she stared back, Connie could see that he hadn't aged all that much. His ragged hair and scruffy appearance gave the impression of a street person, yet he would only be in his forties, a few years younger than her mother.

But his features were harder, sharp, less kindly than she remembered. His overalls paint-splattered and grimy. Not the BJ of fifteen years ago. Like two different people. Out of instinct, Connie took a step back, exhaled. "BJ." Her voice barely above a whisper.

He jammed his hands in the pockets of his overalls. "Short stuff." He remembered the nickname he gave her. "You...Simone," he murmured, distressed.

The comparison to her mother felt benign most of the time. This time it alarmed her. Connie's blood ran cold with BJ gawking like he saw a ghost. He made a move toward her. Possibly to reassure himself that she was flesh and blood and not an apparition. "I can't believe it's... Simone," he groaned.

BJ's comment like a slap in the face. "I'm not my mother," Connie said through gritted teeth.

His head snapped back. "I know you're not her. What do you take me for?" he growled, his face knotted with frustration.

Now wary, Connie stepped behind the prop table, giving herself a bit of cover. "We've got to talk about the night Mom disappeared. About the three of us in the hallway." Rubbing sweaty hands on her jeans, Connie lifted her chin, determined. "I heard about the cut on your hand the night of the storm and your fall off the grid the next day. I'm sorry about that."

Sound rumbled in BJ's throat, his mouth working fiercely, his eyes widened. Fear replaced frustration.

"I was supposed to be in the house watching rehearsal when the lights went out, but I wasn't. I was backstage. Looking for Mom."

Inching along the cold cement wall that night, counting the doors. The dressing rooms, the utility closet, the storage area. Until she paused outside the room where her mother was arguing with someone.

Without warning, Connie started to cry, her voice quivering, angry. "You were in the dressing room with my mother. I heard voices. She was upset. And then you both came out and you threatened her—"

"No!" he yelled. "I wouldn't—"

"Grabbed her. I tried to pull you off her—"

BJ shook his head violently. "It wasn't like that—"

"She begged me not to say anything, and I didn't for fifteen years." Connie wiped her eyes. "You said you'd see her later. You scared her!" Connie delivered the stinging accusation. "Did you see her later? Did you hurt her?"

"No!" BJ crumpled, body caving, shoulders slumping. His expression sad, pained. "She loved me."

Taken aback, Connie gasped. "Loved you? Look at you! How could she—"

"We had plans!" His eyes flashed defiantly.

Plans? "Did you hurt her because she wouldn't leave Dad for you? Is that how you cut your hand?"

"What?" BJ clasped his arms to his stomach, moaning. "No...I would never..." He dropped to his knees.

Connie took a breath, then firmly, "I never told anyone, not the police, not anyone, because she begged me, pleaded with me, and said, 'forget whatever I saw or heard.' So, I did. I'm not even sure to this day what your words, her words, meant. What passed between you."

Detective Nardone's words rose up to confront her. *If we'd only had a witness.*

Connie pitied the technician on the floor, rocking, muttering things that she couldn't understand. "I feel sorry for you, BJ, but I can't hold back anymore. I came here to tell you I'm going to the police. They'll want to talk to you—"

He sprang to his feet, darted around the prop table, and grabbed Connie's arm, his fingers claw-like, yanking her closer to him. The smell of his sweat overpowering. "I heard things. I saw things too. Ask *her*!"

Connie wrenched away from his menacing face and stuttered, "A-ask *who*? What are you talking about? What did my mother know that frightened you? When she said that night you wouldn't be able to work at the theatre anymore?"

"BJ?" The stage manager's voice echoed through the backstage. "Are you locking up back there?"

Startled, like a wild animal, his face rigid, he hunched his shoulders, withdrawing into himself and hurried into the scene shop.

Connie stumbled off the stage, brushed past the stage manager, and ran through the lobby, gulping moist air as she hit the sidewalk, not stopping until she reached the driver's seat of her loaner car. Grasping at bits of the conversation. BJ had seen or heard something. Ask *her*, he'd said.

Connie rested her forehead on the steering wheel, forcing air into and out of her lungs. For many years she refused to admit to herself that she saw BJ, her friend, threaten her mother the night she disappeared. Refused to consider what he might have to do with her disappearance. One thing was certain: She couldn't live with any more secrets. Her hands shook at the thought that her mother's plea for secrecy would now be relayed to the police.

It wouldn't be easy, and a wave of nausea rolled through her. Connie gagged, opened the door, ready to throw up. She cranked the air conditioner to high. She wasn't up to facing the police now, and couldn't go home, or to Porter's, feeling like this. Needing more than a shoulder to cry on, Connie rummaged around in her bag and located a business card. Tapped numbers into her cell phone.

"Hello?"

"Finn? It's Connie."

Chapter 23

Now

Between the north and south ends of Colmar was a pretty park with a small lake, a running track, and lots of trees and open, grassy areas. They sat on a park bench surrounded by the lush summer greenery of trees and shrubs that provided shade and filtered the light of the late afternoon sun. The Colmar Park was mostly empty—a few joggers on the running track, two young women sunbathing on a blanket near the pond, a mother pushing a stroller on a footpath. An idyllic setting for a summer afternoon. The environment was soothing. And Finn was right—the location was ideal for privacy.

Connie had offered to come to his office in Clifton, but he'd suggested the Colmar Park instead. He'd met her here an hour ago and she assumed she looked as distraught on the outside as she felt inside. Revealing everything to him—the stormy night fifteen years ago, seeing her mother and BJ in the backstage hallway, the promise, the confusing dialogue, the rock, her brakes, her suspicions about Rosa, the trauma of meeting BJ, and her father's questionable alibi—was a surrender of sorts. She could breathe more deeply. "I made a promise to my mother, and I had to keep it."

"Yes. What do you need from me?" Finn asked. "I realize you've done the therapist routine before."

"Apparently unsuccessfully."

He smiled. "You've been carrying quite the burden. Time you laid it down, don't you think?"

"Talking to the police will help."

He nodded. "It should. Tell them everything. The truth."

"My sister thinks I need to grow up. To get over being the child whose mother abandoned her."

"What do you think?"

"Yeah. Okay. I agree with her." Connie scraped her sandal against the concrete beneath her feet.

Finn placed an arm on the bench back, turning to face her. "But?"

"Honestly?"

He shrugged. "Any other way?"

"I won't 'get over' it until I feel I've done all I can to find my mother's murderer."

Finn looked off into the distance. "Understandable. But you're stepping into some dangerous territory."

"I know."

"I think you have to rely on law enforcement. Promise me you'll be careful and call me if you need anything."

"Sure. Do you mind answering a question?"

"Depends. I avoid politics and religion."

She laughed. His eyes crinkled at the corners. Warm, deep brown pools.

"Was it hard coming back here to Hallison after you left the seminary? I mean, how did your family and other people react?"

"Disappointed at first. We were…are…a solid Irish Catholic family. Mom loved having a son as a priest. Dad didn't care one way or the other. The neighbors, though…well…Hallison. It was difficult. I stayed with my folks for a few months before moving to Clifton."

"I didn't think I could handle coming home. I pretend I'm okay with being here, and I do miss Hallison, but…I still have a lot of…"

"Anger? Resentment?"

"I was going to say control problems. I want to lash out. Have done a few times since I've been home. I'm trying to get over the 'reckless teenager' bit."

He nodded. "It may take time. But contrary to what the experts say, you can go home again. You have to block out all the crap."

"Thanks Finn. Brigid's lucky to have you as a brother."

"We're not in my office. Just good friends. Come here." He wrapped his arms around her, and she settled into his chest, inhaling a woodsy, spicy aftershave, feeling him breathe into her hair.

It was difficult to think of the Flint estate as partially belonging to Charlie, raised on the streets of Newark, even though he assumed the role of the upper-class gentleman without effort and had installed his mother Deirdre as the matriarch. She also played the part, despite retaining an Irish brogue.

Off the parking area behind the house was a patio where her hosts had set up a drinks cart and a grill emitted a stream of pungent, mouthwatering smoke. Grilled food in a backyard. Her stomach rumbled. Of course, the terraced patio and decks were no simple backyard, and the outdoor kitchen was complete with an island, fire pit, and glass and chrome patio furniture. Charlie leaned over the fire poking at contents under a hood.

"You're cooking tonight?" Connie gave him a peck on the cheek.

"Absolutely. This is my domain." He grinned and gestured at the portable bar. "We're being informal. Find yourself something to drink.

Jackie will be out in a minute. She's finishing up a salad. Mom is away spending the night with friends from the old days." A note of relief in his voice.

Connie picked up a chilled bottle of white wine and filled a glass. "Does Jackie need help?"

Charlie flipped whatever was browning on the grill. "She's good. This gives us a chance to talk."

"I hope I'm not a bother. You and Jackie have been so hospitable."

"Honey, you're welcome here any time." He lowered the hood and smiled.

Outdoor lanterns dotted the perimeter of the patio, casting a golden haze over the grounds as the sun slipped beneath the line of trees that marked the rear of the property. "You said there were arguments between Mom and Dad, talk of an affair, divorce."

Charlie waved his fork. "I shouldn't have shot off my mouth."

"That's okay. But I'm wondering…the talk about an affair. Who was it supposedly with?"

He picked up a glass with whiskey on the rocks and motioned to a chair. "Have a seat. I'm only passing on what your dad said, or rather what he hinted at one night when he was in his cups. Never said who. Only that he was worried Simone was seeing someone else." He leaned into the cushions of the patio chair. "I wish I had been around that night."

"When Mom disappeared?"

"I might have been able to do something."

"Like what?" Connie asked, curious.

"Something. Simone called me. She left a message for your father but wasn't sure he'd gotten it, so she called me to come and get you," he said, swirling the cubes in his drink.

"But Dad picked me up."

"Right. By the time I got to the theatre you were already gone."

"You were in the theatre that night?"

He shook his head. "I didn't get past the lobby. Somebody...can't remember who...said you'd left. I went home."

They sipped their drinks. "I got an estimate for the car repair today," she said.

"Ouch. Can I help? I gotta a friend who owns a garage."

"All good, but the mechanic said the brake line had a slow leak. Like it might have been damaged."

Charlie set his drink on an end table. "Damaged?"

"Coupled with the rock incident, it has me on edge."

He darted to the grill to save dinner. "You need to go back to the Hallison PD and report that information." Then he refilled his glass. "And take precautions. I still have a few buddies around the force. Let me make a call or two. See if we can't keep an eye on things while you're in town. Are you planning on leaving soon?"

"Dinner!" Jackie stood at the open glass door, a large wooden bowl in one hand and platters in the other.

Connie jumped up. "Let me help you." She took the salad to the table while Jackie offered the dishes to her husband—he lifted steaks from the fire to one plate, grilled vegetables to the other.

Dinner was delicious and relaxing. After a couple glasses of wine, she could have remained in her comfortable seat forever. The patio lights formed a bubble of security around the table and chairs, the rear of the Flint estate draped in black, lit only by the early fall moon.

During a pause in the conversation, Connie announced, "I was at the theatre again yesterday. The lighting technician? BJ?" Suddenly nervous at bringing up his name because tomorrow would seal his fate.

"I didn't know that he was injured the day after the storm. Fell off the grid and fractured his leg. He walks with a limp."

"Yes," Jackie said. "Terrible. He didn't work at the Flint for a brief period. I guess I was gone when he came back." She twisted in her seat to face her husband. "That reminds me, we have a board meeting next week. You'll come home in time?" Then to Connie, "Sometimes we're like ships in the night. I don't see him for days. And then I have to follow after him and clean up his mess."

Charlie laughed, uncomfortable. "That's a slight exaggeration."

Connie nodded at them as if she understood, which she didn't, and covered her glass with one hand. Any more and she wouldn't be able to drive back to Hallison. "BJ and I talked. Briefly. He said some things about the night Mom disappeared." On the verge of spilling everything that she'd heard from him, Connie caught herself. Not yet. She planned to speak to Detective Nardone first thing in the morning.

Her hosts exchanged glances, waiting. In the silence, the only sound was Charlie pouring a splash of wine into his glass.

Connie avoided Detective Nardone's gaze, her shoulders hunched up to her ears, and tapped the rim of her coffee cup. Self-conscious. They'd been sitting in the Hallison town diner for an hour, Connie disclosing everything she remembered from the night her mother disappeared. As well as her conversation with BJ yesterday.

Nardone reached across the table and covered her hand. "You were a kid, frightened, confused, your mother asking for a promise. Don't be too hard on yourself."

"I'm so sorry."

"Your confessing what you witnessed that night wouldn't have changed Simone's death. Trust me."

This trust thing was new territory for Connie. The collapse of her life in Hallison left a dent in her faith in humanity—hard to rely on people if you feared they might discard you.

"By the time the missing person's investigation was in place, she was probably gone," he said gently.

Dead. "Maybe BJ knows something? I've been thinking through everything and now I'm sure they were threatening each other that night. Mom and BJ. Each knew a secret about the other."

"Let's let the cold case unit sort it all out."

"There was talk of an affair at the time. A divorce. Things weren't one-hundred percent with my parents…"

"You came forward now. I hope you can find a little bit of peace in that."

"I don't think I'll ever make peace with my mother's death."

"Yeah." He was quiet a moment, then shook a finger at her. "Hey, it was good advice to report the damaged break line to the Hallison police. ASAP."

"I will."

"By the way, the red Ford Tempo that was spotted on the parkway? Nothing ever came of it."

Another loose end. "Did anyone ever find a blue tote bag, a carryall? My mom had it with her at the theatre that night. In fact, it tended to go everywhere she went."

He frowned and shook his head. "Nothing like that was ever discovered."

Chapter 24

Now

Though Louis Nardone was leaving town in a couple of days, he generously agreed to accompany Connie and her father to a meeting with Detective Rutherford. First, she needed to come clean to her father and sister. Which, after fifteen years clutching the truth about that night to her chest like a prized possession, proved as difficult as she imagined it would be.

Her hands clammy, Connie pulled Gaby into the living room, sat her down on the sofa next to her. Across from their father in his recliner.

He turned off the television and narrowed his eyes, glancing first at Connie, then at Gaby. "What's this about?"

Gaby shrugged and looked to her sister. "Connie?"

With both of them staring at her, the silence in the room swelling, Connie had no choice but to plunge in and tell all: from the moment the lights went out in the theatre until she ran to the lobby to wait for their father to pick her up. Her voice halting, she recounted the events that took place backstage. Their mother and BJ in the dressing room. Then the fight in the hallway. And her promise to forget what she'd seen and heard.

"I'm sorry. I promised Mom…"

The silence heavy, oppressive. Their father sighed, Gaby sniffed.

"I figured there was something going on at that theatre," her father said. "Late nights. Phone calls I wasn't supposed to overhear." Her father leaned back in his recliner and closed his eyes.

Connie ignored the knot in her stomach. "Charlie said you hinted at an affair…at a divorce." She fired a glance at her sister. Gaby's head was bowed, her hands clasped in her lap.

Her father opened his eyes. "Charlie doesn't know the whole story. Never did." He withdrew into his cocoon of grief, as though losing his wife while she was still alive was one more tortuous moment in a fraught marriage.

Where were you from ten p.m. to five a.m.? she wanted to ask her father. His timeline was still a problem to Connie.

Gaby lifted her head and walked to the kitchen, Connie on her heels, and made another pot of coffee. "Gaby? Say something."

Her sister pulled mugs out of the cabinet, her mouth a tight line of tension. "Say what? I wish you'd been honest about what you saw that night? I understand why you weren't. Mom and all… Still. Would knowing about that fight have helped the police? I don't know."

"She begged me to promise not to say anything. I couldn't betray her."

After a beat, Gaby turned to her sister. "You were young. It had to be terrifying. Who knows what Mom was thinking? Or doing." She poured coffee and handed a cup to Connie.

She was astonished at their reactions. Neither Gaby nor her father apparently blamed her for withholding information. "I hope you and Dad can get through this." Connie blew on the hot liquid, her face averted.

Gaby cocked her head as though baffled. "That's what you never got right, Connie. We're family. We get through things together."

Family.

Detective Rutherford wasn't nearly as forgiving. Grilling Connie, drilling into her past. "So, you failed to tell the truth about what happened that night."

"Her mother made her swear not to say anything," Nardone interjected. "She was thirteen. A scared kid—"

Rutherford turned on him. "And you failed to interview her? Let her slip through the cracks?"

"Stop! It wasn't his fault," Connie blurted out.

Detective Nardone waved away her defense of him and laced his fingers across his ample midsection, calm and reasonable. "We were covering a lot of territory. More than twenty interviews in the theatre alone. Plus the neighborhood, friends, family. They're all in the file."

"Water under the bridge," her father muttered.

Rutherford had mutated from call-me-Tom-and-trust-me to I'm-the-top-cop-who'll-have-to-clean-up-your-mess. His history with her father may have been all that kept him in check. He made notes on a sheet of paper in front of him. "We'll bring this BJ in for questioning," he said, brusque and formal. "I'll be in touch." He shook her father's hand, nodded to Nardone, ignored Connie.

What a jerk.

Two hours later, bent over her glass of wine, Connie picked at a damp spot on the napkin that served as a coaster, happy hour well underway at Porter's. The spirited bar chatter a contrast to her miserable mood.

Brigid patted her belly, weeks away from the impending birth date. "All I can say is...wow."

"Pretty much every reaction I've gotten today, with a few choice words thrown in by the cold case detective." She downed the rest of her drink.

"You were a kid."

"That's what Gaby and Louis Nardone said—"

"Trying to honor your mother. Hey, if my mother had made that kind of a plea, I'd have zipped my lips too."

"Now, Dad thinks Mom was having an affair. I can't see it. Not with BJ." Her sophisticated mother and the scruffy lighting technician? Hard to imagine. Of course, the younger BJ was much more appealing.

Brigid glimpsed Dack behind the bar. "Hard to tell what might make someone stray."

"My parents were having trouble, but that idea never entered my mind. Or the thought of a divorce."

"Your mom was glamorous. I remember a CYO dance in the church basement when we were in eighth grade. She was chaperoning. The boys were more interested in her than us!"

"When she started dancing, she was something."

"Father O'Flaherty had to calm her down." Brigid chuckled.

Even as a thirteen-year-old, Connie was aware of her mother flirting, loving the attention.

Happy hour swirled around them. Brigid hugged Connie. "People will move on. You did the right thing coming forward now."

"Thanks," Connie said, grateful for the support. "I'm still wondering what Mom had on him back then, what he meant the other day by 'ask her.' That he claimed to know things he never revealed. When I told Rutherford what BJ said, he blew me off. Said they'd question him themselves."

"Asshole," Connie and Brigid said in unison, joining pinky fingers.

"By the way, you're coming to the anniversary party tomorrow night, yes?"

Damn. The thunk in the pit of Connie's stomach was so strong she was sure her friend heard it. There had to be some way to avoid the neighborhood bash Brigid had been yakking about for days. She wasn't in the mood for an event in Saint Gabriel's basement. She remembered a couple of wedding receptions down there when she and Gaby were kids. Running all over the place, bumping into couples on the dance floor, generally raising a ruckus as Grandma Tucker used to say. Images of herself, the fair-haired younger daughter, letting her sister take the blame for their "ruckus."

"…this great DJ and a terrific caterer and open bar…" Brigid was saying, so enthused about the party, failing to notice Connie's reluctance to commit.

"What if people find out about BJ and me and Mom? That he's now a person of interest."

"So what? Anyway, how would they? Cold case stuff in the county prosecutor's office? Nah."

"It would be awkward. Like I was a little-girl-lost for fifteen years, staying away, afraid to deal with reality. To tell the truth. I'll feel like Scarlet O'Hara entering the ball after killing off her husband."

Brigid shrugged. "Don't wear red."

Chapter 25

Now

The anniversary party was a Who's Who of the old Newark and Hallison neighborhoods, with a smattering of friends and relatives from surrounding towns. Everyone loved Brigid's parents and had no doubt come from all over the Garden State to help celebrate with them. It had taken a considerable amount of coaxing on Gaby's part before Connie agreed to go for an hour or so. By the time they descended the stairs to St. Gabriel's hall, the party was in full swing.

The place had been spruced up since the days Connie had attended events there. Its warped knotty pine walls were now painted a soft beige, the linoleum replaced with a smart black-and-white tile design, and recessed lighting offset the low ceiling. Colorful crepe paper streamers were strung from one corner of the room to the other, dipping and bobbing, and wound around pillars. Balloon bouquets graced the banquet tables covered with yellow paper tablecloths. Altogether, the decorations were festive, promising a fun party.

The DJ stood at a table at one end of the room and the bar, supervised by Dack, at the other. On a makeshift dance floor couples bumped and rocked to Motown, while, true to form, a dozen little kids played tag in and around the tables.

Connie scanned the crowd, aware that a handful of people had already noticed their arrival and were speaking in small groups. She was right. It was *Gone with the Wind*. Her fear had come to pass. Brigid had called earlier in the day to warn her that the story was out. Her mother's cousin who lived in Newark worked in the county prosecutor's office, and word had leaked about Simone, BJ, and Connie the night of the storm. The fight and the promise. The person of interest.

And Hallison being Hallison, neighborhood gossip being what it was, the story had spread throughout the party by the looks of it.

She closed her eyes and heard Finn's instruction: *Block out all the crap.*

Connie made a beeline for a table closest to a wall where she could plop into a metal folding chair, sip wine, and avoid the throng of a hundred or so people. By the buffet line, Brigid's mother played the grandma role, separating pugnacious grandsons and holding them at arm's length. Meanwhile, Brigid held her youngest on her lap, wiping food from his mouth, grinning and chatting with two women who Connie vaguely recognized from high school days.

"Want a drink?" Gaby asked.

"White wine, thanks."

Gaby walked across the room, speaking to folks, kissing cheeks and shaking hands, forestalling any potential rumormongers with bulletproof sisterly solidarity. If Connie was Scarlet O'Hara, that made Gaby the loyal Melanie. She admired her sister's social skills. At the bar Dack greeted her warmly and poured drinks. He must have inquired about Connie because he caught her eye and lifted his hand. Brigid glanced her way at the same time and waved like a wild woman, setting her youngest in a chair and grabbing her oldest to keep an eye on his brother. She marched across the dance floor and hooked arms with Connie, leaning in to her ear. "You hanging in there?"

Connie glanced around, pulse thudding. "Feels like everyone is staring."

"They are. At the great-looking gal come home to honor her mom." Brigid squeezed Connie's hand, urging her across the basement. "See who's here?" She plonked her down between two women. Definitely from high school.

"Connie!" one cried, her curly hair bobbing as her head bounced. "I want to hear all about California." She pulled Connie into a hug. "You look fantastic."

Connie had taken Brigid's advice to avoid wearing red, or anything too flashy, settling for black slacks and a white cotton blouse.

"Candy!" Candy Fleming, sweet and sugary like her name. Full of compliments, easy to befriend, always willing to go along. She and Connie and Brigid had been classmates since grade school and sat together in homeroom their freshman year. "So nice to see you."

Brigid beamed. Next to her the other woman brushed bangs off her face, her lips curving upward, her eyes frosty. "Hi Connie. Heard you were in town."

"Tammy." Her teenage nemesis, or rather, Connie had been Tammy's nemesis. Always competing for the same roles in shows for two years, usually awarded to Connie. Clearly, still holding a grudge fifteen years later.

Brigid asked, "Where's Gaby?"

"At the bar getting us drinks." Actually, her sister was chatting with Mrs. Delano, who occupied a table with Deirdre O'Shaughnessy—there was no sign Charlie had accompanied his mother—and Rosa. Connie's spirits plummeted. It was bad enough to imagine what everyone was saying about her, but to witness her neighbor's jubilant smirk as she gestured to Connie was crushing.

Candy murmured into Connie's ear. "I'm so sorry about your mother." She squeezed her hand. "Such a sad time."

Connie nodded, grateful.

They relived high school days, who attended the reunions, who looked older and who younger, marriages, divorces, and children.

"Connie," Candy said, "I remember you as Maria in *The Sound of Music*, singing and dancing with all those little kids. And you were only a freshman!"

"She was a star even then." Brigid lobbed a casual glance at Tammy, who smile-frowned.

"Fun times," Connie said, although not really: Her mother had disappeared a few months before.

Gaby delivered her sister's wine, settled in with them. Brigid changed the subject and had the group chuckling over Dack's antics with the kids. Within the hour, the remains of baked ziti, chicken marsala, and beef with peppers and onions sat scattered around the table.

More relaxed now, Connie drank her wine and let the past wash over her. It was pleasant to see Hallison friends, most of them, to savor the sounds and smells of a church basement social. To ignore gossip that might be circulating in the crowd.

"Hey, is that Father O'Flaherty?" Candy asked. He'd been the pastor of St. Gabriel's when they were kids.

"That's him all right. He's gotten old," Brigid said. The priest, in a black suit and traditional Roman collar, had a walker and moved with difficulty. "He must be about a hundred by now."

"I thought he was a hundred when we were in grade school," Connie said, and the table giggled. "Oh, and the days when he gave out report cards?"

Candy winced. "I was terrified of him."

"Not me," Brigid bragged.

"Who are you kidding? You almost peed your pants when you got called to his office for making out in the old cloak room."

Brigid tossed her head. "Johnny Mac. He was cute and worth getting chewed out. I got sent to confession that week."

"He can't still be the pastor," Tammy said.

"Nah. Father Pete's in charge." Brigid pointed at a young man, in khakis, sandals, and a short-sleeved shirt. Connie recognized him from her mother's funeral.

Next to him sat Finn, drinking a beer and appearing super-chill.

"Times have changed. Anybody need a drink?" Candy took orders and Gaby offered to help her transport them.

Tammy left to visit with other friends and Brigid stretched out her legs.

"Getting tired?"

Brigid grimaced. "No more than usual. How's your father taking the BJ news?"

"He didn't want to come today. I think he was nervous about facing people."

Candy and Gaby returned, their hands full of glasses, and distributed drinks. The DJ invited everyone to rise and toast Brigid's parents as he played "Happy Anniversary" and they sang along. The celebrating couple blew out dozens of candles, with the help of their grandsons, and the crowd cheered and clapped as they cut the cake.

"You guys did a great job with this party," Connie said.

"Mostly my sister," Brigid sighed. "She loves this stuff. I could have stayed home and put my feet up tonight." She started to sit again.

"Oh no you don't!" Dack put an arm around her. Brigid rolled her eyes and Connie grinned. "We have to have at least one dance."

The DJ played a slow song, and folks drifted into the center of the basement. Connie and Gaby worked on their drinks and watched the anniversary couple snuggle together.

"You were gonna pin this murder on me, huh?" Rosa growled in Connie's ear.

Connie whipped her head around, her face inches from her neighbor's. So close she could smell Rosa's stale cigarette breath.

"And there you are," Rosa kept on, "too scared to tell the truth fifteen years ago. Maybe save your mother's life. That's what everybody's saying."

Were they? Shaken, she tried to ignore her, but Rosa had pasted herself against her arm. "How's that rock investigation going?"

Block out all the crap. Connie turned away.

But Rosa loomed above her, face leering. Not to be easily dismissed. "I saw Si-mone that summer late one night. On Third Street."

The music ended and the DJ shouted "congratulations" into the microphone. Connie could barely make out Rosa's words.

Her neighbor stooped down, now eye level. "Getting dropped off at your house. Kissing the driver. And not like"—she created air quotes—"a cousin. If you get my drift."

"What are you talking about? Who?" She grabbed Rosa's sleeve, but Rosa yanked herself free, laughing, enjoying the moment.

"Figure it out yourself, you're so smart." With a sly grin, she sauntered out of the basement.

Gaby touched Connie's clenched hands, the knuckles white. "What was that about? You okay?"

Connie nodded. Taking a deep breath. *Calm down,* she told herself. *It was only Rosa.* The jailbird who hated her mother. She couldn't be trusted to tell the truth.

"Care to dance?" Finn had appeared above her.

"I don't think—"

Without waiting for Connie to finish declining, he took her hand, pulled her to her feet, and led her to the dance floor, weaving in and out of couples until they found a spot across the room near the bar. He placed an arm around her waist, she laid one palm in his, the other on his shoulder as they moved to the music.

"Thanks for the rescue," Connie said.

Finn's eyebrows shot up in surprise. "Is that what this is?"

"Our neighbor. Saying some vile stuff."

"Ah. The neighbor."

The cloak of good cheer that had settled over the event dissolved in the wake of Rosa's vicious attack on her mother. Kissing someone in a car on Third Street late at night. Obviously not her father. Was this proof of an affair?

Finn expertly twirled Connie away, then back into his arms. Despite her upset, she was impressed. "Wow, you learn steps like that in the seminary?"

"You forget, I've been out five years. Plenty of time to perfect dance moves." He pulled her a smidge closer. Nice.

He paused as the song ended, still holding her hand, remaining on the dance floor. As the next number began—an old Beatles' tune, way more upbeat—he led her to the edge of the now-crowded dance floor, snagging two chairs at an empty table. "Talk to me."

Connie turned her back on the party. "I feel like people are gossiping about me. Not to mention my neighbor."

Finn squeezed her hand. "Breathe and remember what I said."

"Yeah. Block out all the crap. I've been using that a lot lately."

He gave her a hug and pulled her once again onto the dance floor.

With Rosa gone, Connie felt more comfortable sitting at Mrs. Delano's table with half a dozen other women. Her neighbor, silver hair styled for the party, in a lovely pale green and blue summer dress, was enjoying herself. Connie studied her, speculating on how much she knew about Rosa's behavior. The rock through the window. Her taunts and threats. No way would she raise the subject tonight and ruin the party.

Brigid's mother, in a stylish tunic and leggings, lifted her hair off the back of her neck and pulled out a chair next to Charlie's mother, Deirdre. "I need a break."

Deirdre tossed back the rest of her whiskey. "Charlie's my ride home. Anybody seen my son?" Her brogue was thicker the more she drank.

"How is your son?" one of the women asked.

Deirdre smiled wickedly. "Works in corporate security for the Flint family. They have their fingers in lots of pots." She winked. "He was the smartest one in that gang he ran with. Always understood which side his bread was buttered on."

"We dated back then," Brigid's mother said.

The table swiveled heads in unison, eager to catch this surprising bit of ancient romantic history.

Brigid's jaw dropped. "You and Charlie?"

"Once or twice." She touched Connie's arm. "I also dated your father a few times before Simone and he were married. Simone dated both of them too."

"You and Dad?" Connie asked.

"I can still see the church basement at Holy Family. One of Liam's cousins got married and the whole neighborhood was invited. We all bought new dresses. Simone too, I think. She was stunning..." Her voice drifted off. "We all looked good. Especially Simone."

"Is the wedding where you met Dad?" Brigid asked, bouncing her youngest on her knees.

"No. That was later. They grew up together, Charlie and Liam. High school football team, police academy. People took them for brothers. Except that Charlie was tall and dark and Liam short with auburn hair and very serious. Charlie was the ringleader and they were always together."

"That they were," Deirdre chimed in.

Connie had heard some of this before. At her mother's funeral.

Gaby drifted over and they made room for her at the table.

Then Deirdre continued, "Charlie teased your father about his height and being awkward on the dance floor. Liam tried to compete with him and always fell short. Insecure, I imagine. Until he married your mother." It was quite a pronouncement.

"Mom, more coffee?" Brigid cut in, trying to steer the conversation to a less sensitive subject.

But Connie wasn't ready to move on. "Mom, Dad, Charlie, and you..." She nodded at Brigid's mother. "You all were friends back then."

"We all ran around together sure. I didn't know Simone too well, at first. She was several years younger than me and I graduated high school before her. All of us had a good time going out together...dances, movies, trading off dates."

"Mom, you were a regular social butterfly." Brigid handed her toddler to her mother and stretched her back.

"Until I started dating your father. Then there was only one man for me." She patted her daughter's knee.

Deirdre sat up, seeming more sober. "Liam had his eye on Simone that first night, but Charlie was faster on his feet. She didn't stand a chance. In the beginning, she and Charlie dated on and off and she went out with your father when Charlie was busy," she said, with a condescending nod to Connie and Gaby.

The sisters shared a look.

"I was a consolation prize too." Brigid's mom laughed. "Liam was never interested in me." She sighed. "They were a handsome couple. Charlie and Simone. Later, of course, when the time came, the Tucker family considered Liam and Simone a mixed marriage."

"Why? They were both Catholics." Brigid rolled her eyes.

Her mother raised a hand in protest. "Yes, but a first-generation Irish man and a very young French girl? It wasn't done in his Newark neighborhood."

Connie considered the conversation. Their mother married Liam and not Charlie. She dated both of them, and she and Charlie were a "handsome couple." So why did she end up with Dad? "Charlie's wife Jackie is a lovely woman."

Deirdre scoffed. "Charlie O'Shaughnessy was the talk of the town, a ladies' man. All the girls wanted to be with him." Her smile reminiscent of the Cheshire Cat's—knowing all, saying little.

At that instant, the "talk of the town" himself appeared, obviously in a hurry. "Ladies." Charlie tapped his watch. "Mother?" It required five minutes to pry Deirdre from her seat, say repeated goodbyes, and check the contents of her purse to reassure herself that nothing was missing. At last, Charlie and Deirdre wound their way to the exit.

After a beat, Connie asked Brigid's mother, "Charlie and Mom were a serious couple at some point?"

"For nearly a year," she answered. "Your father was in love with her too. He knew he was second fiddle, but he'd have married Simone under any circumstances."

Mom chose Dad in the end. That said something about their marriage. Though he had gotten her pregnant before they walked down the aisle.

"It was very sudden. One minute Simone was with Charlie, and the next she was engaged to Liam," Brigid's mother said. "All she ever told me was that Liam would make a better husband. A better father. More reliable. She could trust him."

Though Gaby bobbed her head at this, confirming her feelings about Charlie, it certainly didn't make their parents' marriage sound overly romantic. Particularly because it began as a shotgun wedding.

"You're up!" Brigid put an arm around Connie's waist as the strains of "Dancing Queen" shifted the party mood from relaxed to raucous. "I. Love. ABBA!"

Brigid dragged Connie to the dance floor, with Connie pulling Gaby behind her, the sisters surrendering to the atmosphere. Bumping and lurching. Connie caught Gaby's eye and smiled. Gaby grinned back. Their mother's favorite number. For once they could take pleasure in her memory without remorse or sadness. Partygoers formed a circle and people clapped and shook their way into the center of the ring, each doing their own thing.

When Brigid pushed Connie to move forward, she whirled around and around like her mother, blond hair flying, her head thrown back. The room spun, the music crushing but irresistible, the other dancers a blur as Connie rotated, a tight circle within a circle. The wine had gone to her head, taken her beyond the church basement of St. Gabriel's into the Tucker living room on Third Street, unaware of other people trying to get their solo turn. She was thirteen and her mother was twirling to ABBA's rhythm, wild and free.

Amid the whirl, Connie registered Brigid's eyes popped wide and Gaby's expression transformed from delighted to grim. No use trying to stop, though. Her body operated under its own power. Eyes closed, she heard her mother say, "Someday we will share the stage." Tears flowed, the floor tilted, and Connie would have fallen if a couple of people hadn't caught her. Someone led her off the dance floor to the women's room, where she collapsed on a toilet seat, ugly-crying, and then retching.

Chapter 26

Now

"One too many white wines." Dack drove with one hand on the steering wheel, the other hanging out the window, the night air cool and refreshing.

"I guess," Connie answered, leaning against the headrest.

The alcohol had surely contributed, but more likely the dizziness and nausea were brought on by spinning nonstop and being thrown back into her past with her mother.

Gaby, silent in the back seat, had looked at Connie strangely as she was escorted to the bathroom and once Connie had returned, demanded that they go. Now. Brigid had taken control, enlisting Dack to drive the sisters home. They'd walked to St. Gabriel's—it was only a few blocks from the Tucker residence—but Connie was in no shape to negotiate even a short walk.

Dack pulled into the Tucker driveway. "Look at that. Still have that Town Car. Your dad loves that thing, right?"

"Right." Connie cleared her dry throat, her mouth sour. "Thanks for driving us." She fumbled with the door handle. God, her head was pounding—she needed aspirin, water, and a bed.

Gaby was already outside the car. "Yeah, thanks, Dack," she called in through the open passenger window before marching up the path to the front door.

"Your dad hated me when we were in high school."

"I don't think so—"

"Sure, he did. That night he caught us making out on your porch and threatened to castrate me if he ever found us like that again." Dack chuckled. "Good thing we had my dad's pickup."

"We were never that serious—"

"Yeah, we were."

To Connie, Dack was a high school boyfriend who was somewhat easy to forget. She couldn't imagine he felt any different.

"Anyway, your old man and I became buddies. Bartending together. Believe that? We talk about stuff." Dack rubbed the wheel, gazing out the windshield. "He said once he was sorry he sent you to California and missed you."

Now that *had* to be a figment of Dack's imagination—

"Really nice to see you, Connie."

"Especially like this." She tried to laugh. It came out like a croak as she swung the passenger door wide open.

"I felt bad after you left that summer."

Of all times for Dack to relive their teenage years. "We were so young. I was fifteen. Who knew what we'd want later on."

He turned sideways. "I already knew what I wanted."

"Dack…" Connie closed her eyes and saw her bed.

"Anyway, you need some sleep."

"That I do."

Gaby had switched on the hallway light, leaving the rest of the house in the dark. Good. She wanted to avoid any conversation with her sister. She'd turned a pleasant evening into a fiasco for both of them.

Connie filled a glass with water, drank it down, then refilled it and climbed the stairs to the second floor, treading softly past Gaby's bedroom. On the threshold of her own room she heard footsteps.

"What happened to you tonight?"

With her back to Gaby, Connie exhaled, pushing the party away. "I had too much wine. I got lost in the song. I was spinning and dancing and then all of a sudden—"

"You saw Mom."

"Gaby, I'm sorry. All the dancing and drinking. I got so dizzy and then I lost it."

"You saw Mom dancing, didn't you?" Connie heard sadness in her sister's voice.

A beat. "Yeah. I did," she whispered. "'Dancing Queen' brought it on."

Gaby fiddled with the bedroom door handle. "I remember that night right before…"

"She disappeared." Connie crossed the few feet separating them. "I can't get the image out of my mind. Mom twirling in the living room."

"Cranking the music up so loud. Dad would have had a fit."

Another beat.

Connie hugged Gaby. "Good night."

"Connie?"

"Yeah?"

"You didn't only see Mom dancing, did you?"

A chill moved down her spine. "What?"

"It was like… you *were* her. Dancing. Is that why you're so determined to find her killer?" Gaby rambled on. "Everyone always says you two look identical, but tonight…you were so *much* like her. It's like…a part of you died with Mom, and now you need to go find it."

"I didn't die!" Connie said to Gaby's closed door.

193

What the hell was she talking about?

Connie nursed a hangover, head propped up in her right hand.

Her father's fingers had been drumming on the table, but now they fell silent as he regarded his younger daughter. "Some party last night."

"Uh-huh."

He glanced at Gaby stirring scrambled eggs in the pan. No comment there.

"Who all came?" he asked.

Gaby gave a rundown of attendance, pausing to insert updates on neighbors' and friends' lives. "Deirdre O'Shaughnessy was there, but not Charlie or Jackie. Until he had to pick her up. He wasn't too thrilled."

"Deirdre. Huh. Never liked her. She never liked me. Always thought your mother was too good for me."

Gaby refilled their coffee cups, Connie grateful for the added caffeine. Still suspicious of her father's actions the night her mother disappeared, yet hesitant to confront him about his timeline, she was curious about the anniversary party conversation. "She talked about you and Charlie and Mom back in Newark."

Gaby set three plates of eggs on the table. The aroma made Connie's stomach roil.

Her father glared at Connie, stuck a fork in his share of the eggs. "What does she know? Busybody. Always had her nose in everybody else's business. She didn't like Simone either, no matter what she says."

"Why didn't she like Mom?" He had Connie's full attention now.

Her father gestured indifference. "I think she was jealous. Had to compete for Charlie's attention."

Pushing his breakfast aside, Liam stood, grabbed his keys and a light jacket. The weather had turned breezy overnight, the temperature dropping into the low seventies.

"Where are you going?" Gaby asked.

"Out."

"Where?"

"Out. Can't a man have a little privacy?"

"Porter's isn't open yet," Gaby said.

"I'm not going to Porter's!" he shouted and slammed out of the house.

The sisters exchanged glances. This wasn't good, they seemed to be saying. "Should we go with him?" Gaby said.

"Or follow him," Connie added.

Gaby sighed, "I'm too tired to play detective. You go. I'm going to work. I've missed enough days."

Liam cranked the engine of his Town Car and eased down the driveway into Third Street. He turned right. Connie watched him take off, then hurried outside, flipped the ignition switch of her loaner car, and followed him. Down Mercer, then Lennox, his route triggering her curiosity. Not to Newark to visit relatives; he rarely went there anymore. Not to his security job; he'd taken off for the foreseeable future since the accident. When he entered the parkway, though it was easy enough to track him, Connie was more confused. Until he took the Colmar exit. He was going to see Charlie. They cruised through the Uptown area, bypassing Chappelle Road. The Flint residence.

"What the...?" Connie said aloud. "Where the hell is he going?"

When they reached Downtown Colmar, the bottom dropped out of her stomach. There could be only one place of interest to Liam Tucker in this part of town. The Flint Theatre. He came to Colmar to find BJ, she was sure. And do what? Connie lost the Town Car in traffic, craning her

195

neck to peer around a truck and two cars in front of her. By the time she reached the theatre, her father's Lincoln was parked in the lot next to the café.

She dashed from her car to the theatre lobby. Empty. It was too early for rehearsal, but not for technicians and designers to be hard at work—

The doors from the house banged open. Shouting. BJ limping, arms gesturing wildly. "Stay away from me. I didn't do anything!" His face red, his breathing ragged.

Connie's father was on him, had him by the strap of his overalls, tugging the technician toward him. "You son of a bitch!" he yelled. "You tell me the truth!"

"Leave me alone!"

"You slept with my wife!"

BJ whirled in his grip. "We loved each other."

"Did you kill her?"

"Stop!" Connie thrust herself between the two of them. Her father reared back, ready to swing his fist at BJ. She ducked under his arm, the punch mostly hitting air, a glancing blow on the technician's shoulder.

Ted ran out of his office. "What's going on?" He clutched Liam from behind. "Hey! Hey!"

Connie turned her attention to BJ. "Are you all right?"

As he limped out of the lobby, his eyes full and ready to overflow, he shouted, "We didn't sleep together! And I didn't kill her!"

Ted released her father, after giving BJ time to vacate the theatre premises. "Liam, you have to calm down. The police have questioned BJ and released him. There's no solid evidence—"

"Only what my daughter saw that night." Her father whirled to confront Connie, his eyes daggers, panting. Accusing. "Well?"

"Dad. Stop," she ordered.

He waved her off, marched out of the lobby, and disappeared down the sidewalk.

"Ted...can we talk for a minute?"

The director exhaled loudly. The space between them cold. "Only for a minute. Got a lot on my plate today."

Connie followed him into a windowless, crowded room off the theatre lobby that tried to accommodate two desks, a computer, and bookshelves. It smelled of day-old fried food. "Excuse the mess. Have a seat." He sank into the desk chair. "So?"

She took a deep breath. "I'm sorry about all this. BJ..."

Ted tapped a pen on his desk blotter. "I can't imagine BJ played any part in Simone's death. He's not that kind of man."

"He told me they had plans to go away. They loved each other, he said. You heard him just now."

Ted examined his hands, dipping his head. "They were friends during that time, during the rehearsal period. Even before in previous productions. In love?" he shrugged. "I never saw it."

"BJ was kind to me, very patient. Teaching me scene shop and lighting stuff. I give him that. A few days ago he told me he knew some things...that I should 'ask her.'"

The director raised his hands to signal he had no idea what she was talking about. He was over all this, Connie thought.

"What about some kind of secret BJ had?"

"What secret? Look I have to go—"

"That night when my mother and BJ fought in the hallway, and he threatened her, physically," Connie added for emphasis, "my mother warned him, saying she'd tell you his secret. That he'd be out of the Flint Theatre. Do you have any idea what she could have meant?"

Ted's expression went slack. He squirmed in his desk chair and shook his head. "Not sure what you want from me."

The truth. "Could you put me in touch with Angela Westerman?"

"Why do you want to contact her?" he asked, wary.

"You said she was a good friend of Mom's. I'd like to talk to her."

Wordlessly, he searched the contacts in his phone and sent Angela's information to Connie's cell. "Played the upstairs neighbor in *Streetcar*. Eunice."

"Thanks, Ted."

"Not sure what she's doing these days. Hasn't been around much. Never acted with us again. I think she was so devastated by Simone's disappearance that she quit. Theatre no longer interested her." He shuffled papers on his desk and checked his watch. "If that's all?"

Chapter 27

Now

Connie figured the theatre wasn't the best place to be after the morning's near fistfight between her father and BJ. In any event, she wanted to avoid the stares and comments of cast and crew that would inevitably crop up if she poked her head into the house. Connie debated staying in Colmar; she wanted to finish the conversation with BJ. Sooner or later he'd come back after he calmed down. She'd give him an hour or so and then try the loading dock entrance to the backstage area. She'd used it many times as a kid.

Next door in the café, she ordered coffee, situating herself by the window that overlooked both the sidewalk and the parking lot adjacent to the theatre. She took out her phone to check email and texts. There was little to view. Only a few messages from her boss in San Diego wondering if/when she was coming back. Good question. After an hour, she bought lunch, read the news on her phone, and checked the time every five minutes. It's possible BJ was too shaken to show up at the theatre. No, he was a professional. The show opened in five days. Give him time.

Connie considered BJ's words: We didn't sleep together. Her father wanted the truth, too. She'd never doubted for a minute that her parents loved each other when she was growing up. Whenever she envisioned the two of them during the past couple of weeks, it was the rancor and resentment that surfaced. It wasn't always like that.

Chapter 28

Then

Summertime. Connie was seven. The Tucker family piled in the used Saturn that her father swore by. Down the Jersey shore for a week. Seaside Heights. A cheap little bungalow with one bedroom, a foldout sofa bed for Gaby and Connie, and a kitchenette. The sisters were ecstatic to be a block from the beach during the day and a five-minute walk to the boardwalk at night. They built sand castles, dove in and out of the waves, and pestered their parents for candy money. The smell of suntan oil and hot dogs and saltwater. The sun so strong it burned skin to a crisp.

Meanwhile, her mother and father sunbathed, swam out to the edge of the deeper water, and distributed sandwiches and sodas for lunch. Their father and Connie burying Gaby in sand up to her neck. Their mother snapping photo after photo.

Dinner at seafood shacks, sitting at picnic tables, and watching the sun dip lower in the sky, the humidity bothering no one. Peaceful and congenial. Their father asked their opinions on topics and the family discussed everything from where to eat their next dinner to why the ocean was sometimes green and sometimes blue.

One afternoon, while she and Gaby constructed a canal in the sand to siphon waves out of the ocean, her sister poured a bucket of water into the channel. It wasn't supposed to happen that way. Angry, Connie took a step toward the family towels, where they'd dumped beach cover-ups, shoes, and a cooler, to appeal to her father to set Gaby straight. She stopped.

"Lower," her mother murmured, lying on her stomach, the straps of her bikini top on her upper arms.

"How's that?" Her father spread suntan lotion on her mother's back, massaging the cream from her neck to her waist.

That night after dinner, Connie and Gaby played checkers on the porch by the yellow light of the bug lamp while her parents danced to a tune on the portable radio in the living room. She glanced through the screen door. Her mother sang along to the music, something about always loving someone.

"You better," her father murmured.

Then they laughed at a private joke. Her head thrown back, her hand curled in his.

Chapter 29

Now

The beach. The dancing. Foreplay. Though at the time she never would have been able to name what she'd witnessed. The memory made Connie's eyes sting, for what her parents lost. For what could have been. She needed the truth about her father's actions the night her mother disappeared. The timeline that didn't mesh with her recollection. Confronting him directly wasn't the best option because there was no guarantee he'd be honest. She'd find another way to unearth the truth.

She stuffed her cell in her bag. BJ had enough time to recover and return. The Flint was his life, Ted had said.

She walked to the entrance of the café, pushing the door as Jackie, on her phone, pulled it on the other side. They smiled at each other.

"How are you doing?" Jackie reached for her. "This is such a difficult time for you, isn't it?"

Connie allowed herself to sink into Jackie's arms. She was the first person to ask how Connie felt, what keeping the promise to her mother for all those years had cost her. "I'm okay. Feel guilty. Like I should have spoken up."

"You did what you thought was right." Arm around Connie's waist, Jackie led her to the table she'd just vacated.

For once someone didn't excuse her behavior because she was "a kid."

"What are you doing here?"

"I followed Dad to the theatre. He went ballistic this morning, cornering BJ, taking a swing at him."

"Liam was here?" Jackie asked, agog. "Fighting?"

"I know, right? What a mess. What about you?"

"Executive board meeting. Emergency repairs to the lighting grid system that Ted says needs shoring up before the show opens. It could be expensive. I want to catch him during a break in rehearsal. Charlie should be here soon, if he remembers. I swear I'm like his PDA. The digital assistant, not the display of affection." She laughed.

The two of them were dedicated. Of course, it *was* named the Flint Theatre.

"Here he is." Jackie smiled at her husband walking in the café door, holding out a hand that he took and squeezed.

Charlie kissed his wife's cheek, touched Connie's shoulder. "Called your dad and got no answer."

Jackie motioned to Charlie. "There was a slight argument here this morning. Liam and BJ. I'm sure Connie doesn't want to revisit—"

"Here?"

Through the window, Connie caught a flash of overalls and a red ball cap on the sidewalk next to the parking lot. BJ. She'd known he'd return. He cut through the lot and walked to the rear of the theatre. Jackie and Charlie followed Connie's gaze as she stood.

"Nice to see you both." She swung her bag over her shoulder.

Charlie grabbed her hand. "Where are you going?"

"To ask BJ who the woman was he apparently saw with Mom sometime the week before she disappeared. To ask him what he overheard. To find out once and for all what happened." To discover what was between him and her mother.

"Didn't the police question him?" Jackie asked.

"Yes. And released him. Who knows what he told them?"

"Presumably, the truth," Charlie said.

"Look, I want to get back to California. I want my old life back. And everyone is crazy busy at the theatre with the show opening, so I can't come later and bother them. Time's running out." Connie offered a quick kiss to both of them and sped out the door.

She cut through the parking lot flanking the café as BJ had and entered a lane that ran along the back of several businesses, including the café and the theatre, that serviced a series of loading docks and dumpsters. Back entrances to all of the shops were located here. Behind the Flint Theatre, she climbed a few steps to the cement block that held a half-full dumpster.

Connie paused outside the open, heavy metal security door, then crossed the threshold into the scene shop. Overhead lights glared. She hadn't been in this part of the backstage area for fifteen years, yet it was all instantly recognizable: stacks of painted flats resting against one wall, the tool cage open, lumber piled haphazardly in a corner, paint buckets forming a pyramid. She savored the backstage smells.

In the past she might have considered chasing BJ impulsive, even reckless. But not now. She was clear with purpose. The technician was a key to her mother's disappearance. Still, her heart beat faster. The surroundings eerie, though familiar. And quiet. From a distance, she could hear someone yelling orders. The stage manager. The empty scene shop indicated work might be done for the day, leaving BJ to lock up back here. As he often did when she tagged along after him years ago. She walked to the door leading from the scene shop to the rest of the backstage area.

A hand snatched her shoulder. Connie gasped.

"Shut up!" BJ muttered. "Why're you following me?"

Connie flinched, jerking away from him.

"Bad enough your father's throwing punches. The police are interrogating me, thanks to you."

Fear of her old friend mingled with determination. The latter won. "I'm sorry. I want to understand what there was between you and my mother. What really happened that night."

BJ lifted his chin, relaxed his stance, and removed his cap. For the first time she could see his whole face, hair and beard streaked with gray, eyelids drooping. He crammed his hands into the pockets of his overalls. This scruffy individual, obsessed with her mother, could not have been the reason her parents were talking divorce, could he?

"I already said."

"I need more, BJ. Tell me everything. Please."

He quivered, stabbed glances to his right and left. Took hold of her arm, pulled her into the empty tool cage. "You accusing me of something?"

"You said you weren't having an affair. That you loved her. Then what was the argument in her dressing room about? You told me you saw things, heard things."

His mouth moved but no sounds emerged. Then he hung his head. "I loved her. I would never hurt Simone."

The fluorescent lights of the scene shop ceiling buzzed. He closed his eyes to conjure the memory of the last time he saw her mother. "She was scared. She had trouble at rehearsal all week."

Connie flashed on leaving the house that last night. Her mother was agitated as she kissed them goodbye before Connie begged her to attend the rehearsal. As they drove through the rain to the theatre, worn wipers slapping the windshield, as she applied highlight and shadow in the dressing room, something had been bothering her mother.

"I told all of this to the detective."

That would be Tom Rutherford. "Now tell me."

He sighed. "They were into act two when the power went out. Everything's black. No cell phone flashlights back then. She went looking for you. Into the dressing room." He heaved another sigh.

"And you followed her…" Connie coaxed him.

"To talk. Just to talk. Like I told the officer. I wanted her to come away with me," he said, vulnerable, pathetic even.

"But she said no, didn't she?"

He nodded.

"You didn't really have any plans, did you?"

His head barely moved, a whimper in his throat—agony for BJ to admit his obsession with Simone was not reciprocated.

"And this made you mad? Getting rejected? I heard you say you'd 'find her.'"

"To talk some more. I had to convince her!"

"*Did* you find her? Did you two fight and somehow…you killed her…accidentally?"

BJ turned red, then glum, facial muscles sagging. "It was no use. She loved someone else."

"My father."

"Him? He didn't stand a chance. But I never told the detective this." He exhaled loudly.

"Then who? You said you saw and heard—"

BJ cut her off, defensive, aggressive. "Besides why would I hurt her when there was a cop hanging around the theatre that night?"

Wait, what? "A cop? Someone in uniform?"

"I guess so."

Her father, in uniform, came to the theatre later to pick her up. But before the rehearsal? And what about Charlie? He was dating Jackie then. He could have come to the theatre. Though, Connie hadn't seen either of them that night before the blackout.

"Who was it?" she asked.

"I dunno. Just saw the patrol car out front after the run-through started. Couldn't see who was in it."

Grasping at straws, Connie asked, "The theatre hired a cop for security?"

BJ shrugged, his eyes glistened. "After I saw you two in the hallway, I went out to check the generator."

"You didn't see her leave?"

"I never saw her again." BJ slammed his cap on his head, brushed past Connie.

"BJ! Wait! What was the secret Mom held over you? Why was she threatening you? What did you have on her?"

He pivoted to her for a second, alarmed, before practically running to the stage.

"Who was the woman with Mom? The one you overheard?" She rushed after him but by the time she reached the wings, BJ was standing in the house, talking with Ted. No point in hanging around now.

Connie trudged back to the parking lot, banged the car door shut, and flipped the ignition key. According to the message her mother left, she hinted she might be going away soon. If BJ was telling the truth, his revelation begged the question: Who was her mother in love with?

Chapter 30

Now

Today BJ offered vital information, assuming he was telling the truth. He didn't have an affair with her mother, and she was in love with someone else. Not her father. But maybe her mother had confided in Angela. Connie called the Westerman residence from her car on the road to Hallison and, after five rings, a generic message requested that she leave her name and number.

"Hello Angela. I'm Simone Tucker's daughter, Connie, in town for the funeral." She paused. "I...understand that you were close to her. Worked together at the Flint Theatre. Would you be willing to meet with me? I'd like to talk." Connie provided her phone number. "Thanks. Bye."

Still no idea about either her mother's or BJ's secret.

She brushed her bangs off her forehead and ramped up the air conditioning. Perspiration trickled down the inside of her blouse, the dampness annoying. Rush hour traffic forced her to crawl at a snail's pace. Better this speed than playing bumper cars with crazy drivers that might result in another accident. At one point on the parkway, when the line of cars was at a standstill, she left a voicemail for Detective

Nardone. He was leaving town today, but before he did, she had a question for him. Until she got an answer, there was one place that could lift her spirits and tonight she needed a mood-enhancer and supportive ears.

Half an hour later she sat at her favorite scarred table in the rear corner of Porter's, her back to the rest of the bar, which included her father behind the cash register. Smiling and jawing with customers. No sign of his earlier anger at the theatre. Opposite her sat Brigid, happy to use her break-out-of-the-house card, and Gaby, who had required significant wooing to get her in here after a busy day at work. The volume ebbed and flowed around them. Aromas of cooking grease wafting out of the kitchen every time the swinging door was flung open.

They dipped chips into guacamole—Gaby drank beer, Connie had seltzer to keep her mind on the task at hand, and Brigid a Virgin Mary.

"You recovered from the anniversary party?" Brigid scooped a hunk of guac onto a bite-sized tortilla chip and popped it into her mouth.

"I was a hot mess that night."

"Yep. Like the old days."

"What are you talking about?" Connie scoffed. "I never got that wasted when we were kids."

"Uh...yeah you did. Lots of underage drinking that last year. The boardwalk in Point Pleasant, my aunt's wedding—"

"All right!" She shot a glance at Gaby, who stayed neutral, eating and drinking. Silent. "I have a couple of things I'd like to tell you two."

Brigid leaned into the table, eager for Connie to dive in. Gaby crossed her arms. Cautious. After taking a sip of her drink, Connie began with this morning at the theatre and her father's scuffle with BJ— a "holy shit!" from Brigid, a shocked expression from Gaby.

"Good thing I followed him."

"Poor Dad," Gaby said, glancing at their father behind the bar.

"Poor BJ. Luckily, Dad's punch didn't land."

"And you couldn't have stopped it before it started?"

"It was already happening as I arrived. Nobody was hurt, BJ certainly wouldn't press charges at this point—"

"Charges?" Gaby yelped.

"Calm down, Gaby." Connie scanned the bar. No one paid them any attention. "There's more." She emptied her glass and recounted her conversation with BJ in the scene shop.

Brigid eyeballed first one sister, then the other. "The person of interest."

Gaby spoke slowly, as if each word was painful: "He said that Mom was in love with someone…but not…"

"Dad."

The arrival of their dinners poked a hole in the balloon of privacy that surrounded the table. "Enjoy!" the perky waitress commanded.

"Gaby, I'm sorry this is coming out." Connie waited for her sister to comment, then smacked the bottom of the ketchup bottle and handed it to Brigid. "But isn't it better to know the truth about Mom and whatever happened that night?"

Gaby swallowed a bit of her sandwich. "Not if it's going to hurt Dad."

Brigid cleared her throat. "You wouldn't want an innocent guy to go to jail, would you?"

Gaby wiped her mouth. "BJ doesn't sound too innocent to me. Stalking Mom, lying to the police the first time, threatening Connie, attacking Dad."

"Dad attacked him, for the record."

Gaby tossed her napkin on the table, pushed her partially-eaten dinner aside. "You've heard my opinion for what it's worth: Leave. It. All. Alone."

"Why are you so against learning the truth?"

"What's past is past. It won't bring her back. For the last time, let it go."

"I can't," Connie whispered.

"Why not?" Gaby's voice again rose a decibel or two, though in the crowded bar, no one noticed.

"You weren't in the theatre that night. You didn't see Mom and BJ fighting. Hear Mom plead with me to tell no one." Connie slumped in her seat, her breath expelled in a puff of frustration.

Gaby reached across the table, touched her hand. "I'm sorry for that. Truly sorry. But what you're doing…it's not going to help. You have to move on."

"That's hard to do when your life is threatened."

Brigid stopped chewing.

"That 'accident' on the parkway? The cars piling up and me unable to brake? Might not have been an accident. Fluid drained from the brake line."

"What?" Gaby exclaimed. "Have you gone to the police?"

"Not yet."

"Damn, Connie," Brigid murmured. "This is serious, kiddo."

"I'm picking up the car tomorrow. I want to speak with the mechanic first and then I'll go see the Hallison police. I'm wondering if it's Rosa? First the rock and now this?"

Gaby shook her head. "Why would Rosa, why would anyone want to do this to you? To us?"

"To shut you up?" Brigid offered.

"Then maybe it's time you worried about consequences." Gaby rose and dropped some bills on the table.

"Wait a minute. I have to ask you something." Her sister stood over her. "You remember Mom's blue carryall? The tote bag she carried around with her everywhere?"

Gaby frowned. "What about it?"

"Did you see it after that night? She had it with her when we left the house and in the dressing room, but Detective Nardone said it was never found. Now I'm wondering—"

"Connie! Stop!" Gaby left the table, pausing at the bar to have a word with their father before she exited Porter's.

"Some bad blood there," Brigid said.

"I don't understand why she's so defensive about Dad. Why neither one of them is anxious to pursue Mom's murder. Gaby's actually angry I'm digging into the past."

Connie flagged the waitress. *The hell with it.* She ordered wine and nibbled on a French fry.

"She's right about one thing, though. You gotta think about consequences. If pursuing your mom's murder is pissing somebody off, you better turn all your fact-finding over to the cops." Brigid slurped the last of her drink through the straw. "We're talking some high-level danger. You gotta be careful."

"Don't worry. I can take care of myself. I have my pepper spray if anything goes south. I used it once in San Diego. I was walking home early one morning, and this guy followed me, right to my front steps. I sprayed him. Stopped him in his tracks. Long enough for me to get in the house."

Brigid assessed her as if in a new light. "Wow."

"So," Connie said, "the night of the anniversary party, Deirdre and your mom talked about the triangle. Dad, Charlie, and Mom. Could my mother have been in love with Charlie? I mean, they dated before she married Dad and he was around a lot, teasing and being playful when we were kids. But Dad was his best friend."

"Charlie and your mom? I can see them as late teens, twenty-somethings, all into one another. But by the time Simone was married to your dad? With two teenage daughters? Nah. Anyway, Charlie himself was married, right?"

"He got married the year after Mom disappeared. Not long before I left for California." Connie took a drink of her wine. "That was a good move. I like Jackie. So thoughtful."

They paid their bill, walked out the door, and hugged. "You're a good friend," said Connie. "Putting up with me."

"Hey, we go way back." Brigid toddled off to her car, waving as she sank into the front seat.

The night was balmy, the air fresh with a slight breeze drifting through the neighborhood. Walking would feel good. On the curb ready to cross Ferry Street, her cell rang. It could be Mom's friend from the Flint Theatre. Angela Westerman. Connie eagerly rummaged through her bag. Caller ID said Unknown. "Hello?"

"Connie Tucker?" a male voice asked, the background noisy.

She recognized the voice. Retired Detective Nardone. "Hi. Thanks for getting back."

"Sure. I'm at the airport. You can hear the PA." He chuckled, breathless, then coughed.

On cue, the public address system announced a departure and gate. "Do you have time to talk?" she asked.

"My flight was delayed. What can I do for you? Heard anything from the cold case unit?"

Connie clenched her fist to drain the tension from her voice. "No. I've called a bunch of times and no one gets back to me. I suppose they'll contact Dad if there's an update."

Another announcement, this time alerting passengers to a pre-boarding process.

"Oops, that's my flight to Seattle. Sorry."

Connie jumped in: "You said my father's car was in Hallison from ten or so the night Mom disappeared into the next morning. I suppose you might not remember who corroborated that."

Nardone's laugh ended with labored breathing. "Normally I don't recall witness names after this many years. But like I said, your mother struck a chord with me and anyway, the name was so unusual I must have tucked it away in my long-term memory bank. Basil."

"Basil?" Who the hell was Basil? Surely, she'd recognize the name of anyone close enough to her father to provide an alibi.

"Basil Porter."

After wishing Nardone best of luck in his new home and ending the call, Connie halted on the sidewalk in shock for two reasons. One trivial: No wonder Old Man Porter had rejected his first name. And the other critical: Did the Old Man lie to protect her father? They were good friends, but violate the law?

Connie started to walk down Ferry Street, and then around the corner, weighing the day's events. Clearing her head. Sorting through evidence. Gaby and Brigid were right: She had to think about the consequences of naming suspects. Rosa had a motive, if hatred and envy were motives for killing, and certainly access to Connie's car to tamper with the brakes. But Rosa had no reason to be at the theatre, and indeed, Connie had not seen her there that night. BJ was the most obvious suspect. He had opportunity, motive—her mother's rejection, his obsession, and the disclosure of his secret—and the means. She had witnessed him threatening her mother.

Either Rosa or BJ being guilty would not upend Connie's world. But her father? Motive: Her mother in love with someone else, planning on a divorce, leaving him. Opportunity: He was not home between ten p.m. and five a.m.

Alibi or no, she had to face facts and consider what it would mean if her father was guilty of murder. It would destroy what little was left of their family. Is this why Gaby was so reluctant to even discuss Mom's death? Was she afraid that their father was somehow involved?

Connie had to find out. Her father was scheduled to tend bar at Porter's for a few more hours. Gaby, probably still irritated with her, had said she planned an early night—once she was in her bedroom with ear plugs, sealing her from noise inside and outside the house, her sister claimed she couldn't hear a thing.

Good.

Chapter 31

Now

Connie tiptoed up the stairs to the second floor of the Tucker home, careful to avoid the center of each stair—the creaking zone, familiar to Connie from long-ago days of escaping the house undetected.

The closed door of their father's bedroom reminded her she was trespassing on his private domain. When she and Gaby were little, the wide-open door invited the two girls to play trampoline on their parents' bed, bouncing and jumping until their mother would enter and join in their game which invariably ended in a tickle session. That was then.

She had no idea what she expected to find hidden behind that door. Yes, she did: some clue to confirm his guilt or innocence. What else?

Fingers twitching, she touched the handle's cold, tarnished metal, twisted it, then stood on the brink of the bedroom. Taking a last glance down the hallway, she slipped inside. The air conditioning a low hum, the cool air bathed the room in comfort. With her cell flashlight, Connie saw that the blinds were closed, floral curtains drawn. Her eyes, adjusting to the shadows, identified familiar furniture—the bed, a bureau, and a dressing table. He had kept the room unchanged, including the now worn green area rug.

First stop was the closed closet. Khakis, polo shirts on hangers, and two suits hung neatly, a shelf with folded sweaters and a couple of hats she'd never seen her father wear. This kind of organization suggested Gaby's influence, the attic notwithstanding. Nothing hidden in the corners, no blue carryall stuffed behind boxes of old clothes. On the floor behind a pair of dress shoes, slippers, sneakers, and winter boots was a gray, metal, locked container. Connie knew what it held: a gun and ammunition. When she was twelve there had been a rash of home invasions in Hallison. Her father had insisted her mother have a legal handgun in the house. They'd argued about it—her mother resisting until her father assured her that they'd keep it in a safe place—away from their daughters' snooping eyes. Connie had eavesdropped on the conversation that day and saw the gray box. Then it disappeared, hidden away in the house. Until it surfaced this day.

She shut the closet door.

The dressing table. In the past, a feminine hand mirror and matching hairbrush lay on a lace runner that covered it. When Connie was four or five, she loved to steal in here and inhale the scents of her mother. Mysterious bottles and jars. Perfumes and makeup and jewelry. All gone now. The dresser bare, the drawers empty. Removed from her father's life for these past fifteen years.

Closing the last drawer, she dropped her phone. A violent clatter on the floorboards, its flashlight's beam bouncing off the walls. Connie snatched it up and stiffened.

The house remained quiet.

She darted to the bureau that her parents had shared. Her father's things in the top three drawers that she and Gaby, sneaking into the forbidden zone as little kids, had studied in amazement. Tee shirts, shorts, in one drawer, pajamas, socks, and handkerchiefs in another. Assorted personal items in the third—change jar, holy cards, rosaries, old driver's licenses.

Her mother's clothing had always been placed in the bottom two drawers. The top drawers hadn't changed, but the bottom two were now as empty as the hole left by her mother's death—except for a small, soft object, covered in pretty pink cloth. A lavender sachet, like the one in the suitcase at the theatre. Her mother tucked sachets in all of their bedroom drawers. As Connie lifted the pouch to hold it to her nose, something dropped off.

A piece of jewelry had been wound around the sachet.

Downstairs, a door thumped open, shooting a bolt of electricity through her. Tightening her grip on the pouch and the jewelry she closed the drawer and eased into the hallway. Shutting her father's door, she exhaled to quiet her nerves and listened. Kitchen cupboards opening and closing. "Gaby? Where's the aspirin? Damn headache again." Her father.

Connie's sister ran from her room into the hall, yanking the plugs out of her ears. So much for blocking out noise. "Dad?" She turned to look at Connie. "What are you doing?" She stared at her sister's hand.

"On my way to bed."

Either Gaby was too distracted by their father calling her or had decided to resist any urge to decipher Connie's behavior. She tied her robe closed and tromped down the stairs. "I'm coming."

Heart pounding, Connie fled to her bedroom, closed the door and flopped onto the bed to do battle with her labored breathing. She'd had a narrow escape. Then she glanced at the hand Gaby had scrutinized. Still clutching the lavender sachet and what had been attached to it. Connie hadn't discovered the missing blue tote, but she had found something else. Her mother's necklace. A tiny gold cross on a thin chain.

A precious First Communion gift from her own mother, Grandmother Bernard. Another object that she always kept with her.

Her father had somehow come into possession of this prized treasure.

Connie woke with a headache, her mind spinning. A hot shower and two cups of strong coffee didn't help—only made her edgier and more irritable. Finding the necklace and learning of the Old Man's covering for her father had only added weight to the burden she shouldered. She dreaded having to confront Porter. If he'd lied about her father and provided a false alibi, he'd done a great job of hiding his guilt around her. That this grandfatherly man could be involved in concealing a crime as horrifying as her mother's murder was unthinkable. That he could be a threat to Connie even more inconceivable. Still...

In the parking lot of the body shop, her car was good as new, the bumper and side door pristine. The mechanic confirmed that the brake line had to be replaced. If he thought something was amiss, someone responsible for an unlawful act, he didn't let on.

"Rental car, right?" the mechanic said.

"Yes. Didn't want to return it banged up." Connie tucked the credit card receipt into her bag.

"Good idea. Don't forget this." He held a small black box in his palm.

"What's that?"

"Your GPS tracker," he said, putting the gadget in Connie's hand.

"My what?"

"It fell off the underside of your car. It's a good model. I've seen some that plug into your OBD port, but this is wireless. Great anti-theft device."

"Does this mean my car has been...tracked?"

"Yep. This baby collects data every second and every few minutes uploads to a server. Trip history, vehicle location. The works."

A chill raced from her head to her toes. She thanked the mechanic, settled into the front seat, and inspected the GPS tracker in her shaking hand. Outside, the day had turned dark, the sun buried behind thick gray clouds. The forecasted rain would soon descend.

Someone wants to keep track of me. Where I go. What I do. Who I talk to.

Detective Keogh of the Hallison Police Department peppered Connie with questions: Why hadn't she reported the brake issue immediately? Why wait until it was repaired? There might have been physical evidence on the automobile that was now destroyed. Who had access to her car? Who else drove it? Etc. etc. The onslaught made her weary. He bagged the GPS tracker as evidence—though by now it had been handled by her and the mechanic at the very least—and told her to stay out of the car until he could investigate. He'd be in touch. At the last minute, he half-smiled. A little sympathy. The tracker could have been placed on the car for previous renters, but he'd have it examined.

Except that in her gut Connie knew it was meant for her. She'd stepped on someone's toes. And despite the advice everyone offered her, she'd waded into something deep and dark and she couldn't climb her way out of it until the obvious question was answered: What had happened to her mother that night?

By the time she'd left the Hallison Police Department Connie was emotionally drained. Now she sat on the porch swing, tapping her toes on the ground to keep the glider swaying in the afternoon heat. Lifting her hair and sweeping it into a ponytail, she debated when to approach Porter about his part in her father's alibi. When to approach her father about the necklace. When and how to approach BJ about his cryptic "ask her."

She glanced back through the front window—her father slept in his recliner, taking the day off from work. Gaby had texted an hour ago saying she'd cook dinner for all of them later. Connie was on her own for a few hours. Her eyes closed to the buzzing of insects diving into her sister's hanging flowerpots.

She drifted off, awakened by a car door slammed in the Delano driveway. Rosa emerged from the driver's side of the SUV, and buried her head in the back seat, while Mrs. Delano remained in the passenger seat. Connie made a split-second decision: She refused to allow Rosa to obstruct the relationship that she and Mrs. Delano had developed so many years ago. She hopped to her feet and marched to her neighbor, who was struggling to negotiate her purse, a bag of groceries on her lap, and the vehicle's door.

Connie pulled on the handle. "Let me help you." She grasped the brown bag and stretched out her hand to Mrs. Delano, who released the seat belt, hugged her pocketbook close to her body, and grabbed Connie's arm.

"Hey, cut it out," Rosa fumed. "Let her go."

Connie paid no attention and helped Mrs. Delano out of the vehicle. "There you go."

Her neighbor smiled with appreciation. "Thanks Connie," she whispered. "I turned my ankle this morning."

"Are you okay?"

"Much better."

Rosa appeared at her mother's side, pulling her away from Connie.

"Take it easy," Connie said. "You'll hurt—"

"I can take care of her."

"Apparently not."

"Please, lower your voices," Mrs. Delano pleaded and took the grocery bag from Connie's arms. "The whole neighborhood will hear you." She limped onto the porch.

"As if I cared," Rosa said to her back, though she did drop the volume. Both she and Connie watched Mrs. Delano enter the house.

"You threw the rock through our window," Connie said. "What about my brakes?"

Rosa snapped to attention. "No idea what you're talking about. If I wanted to cause some real damage I would have. Stay away from us and maybe you won't need to run to the cops." She climbed back into the SUV and switched the ignition key.

Connie grabbed the passenger side door and swung it open. "Tell me the truth. Who did you see my mother with that summer? Who was she..."

"Kissing?" Rosa started to laugh as though she found the question funny. Then stopped abruptly and squinted at Connie. "You got no idea, do you? Who your mother really was?" She shook her head. "I feel sorry for you Tuckers."

Connie slammed the car door and Rosa roared away. *Sorry for us.* Rosa Delano, sorry for the Tucker family. Whatever she had seen was that damaging or shocking.

She waited until the car had turned the corner at the end of Third Street, then stepped onto the porch and knocked on her neighbor's screen door. "Mrs. Delano?"

"I'm in the kitchen."

Connie entered the home where she'd spent so many hours as a kid and inhaled the aroma of childhood comfort. Something baking. Mrs. Delano stirred a pot bubbling away.

"Smells good."

"Homemade vegetable soup. Want a bowl?"

"No thanks. Gaby's cooking tonight. But I'll take one of these," she said and pointed to a plate of oatmeal raisin cookies.

Without asking, Mrs. Delano removed two mugs from the cabinet and seized the coffee pot.

Connie pulled a chair from the table for her to sit on. "Why don't you get off your feet?"

She brushed away Connie's concerns and sighed. "I'm fine, and I'm sorry about Rosa. She could never quite accept anyone in your family."

Connie took the woman's hand. "It's painful for you. She and Mom didn't get along. They had fights about Gaby and me sometimes."

"Yes. Rosa was so jealous of your family. Especially you, Connie. So lively, fun-loving, always smiling as a child. And beautiful." Mrs. Delano touched Connie's cheek. "It's been going on for many years…she can't find herself. And then she gets in trouble." The older woman wiped away a tear.

The drugs Dack and Brigid mentioned. Rosa out on bail.

You know," Mrs. Delano said, "she was sent away for a year the month before Simone disappeared."

"What?"

"You might not remember. You and Gaby were only…"

"Thirteen and fourteen."

Mrs. Delano's face fell, her eyes brimming with tears. "She had such a hard life before she came to live with us. I hoped a loving family would make a difference. I kept hoping that things would change."

Connie's thoughts were swimming. Rosa wasn't around the neighborhood when her mother vanished. She couldn't have been involved. There would be no point in her tampering with Connie's car, unless for sheer spite. Which was always a possibility.

"Her lawyer said it could be longer this time." Mrs. Delano blew her nose.

Two hours later, the clouds had shifted off to the east, replaced with an early fall sunset that streamed in the window of the Tucker kitchen. A blue and red sky. The three of them ate Gaby's meat loaf, twice-baked potatoes and fresh string beans. Gaby and her father made small talk—the Yankees' slump, tomorrow's weather forecast, the library's new literacy program—studiously avoiding any topic having to do with their mother, law enforcement, theatre, or the past.

Her sister tried to engage her in the fragile conversation, but Connie's mind was full of certainty of Rosa's innocence and the possibility of her father's guilt. She couldn't shake the image of the necklace in the sachet. Her mother had never gone without it. How could her father have come by it? And what of her father's alibi for that night? She only half-listened to her sister and father chat, occasionally stealing glimpses of him: relaxed, smiling, his color good, healthier-looking than at any time since she'd returned to New Jersey.

Tomorrow, she would force herself to question the Old Man, as fraught—and hazardous—as that interview might be. Depending on what she learned from him, Connie would have to decide about her father—how and when to approach him. If at all. And then deliver whatever she found out to the cold case unit. That was all she could manage.

Her cell rang but she ignored it. Whoever was calling could wait until she'd finished eating.

It was hours later as she lay on her narrow bed, paging once again through family photo albums that reflected so many happy times for the Tuckers, that she remembered the call.

It was Angela Westerman. The message was brief and to the point. She knew Simone from the Flint Theatre ages ago but hadn't been well lately and wasn't up for company. With a clipped "Have a good night" Angela clicked off.

The call made Connie antsy, left her feeling up-in-the-air. She pulled on a pair of jeans and a black tee shirt, grabbed her bag, and stepped into the hallway. Her father's bedroom was quiet; he retired upstairs after dinner. She could hear faint television voices emanating from her sister's room. She tiptoed down the stairs and let herself out the front door, texting Gaby on her way to Porter's. No point in panicking her sister if she discovered Connie's absence. No point in waiting until tomorrow to have this out with Old Man Porter. A bar with customers was as safe as any place to talk murder and alibis.

Almost eleven, the bar winding down, only a few lingerers in the place, seated at a table or two. Connie, stomach twisting, pulse racing, motioned to Porter and moved to an empty one.

He gave her a "one minute" sign and closed the cash register, offering a word to Dack.

"How's the old man doing?" he asked as he sat heavily.

"Taking it easy tonight." She clasped her hands tightly.

"You okay? You look strange."

"I'm fine. Could I ask you something?"

"Sure, toots, anything." He was the grandfather now.

"I've had a lot of questions about Mom's disappearance. So, I tracked down the detective who ran her case. He's retired now."

"Uh-huh." The Old Man's expression innocent, interested, definitely not anticipating an ambush.

"He told me Dad's alibi for that night. That he didn't get Mom's message at first, but later when he did, he picked me up and came home around ten and was in for the rest of the night."

Porter nodded. Again, not expecting anything.

Connie took a deep breath to stay calm. "You corroborated his story."

"That's right."

"But it's not true," she blurted, accusing him. "You lied for Dad."

Chapter 32

Now

Stunned, Porter's jaw dropped, his features drooped. At that moment, he looked all of his eighty-some years, as though his past had caught up with him. He rested his arms on the table, his eyes ablaze with defiance. With loyalty. "Nobody needed to know. Not the cops. Not anyone."

"What?"

"Your dad is a good man. He suffered a lot. He wanted to keep things secret."

"Tell me."

The Old Man bowed his head and sighed. "Your folks' marriage was on the rocks. Simone was not happy. He tried to make her happy, but... she was upset, those days."

Fluorescent lights flickered on, the glare a harsh dose of reality. Closing up the bar was imminent. Dack and the waitress avoided the two figures huddled together and purposefully focused on cleaning other tables. Connie and Porter sat isolated in their own bubble, swaddled by memories of the night when her mother went missing.

Connie marveled at how successfully her parents hid the full truth from their daughters—neither she nor Gaby had an inkling. They probably intended to tell the two of them "when the time was right." Old Man Porter was the third person—after Diana and BJ— to describe her mother as upset, unhappy. The joyful, vivacious figure making up stories and dancing in the living room, upset.

Connie leaned in. "Were they planning to...?"

"Simone told him that day she wanted a divorce."

There it was. "Charlie mentioned talk of a divorce, but Gaby and I, especially Gaby, dismissed it. But that doesn't explain his alibi and your covering for him. I was home by about ten, but I heard Dad come in at five a.m. Where was he during those hours?"

Porter sat up straight, drew a hand across his cheek. "With me. Here. I told the police I was with him at your place until one a.m. His car parked in the driveway."

He jerked his head in the direction of the back room, where more than one Porter's customer had slept it off after a bout of too much carousing. "Devastated that night. Didn't want anyone to know. Too hurt. He dropped you off and walked here. He figured Simone would be home in the next hour, so you and your sister wouldn't be alone all night." The Old Man leaned back in his seat. "He didn't count on her going missing."

Connie's mind whirled, frustration rising. "Why not tell the police the truth? Would it have made a difference if Dad was passed out here and not in his own home?"

"Maybe. Maybe not."

"It might have made a difference to me."

Porter's voice vaulted into the space between them. "I did what a good friend should do...support a man in trouble. It was bad enough

Simone was gone. He couldn't bear admitting his drunken state to a bunch of fellow cops. He was too proud."

"Dad slept it off in the back room."

"After Simone was gone, his world fell apart. He lost himself as well as losing her." Porter reached across the table and took Connie's hand. "And then he lost you. Sweetie, he had no choice...you needed something he couldn't give you."

"What was that?" she asked, the old defensiveness rearing its ugly head.

"A mother."

The Old Man, sorrowful, hoisted himself to his feet and trudged away.

Outside, Connie turned one way, then the other, unsure of what to do. She paced the block in front of the bar. According to the Old Man, her father couldn't have been responsible for her mother's disappearance. He was getting drunk and then sleeping it off. Could she believe Porter? He could still be shielding her father. *No.* He'd never lied to her before; had always been one of the most stable adults in her life.

She didn't have a choice. She had to believe him.

Without acknowledging it consciously for fifteen years, Connie had questioned her father's absence from the house between ten p.m. and five a.m. Subconsciously, she'd blamed him for her mother's absence. It was possible his only crime had been loving his wife too much and getting drunk because he couldn't face life without her. If only the Old Man had leveled with the police about her father's alibi...

The night's revelation left Connie more disturbed than ever. She weighed the potential suspects: besides BJ and Rosa, and possibly her father, did her mother have other emotional connections in her life fierce and passionate enough to trigger the violent act that ended her life?

According to BJ, she was in love with someone; according to Rosa, her mother and someone were seen kissing in a car on Third Street.

Her death could have been a random act. A diabolically insane person could have committed the killing. Fracturing her skull, strangling her mother with her own scarf, burying her in deserted woods. Surely the investigation had considered this possibility.

Then there was the tracker on her rental car and the cut brake line. What were they about?

Connie turned toward Third Street. Everyone was right: Leaving the cold case detective, however much he turned her off, to do his job was the best route to follow. Hoping and praying that someday, someone would be caught and pay the price for her mother's death.

The house was dark when she unlocked the front door. Creeping up the stairs, Connie wondered at her sister and father: however sad, however grief-stricken they might be, both had demonstrated the ability to switch off their minds and succumb to sleep. Tonight, Third Street was quiet, the air coming through her window calm and steady, as if the neighborhood were giving Connie a break. Letting her release the heartache so she could rest.

Her cell phone jingled. A text coming in. Connie rolled over in her twin bed, squinting against the warm golden light streaming into the bedroom, the house equally as silent as the night before. She glanced at the phone: six thirty a.m. Pretty early for someone to be texting. Unless it was an emergency. The notion compelled her to tap on the message from a number she didn't recognize: *You want to know who 'she' was? Come backstage this morning. 9:30. Use the loading dock. BJ*

Connie dropped the phone onto the sheet as if it burned her hand. How did he get her cell number? More importantly, he was willing to talk, finally, after she'd pursued him for days. She texted back *Okay* and scanned the room as if uncertain what to do next. Three hours. No way did she want to bump into Gaby or her father and discuss the Old Man's alibi story; she'd have to deal with that later. The two of them would be rising soon for work, or whatever her father had planned for the day. She had two options: hunker down and wait an hour or two, or dress now and leave. A second later she grabbed clothes and a jacket, her bag, shoes, and the cell off the rumpled sheet.

The clanging of Gaby's alarm clock jolted Connie as she hurried past her sister's bedroom door. She flew down the stairs as if pursued.

The morning air was fresh and cool, and her jacket felt good as she headed to the Hallison town diner. Thirty minutes later she faced scrambled eggs and a cup of coffee, the caffeine a wake-up boost, sorting through her feelings and what the meeting with BJ might mean. She had to be prepared for whatever he had to say. Whoever the "her" was.

A thought flickered: The last time she saw the technician he was destroyed, broken down by memories of the past and his illusions about her mother. But now? She assumed this was a good faith meeting, not a way to ambush her, threaten her in some way. With the Flint production opening in a few days, the final dress looming ever closer, the crew might be hard at work. But no, probably not at nine-thirty. There was a reason BJ set up the meeting for that hour: the theatre would be empty. No one would know she was there.

Shivers scuttled down her spine; she pulled the jacket tighter around her middle, Finn's words to her emphatic as they sat on the park bench and he comforted her: "...promise me you'll be careful and call me if you need anything." She punched his number into her phone and left a voicemail. Now, at least one other person knew where she was.

Connie had agreed with Detective Keogh in principle—stay in Hallison, out of her rental car until the tracking incident was sorted out.

This trip, however, was a necessity. The ride to Colmar bittersweet. This was no doubt the final time she'd visit the place where she had last spoken to her mother, the last time she'd visit the place where she'd amassed fond memories and old friends. Connie had no idea when she'd return to New Jersey, but whenever that was, the Flint Theatre would not be on the agenda.

Today's trip was about one thing: BJ's revealing the name of the woman he saw with her mother the week she disappeared.

The parking lot was empty, save for two cars, and Connie slipped into a space in the rear. Within a couple of minutes, she stood at the back entrance of the theatre on the loading dock, her pulse thudding. It was nine twenty-five. The door was ajar—BJ wanted to make certain Connie could access this entrance—and she eased it open. Lights were full up in the scene shop, but no activity. She treaded with care around a table saw and half a dozen two-by-fours leaning against it. As if someone had been interrupted in the middle of completing a job. She smelled fresh sawdust.

The door to the hallway that ran past the dressing rooms was open. He wasn't in the scene shop; he had to be on the stage.

"BJ?" she called.

Connie moved through the door and into the hallway, deliberately ignoring what had been her mother's dressing room that fateful night. Stage lights were up to half, leaving shadows scattered around the playing area. No sign of the technician here, either.

She was present, as requested; he was not. She didn't intend to hang around indefinitely, especially once Ted and the cast arrived. Flats on the other side of the stage formed the walls of the room where the play's action took place. She'd check over there, wait a few more minutes, then leave. Disappointed, but unwilling to be made a fool of.

As Connie crossed the stage, she imagined BJ having a good laugh at her expense.

In the half-light, a form in a fetal position materialized on the floor. She recognized the overalls and ball cap lying next to him. "BJ? What are you doing there?" she said, edging closer.

She stopped and gasped. Blood draining from her limbs, panic racing through her veins. His body was crumpled, one arm outstretched, almost reaching for help. His features contorted like his last thoughts had been angry. His eyes open and staring. She screamed and covered her face.

Someone else screamed behind her.

"What were you doing here?" the stocky Colmar police officer asked, standing in the aisle beside her, tapping a pad against his thick fingers.

Connie sat in the house, facing the stage where EMTs had covered BJ and were preparing to move him out of the theatre. Holding a glass of water someone had thrust at her. "I was supposed to meet him. At nine-thirty."

Next to her, Diana, the Flint's leading lady, held her hand.

The cop looked around. Weirdly impassive, as if such scenes barely rated his attention. His hooded eyes found her again. "Were you working for him? Rehearsing?"

She shook her head. "No. He was a friend from the past. I was saying goodbye before I left town." No way would she mention the real reason she'd shown up at the theatre. She started to tremble as the full impact of what she'd discovered hit her: BJ was dead.

"It's too awful." Diana removed her sunglasses to expose red-rimmed eyes. She'd been the second one to scream, to see BJ on the stage floor. "To fall off the grid a second time?" She choked on her words, her lips quivering. "He was such a part of the Flint Theatre...first his leg and now this. A horrible accident." She gasped. "The catwalk and the grid were unsafe. No one should have been up there. Not even BJ."

"And you were here because...?"

Diana slumped. "I came in early to walk around the set by myself. The stage lights were up halfway and the house out. As if rehearsal was in progress. I didn't see anyone, so I went onto the set and they were there...BJ and Connie."

Ted stood in the background, agitated, arms crossed, answering questions posed by another officer. He'd cast a surprised, quick look at Connie upon his arrival: What are you doing here? He seemed to be asking, much as the officer had.

Finished with Diana and Connie, the cop snapped the pad shut, nodded, and strode to the back of the house.

Connie's mind raced. Images flashed: BJ backstage, the last time they talked; BJ taking her up to the catwalk; BJ with her mother, the night of the storm. "I don't understand," she stuttered to Diana. "He knew that lighting system better than anyone. He wouldn't have done anything unsafe." She studied the catwalk over the stage, a section of broken railing hanging free at a precarious angle.

"I can't get that picture of him out of my mind," Diana sobbed. "Lying there..."

Connie heard BJ's command to her thirteen-year-old self. "Never go up top without safety gear." She'd always seen him wear a belt or line.

"I didn't see any safety equipment on him. Did you?"

"What?" Diana asked, distracted.

"A safety belt? Or a line he could attach to the guardrail?"

She shook her head. "I have to get out of here." She swiftly moved up the aisle and out of the theatre.

With no reason to remain, Connie followed her out. A crowd had formed on the sidewalk outside, drawn by the presence of three cop cars parked diagonally across the street. Next to them was an ambulance.

Dazed, Connie considered the sickening accident. BJ on the rail, failing to take precautions. The cost of a grid fix had been discussed among Ted and the cast members. Jackie said the board was meeting to decide on repairs. BJ must have known all this. He wouldn't deliberately risk his life.

One thing was certain: Now she would never learn what secrets BJ had harbored.

Chapter 33

Now

"What were you doing there?" Gaby asked, rubbing Connie's back.

It was a soothing gesture from her sister. They sat outside on the Hallison Public Library patio. Connie had gone to see her after leaving the theatre, traumatized and dejected. Convinced that with BJ's death, hope for a resolution to her mother's murder had diminished.

"He texted me early this morning. Said to come to the theatre if I wanted to know who the 'her' was—the woman he'd seen with Mom the week before she disappeared. He said he'd seen and heard things. I kept asking who she was, but he never said. Then suddenly I get his text."

"Why's this woman such a big deal?"

"I don't know, but BJ seemed to think she was connected to Mom's disappearance. That whatever got said really upset Mom."

"There had to be a number of women in the theatre that week."

Connie nodded, glum. "On my way here, I called Charlie to ask about the grid repair and BJ's accident. Probably one too many questions, because he cut me off and invited me to dinner. A chance for me to say goodbye."

Bees buzzed around a flower bed on the perimeter of the patio while the Tucker sisters sat in silence.

"Do you have to leave?" Gaby said. "What about staying? For a few months. Or indefinitely."

"Indefinitely? What would I do here?"

Gaby shrugged. "What are you doing in San Diego that you couldn't do here?"

Bartending. The universal line of work.

"What do you want, Connie? I mean here, now, with this?"

She looked askance at Gaby. "What I've always wanted. To find Mom's killer."

"Is that all?"

"Why? What do you want?"

"What I've always wanted. You home."

Connie's eyes burned. Gaby rose. "Have to get back to work."

"You want to come with me tomorrow night? To Charlie's for dinner?" The afternoon humidity lay like a blanket around them.

Gaby wiped dampness off her brow. "I don't think so."

"Oh, come on. It'll be the last time I see Charlie and Jackie. Except maybe for BJ's funeral."

Her sister frowned. "So terrible. I'm sorry you had to find him."

"Apparently, the part of the guardrail that gave way should have been repaired long ago. I wouldn't be surprised if there's a lawsuit. Charlie and Jackie must be freaked out."

Gaby shot her a sideways questioning glance.

"They're on the theatre's board. I have a feeling the Flint estate may have to cough up some big bucks."

Walking the few blocks home in the sweltering heat, Connie heard her phone buzzing in her bag. She'd turned it to vibrate at the theatre when the police started asking questions. Two doors from her Third Street home, she checked the caller ID and tapped Answer.

"Hi, Finn."

"Connie. How are you?" he said in a rush.

She now stood at the end of her driveway and stared at the Tucker porch. And Finn.

"Fine." She clicked off and met him on the front steps.

He held her tightly, kissed her cheek, and led her to the glider. "I missed your call. Was with patients. When you didn't answer your phone a couple of hours later, I went to the theatre to find you. You'd already gone."

"You didn't have to do that," she said, though grateful and pleased he did.

He tucked stray hair behind her ear. "My God. I heard what happened. What were you doing there?"

For the third time, Connie answered the question, this time telling all.

"Poor BJ," Finn said when she was done. "So, you never got the answer you wanted from him." He sighed. "Really unfortunate. Having that woman's name might have put your mind at ease."

"Thanks Finn. Nice that somebody cares."

"Lots of folks care about you, Connie. For example, Brigid said you'd better not wait another fifteen years before you get back to Hallison." He laughed. "I think she wants you to be a godmother."

This drew a dry laugh from her. "I don't think I'm godmother material. Flattered, but not really in my wheelhouse." She sighed. "If the cold case unit arrests anyone, I'll be back for the trial."

"You think there's a possibility?"

She shrugged.

"Hey, you did your best when it came to your mom. She'd be proud of all you've done."

"I'm not sure about that," she said. "Hold on." She went inside for a minute and returned with two cans of soda, handing one to Finn.

"Brigid's going to miss you," he said.

"Me too."

"Me three." He smiled. "It's been nice to get to know you again."

Another mocking laugh. "An adult instead of a juvenile delinquent."

"A beautiful woman, a hell of a dancer, and a loyal daughter."

"Stop! You'll make me cry." She dug her sandals into the floorboards to start the glider swinging. The guy had skills. Finn said exactly what she needed to hear these last weeks.

He stretched his arms along the back of the swing. "I've been thinking I need a vacation. Do a little traveling."

"That's nice. Any place in particular you're considering?"

"Uh…Southern California?"

Connie gawked at him.

"Yeah. San Diego." He brushed her lips gently with his own and raised his drink. "Here's to your mom."

Finn. Brigid's big brother. She nestled into the crook of his arm, releasing the day's ordeals. For a moment.

Chapter 34

Now

Connie had suggested a restaurant for this last supper and Jackie said, "Nonsense." Her mother-in-law preferred eating at home. Gaby declined to join her and there was no question whether her father was interested: "Colmar's too rich for my blood."

The meal was served in the formal dining room as before, a rich beef bourguignon and a warm, crusty French bread. The conversation was polite, skirting BJ's accident at the Flint Theatre, veering into Charlie and Jackie's first meeting at a PBA fundraiser. The past—Charlie and Jackie's past, anyway—the safer destination. From that point forward, Jackie gradually introducing Charlie, still on the police force at the time, to the possibility of life as an employee of the Flint Corporation. He'd at last traded the uniform for Armani, resigning from the Newark police department when Connie's father resigned. The two partners leaving law enforcement at the same time.

Deirdre left the table after dessert and Connie could wait no longer. "So awful about BJ."

Jackie shook her head. "I warned the board about that grid. There was no appetite for a permanent fix. Replacing the entire thing. Instead, they planned to retrofit the existing pipes and railing before the show opened."

"Too late."

"Yes. Unfortunately," Jackie said. "With BJ's death, hard to say what Ted will do now. Postpone? Cancel?"

Like they canceled *A Streetcar Named Desire* after her mother disappeared.

"The theatre didn't have the budget for a complete renovation," Charlie said.

Jackie stirred her coffee. "We could have used the emergency fund."

"You mean our money?"

"My money." Jackie's smile forced.

Charlie returned her forced smile. "Of course. Anyway, what was BJ doing up there? Ted said the grid was off limits until the repairs were complete."

In the silence that followed, Connie took the opportunity to release some air out of the tension valve. "BJ loved that theatre. He introduced me to everything backstage when Mom was in rehearsal."

Jackie nodded with affection and Charlie refilled Connie's glass. One more wouldn't hurt. Her head was woolly, her body relaxed, perfect for introducing a difficult topic.

"I confronted BJ about that night. He told me that Mom was in love with someone and it wasn't Dad."

Jackie reached for Connie's hand. "Don't put yourself through—"

"Old Man Porter said she told Dad that day she wanted a divorce." This silence different, heavier. She sipped her wine and went on. "And he spent hours at the bar that night after he dropped me off, too drunk to make it home. Sleeping it off until morning. When he figured she'd be there. Only she never came home."

Jackie shook her head. "Honey…"

"That was Dad's alibi."

"I knew they questioned Liam," Charlie said.

"Detective Nardone told me the spouse is the first person they go to." Connie shrugged. "I'm wondering…BJ said he saw and heard things that week. Told me 'ask her'."

"Who?" Jackie asked.

"Some woman BJ saw with Mom. Never heard from him who it was." Connie explained BJ's text to her the morning he died. "That's why I was at the theatre. What could he have seen or heard? Did anyone at the theatre ever mention anything like this?"

Charlie and Jackie signaled they were unaware.

"BJ said there was a patrol car outside the theatre that night. Could that have been Dad?"

Another freighted silence.

"I don't know. We weren't riding together that night. Because of the weather, I was sent to the Ironbound. Flooded streets everywhere and power lines down," Charlie said. "Newark needed a police presence. I took a short break to pick you up around ten, but like I said, you were already gone."

Connie excused herself to find the powder room. Down a hallway and to the right, Jackie said. She wiped her face with a wet cloth to clear her head, her eyes drooping. On her way back to the dining room, she peeked in the library and confronted a floor-to-ceiling wall of books, many leather-bound, with deep green velvet curtains covering the windows. She stepped into the room and squinted at the books. A fortune in first editions. She pictured Gaby agog at these groaning shelves. A warm glow from lamps scattered here and there lit the room.

Charlie's mother, seated at a square table, played cards. Deirdre glanced up, gestured to an empty chair across from her.

"Solitaire," Connie said and sat.

"My favorite game. I always win, but don't tell Jackie or Charlie. They'll say I'm making it up." A smile. More serene now, and sober, than at the anniversary party. Tension had fallen away from the old woman like melting ice, dropping her shoulders and leaving a softness behind.

No sign of the overbearing gossip from Connie's childhood.

Deirdre laid out the deck, moving cards from place to place rapidly, her concentration absolute. "Do you play?"

"No. I used to play gin with my father when I was a kid." The two of them, picking up and discarding, laughing and teasing each other. Gaby wasn't interested.

The older woman studied Connie. "We used to call your mother Mona."

"Mona? I never heard that name."

"When she was younger. Then out of the blue she would answer to nothing but 'Simone.' Said it was going to be her stage name. She wanted to act when she was only a girl."

Like me.

Charlie appeared in the doorway, drink in hand. "There you are. Jackie thought you might have gotten lost."

"I was having a nice visit with your mother."

He cocked an eyebrow, questioning whether anyone could have a "nice visit" with Deirdre.

"We were talking about Mom. Her nickname was Mona."

"Mona? Who told you that?"

Deirdre continued with her game of solitaire. "That was what we called her." She slapped the cards with more energy. "I knew more about her than you. She wanted out of Newark. Always dreaming about marrying some rich man."

"Guess that didn't work out," Connie said.

"Connie?" Now Jackie appeared, bearing a tray with coffee, mugs, creamer, and sugar. "Did you get lost?" She frowned at Deirdre. "Let's go to the parlor."

"And you"—Deirdre pointed to her son, though kept her eyes on her cards—"were always a ladies' man. Couldn't control you."

Charlie laughed. "Can't argue with that."

Jackie produced something that sounded like a laugh and said, "Had to practically bribe you to walk down the aisle." She handed her husband the tray.

"Hard to relinquish those bachelor days."

Deirdre snorted. "I could tell you more—"

"Mother."

"Triangles," Deirdre said, her focus on the cards fierce. "Always mixed up in triangles."

Charlie sighed. "My past is of no concern. Sorry, Connie."

Connie grinned. "I'm kind of enjoying this."

Another hour and more drinks later, Connie was in no condition to drive. She texted Gaby she planned to spend the night with Charlie and Jackie, then followed them up the winding staircase to the second floor. Jackie walked down a long hallway, with a series of closed doors on either side, pausing in front of a guest room, a bedroom she described as cozy where Connie would feel at home. *At home?* In a room with a king-size bed, sitting area, and huge bathroom? Brocade drapes covered windows that overlooked the terraced gardens behind the house. Connie compared it to the Tucker residence on Third Street. No way was this home.

"Text me if you need anything." She hugged Connie. "I'm glad you decided to stay. It's nice having you here. Good night."

In the middle of the bedroom Connie spun slowly, absorbing everything. How the one percent lived. For the briefest of moments, she was jealous of Jackie's upbringing, to have all this as a child instead of Hallison. Courtesy of a basket of guest toiletries, she brushed her teeth in the luxurious bathroom—marble vanity, recessed lighting, spa tub, glass shelves holding potted plants. How often was this bathroom used, she wondered.

The air conditioning kept the room at a perfect temperature, comfortable for sleeping, not too warm, not too cold. The sheet tucked over her shoulders reminded Connie of the overnight stay in the hospital for her tonsillectomy, where the starched sheets and muted lighting had lulled her to sleep. Even bustling nurses in and out of her room had been soothing, restful.

Unlike the later hospital visit the year after her mother disappeared…following the nightmares and the pills.

Connie dropped into a dream of a Hallison High School production. She forgot her lines and panicked, startled awake by a loud noise. Head pounding. Too much alcohol. She opened her eyes in the dark. Couldn't be morning. No light seeped out from the borders of the drapes, but something woke her up.

She tiptoed to the door and cracked it open a couple of inches. No activity in the hallway.

Then light from one of the first-floor rooms flooded the foyer. Voices drifted upward, soft at first, becoming louder. One light and insistent, the other deeper and firm. Jackie and Charlie.

Jackie: "You are not going to…"

Charlie: "Didn't say I was…"

Like her mother and BJ arguing in the dressing room years ago.

In a cold sweat, Connie stepped into the hallway. They'd lowered their voices. It wasn't polite to eavesdrop, Mrs. Delano told Connie and

Gaby repeatedly as kids. If people wanted you to hear what they were saying, they'd tell you. That had never hindered Connie or her sister. Even now, this was none of her business, and yet...

Charlie: "That's enough...!"

Another sharp sound. Breaking glass. Connie flinched, lurching backwards.

A figure entered the foyer below her, a shadow moving to the bottom of the stairs. Connie darted into her guest room and eased the door shut. Footsteps drew nearer in the hallway, someone pausing right outside. Connie held her breath, her pulse on high alert, afraid of any noise escaping from her room. After a full minute of silence, Connie slinked back to bed, unnerved by the sounds in the night.

At seven-thirty, Jackie texted, *Off to the gym*, but invited Connie to relax and enjoy breakfast in the dining room. It was too late to go back to sleep, though the covers were inviting, and that bathroom had yet to be fully explored.

Connie took advantage of the spa tub and accessories, plunging her body below the surface of the water, lathering herself with a lavender body wash. Such luxury. The shower at the Tuckers leaked periodically due to inadequate caulking, the grout between the floor tiles, though clean, warranted a decent scrubbing with bleach to remove years of stains, and she shared it with Gaby and her father. Which sometimes meant a quick trip in the morning. She settled deeper into the tub.

When she at last made it downstairs, she found a place at the dining room table had been set for her. She poured coffee from an urn on the sideboard and her breakfast appeared—poached eggs, fruit, a basket of croissants with marmalade, and bacon—courtesy of a pleasant, middle-aged woman in a starched uniform who introduced herself as Lena. Connie had seen her on previous visits but never heard her name.

"Good morning. How's your head?" Charlie stood at the entrance into the dining room, ready for the day in a suit and tie, hair slicked back. Aftershave formed a scented halo.

"Better." Connie bit into a strip of crispy bacon. "Handsome dude."

He poured himself a cup of coffee and gulped the contents. "Work uniform."

"Different from the cop uniform."

He gestured at his jacket. "Have to dress the part. All the world's a stage."

"Can you sit for a minute?"

He checked his Rolex. "A minute," and took a chair across from Connie.

"I didn't get a chance to thank you for everything you've done for us. For me. The repast, hospitality here."

"Porter's." Charlie grimaced. "Hard to get that smell out of your clothes."

"You and Dad certainly put in the hours there in the old days."

"Those were the old days. Anyway, ancient history." He glanced again at his watch and crossed one neatly creased pant leg over the other.

"About the patrol car at the theatre that BJ saw. Maybe the theatre needed extra security for some reason?"

Charlie rattled change in his pants pocket. "Let me make a call today and see if I can't get some answers for you. With the storm that night, Colmar, like Newark, might have stepped up a police presence. Especially with the power outages. I'll get back to you."

Chapter 35

Now

The cemetery was Oak Park. Where Connie's mother was interred. The earthy smell of new-mown grass reminded her of summer days running in the backyard, dancing in the lawn sprinkler with Gaby. Her mother rested on a green knoll up a slight hill and off to the left from BJ's gravesite. It had been less than a week since his fall from the lighting catwalk. A quick burial apparently preferred. His family—parents and a sister—passed on an open casket viewing and a church service; a few prayers at his grave the only death ritual permitted the deceased. However, the atmosphere of this funeral service was markedly different than her mother's, where sadness and melancholy had dominated. A kind of passive acceptance of the inevitable.

No acceptance on this day at Oak Park. Terrible loss and rage permeated the short ceremony, as if his family were screaming at the assembly: *How could this happen?* Their dear son and brother had given his life to the Flint Theatre. Somebody was going to pay for this tragedy. If the mood of the hour was any sign, and the newspaper scuttlebutt true, the theatre was in for an economic jolt: someone *would* have to pay out.

Charlie and Jackie, both in somber dress with miserable expressions, stood at the back of the crowd. Connie imagined a strained dialogue on the ride home about money and the replacement of the grid system and guardrail. Standing next to them was a group of unfamiliar individuals—possibly the theatre's board—and familiar folks. Ted, beside himself; Diana; the stage manager; and the rest of the cast. And another woman, in a black suit, head covered with a wide-brimmed hat and large sunglasses.

The minister finished his brief eulogy, seemingly ready to flee the barely contained wrath of BJ's parents, offering them words of condolence, shaking their hands, then moving swiftly away. The next wave of mourners included the theatre folks, who were greeted with dour faces and curt nods. Connie nodded to Charlie and Jackie and turned to the group from the theatre. A conversation drifted her way.

"Angela," Ted said with genuine warmth to the woman in the wide-brimmed hat. "So nice to see you."

Diana offered a hug, which earned a quick one in return.

Angela. *Angela Westerman?* The woman said something that apparently troubled Ted, since he frowned, shuffled his feet, and left. After a final word, Diana trailed after him.

Connie slowed her approach to the woman, not wanting to pounce on her. "Angela Westerman?"

Despite her efforts, this brought the woman whirling in her direction, adjusting her hat.

"Sorry. Didn't mean to startle you. I'm Connie Tucker." She smiled, uncertain.

Angela gasped, staggering as she reached for Connie's arms. "Simone," she murmured, gripping her elbows tightly.

"I hear that a lot." The likeness to her mother, once a source of pride, had become a burden. "I'm sorry to approach you here. I don't mean to ambush you, and I did receive your voicemail, but I live in San Diego and will be leaving in the next few days and I would like to speak with you about Mom," she finished in a rush.

Angela hadn't taken her eyes off her, staring as though she could drink in her whole being. "I'm sorry, what did you say?" Connie's monologue had blown by her.

"Could we talk?"

After a beat, where Angela seemed to weigh the pros and cons of allowing such a meeting, she glanced behind her. The crowd had dispersed, the family on their way to a waiting limo. She breathed from a deep, obviously painful place and met Connie's eyes. "Did you drive?"

"Yes."

"Then follow me." With that, she headed briskly to her car, Connie hurrying to her own.

They drove back to Colmar, winding through the north end, downtown, and finally Uptown, where Angela entered a private road that climbed to the highest point for miles. Rock View Way. Connie remembered this drive and the view of the New York skyline from a cast party. The show before *A Streetcar Named Desire.* She parked where Angela indicated and when they passed through a side entrance into a foyer and beyond, Connie and Angela emerged into a glass-enclosed living room, perched on stilts, built into the side of a hill.

"I was here for a cast party." Connie gazed out the window. "This view is incredible."

Angela removed her hat and sunglasses, revealing a classic beauty. Her hair a luxurious brown, deep-set, penetrating green eyes, her cheekbones chiseled. She would be about her mother's age. "Please. Have a seat."

Connie accepted a glass of wine—no repast after this funeral—and settled into a beige plush sofa while Angela vanished into the interior of the house. She closed her eyes and traveled back in time to the previous theatre gathering here until Angela returned with a tray of assorted snacks. "Help yourself. I can't eat them, but don't let that stop you." She gestured toward various chips and dip and nuts. Enough to feed half a dozen guests.

"I remember Mom dancing in this room. The life of the party. Conversations around the room, the music thumping. She grabbed my hand and pulled me up into a boogie circle with her, her arms swinging over her head. Like a wild woman."

Connie smiled. Angela too.

When the music had transitioned to something slower that night, her mother, catching her breath, had slid a flute off a silver tray as it floated past. "Champagne," Connie said now. "My first taste of alcohol. The bubbles tickling my nose. Then someone tapped a glass to get our attention."

"That would have been Ted. His toast to the cast and crew. Praising them," Angela said, wistful.

"Mom complained about her feet hurting. I said let's go home then, but she said no, that she'd paid dearly for that night and planned to enjoy it."

Angela remained composed, hands folded in her lap. "Over fifteen years ago…"

"And yet the memory's still so razor sharp. I wanted so badly to be on the stage with her." Her heart wrenched. A pang of profound loss, a numbness creeping up her arms and legs. So much they could have shared, had her mother lived.

The silence was finally broken by Connie. "Ted said you and Mom…I think his words were 'thick as thieves.'"

"Yes. We were good friends."

"And you left the theatre after she disappeared. Must have hit you hard."

"Simone...your mother...was a special person. In many ways too good for the Flint Theatre. She talked about moving to New York to audition."

"New York?"

"I think she kept her plans secret."

The message her mother had left her: *But their Mama wasn't happy... And if she should ever have to go away, she wanted them to know how much she loved her girls, how much she'd miss them.* This was what she was trying to tell Connie.

"This shocks you," Angela said.

Connie explained her final gift from her mother and, before she could help herself, poured out her life and her heart. First to Finn, and now to Angela, a complete stranger. Everything she saw and heard the night her mother disappeared, the exchange of threats between BJ and her mother; the rage she flung everywhere afterwards and the resulting exile from New Jersey; the need to find out who had murdered her mother; the scary incidents with the rock and the brakes and the tracker; her assumptions, however wrong, about BJ; her discovery about her father's alibi; even the past, when Simone, Liam, and Charlie formed a triangle of both requited and unrequited love.

When she finished, limp, utterly exhausted, Connie's eyes were wet, her glass empty. The late afternoon sun streaked across the sky, sending shimmers of light through the glass of the enclosed room.

Both of them sat in silence for a moment.

"Charlie O'Shaughnessy married Jackie Flint," Angela said.

"Yes."

"Jackie played the Nurse in *Streetcar*. We talked off and on during rehearsals. We weren't close friends."

Connie blew her nose and wiped her eyes. "When BJ told me my mother was in love with someone, not my father, I thought it might be Charlie. He was always around when we were growing up. Like a puppy dog trailing after her."

Angela swallowed the rest of her drink. "I don't think Simone was in love with Charlie. But he was there the week of dress rehearsals," she said. "Hanging around backstage. In his uniform."

Then it struck Connie. "Jackie was in the show, so Charlie must have come to the theatre to see her."

"Yes. I think they were dating then. Lots of people in and out of the dressing rooms. You know how it was the week before a show opened."

"Yeah," Connie said with a smile.

Angela smiled too. "Rehearsal bedlam. One night I watched Charlie enter Simone's dressing room." Angela's eyes narrowed. "Whatever he said disturbed your mother. I came in at the end of their conversation, and when Charlie saw me, he left in a hurry."

Suddenly aware of her heartbeat, Connie said, "BJ told me she was scared the week she disappeared." She examined the woman in front of her. "Did you mention Charlie's behavior to the detective?"

"I didn't think anything of it at the time," Angela said. After a beat: "You think there was more to it?"

Connie shook her head. "I don't know. You're sure she wasn't in love with Charlie. Why?"

Angela Westerman sighed, dropped her head, and whispered, "Because she was in love with me."

Chapter 36

Now

Connie concentrated ferociously to keep her mind on the road, despite the knot in her stomach. After hearing Angela's bombshell and details—she and Simone had gotten together some time after the cast party at her house, had been together for a few months; they had discussed moving to New York together, with her mother approaching the topic of divorce the day of the storm—the actress admitted that when Simone disappeared, she did withdraw from acting. Angela knew fifteen years ago it had to be foul play. Simone would never have run off without a word to her.

Her mother. With a woman. Connie struggled to get her mind around the fact. Her father no doubt oblivious. Angela was so beautiful, so kind, Connie could see her mother falling in love. Rosa's words about her mother cropped up: "…late one night…getting dropped off at your house…kissing the driver." Probably Angela. Maybe she was also the sender of the opening night flowers from Broad Street Florists, too.

All of which begged the question: When her mother wrote the message to Connie, did she still imagine they would "share a stage together"? Angela was certain her mother had not run off, but that was exactly what she planned on doing. Without her children. Connie's wounded heart emerged. The abandonment that slammed her after her mother's disappearance reared up. Even though she was an adult and had been living on her own for years.

"BJ told me to 'ask her'," Connie had said to Angela. "Did he mean you? Did he see you and my mother together? Did he think you knew something about her disappearance?"

Angela was emphatic. "BJ knew nothing about us. No one did. I suppose that's why he fostered the fantasy about Simone."

Connie wasn't so sure that was the case. The relationship between Angela and her mother could have prompted BJ's outburst the night of the storm, his warning her mother: "I saw what you did."

Her father was right. Her mother *was* having an affair. Just not with BJ. But what about Charlie's appearance in the dressing room that week? Angela had said her mother was upset after a conversation with him. With Uncle Charlie. What could he possibly say that would upset her mother?

The house was empty when she pulled into the driveway. Gaby had texted that she wanted to speak with Connie. Ditto. Their last conversation had taken place before Connie had attended BJ's funeral, before she learned that her mother and Angela were in love.

But at present, her mind whirled with notions about Uncle Charlie. If she thought back, there were things these last three weeks that confused her: contradictions between Charlie and her father about their shared past, including their time at the police academy; their totally different stories on Detective Rutherford's career path. Angela witnessing Charlie in her mother's dressing room, leaving her distraught. Was there some way to get to the bottom of it?

At the Hallison Public Library, Gaby was busy in the stacks, not at a computer terminal or on the phone. Connie hurried to her. "Got your text. I have a lot to tell you about Mom, but first—"

"Later." Gaby scanned the aisle. A young boy stood at the far end studying the spines of books, tilting his head one way and then the other.

"When?"

Gaby checked the clock on the wall behind them. "I'm off in half an hour. Porter's?"

Connie hadn't been in the bar since the night of the conversation with the Old Man about her father's alibi. "No. I'll see you at home. Where's Dad?"

"He went into work earlier today. Not sure what time he'll be home."

"I got a favor to ask."

Gaby, guarded, pulled Connie into an empty carrel. "What?"

Despite twinges of guilt—this was their Uncle Charlie she was talking about—Connie dove in, describing her concerns. "I hate to think this, but could Charlie be lying?"

Gaby sighed and turned to the door of the carrel. "Again, Connie, it's all in the past."

"I don't think so. Deirdre claims Mom, Dad, and Charlie had secrets—"

"Deirdre! Deirdre?" Gaby blinked. "That's your source of information? I'll see you at home."

Connie blocked her sister's exit. "Do you know any way to access old police records? Or someone who does? Maybe someone in HR? Since you're in the research business—"

Gaby stared at her, wild-eyed. "You must be kidding! Police files?"

"Shh! There's probably stuff on the Internet. Maybe a deep dive—"

Gaby lowered her voice. "Your obsession with Mom's death is going to get you in serious trouble. Let the cold case guys take over. Who cares about Dad and Charlie in the past?"

"Mom's past too. There're things that are inconsistent."

"No. I don't have the authority to do that. I wouldn't know how to do it. And, for the record, I now think you've gone overboard. This idea of yours is crazy." Gaby crossed her arms, eyes flashing defiance.

Connie gripped her sister's shoulders. "Please! This may be the last chance we'll have to do this. Will you see what you can find out?"

Gaby stared at Connie. "I'll *see* you at home."

They rocked on the porch with glasses of lemonade and a plate of brownies Mrs. Delano had dropped off. The day cooling, the sun's rays sinking behind the line of houses across Third Street. Their earlier conversation in the library the elephant in the room. Neither mentioned it, but there it sat.

And Angela Westerman? When to introduce her into the conversation? She swore no one knew about their affair. BJ might have. But what if someone else found out and it set off a rage reaction?

Finally, Connie confessed. "The problem was me all along. I kept thinking Rosa or BJ or...maybe even Dad—"

Gaby scowled. "Dad?"

"—knew something about Mom's death. I can see now how wrong I was."

Somewhat appeased, Gaby sighed. "And now you're wondering about Charlie. You don't really think he had anything to do with..."

Connie hung her head. Her beloved Uncle Charlie, the man she ran to whenever a roadblock appeared, the only one, besides Old Man

Porter, she didn't resent when she was sent away from home. "I don't, really. But there are loose ends. You have a sense about him, don't you? Even as kids you didn't like him."

"Told you before...something never seemed genuine," Gaby said. "But to connect him to Mom's death? No. Not buying it. You're the one who always defended him."

"Yes. I did." Painful to even question Uncle Charlie's guilt or innocence. "Somehow I think Mom's death is connected to her past."

"The triangle you keep going on about?"

Connie ignored Gaby's tone. "Help me figure this out. Mom was into Charlie, the perfect couple. Then, like, without any warning, she was engaged to Dad. Why?"

"There could be lots of reasons why." Gaby frowned. "Anyway, getting jilted, if that's what happened, doesn't necessarily make someone capable of extreme rage and extreme violence."

"Oh, no?" A beat of silence. Connie set her empty lemonade glass on the ground. "What did you want to tell me?"

Gaby smiled for the first time since the library meeting. "Dad perked up this morning."

Their father had plenty of good reasons to be morose; fewer to "perk up."

"He went down to the basement to clean out some boxes of old tools. Stuff. But he came upstairs with his dress uniform. The blue one, with the ribbons on it."

"I remember him wearing it a few times. To funerals, he said."

"Anyway, I coaxed him to share the story behind each one. A service commendation for twenty years on the force, a merit award for professional conduct, something for an outstanding arrest of a Newark drug kingpin." Gaby shook her head. "Who knew?"

"Not us," Connie said.

"And then there was a medal for bravery." Gaby sat forward, pride in her voice, eyes shining. "He risked his life by saving a little boy in a burning building. I had to worm it out of him, but he was on patrol duty when it happened. The place went up like a tinderbox, he said. He didn't think twice and charged into the fire."

"That was the story Old Man Porter mentioned. What did Charlie do?" Connie asked.

"Charlie?"

"Did he go into the burning building too?"

Gaby eyed her sister warily. "Why?"

"When did this happen?"

"Right before he got engaged to Mom, Dad said." Gaby beamed. "He figured she was swept off her feet by his heroics."

"That might explain her pivot from Charlie to Dad, if she was. The timing's interesting." Connie stuffed the last bit of a brownie into her mouth.

"Meaning what? You think this is tied to her murder? Connie"—Gaby's attitude softened—"everything doesn't lead back to Mom's death. It's possible they'll never discover the killer. Anyway, it was nice to see Dad upbeat."

"I agree." Connie patted her sister's shoulder. "I'll be back later." Her father's courage may have seduced her mother, causing her to turn from Charlie and marry him; however, there was the matter of Charlie's appearance in her dressing room that last week.

"What were you in such a hurry to tell me at the library?" Gaby asked.

Angela Westerman and Mom. "It can wait." It would rock her world whenever Gaby heard the story.

"Where are you going? Dinner?" Gaby called out as Connie bounced off the front porch and started for the street.

"Porter's."

"You said you didn't want to go there tonight."

"Changed my mind."

Chapter 37

Now

Happy hour in Porter's ending, the crowd thinning, Connie snagged a seat at the end of the bar, two empty stools away from the closest customer. Dack brought her a glass of wine and offered to put in a food order. Connie declined the offer; she didn't intend to be here that long.

Just long enough to get an answer. At the cash register, her father looked up and waved. Connie lifted her hand in response. There was unfinished business with him.

Old Man Porter lugged a case of beer from the backroom and plopped it behind the bar. He didn't even acknowledge Connie. Didn't matter. She'd approach him.

Connie was convinced her mother's death was tied to the past, to her relationship with Charlie and her father. Possibly to something that occurred years before her murder. What drove her to reject Charlie and choose Connie's father? Something had to trigger the decision. What happened and who knew about it? Who did she trust?

Your mom was like a daughter to me, Porter had said.

Daughters and fathers. Complicated relationships. Something Connie understood. She caught Porter's attention and motioned to him. He hesitated, then lumbered over and wiped the bar that was already clean. "You're still here?" he teased, the moment awkward. "Thought you were on your way back to the land of sunshine." Tension like a curtain between them. Something Connie had never experienced with him.

"Soon," Connie murmured, loud enough for him to hear. She beckoned him closer. He leaned across the bar. "You've been a good friend to my parents over the years."

He straightened.

"Hiring my dad way back when, putting up with Gaby and me as kids. The alibi for my father. Treating my mother as your daughter, you said."

His eyes narrowed. "I loved your mom."

He began to turn away, but she reached for his hand.

"I'm learning that a lot of folks did," she said. "Before Mom got engaged to Dad, did she talk to you about...anything?"

Porter tossed the bar towel over his shoulder, a little impatient. "Like what?"

"Anything that might have scared her? Pushed her to marry him?"

He stiffened, playing with the unravelling hem of the cloth, avoiding her eyes.

"Please tell me." Desperation tinged her voice.

The Old Man hesitated, then, after a glance down the bar at her father, yielded. "One night she came here. Alone. I was about to close when she walked in. Crying. We had a party celebrating Liam's medal ceremony."

"For rescuing the boy in the fire."

"Yeah. Might have been the next night. She said a horrible thing. Said someone"—Porter closed his eyes, his face sagging—"got rough with her. Tried to force himself on her, tore her dress. Never mentioned his name, but..."

Connie's pulse jumped, her palms instantly sweaty. "Charlie." She barely breathed the word.

The Old Man's eyes sparked, then went black. "O'Shaughnessy always was jealous of your dad. When Liam won the award...well...Charlie tried to make it like *he'd* been the real hero." He snarled, "Lies. All lies." Took a deep, savage breath, then let it all out. Found her eyes again. "She broke it off with him. He wasn't the man for her. Simone turned to your father. Charlie didn't take it well. Especially when your parents got married."

Her mind screamed *No!* Uncle Charlie...guilty of assaulting her mother. She clamped her hands on her shaking legs. "Did it bother Dad that Charlie still...loved Mom? I mean, he was around when we were kids, being Dad's partner. Really nice to all of us. We called him Uncle Charlie." She heard desperation in her voice. *Please let this not be true.*

Porter shook his head. "I never told your dad about the night Simone came to me. Liam...he's not the forgive-and-forget type. One of them would've ended up dead."

"But it was Charlie Mom called to pick me up and take me home the night she disappeared. She must have trusted him."

"Oh, he cleaned up his act all right. The night after Simone came in here crying, we two had a one-on-one...me and O'Shaughnessy. And a baseball bat." He jerked his head toward the room at the back of the bar. "I threatened to turn him in. He left her alone after Liam and Simone's marriage. At least...that way." The Old Man turned away, weary. "Too much pain. Too much."

264

A notion pricked at the bottom of her mind, forcing its way to the surface. The end of her parents' marriage. "So, Charlie knew," she said dully.

"Huh?"

"That Mom and Dad were talking divorce."

Charlie had said their father hinted at a divorce in the weeks before her mother disappeared. Knowing that, was it possible Charlie's long ago obsession with her was revived? That the knowledge gave him hope and drove him to pursue her mother again?

When Connie returned home from Porter's, Gaby was humming and cooking, the oven emitting inviting aromas. "Back already? Did you see Dad? He's off work in half an hour so I'm whipping up a chicken casserole."

Connie begged off, complaining of a headache, and headed to her bedroom. Tried to busy herself with email and texts, a couple from her boss, again wondering when she was returning to work at The Shack. Activity didn't help end the distressing mental loop: Uncle Charlie. A serial liar. Guilty of assaulting her mother. But that didn't make him a murderer, she argued with herself. She envisioned all of the happy times when they'd laughed together before her mother disappeared...and after. No. Not possible.

Connie tossed and turned for hours, disheartened. Intermittent sleep ended abruptly at seven a.m. when a garbage truck rumbled down Third Street. The sounds of brakes squealing, engine grinding, drifted through her bedroom window.

Connie rolled over and sat up. Since she was awake, she might as well make the most of it. Yanking on shorts and a shirt, she grabbed her bag, stole down the stairs, and let herself out of the house.

Inhaling the moist Hallison morning, she drove to the nearest Starbucks for coffee and a Danish. The route took her to the edge of town and once she'd fortified herself with breakfast, Connie wound through backroads, vaguely acknowledging that she'd, once again, defied Detective Keogh's recommendation that she stay out of her rental car.

Skirting Colmar, she allowed her inner driver to take control. It soon became clear it was taking her to the construction complex where her mother's remains had been found. Not sure what the point of coming a second time was. Still not sure what she'd hoped to achieve with the first visit, as Gaby pointed out. Connie pulled up to the chain link fence surrounding the construction zone, still displaying the danger and warning signage. Somehow this site felt more like a permanent grave for her mother than the formal plot in Oak Park. Someone had found the perfect, remote spot to bury her mother. Until the land was developed. What were the odds her remains would be discovered?

As before, workers in hard hats and safety vests crawled around the skeletons of buildings that would soon be home to an untold number of residents. She doubted anyone would remind them that a woman had been buried in their backyard. Connie stood at the fence, forehead resting on the cold metal of the chain links. *Oh, Mom...*

The foreman in the distance waved his walkie-talkie, motioning to other men, examining a section of the construction, noting on his clipboard. No need to trespass and bother him today. She merely wanted to say goodbye and send love.

A booming clang pierced the air as two steel girders collided, the foreman now yelling, running in the direction of the errant crane. Connie stepped away from the fence, glancing upward to see the construction damage, her sight captured by a white and black sign she hadn't noticed before: Flint Development. They owned this property?

"They have their fingers in lots of pots," Deirdre said at the anniversary party.

She pushed herself to sort through the facts. Charlie and Jackie married after Connie's mother disappeared—their wedding, a huge gala affair in New York City. He was still a Newark cop at the time. Later, Charlie worked at the Flint corporate headquarters in New York, which included an international banking component. He never mentioned property development. Detective Rutherford said back in 2004 this area wasn't slated for development because it was supposed to be designated Green Acres.

When did the Flint Corporation purchase this land? If Charlie had any idea that a condominium project would one day appear on this property, if he was responsible for her mother's death, he wouldn't bury her on land that he knew could be developed one day. That wasn't a smart move, and Charlie was, if anything, smart.

Connie aimed her rental car for the curb on Third Street, so distracted she accidentally scraped the tires along the cement. She sat behind the steering wheel, weighing the uncertainties of Charlie's actions. On that stormy night her mother disappeared, the construction site was close enough to the theatre, yet still isolated, that Charlie could have buried her and returned home within hours of her death. He supposedly wasn't at the theatre so the police wouldn't have questioned his whereabouts that night.

If Charlie wasn't guilty, her father's alibi solid, and BJ—though no longer in a position to defend himself—not really a suspect in her mind, where did that leave Connie's weeks of digging into the circumstances of her mother's murder?

She tramped into the house. "Gaby?" She needed to share all she'd discovered in the last twelve hours: Old Man Porter's revelation about

Charlie's assault on their mother and the Flint corporation's ownership of the construction site.

Her father looked up from the sports page of *The Star-Ledger*. "Your sister's at the library."

"Okay." She had to, finally, buy a ticket to San Diego, call Chick about returning to work.

Her father put the newspaper aside and removed his reading glasses. "Sit down for a minute, will you?"

She hesitated. The deadly calm of his manner disturbed her. They hadn't talked alone since the day she arrived, not counting the trips to and from the county prosecutor's office. Come to think of it, her father seemed almost serene the past few days. Ever since BJ's accident. Though his alibi cleared him of her mother's death and made him innocent in the eyes of the law, Connie was still wary of him.

Tension spread from her neck into her shoulders. She needed to say a few things to him and there was no time like the present. Connie could stop blaming her father for doing what he thought was right, even if it meant dooming her to teenage years in a cold and unloving environment. Nervous energy cascaded through her body and she rubbed clammy palms along her thighs. She forced herself to sit down. "I've been meaning to talk with you."

He steepled his hands, covering the lower half of his face, exposing the heart tattoo on his left arm. He cleared his throat. "Connie, I—"

"It's okay, Dad," she said softly. "I understand what you did. You thought sending me to live with Aunt Marie was for the best—"

"No, that's not—"

"I'm over it. I forgive you, the past, all of it—"

"Connie!"

She drew back, her father's sharp tone like a verbal blow.

"Sorry. I don't want to talk about the past." He ran fingers through his curly graying hair.

Despite the show of tranquility, his hand trembled. Because of this conversation?

"Then what?" she asked, impatient, the old defiant Connie emerging. Her foot tapped the table leg.

Drumming his fingers on the table, he avoided her eyes. "I think it's time for you to go."

The words stung, her cheeks flushing. She planned to buy a plane ticket this morning, yet in the back of her mind she imagined her father begging her to stay. Indefinitely, like Gaby said. To make up for lost time. As a way of making amends. Not sure what her response would have been, even so, Connie wanted to be asked. Wanted him to acknowledge the mistake he'd made those many years ago. "I plan to." Her back stiffened.

"Now."

Connie pushed forward in her chair. Her voice rising. "What's the rush?"

The drumming picked up speed. "We need to…things are…" He sighed. "I want us…things here to get back to normal."

Stunned, Connie shook her head. The kitchen closing in on her, the familiar anger a red-hot ball that strangled her speech. "Normal? Things are never going to be 'normal' around here—"

"Gaby wants this too—"

"Our mother, your wife, was *murdered*. Her funeral only weeks ago. Are you telling me you can forget all that so things can go back to 'normal'?" She was yelling, her breathing irregular, her chest rising and falling.

His peaceful features went slack, then ashen. "You got to let this go. It's driving me…us…crazy."

"Who's 'us'?" Gaby hadn't mentioned anything to her about Connie "driving her crazy."

He shifted in his seat. "Everybody. Gaby, the Old Man, Mrs. Delano, Tom Rutherford."

Her beloved Mrs. Delano? Old Man Porter? They all wanted her to leave? Her heart sank.

"Even Charlie."

"Charlie?" He'd seemed so eager to help Connie sort through the past. Now he was eager for her to go.

"Pestering him and everybody else with questions. Pushing people to remember that night. It's not right. You gotta stop."

"What about Charlie?"

"Huh?"

"When I said he told me you hinted at a divorce, you said he 'didn't know the whole story.' What whole story?"

He waved a hand. Conversation over.

"What didn't Charlie know?" she pressed.

"What difference does it make? Your mother's not here to—"

"Dad," she said, her tone easing. "Talk to me."

His body appeared to sag under the weight of his secret. He heaved a sigh. "That night, after I picked you up at the theatre and brought you home…" He licked his dried lips. "I left the house for a bit…"

"And went to Porter's to drink and then slept it off there."

As if the words packed a punch, his body caved inward, thrusting him backward in his seat. "How…?"

"The Old Man. Detective Nardone told me he was your alibi."

"Should have figured you'd find out," he muttered, "the way you kept nagging every—"

"Driving everybody crazy. Right. What about that night?"

Her father dropped his head into his hands. "Your mother left me a message. Made a decision about the divorce." When he looked up at her, his piercing blue eyes sad, a single tear rolled down his cheek. "She was calling it off."

Calling it off? Calling off the affair with Angela, too, and the plan to leave her children? "Why?" Connie asked, her mind a jumble.

He shrugged. "She said something happened at the theatre that made her change her mind. That we would talk as soon as she got home."

Your mama almost made a terrible mistake, her mother had said, hugging Connie backstage in the hallway.

"Only she never made it home," Connie said.

Her father wiped his eyes with the sleeve of his polo shirt. "And I never got the message until the next day, because..."

"You were..."

"Drinking at Porter's."

"So, that's the whole story. Charlie didn't know about Mom's change of heart." Would that last night have been different if he had? She breathed deeply to ease the pain in her chest.

"Why would he know about it? It was between your mother and me," he said with vehemence.

The kitchen was quiet, save for the ticking of the wall clock. Connie tilted her head to get a better angle on her father. "Did it bother you that Charlie and Mom were together, back in the day? I mean, they were a couple and then they broke up and she married you." She held her breath. It could prove to be a hazardous question.

Instead of the explosion she anticipated, he threw back his head and released a harsh guffaw. "That's what everybody back then wondered. Why would Simone..." His voice wobbled, then turned wistful: "Why would beautiful, happy, belle of the ball Simone marry the runt of the litter when she could have had anyone. Including the neighborhood prince charming."

"Charlie."

"Yeah. I never really understood why she chose me. But she did."

True to his word, Old Man Porter had never shared what Charlie had done to her mother and sent her into the arms of Connie's father. Porter said he wasn't the "forgive-and-forget type."

"Charlie never held a grudge," her father said. "He got over it." He stretched an arm to Connie as if to touch her shoulder. Then withdrew it, rose, and shuffled to the hallway.

"Dad?"

He pivoted back to her.

"What ever happened to Mom's necklace?"

"What?" He seemed confused.

"The one with the gold cross on a chain. She never took it off. It wasn't with her personal effects."

As before, her father scrutinized his daughter, assessing, wondering why the question. Then he exhaled, as if bone weary of rehashing details of her mother's past. "The chain broke. I had it replaced but didn't have a chance to give it to her."

A simple answer. From an innocent man.

One hand resting on the frame of the kitchen's entrance, her father said, "You might not believe this, but I'm going to miss you." He trudged up the stairs to his bedroom.

She swallowed to relieve the lump in her throat, following him into the hallway, watching his progress to the second floor, his back hunched.

He'd just gone out of sight when Gaby walked in the door. "Where's Dad? What's the matter with you?"

"He's going to take a nap." Connie blinked back tears. "We have to talk—"

"In the kitchen." Gaby strode off, not waiting to see if her sister obeyed her command.

Connie reentered the kitchen behind her.

"Sit down. Please." Gaby pulled a chair away from the table for herself and perched on its edge. She withdrew a sheaf of papers from her bag and tapped them on her thumbnail, then placed them on the table. "Someone who used to work with the Newark PD archives comes by the Hallison library now and again." Gaby twisted her curly hair into a ponytail. "I did a favor for her once, so I asked her."

"To…?"

Gaby lowered her voice, taking a quick glimpse out of the kitchen archway. "To see what she could find on Charlie."

Chapter 38

Now

Connie held her breath. Gaby had done as she'd asked.

"Here's the main facts." In a dispassionate tone, Gaby relayed the information her acquaintance had gleaned from archived, practically buried, files that dated back to the nineteen nineties. Gaby's librarian's mind had organized the material into three main categories. First, the issues at the police academy—Charlie's penchant for trouble with fellow trainees and his tendency to settle disputes violently. He was called down for two fistfights and other minor skirmishes. He barely graduated. Certainly not top of his class, as he'd bragged to Connie. Next, there was his time with the Newark Police Department. Amazing, given his record at the academy, that he was hired. Or maybe not so surprising. Knowing Charlie, he'd charmed his way into a job and, fortunately, was paired with their father, no doubt the steady, reliable half of the duo. While with the Newark PD, he had a couple of run-ins with Internal Affairs for excessive use-of-force complaints, and not only with the homeless guy. But nothing stuck. He was Teflon...everything slid off him.

Charlie O'Shaughnessy was a street kid, a bare-knuckle brawler from Newark, where he supposedly saved their father's life, and being clad in Armani couldn't hide that fact, couldn't conceal the reality of his lies and criminal behavior.

"I saved the best for last," Gaby said.

Something in her impassive voice shook Connie. "There was an assault charge against him that got buried. The woman refused to testify."

Connie's heart slammed in her chest. Was that incident before or after the night her mother showed up at Porter's, crying, distraught?

Gaby thrust the papers back in her bag. "It's here in black and white. That fun, charismatic-guy persona hid a lot of bad stuff over the years."

Connie cleared her throat. "I appreciate what you did. Risking your neck. Thanks."

"Yeah...well." Gaby folded her hands and leaned into Connie. "You think this is enough to make him a suspect in Mom's murder?" she asked, even now somewhat skeptical.

"No. I don't know."

Connie related the Old Man's story about Charlie's assault of their mother. Gaby bit her lip, her face darkening. Then, she described her visit to the construction site and the signage bearing the Flint family name.

"The corporation didn't own that property back when Mom was killed."

"He should have been jailed for what he did to Mom back then," Gaby said.

"Of course, but there's nothing concrete to tie him to her disappearance. We need something more."

Gaby frowned. "I think you should call the cold case detective."

Again. Her father was right about her driving Detective Rutherford and the cold case unit crazy. "Yes. Let's not mention anything to Dad. Yet."

"Of course not."

Connie debated how to reveal their mother's romantic past with Angela Westerman. "So…"

"What?"

"There's something else I need to tell you."

Gaby's shock at Connie's revelation was only exceeded by her dismay at the thought that their mother had planned to leave Hallison. As the sisters huddled together sharing this news, Connie reminded Gaby about the message their mother had left shortly before she disappeared: she was calling off the divorce. "At least that's what Dad said."

"So much we didn't know about Mom and Dad," Gaby murmured. "I feel like they're strangers."

"If Mom really did plan to cancel the divorce, who would be affected by it? Dad, of course."

"Angela? Could she have been upset enough to be considered a suspect?"

"She's not the type," Connie said, doubtful.

"Type of what? Murderer?"

Connie shrugged. "BJ is dead, and I'm not a hundred percent sure it was an accident—"

"What?"

"—so there's Charlie." She closed her eyes. Saying his name in the same breath as "murderer" still unbelievable, throbbing like an open wound.

"You've got to call Detective Rutherford. Tell him what you...what we found out, ask if he thinks the information is relevant." Gaby pulled lunch out of the refrigerator.

"I will, but he'll call Dad, who already wants me gone. To return to 'normal,' he said." Connie nibbled on a carrot stick.

Gaby turned to her. "Dad said that?"

"Uh-huh. Thinks I'm driving everyone nuts. The Old Man, Mrs. Delano—"

"Can't believe that. She loves you. Us," Gaby corrected herself.

Connie eyed her sister. "Dad thinks you want me gone too."

"No. Not true," she said firmly. "We've just found each other again. Why would I want you gone?" Gaby embraced her sister, and they stood a moment in silence.

Connie grabbed her bag off the table. "I'll be back later."

Gaby followed her to the front door, exasperated. "Where are you going now? Aren't you calling the detective?"

"I will, but first I want to make a final visit to the theatre."

"Why? Stay away from there. Stay away from Colmar."

Connie paused and turned back. "Once we talk with Detective Rutherford, it's all over. Whatever loose ends there are will be his responsibility. But...BJ...if his death wasn't an accident, I feel I owe it to him to take my doubts to the prosecutor's office. Maybe at the theatre I'll see something."

"Connie, let's put this to bed. I'll come with you after work. Then we'll call the detective."

"The theatre's no big deal. I can say goodbye to Ted and Diana, if she's there."

Thunder rumbled to the east, somewhere over Newark. "Connie...please."

"I'll be back in an hour or two and then we can have a nice dinner together. Order in or try a new restaurant." Connie planted a kiss on Gaby's cheek. "Stop worrying. I'll be fine."

"Come straight back here after the theatre, understand?"

Connie crossed her heart, as they used to as kids. She glanced at clouds sailing across the sky, blocking the sun, turning the day gray. Rain would come eventually, the weather app promising minimal accumulation early on, the possibility of a thunderstorm much later in the day.

The weather app was wrong. By the time Connie reached Colmar, what began as a light shower had segued into a full-fledged downpour. She texted Gaby she'd made it to the theatre.

In the parking lot she slid her rental into a space next to Ted's Toyota. Ducking her head under a newspaper she'd left in the front seat, Connie ran to the entrance and hurried into the lobby, shaking droplets off her jacket.

She absorbed the silence.

Ted's office door was ajar, revealing a sliver of light and the sound of a printer. She stepped quietly to the theatre and entered the house. No rehearsal in progress.

Lighting in the theatre muted, she eased into a seat in the third row and examined the stage, then the grid above, draped in yellow CAUTION tape. There had been no safety line on BJ's body that he would have clipped to the guardrail. When he'd fallen fifteen years before, the result was a break so bad that his leg never healed properly. Surely he'd have taken precautions now. Unless something or someone didn't allow time for that to happen.

"Surprised to see you here."

Connie recoiled into her seat. Ted stood above her in the aisle.

"I hope it's okay. I came to say goodbye before I leave town."

"Is that happening soon?" he asked, unsmiling.

"Yes." He wanted her gone. Connie was a nuisance, digging up the past, reminding everyone of a disturbing time. She understood Ted's reluctance to extend any more hospitality. "What's happening with the show?"

Ted glanced from Connie to the grid. "We've postponed the opening. Everyone's lost heart."

This had to remind him of fifteen years ago and cancelling *Streetcar* after her mother disappeared.

"Anyway," he said, "we need to wait for the emergency repair."

A crack of thunder shattered the quiet of the theatre. "Why didn't BJ wear a safety belt the day he fell?" Connie asked.

Ted backed up a step. "What?"

"Neither Diana nor I noticed a safety belt or line on him. I think he'd have used one after his terrible fall. He was forever telling me as a kid to never go up top without safety gear."

Ted stared at the grid again as if looking for an answer. "I can't talk about the accident. Insurance issues."

More like lawsuit issues.

He tapped his foot. Nervous. "I need to lock up soon."

"That last night, before my mother disappeared, she and BJ fought in the hallway outside the dressing room."

"I know all that." His phone rang and he checked the ID.

"When BJ threatened to reveal something about my mom she freaked out, she said he didn't know what he was talking about, said if he didn't shut up she'd tell *you* his secret. That it would get him fired from the Flint Theatre."

Ted remained motionless. His face blank.

"I asked you about this the day BJ and my father mixed it up in the lobby, but you never gave me an answer. *Do* you know what it was? His secret?"

"Why do you need to know? The man is dead." Ted's vehemence caught Connie by surprise.

"I just wondered if it had anything to do with his death. A secret from his past that still haunted him fifteen years later."

Ted turned to go, then stopped and glanced over his shoulder. "It had nothing to do with his death. He'd been clean for over ten years. And for your information, BJ himself came to me. Offered to resign. I persuaded him to get help." Shoulders slumped, he hurried away.

"I'll be right out," Connie called after him.

Drugs. Her mother had witnessed BJ using or dealing. Either way, even marijuana was illegal in 2004. Smoking dope wouldn't have been an enormous crime. It was everywhere. But selling the product—whatever it was—to others? Especially in the theatre? That might have gotten Ted's attention and forced him to release BJ. Except that Ted was capable of more compassion than her mother imagined.

In the dim light, Connie walked onto the stage, seeing BJ as he was the day he died. On his side, his body broken, his face distorted. Assuming it wasn't an accident—and Connie didn't believe it was—BJ clearly possessed knowledge that made him dangerous, threatening enough that he had to die. She stood under the catwalk staring upward at the empty space where the broken railing had been removed. If BJ fell accidentally, the trajectory probably would have landed him within a few feet of the grid. But when she found his body, it was three or four feet farther downstage. As if he had jumped. Or been pushed. Had anyone else noticed this?

Suddenly the theatre felt cold, stony, unwelcome. Hiding a secret.

From the back of the house, a figure emerged. Then the overhead lights switched on. "Connie?"

She shivered, all of a sudden chilly. "Jackie. Hi." Jackie was here. Charlie too? She couldn't face him and pretend she didn't know what she knew.

"Ted said you were saying goodbye."

"I was wondering about BJ."

"The board met this morning and approved the repairs. It has to happen quickly in order for the season to move forward."

Connie nodded and walked off the stage, following Jackie into the lobby. No Charlie. Good. Though it was mid-afternoon, the sky was black and a deluge pounded the glass of the front doors. "Wow. Didn't see this coming."

Déjà vu. The theatre. Rain. Wind. Lightning. Thunder. That night. Her insides quivered. She had to get out of here, a wave of claustrophobia raising her pulse.

Jackie agreed. "I don't think this kind of thing was predicted."

Ted emerged from the office, locking doors and pulling on a slicker. "Bad out there. Roads out of Colmar are flooding. Hallison, too, I heard."

"Connie, that's not good," Jackie said.

"I'll be fine as long as I leave now." Her heart in her throat.

"Come to our place—"

"No, but thanks." She headed for the dark beyond the glass. The street outside the Flint Theatre had transformed into a swiftly moving stream.

"At least stay until it lets up some," Jackie pressed. "I'd appreciate the company. Charlie's away overnight in New York and Deirdre...well." She grimaced.

281

Connie paused. Charlie was away. She'd tell Gaby that when she texted to say she'd be late getting back to Hallison, so her sister wouldn't freak out. "You're right. It might be better to wait a bit. Thanks."

The windshield wipers slapped a steady rhythm, challenged by the onslaught of the storm, as Connie maneuvered her car to the Flint estate, trailing behind Jackie's Mercedes, slowing when she approached half a foot of standing water. Her grip on the steering wheel claw-like, headlights sending faint white strips of illumination onto the road, she followed Jackie through the water.

The car bounced off an unseen pothole, delivering an unnerving jolt. She bent over the wheel, willing herself to ignore the slashes of lightning brightening the sky. Jackie had disappeared ahead.

When Connie splashed down Chappelle Road and turned into the driveway, she found the normal exterior lighting of the Flint mansion extinguished. In fact, none of the homes on the road were lit up. The day turning into night. The pounding storm. Connie's nerves frayed. Without light anywhere on the grounds, the Flint house was an eerie hulk, its beauty and grace invisible.

In the parking area behind the house, Connie slid into an empty space next to the Mercedes. She lifted the collar of her jacket and ran to the back entrance, meeting Jackie at the door, heavy Turkish towels in her hands. One for Connie and one for herself.

"Downed transformer has knocked out this whole end of town," Jackie informed her.

A battery-operated outdoor lamp cast a glow over the kitchen. Entering the house this time—even without Charlie—felt different.

Jackie took her jacket while Connie squeezed water out of her hair, drying her face and neck. Her sneakers were saturated, along with her socks.

"You can leave your shoes here," Jackie said, pointing to a slatted wood rack that already held her own.

In the well-equipped, stainless-steel kitchen, Lena, the housekeeper, offered Connie a subdued nod, then busied herself at a counter.

"We'll have a fire in the library to take the chill out of the air. We can have a drink in there. Hot toddy?"

A little early for happy hour, though outside it could have been midnight. "Wine's fine. I appreciate your invitation," Connie said.

"Nonsense. The trip to Hallison in this storm would be a nightmare."

They moved down the candlelit hallway that led to the foyer ahead, the library situated on their left, where a blazing fire had already rendered the room toasty. On Connie's previous visit, lamps had cast a warm glow over the room; now they'd been replaced with more candles on end tables, a coffee table, and at the square table where Deirdre, once again, played solitaire. The old woman squinted at Connie, offered a replica of the housekeeper's noncommittal nod and returned to her cards. Classical music floated softly, its source invisible. The wall of books was merely a dark shadow, as the drawn velvet curtains kept visions of the wind and rain at bay. Connie could imagine the storm happening elsewhere. Altogether, the room was congenial and inviting.

"Would you like to change out of those clothes?" Jackie asked, solicitous.

Her pants were soaked several inches up from her ankles. She debated. Leave the warmth of the library to strip out of pants that would dry in an hour? No. "I'm good. The fire will take care of them." She squished the thick pile of the rug between her toes, accepted a glass of chilled white wine, its crisp tang welcome, and curled up on the vast sofa. Then it struck her: She needed to tell her sister she was safe.

"Sorry," she said as she texted. "Gaby'll worry if I don't get in touch." And tell her Charlie was away overnight.

"Nice to have a sister. Someone to worry about you." Jackie popped the olive off the swizzle stick in her martini into her mouth and took a swallow.

"Yes, it is," Connie said as she completed the message and sent it.

"I wanted a sibling when I was growing up, but it wasn't in the cards. One thing Charlie and I have in common. Only children."

Jackie would have been young enough to have kids when she married Charlie. Had they considered raising a family? Not a question Connie was comfortable asking. But Charlie had seemed to like kids or had at least been good with Connie and her sister. *Regardless of his violent behavior with others.*

The crackle of logs shifting in the fire, muted strings, and the slap of Deirdre's cards were the only sounds in the room. The older woman hadn't moved beyond that first nod when Connie entered. Now she looked up. "Charlie had a younger brother. He died when he was only one. Pneumonia."

Jackie cocked her head, as if speculating on the truth of Deirdre's statement. "Charlie's never mentioned this before."

"Charlie was four at the time. Jealous little devil he was. Tormented the baby."

Connie swallowed her wine. *Charlie a tormentor.*

Jackie pulled a throw cover around her shoulders like a shield against Deirdre's version of Charlie's childhood. "We'll have a snack in a minute. Are you cold, Connie?"

The fire snapped and popped. "Not anymore." Her pants were drying nicely.

The housekeeper entered with trays of sandwiches—steak and caramelized onions on ciabatta and roast chicken and Waldorf salad on crusty rolls. This was Jackie's "snack." More like an early dinner—and a delicious one, from the looks of it. Connie, ravenous from having missed lunch, filled a plate. Between the wine, the food, and the fire, she had relaxed, almost ready for a nap. Yet she had to force herself to ward off drowsiness, to stay alert in order to drive back to Hallison as soon as the storm let up.

"This is fantastic," Connie said between mouthfuls of chicken and Waldorf salad.

"Lena does a wonderful job." Jackie gestured toward the sandwiches. "Deirdre?"

Jackie's mother-in-law waved away the offer and concentrated on her game, all talk of Charlie's dead brother terminated. Connie and Jackie ate and drank and chatted about growing up in Colmar versus Hallison, family vacations, and childhood memories. Connie marveled that she and Jackie had so much to share, despite their lives having been lived out in wildly dissimilar circumstances. Deirdre continued to play solitaire, only occasionally raising her head to glance at them with undisguised indifference.

Connie's phone buzzed—a text from Gaby. She read the succinct message—COME HOME—and typed an answer: *I will when the storm settles and roads are safe.* Her cell was on low battery. Never mind. She'd be on her way before too long. "Jackie, you're a lifesaver," she said as her host topped off her wine. Good thing she would be sticking around for a bit.

A thud from the back of the house interrupted their conversation as a draft blew down the hallway outside the library. The candles flickered.

Connie shuddered. Something wasn't right.

The shadow at the door of the library moved. "What am I missing?" *Charlie.*

Chapter 39

Now

Jackie rose from the depths of the sofa to give Charlie a kiss—he turned his head at the last minute, so it landed on his cheek and not his mouth. His eyes bore into Connie's.

"Hi," Connie said, her heart thumping at the back of her constricted throat. "I'm waiting out the storm. Still raining?" Her voice bright and easy. And fake. She set the plate with the remains of her sandwich on the coffee table. She'd lost her appetite.

A block of fear had planted itself squarely in her gut. There wasn't much that scared her, not since she'd left home fifteen years ago. She'd been anxious about coming home, and more recently, wary of BJ and her father. Rage had been a constant companion for years. But sheer terror? Unfamiliar to her. Until now.

Even without documented proof, Connie was suddenly certain Charlie had killed her mother.

What would he do if he suspected she was on to him? The image of her mother strangled with her own scarf rose up before her eyes.

Charlie, ignoring Jackie and Deirdre, crossed the room to stand directly opposite her. "How's my goddaughter?" He bent down and

286

hugged her. An awkward bit of business with her sunk into the sofa cushions.

"All good," she said into the fabric of his coat's lapel, her voice muffled, tendrils of his damp hair brushing her cheek.

He straightened and removed his suit jacket, dropping it on a chair near Deirdre. He looked the same and yet different. Malevolent. "Mother," he said as he passed her on his way to the fireplace.

"Drink?" Jackie asked, her manner frosty now, one hand on the whiskey decanter. "Your conference was canceled?"

"Yes, and yes. Highways are flooded. No one's going anywhere tonight." He rubbed his hands with vigor, his features unruffled notwithstanding what must have been a stressful ride home from the city.

Connie emptied her wine glass in a single gulp. Gaby would be worried out of her head if she knew Charlie had shown up. She had to get away from Colmar and back to Hallison. She had to get home. Connie was done investigating. Time to defer to Detective Rutherford. "I'm going to give it a try, at least. Gaby needs me at home."

Charlie angled his head at "needs."

"It's Dad. He's not feeling well." Connie rose. "Thanks so much for your kindness. I've been here a lot and—"

"You can't drive in this," Jackie said. "No lights in Colmar and who knows where else? There's standing water in the roads—"

"I'll make it. Drove through a mud slide once in California."

Connie tried to smile gamely but Jackie wasn't having it. Charlie sipped his drink, quiet for once, and Deirdre looked on, attentive at last, curious to see how this would end.

"Nope." Jackie crossed her arms. "Can't let you do this. Charlie?" She appealed to her husband for reinforcement.

He shrugged. "If she wants to go, we should let her go. Drive carefully," he said, reverting to the supportive, soothing Uncle Charlie.

Without missing a beat, Connie slipped past Jackie, waved a limp goodbye to Charlie and Deirdre, and darted for the kitchen, her host in pursuit. "I don't understand," Jackie said. "What's the rush? Call Gaby and explain. She'll understand. She wouldn't want you to take unnecessary chances."

Connie had her arms in her damp jacket, her sneakers halfway on, wet socks stuffed in her pocket. She couldn't explain to Jackie that her husband, as of yesterday, scared the shit out of her. The sooner she escaped from the Flint estate the better. She dashed out of the house, smack into a wall of water, the deluge relentless, Jackie yelling after her.

Inside her car, she whispered a prayer of thanks, locking the doors and cranking the engine. It ground over and over. Nothing happened.

Panic rose in Connie's chest. Squeezing her heart and lungs, sending a rush of adrenaline coursing through her body. She tightened her grip on the ignition key and cranked again.

A tap on her window. A jolt. Charlie. Ducked under a rain slicker, rivulets of water trickling down his cheeks, his hair matted to his forehead. His normally genial demeanor, distorted by a dim flashlight in the darkness, replaced with a grotesque mask.

"Connie, come inside!" He tried the door handle, his words almost inaudible in the wind and rain.

Connie pumped the accelerator again and again.

"You're flooding it. Come on. Dry off and I'll drive you home later."

All of her instincts told her to ignore his offer, but she couldn't stay in the car all night. She couldn't run, she couldn't drive. It was either the house or remain in the car. At least in the house she wouldn't be alone with him.

Connie trailed Charlie, her sneakers sloshing water again, her pants wet again. In the kitchen, Jackie greeted Connie with another dry towel and ushered her back into the library and the cocoon of warmth.

On the inside, she shook, her brain rattling through next steps. Outside, she was the grateful guest. More food, more drinks—that Connie sipped slowly—more conversation. Time passing. At one point, Charlie left the room and headed down the hallway, returning with a liquor bottle. He poured. "Scotch. Macallan. Fifty-five-year-old stuff. I was the highest bidder at a charity event," he boasted. "Spent a neat twenty-five thousand for the pleasure of sipping this gorgeous liquid. Every shot worth sixteen hundred dollars. Can I get you one?"

"No. Thank you." Connie smiled.

"Jackie?"

"You know I don't drink Scotch." She shifted her focus to Connie. "He likes to show off that bottle. Makes him feel like a rich man." The implication clear: Jackie's money was responsible for his affluent swagger.

The electrified atmosphere, on the verge of ugly, pressed Connie to speak up. "Would you mind if I charged my phone? Battery is almost dead."

"Use mine," Charlie said, extending his cell.

Caught. Any truthful text to Gaby would reveal her situation. She had to mask her real intentions. "Sure." Charlie would read whatever she wrote, so she typed carefully: *my phone's out of charge. this is Charlie's. roads too bad to drive now. I'll text in a bit.* She returned his phone imagining Gaby's distress, her demand to come straight home after visiting the Flint Theatre.

While her hosts played out a whack-a-mole conversation—Connie had never seen this kind of discord between them, fighting over everything from the weather prognosis and the cost of the lighting system repair to a planned European winter holiday—she breathed evenly to clear her mind. What was wrong with her rental car this time? It had run fine getting from the theatre to Chappelle Road. She filled the gas tank earlier today, so…water damage to electrics? Alternator or battery? Everything had been checked at the auto body shop. This was the second time the automobile had put her in jeopardy. It could not be a coincidence. Sweat formed on her forehead.

Jackie interrupted sparring with her husband to check on Connie. "Are you okay?"

"Fine. Tired. Been a tough time and now…I guess it's all catching up with me." Connie fake yawned. "I think I should call Triple A. Maybe I have a dead battery." Untrue, of course. She also wasn't a member of the American Automobile Association. But any lie to get out of this room, on a phone, on her way out the door. It was a desperation ploy.

"Forget them," Charlie said. "I'll call a friend. A mechanic."

"Jerry. Great idea," said Jackie.

"You don't need to—"

"I wouldn't want to see anything happen to you." Charlie punched a number in his contacts and waited.

The odds were high Charlie had fake called.

"No answer. Going to voicemail." He frowned his way through a message to the mechanic, apologizing for the call in the middle of the thunderstorm, asking for help when he could manage it. Clicking off and telling Connie it might be a while before someone could rescue her from Colmar.

She smiled, fake-grateful, and set her system on high alert. Plan B.

Another hour passed. Connie was ready to take the next step. She stifled a real yawn, agreed that she should spend the night, at Jackie's urging, waiting until the tempest had settled. All Connie wanted was to lay down behind a locked door. At ten o'clock, Deirdre excused herself, but not before she provoked her son when he mentioned that Flint's law firm was studying the legalities surrounding the potential theatre lawsuit.

"I dated Sean Carmody before Patrick O'Shaughnessy," Deirdre said. "Sean was a lawyer. Handsome. Shoulda married him." She studied her son. "You're like your father. Good thing you had no children."

"Mother. Please." Charlie's patience was unconditional where Deirdre was concerned. But even he had limits.

"He was a horrible man. Couldn't be trusted, your father."

Charlie sat forward. "That's enough. Good night."

"He was quick with his fists as far as you were concerned."

Charlie flushed, Jackie looked horrified. "That's not true. Dad never hit me." He shifted in his chair to face Connie. "She makes things up."

Deirdre tossed her head. "I know what I know." She left the room.

The house lights flickered on, then off, then on again.

"Let there be light!" Charlie announced, his good humor returned.

Jackie walked up the winding staircase with Connie and paused outside the door to the bedroom where she'd stayed before. "Sorry about tonight. Deirdre. Charlie...things have been a little rocky on that front lately."

"No problem." Connie hugged her good night and stepped into the guest room. Once Jackie's footfalls had faded away, she locked herself in, leaning against the frame, counting her breaths to calm down. In the dark, the raging storm was visible from the window. Thunder cracked. Rain pounded against the panes. *Trapped. Like a sitting duck.*

Connie rushed to the bathroom, switching on the overhead spots. She caught herself in the mirror and saw Simone staring back at her. The blond, wavy hair, the blue eyes. The heart-shaped face. *Mom!*

She sat on the toilet seat, putting the puzzle together. Deirdre's triangle was not a benign, young-friends-growing-up relationship. It had to be a toxic, obsessive affair. Two men passionately in love with the same person and one of them, even after marriage to a wealthy, beautiful woman, stoked his fires of resentment and hope, for years until he saw his opening. Her parents' divorce. That week in the dressing room, Charlie must have bullied Simone, frightening her, seeing his chance to recapture the love affair of his youth. Love festering like an abscess. He was not to be denied again. Did her mother think about the earlier assault? Did her resistance to Charlie's advances somehow lead to her death?

Connie dropped her head into her hands, agonizing, envisioning that last night. The bedlam backstage at the Flint Theatre, people yelling. Chaos. Connie finding her way to a utility closet, then to the dreaded dressing room. She had spent too much time chasing fantasies, first that her mother might be alive and second that innocent people might be guilty. The truth had confronted her at every turn. Heartrending to release her illusions about the glib, charismatic Charlie, who offered to look out for her, to ask old colleagues about the police presence at the theatre that week. Charlie O'Shaughnessy was a liar, a dangerous man, smart and powerful. And a killer. She was in trouble, her life in jeopardy, and the only way out was to escape from this house.

She threw cold water on her face, scoured the bedroom for a spare cell phone charger with no luck. Her clothes still partially damp, her body jittery. The inviting bed was too risky. Once asleep, she might not wake up for hours. And she needed to be alert in a couple of hours. She would wait, upright, on a settee in the bedroom, until the house was quiet. Until it was safe to leave. Until it was safe to borrow one of the automobiles parked in the lot. Jackie had tossed sets of car keys into a dish by the back entrance. Any one of the cars would do.

Connie awoke with a start. Silence all around. The storm had dwindled to light rain, though the wind continued to rattle the old windows. She checked the alarm clock on the bedside table. Eleven-thirty. Another hour might ensure that the household was asleep for the night. Her pulse had slowed, her breathing regular, though her insides knotted, fear chewing into her intestines.

One more hour.

At twelve-thirty, her adrenaline spiking, Connie slipped her phone into her pants pocket and cracked the door, the soft click of the latch reverberating in the hallway. She clenched her teeth, waiting for someone to appear. No one stirred. She tiptoed on stockinged feet down the staircase. Past the chandelier in the foyer and on to the kitchen. The night light guided her to the wood rack where she had deposited her shoes, now semi-dry, her jacket spread out on an island stool. Connie thrust her feet into the clammy sneakers, threw on the outerwear, and found the container with at least four sets of car keys. On top was the ring for the Mercedes. Jackie's car. There would be time to apologize once everything was sorted out and Charlie in custody. Her beloved Uncle Charlie, arrested for the murder of her mother. She shook her head violently to shove the idea away.

Jackie. How would she react to the charge against her husband? Connie would think about that later. As she turned to unlock the door, she spied a knife set in a wooden block holder. Without a second thought she grabbed a paring knife and slid it into her jacket pocket.

Damn it. Outside, the slow drizzle had transformed into another torrent. Connie's hair dripping, water cascaded into her eyes and mouth as she fumbled with the remote to unlock the car, landing on the leather seats, a puddle forming on the floor mat. The dashboard a jet liner cockpit. The bells and whistles of a luxury automobile. Not the ideal car for a quick getaway. She scanned the options, pressed the ignition button, flipped on the windshield wipers. Ready to put the car in reverse and back out of the parking space.

A tapping on the passenger side window. Connie froze.

Chapter 40

Now

Through the tinted glass Jackie's lips moved, forming the words, "Open up." Connie found the release for the door and Jackie bounded into the passenger seat.

"What are you doing?" she demanded, water trickling from her hair down her cheeks. The slicker she wore doing nothing for her head.

"I'm sorry. I need to get home. My car..." Jackie knew her car wouldn't start. She'd witnessed Charlie's call for service. No one showed up. Another nail in the Charlie-is-guilty coffin.

"So, the answer is to 'borrow' mine? Without my permission?" Jackie sounded more exasperated than angry, more disappointed than outraged.

Connie pressed the ignition, the powerful engine quietly extinguished, the only sound the rain pummeling the windshield. "Jackie, this wasn't the best idea, but I'm worried about—"

Jackie reached across her and pushed open the driver's side door. "Get out."

Connie's wet hands slipped off the steering wheel as she resigned herself to whatever came next—Plan B was dead in the water. No Plan

C beyond mute obedience presented itself. Wind rushed into the Mercedes from the passenger side door, still open. Jackie motioned impatiently for Connie to…what? Switch seats with her. Without questioning, Connie ran around the car, sliding wordlessly past Jackie by the trunk, and they exchanged seats. The engine roared back to life.

"You'd better buckle up. Could be a bumpy ride." Jackie waited while Connie fastened the seat belt, then pulled out of the parking spot, spun the car in an arc, and headed down the driveway.

A flash of lightning lit up the interior of the car, Connie wincing, and revealed the tension in Jackie, her death grip on the wheel. The weather had gotten to her too. Or the hour. The clock on the dash read one-fifteen.

"Sorry I woke you up." Connie breathed easier.

Jackie smiled wryly. "In time to see my car being 'borrowed.'"

"Again…I'm sorry."

A tight shrug. "I suffer from insomnia. Charlie could sleep through a dozen alarms. Not me. If I get four hours of sleep a night, I'm lucky." She swerved to avoid standing water, easily maneuvering back into her lane. "What's the problem?" she asked, raising her voice above the roar of rain and the rumble of thunder.

"Problem?"

"With Liam? You said he wasn't feeling well?"

Connie's mind scrambled for an answer, only to be rescued by her fifteen-year-old self. Improvising excuses for missing her "curfew." Lying, really. "Since the accident on the parkway"—which wasn't an accident—"Dad's had these headaches."

Jackie glanced sideways. "I'm sorry to hear that."

"They pass, but I hate to leave Gaby alone to handle him."

"She'll be alone soon enough. When you head back to California."

"I suppose."

"Sounds like you're not sure about that." Jackie slowed at an intersection where the red lights had become blinking yellow lights.

"Gaby would like me to stay. I'm…thinking things over." It was true. Connie had found herself weighing the pros and cons of remaining in New Jersey, despite her father's wishes. She stared at the darkened street through streams of water running down the car window. "Where are we?"

"I'm taking backroads to Hallison. To avoid flooding."

Really? Backroads were surely more likely to flood than the parkway. Still, who was Connie to argue with her liberator? She didn't recognize the area. Houses farther and farther apart, roads deserted at this hour.

"I assume both Gaby and Liam are asleep," Jackie said. "So leaving in the middle of the night perhaps wasn't necessary?"

"Guess I had an attack of insomnia too."

"Huh. You look like you just woke up. Like you're running away from something. Or someone."

The knot of tension that had melted as they drove away from the Flint mansion slithered back into her chest, a strain to take a full breath. How much to share with Jackie? Was Charlie a threat to his wife as well?

"Hard to know where to begin."

"It's about Simone's death, isn't it?" Jackie asked gently.

"It's always been about Mom's death. My entire life, from the day she disappeared. What happened. Who did it."

Jackie sighed. "And you won't stop until you get answers."

"I can't let it go until they catch the person responsible. I want to see someone go to jail for this." *Someone has to catch the bastard.*

"Avenge her death."

"Never thought of it that way, but yeah, I guess so." Connie had no idea where they were. With the windshield so inundated with water, she couldn't see three feet in front of them.

"And you think Charlie is guilty," Jackie said, matter-of-factly.

Blood pounded in her ears. Had it become that obvious?

Jackie filled the gaping silence smoothly. "You don't need to say anything. It's clear what you've been doing."

Connie mumbled, "Huh?" Suddenly nauseous.

Jackie shrugged as if it were the most natural thing in the world. "Building a case against him."

She twisted sideways in her seat. "Jackie, I..."

"I don't blame you." Her smile grim. "If I were you, I'd be doing the same thing. Asking questions. Investigating on your own. Frankly, I never trusted that detective who ran the case." She waved a hand in the air. "Cops. Why did I ever get involved with one? Must have been his charm and good looks. I was susceptible. Your mother, too."

"No, my mother loved my father. She was done with Charlie."

A clipped laugh. "No one has ever been *done* with Charlie. Not Liam, not Deirdre, not Simone. Not even me. Especially me. Can't help myself." Her expression, hidden by the night, impossible for Connie to read. "He thinks he's invincible, but always it's me who has to save him. Charlie gets sloppy sometimes."

No cars behind them or in front of them. Connie's body went numb. The wind lashing the car, the wipers struggling to keep pace with the gushing water. A streak of lightning turned the night into day.

"Jackie...what are we doing here?" The words catching in Connie's throat.

"Saving my marriage, of course."

Connie counted slowly to offset the terror creeping throughout her body. "Let's talk about this."

"I'm sorry, Connie. I was beginning to think we could have been good friends. But you couldn't let it go."

"I don't know everything. Like what exactly happened that night..."

"You don't need to lie."

"I'm not lying."

"You really are too smart for your own good. I told Charlie to encourage you to leave town. For your own good. He's usually so damned persuasive."

Jackie's calm demeanor and steady voice terrified Connie. Her fingers found the door handle while her whirling mind assembled the pieces of the murder to form a whole. Who had access to the theatre's grid system to check out the damage? Who would need BJ to escort her up top? Pushing him off, unprotected, would not have been too difficult. And Mom...

Stall her. Keep talking. Distract her. "You were at the theatre the week before Mom disappeared."

Jackie laughed as though Connie were a child who needed to be reminded of bedtime. "Of course. I was in the show."

"When the lights went out..."

"Onstage, like everyone else."

"BJ told me to 'ask her.' He must have meant you." Connie dipped her head to clear the bits of information bombarding her. "Did he see you with Mom? What did he hear?"

"BJ. Such a simple soul. So trusting. Always backstage. Working."

Connie untangled the mounting evidence. "BJ saw you...what...threaten Mom?" Given Jackie's status as the benefactor of the Flint, BJ—"simple soul" that he was—would have kept that evidence to himself. Until I pushed him to talk.

A gun appeared in Jackie's right hand.

"Jackie!" Connie screamed. "No!" Her mouth dry, pulse pounding.

"My beloved soon-to-be husband, wooing Simone all week. Promising her a future, a life she could never imagine with your father. Then suggesting we call off our engagement." Jackie threw back her head, releasing an ugly grunt. "As if I would ever let that happen." She stomped on the gas pedal and the sedan shot forward, fishtailing a bit and then gripping the road. Piloted erratically with just one hand. "The two of them together. Well. I told her point blank to leave my fiancé alone."

"You warned her."

"He was mine. Not Simone's."

One of them would have had to go. It would not have been Charlie.

"The green monster," Deirdre had said. "A triangle."

"Jackie. Listen to me: Charlie thought Dad and Mom were getting a divorce and he'd have the inside track. But he didn't know that Mom left a message for Dad that night. Calling it off."

Connie was crying now, body shaking. Her mother didn't need to die. Waste and ruin. Needless death. Her breathing short and choppy, she fought off a violent wave of sadness and regret as the Mercedes swerved onto the rattling berm, then back up onto the road. Jackie shot a look at Connie and hesitated as though working it through. Had she killed Simone for nothing?

"Charlie loves *me*, not some childhood sweetheart." Jackie spat out the last words like poison choking her every breath.

Connie's mother had been more than a childhood sweetheart.

Distracted by Jackie's admissions, Connie lost sight of their location. Now she recognized the road leading out of Colmar. The construction site.

She had to do something before they reached the gravel lane and the chain link fence.

The paring knife. Connie clasped its handle in her coat pocket. Images of her father and sister blurred her vision. The turnoff to the construction area lay ahead. Limbs blown off trees lining the road, the wind ripping others free, sending them spinning in the headlights' upper glow before vanishing into the black. Thunder shook the earth.

Hell was breaking open.

"Dad and Gaby are going to miss me." Connie's voice trembled. "Wonder about my car. Where I am. What are you going to tell Charlie?"

"Charlie isn't near as smart as he thinks he is. As for the others…well…no one will think to return to the scene of the original crime. It won't be difficult to make your car disappear."

Jackie was so composed. "You have an answer for everything."

"Have to. Living with Charlie."

The turnoff to the gravel road appeared.

No! Jackie had murdered her mother. She wouldn't murder Connie without a fight.

A jagged white line split the sky with a tremendous boom, exposing Jackie's profile. Her features distorted, her mouth a sneer. The treetops to their left shook violently as though some enormous beast was striding through them. Vicious snaps. Branches plummeted to the ground. Debris scattered all around them, bouncing off the hood of the car.

At the speed Jackie was traveling, with only one hand on the steering wheel, she'd have to concentrate to make the turn into the woods. Jackie bent over the wheel. Jamming on the brakes. Connie counted to three. Lunging, aiming the paring knife for the hand holding the gun. The blade missed her palm but sank into Jackie's forearm. She screamed. A shot fired, ricocheting off the car's roof. The Mercedes bounced and skidded. Spinning in a complete circle. The driver's side slashing toward a tree.

Connie's head bounced off the seat back, her body collided with an air bag. Then, nothing.

Chapter 41

Now

Connie opened her eyes. The rain was a light drizzle again. How long had she been unconscious? The odor of post-lightning ozone hung in the air, rushing through the opened door of the car. Searing pain stabbed her head, her neck, her torso. Burning, yet freezing. Shaking. All was quiet. Moving her head a couple of inches allowed peripheral vision and a glimpse of Jackie, crushed beneath the mangled door and deployed side airbag. Her head wedged between the steering wheel and the dashboard.

Where her face should have been, there was only a mass of splotchy, dark matter.

Connie closed her eyes. Every inhalation hurt like hell. Recalled images and sounds swam before her—headlights shining on trees, the chain link fence picking up and reflecting the illumination, the scraping boom as tree struck metal. The ghostly silhouette of the rising condo buildings in the distance. Flint Development. She passed out again.

Connie heard the siren before she saw flashing red and blue lights, heard a mix of voices, some shouting orders, some soothing, someone telling her that "everything was going to be okay." She was alive. She had survived.

"Can you hear me?" a voice asked.

Her eyes drifted open. The outline of a uniformed paramedic. Behind him, the sky a pale gray-blue. Morning.

Another voice. "Her name's Connie Tucker."

"Connie? Can you hear me?" The question again. Someone slipping an oxygen mask over her mouth and nose, checking her vital signs.

Her mouth, now rigid from the icy air, moved with great effort. "Jackie…" The word nearly inaudible, as the technicians released her from the seat belt.

"Don't try to talk. We'll get you taken care of."

"Oh," she groaned in agony as they removed her from the car and lifted her onto the stretcher.

Movement on her left caused her to shift her eyes slightly to witness activity around Jackie. Jackie's body.

"Too late, she's gone," someone said.

Warmed by a metallic blanket as they rolled her to an ambulance, Connie drifted off.

Machines beeped, nurses and staff bustled in and out of her room in the Intensive Care Unit of the hospital. Shoes squeaking, the smell of disinfectant permeating the air, a battery of tests being run.

When Connie woke up briefly, twelve hours after being rescued, a doctor ran down her injuries—bruised torso, lacerations to her face, a minor concussion, hypothermia—and offered the startled declaration that she was fortunate to be alive. She had survived a horrendous car crash. The driver wasn't as fortunate.

Twenty-four hours later she was transferred out of the ICU and into a room on the third floor. Clicking through television stations and cable, finding nothing of interest. Boredom setting in. Restless, she flipped pages of magazines her father and Gaby had brought in this morning. The sisters had hugged—carefully, due to Connie's bruises—then cried, then laughed.

"Finally, you're awake," Gaby had said.

"How long was I out?"

"Off and on for a day and a half. Since they brought you in from the crash site. You were sedated for the pain." She poured Connie a glass of water. "You were so lucky."

"They keep telling me. But Jackie..."

"I know. Thank God for that truck driver who spotted the wreck," Gaby said. Her eyes full of questions. Unspoken.

"Yes." Connie's eyes added *we'll talk later*.

Her father edged closer to the bed from his position near the window ledge. His eyes glistened, his chin trembling as he touched the crisp, white sheet that covered Connie. "How're you feeling?"

"I'm sore all over. The pain meds help." They met each other's eyes, both of them remembering their last conversation—her father asking Connie to leave, to return to California. Neither of them wanting to acknowledge it.

"You talk to Tom Rutherford?" her father asked.

Detective Rutherford. While in the ambulance on her way to the emergency room, she managed to spit out a few words: "gun" being one; "police" being another; "Simone" being the third. Her father had contacted Rutherford after local cops found the gun legally registered to Jackie inside the mangled Mercedes. No mention of the paring knife. So far. Simpler to keep that bit of information to herself if it never turned up. Jackie's injuries were so extensive, a stab wound on her arm would have been dismissed as insignificant.

"He came by this morning," she told him. "Before visiting hours. I was kind of groggy."

It had been an agonizing conversation, though Tom Rutherford had been appropriately subdued, to his credit listening instead of swaggering his way through their talk. Connie related the events of the night of the accident: her car not starting, Charlie offering to call for help that never arrived, the feeling of being held prisoner at the Flint estate, her escape, only to be caught by Jackie. Then the terrifying ride to the construction site and Jackie's confession: She'd seen Charlie attempting to seduce Simone the week before her disappearance and threatened her, a warning overheard by BJ. Jackie had had no intention of letting Charlie and Simone—or Connie now, for that matter—destroy her marriage.

"She had to remove my mother, BJ, and me from the picture."

"Why you?"

"I asked too many questions."

With no witnesses, and with Jackie incriminating herself for Simone's death, Connie's testimony of the incident was all Rutherford had. Any reservations about her account, and frustration about her "playing detective," he kept to himself. Let the dead—all of them—rest. With Jackie's admission to Connie, the cold case investigation would be closed for good.

"I have to get to the library," Gaby had said at last. "You take it easy, okay? We gotta keep you out of cars." She smiled and kissed Connie's forehead. "I'll stop back tonight."

Her father had sighed. "Connie..."

"I'm glad you came, Dad." She'd grabbed his hand and squeezed it.

"You get better. I want to see you at home soon." He'd followed Gaby out the door.

Brigid and Finn stopped in. She carried flowers, he had a book in his hands.

She shook her head. "Oh, Connie..." Her eyes misted. Wiping her face, she laid the flowers on the rolling bedside table and cupped Connie's chin. "You're going to be this kid's godmother. She'll need a kickass role model."

They laughed, embraced, and Brigid made Connie promise to text later. "Gotta go. Mom's got the baby in the car, and he's been a pain all morning. If this one's a boy..." She rolled her eyes, patted her brother on the arm. "Be good." She walked out.

Finn sat on the edge of the bed. "What you've been through." He kissed Connie on the cheek and touched a bruise on her neck. "Brigid's right about the kickass role model."

Connie smiled and took his hand. "Thanks for coming."

"You think I'd miss the chance to give you a get-well gift and prove a literary giant wrong?" He extended the book and grinned.

She read the title and laughed. *"You Can't Go Home Again."*

"Thomas Wolfe couldn't block out all the crap." This time he gently planted a kiss on her mouth. "Unlike you."

The wall clock indicated time for lunch. Though not the least bit hungry, it would consume some of the seemingly limitless time crawling by. She was an impatient patient. Marking time before lunch's arrival, she skimmed a theatre review of a new Broadway musical. Which reminded her of the Flint Theatre, hoping it would survive Jackie's death.

A shuffling of footsteps at the door caused her to look up. Old Man Porter, hair neatly combed, shirt and tie, all spiffed up for the hospital visit. She set the magazine aside and adjusted the back of the bed, allowing her to sit up. "Come in."

Porter entered, kissed her cheek, and settled into the visitor chair. He smelled of the grill, she thought. Occupational hazard. "'Ya doing okay, toots?"

"Yeah. I should get out tomorrow. Nice of you to drop by."

They sat, silent, for a time. "Jackie Flint," he finally said. "Only met her twice. Charlie stayed away from the bar once he married up." The Old Man extended a brown paper bag. "Hospital food is lousy."

"Thanks." She peeked in the bag. "Wow."

"Burger and fries. Hope they're not cold by now."

Turned out she *was* hungry. She could've kissed him.

Word had spread about the accident via *The Star-Ledger*, and the Hallison neighborhood grapevine was abuzz. What was Connie Tucker doing with Jackie Flint on a backroad in Colmar at two a.m. in the middle of a horrific storm? The newspaper hinted at a Good Samaritan deed on Jackie's part to return Connie to Hallison to deal with a family issue. Never stated what that was. According to Detective Rutherford, the Flint Organization had sicced a spin doctor on the event, airbrushing away any mention of the weapon or Jackie's role in Simone's murder. Painting Charlie as the beloved grieving husband. The Flints had friends in high places.

Connie had had no contact with Charlie since the accident. Though only Gaby knew Connie had blamed him for their mother's murder, after Jackie's confession, Connie suffered a guilty conscience. It was distressing to relive that night when Connie held him responsible, terrified that he would do the same to her.

Their father had reached out to Charlie, but his voice mailbox was full, no longer taking messages. Calling the landline at the Flint home resulted in a neutral communication that advised the caller the number had been disconnected. There was no public funeral service for Jackie, that the Tuckers were aware of, and no burial information in the obituary column of *The Star-Ledger*. None of this was surprising to Connie and a small circle of confidants who heard the true story of Jackie's death. It would be difficult for the Flint family, including Charlie, to celebrate Jackie's life, or honor her death, when the facts bore witness to her hideous end. And guilt.

It was possible Connie had seen the last of Uncle Charlie for a while.

"Don't make me laugh!" On the front porch swing Connie held her bruised sides, listening to Brigid recount the latest mishap in her hectic household involving three rambunctious boys. Four, if she counted Dack.

"Glad you can laugh. It sure as hell wasn't funny when it was happening," said Brigid, indignant. "A gallon of OJ smeared across the kitchen floor and Dack sitting in the middle of it giggling with the kids."

"Perfect."

"I threw them all out of the house for the day. Told them not to come home until dark." She snorted. "Scared the shit out of everybody."

Connie nodded at Brigid's belly. "How many more weeks?"

"Two, if I'm lucky."

They swung on the glider for a while, absorbing the sounds of Third Street on a breezy early fall afternoon. Two weeks since the accident, five weeks since Connie had arrived in New Jersey, fifteen years to the day since her mother had disappeared from the Flint Theatre.

"Today's the anniversary..." Connie began but her voice faded.

"Yep. *The Star-Ledger* rehashed your mom's story, 'cold case, etc. etc.,' along with another update on Saint Jackie. 'Flint Theatre board president, savior of the arts in Colmar...'" Brigid's volume rose with fierce exaggeration. "'How will the theatre, the town, survive without her?'" She frowned. "Such a fuckin' shame she'll never pay for Simone's killing."

"She paid. Committing that murder cost her her life."

Only Detective Rutherford, Liam, Gaby, Brigid, and Finn were aware of Jackie's guilt. To everyone else, what happened to her mother that night at the theatre would forever be an unsolved cold case. Connie was surprised to learn that she could live with that. With Jackie's admission and death, she'd found her bit of justice. And maybe a tad of vengeance after all.

"So, you're really going back to California this time?"

"For now. Who knows about the future."

Brigid threw her arms around Connie. "You better show up for the christening."

"Wouldn't miss it."

In grade school at Saint Gabriel's, there was a reproduction of Da Vinci's "Last Supper" hanging on the wall of the cafeteria. Connie had been fascinated by the painting—the urgency and discord of the gathering as the disciples argued, whispered among themselves. As a kid, she'd wondered what they were saying to each other, while the central figure sat, calm, above the fray.

Now it was Connie's last supper. Last night in Hallison. She sat at the long, wooden, glossy bar and watched the "fray" around her. People gesturing, waving, pointing, speaking softly and loudly. Not that she felt Christ-like, but the mark left on her over the preceding weeks—coming to terms with her mother's death and the rest of her past in the town—had delivered her to a state she recognized in His expression. Tranquility. Acceptance. Finn was correct: You could go home again.

Dack appeared across the bar and pointed to her empty glass. "Get you another?"

"I'm good."

"We're going to miss you around here. Especially the Old Man." Dack smiled, a tad wistful. "Me too. Who's going to hop behind the bar on nights we're slammed and lend a hand?"

"You'll manage." Connie eyed him. "'Course, after your fourth child enters this world, you and Brigid are going to need some extra help."

He groaned. "Don't remind me."

"Here you go, toots." Old Man Porter stepped in front of Dack and placed Connie's supper before her. He patted her hand. "Don't forget where you came from, okay?"

"I won't. And thanks." She raised up from her stool and leaned closer to kiss his cheek.

He shambled away to the other end of the bar where her father held court, roaring, entertaining patrons, pulling bottles of beer out of the cooler, running the cash register. Happy. In his element. With Jackie's death, her mother's spirit could be put to rest.

Porter's had been many things to the Tucker family: a place to relax, a safe haven, a refuge for her father, particularly the night her mother disappeared. And that back room…his alibi.

As she dug into her meal, a question nibbled at the back of her mind. Was it something she'd heard someone say? Tom Rutherford? Her father? Gaby? Brigid, maybe? No…none of them. She swallowed the last of her dinner, washing it down with the remainder of her seltzer. Like gnats flitting around her head, Connie tried to swat the words away, but they wouldn't budge. She let her mind run backward through the last weeks, until she arrived at the correct moment: In the hospital when the Old Man said he'd only seen Jackie twice in his life. Something about that bothered Connie. Gnawed at her. Idle curiosity. Her mother's funeral repast would have been one time he'd seen Jackie. And Porter had said that Charlie no longer frequented the bar after Jackie came on the scene.

She motioned to the Old Man and he raised a finger. In a minute. Gradually he worked his way to her.

"You need something else?"

"No. No. In the hospital you said you only met Jackie twice. At Mom's funeral was one. What was the other?"

Porter draped a bar towel over his shoulder, surprised at Connie's question. "That night."

Connie stiffened, goose bumps rising on her neck. "You mean the night Mom…?"

"Uh-huh."

"Why would Jackie have come here that night?"

Apprehension blocked out the noise of the bar, the room's light shrinking to a pinpoint on the Old Man's face.

He studied her, wary. "Why does it matter? Forget about what happened. It's all over."

"I'd like to know."

Porter shook his head. "Best I can recollect, she came here asking for Charlie. It was late and she hadn't heard from him. She was worried."

"What time was it?"

"Your dad was already in the back room, and we were closing up. So…eleven-thirty, midnight."

Blood drained from her face. "Oh my God."

"What's the matter?" Porter, alarmed, sent a side glance to Liam ringing up a bill. "You wanna speak to your dad?"

"Tell him I'll see him at home." Connie threw a twenty on the bar.

Chapter 42

Now

She slipped out of Porter's before her father could see her exit, the Old Man's eyes monitoring her movements. His revelation threw Connie into a state of dread. If Jackie was at the bar at eleven-thirty looking for Charlie, there was no way she could have followed her mother from the theatre, killed her and buried her body, and ditched the Ford Tempo. It wasn't possible.

Jackie couldn't have done it.

But she must have found out that Charlie had.

Charlie would assume his wife would cover for him. Maybe he told her it was an accident. She had to "clean up his mess," she'd said. Even if it meant killing Connie. BJ was collateral damage: admitting that he saw and heard Jackie and her mother was his undoing. If the police knew about Jackie's threats against Simone, Jackie might become a suspect and unravel the Flint-O'Shaughnessy cover-up.

Connie had been right about Charlie all along.

At the Tucker house, she dashed inside. "Gaby? Gaby!" It was seven o'clock, the dinner hour. On the kitchen table was a scribbled note. "Having supper with a library friend. I won't be late. We can have a last night drink on the porch later."

Good for Gaby; "library friend" meant the security guard. He seemed like a nice guy. Then reality struck: She'd planned on enlisting her sister to join her. Never mind. It was now or never. Her flight tomorrow left Newark at eleven a.m. The clock was ticking.

Her mother's words, three months before the opening of *A Streetcar Named Desire*, challenged Connie even today. Fifteen years later. As a thirteen-year-old, lying in a hammock in the backyard, in the sticky heat of the midafternoon summer sun. Rejected by an afterschool drama program in New York City. Releasing pent-up tears, she'd sobbed, disappointment like an unwanted garment she'd been forced to wear.

Then, her mother had joined her in the hammock, the two of them swinging, silent.

"It's not the end of the world," her mother had said.

"It is to me."

"No. It's only the end if there is nothing else you can do. Think about it. What else can you do?"

Now, Connie twisted the ring her mother had left for her. She knew what else she could do. Had to do. She had no idea if Charlie was still living at the Flint estate. Phone calls weren't answered; the newspaper articles provided no hint of his whereabouts. She'd drive there and see for herself. Leaving New Jersey without confronting this final truth would doom her to a life in limbo. The very place she'd occupied for fifteen years. No way in hell was she going to let that happen.

Gaby would call her reckless, insane, demanding trouble. She'd try to stand in Connie's way. She'd remind her sister that getting anywhere near Charlie was a death wish now. Especially now.

"I have to do this," Connie said aloud. To herself. "He's betrayed the Tuckers. Me. All of us. Charlie is a monster. I want him to know that I know."

Connie stuffed her car keys and charged phone in her pants pocket. "I have to look him in the eye and tell him I know he murdered my mother. And then I want him to admit it. Even if he's never convicted of the crime. I have to hear it from him."

When she was thirteen, Connie's only option after her mother disappeared was to act out. She wasn't thirteen anymore; there was something she could do now. Call on her inner child—not the one who was so badly hurt, damaged by abandonment. But the headstrong, defiant, resourceful one.

Her mother deserved having someone fight this last battle.

First, she raced to her bedroom and ransacked her packed suitcase until her hand clasped the canister of pepper spray. Usually, she kept it on her key ring, but TSA required it be packed in checked luggage when she flew from San Diego to Newark. It had remained in her suitcase once she arrived in New Jersey. Though it wasn't with her the last time she visited the Flint estate, now it would be.

But she knew pepper spray might not be enough to protect her against the violent, narcissistic Charlie. She bolted out of her bedroom and into her father's. Opening the closet door and reaching for the locked metal box holding her mother's revolver. She raced to the basement and her father's worktable. And his tools. Grabbing the largest claw hammer on his work bench, she swung it at the lock on the metal box. Again, and again. The lock wouldn't give, but the old metal frame did, bending until she could drive the claw head into the dent and rip upward.

She withdrew the compact revolver. She'd overheard her father years ago tell her protesting mother that this was a snub nose .22. A relatively lightweight, simple-to-use revolver. The cold steel of the gun's barrel made her shudder, panic creeping up her spine. Could she do this? Shoot Charlie? Hands shaking as she pressed the latch that released the cylinder, she scooped up the six bullets rattling around in the metal box and loaded the weapon. She snapped the cylinder shut, heard it click into place. Praying that the revolver still functioned and that she'd loaded it correctly, praying she wouldn't have to attempt to use it. She sprinted to the rental car—with a repaired alternator—and turned the automobile toward Colmar.

Rage formed a white-hot sphere in the center of her being. More rage than after her mother disappeared. More rage than in that tempestuous year before leaving for California. This was a surge of feeling that blinded her. Took her back to her troubled teenage years. *No!* she screamed to herself. She had to stay in control. That was the difference now. She would use this rage; it would not use her.

She'd become smarter. Connie called Detective Keogh from the Hallison Police department and left a message, explaining where she was going and why. That he should send the Colmar cops to the Flint residence. Her second message was to Detective Rutherford with the same information.

But it was a Saturday night. Both of them probably off-duty. When would they get her message? How long would it take for the police to arrive at the Flint estate?

She couldn't wait.

The Flint mansion remained a majestic structure, the exterior lighting complementing its façade and landscaping. But its glamour had dimmed, as if the house acknowledged the treachery and deceit within its walls. All of Colmar had dimmed for Connie. Her beautiful fantasy of living in this paradise had been reduced to a pile of ashes.

She pulled to the curb several houses away from Charlie's and switched off the ignition and lights. She'd stuffed the gun into one hoodie pocket, the pepper spray in the other. Waiting. Wondering if either Deirdre or the housekeeper were in the house. Could she accuse Charlie in front of his mother or Lena? She'd have to take that chance.

Connie checked her cell, fingers beating a tattoo on the steering wheel. Fifteen minutes to get here. Ten more minutes sitting in her car on Chappelle Road. No message or callback from either Keogh or Rutherford.

Windows on the front of the Flint estate were dark, until a light flicked on in a downstairs room. By Connie's calculation, that would be Charlie's study. Her heart thumped. That had to be him.

She turned on her cell phone to record whatever Charlie said, then exited her car, slipping down the road to the driveway, moving quickly through the side yard to the rear of the house. Evening descending on the backyard of the mansion, the sun on a downward slope beyond the tree line at the edge of the property. Hidden by shadows as she approached the parking area, she broke out in a cold sweat. Reliving the night of her escape from the house. Jackie at the wheel of the Mercedes.

Charlie's Range Rover was parked in its usual spot.

Her body throbbing, muscles taut, Connie pressed the doorbell for the back entrance into the kitchen. When there was no response, she knocked, fingering the button on the pepper spray, grasping the grip of the gun. She touched the doorknob. It turned.

Connie hesitated. The hallway ahead was dimly lit by wall sconces, the chandelier in the foyer dark.

No sign of the housekeeper.

She inched her way to the doorway between the kitchen and the rest of the house, treading lightly. The place was like a tomb—cold and dank. She shivered. Farther down the hall, light leaked from Charlie's study. She moved closer, jamming her hands into her pockets. With a deep breath, she entered the study.

The handsome, charming Charlie O'Shaughnessy hunched over his desk, a glass and the bottle of Macallan on the blotter in front of him. A bottle of water to the side. He looked up as if he expected her, his eyes glassy, unshaven, hair greasy in need of washing. Dressed in a rumpled dressing gown, open at the throat. A messy, depressing scene.

"Join me?" he said, a pointless attempt at nonchalance.

How far the mighty had fallen. For a fleeting moment Connie felt sorry for the man she had loved for so many years. Only for a moment before the rage returned. This was the butcher who had killed her mother. "Too bad about Jackie," she murmured.

Charlie tossed back a slug of scotch before refilling the glass. "She took chances. In the rain that night."

"I was with her." Connie wasn't sure he'd remembered it.

He had no way of knowing what was said between Jackie and herself in the car. He might have believed the newspaper story concocted by the Flint Corporation that Jackie was driving Connie home because of a family emergency.

Charlie stared at her. "Sorry."

"Anybody tell you what happened in the car?"

He took a drink, fondled the tumbler. "She drove too fast."

"She planned to kill me and bury me where Mom was buried. Flint Development." Her voice on a razor's edge, fighting for control. "I thought it was you who murdered Mom, but then Jackie...I thought she was confessing." Connie shook her head. "But she didn't confess...she was protecting you. Her marriage. She knew you were guilty. That's how much you meant to her. She would kill for you."

He waved this away like he couldn't care less, like it had no bearing on his life. Maybe it didn't anymore.

"The gun went off by mistake. Not really by mistake. And Jackie lost control of the car."

"Gun...?" he muttered, confused.

She finally got it, almost laughed. "You're a fool, Charlie. The Flint machine kept that from you like they probably covered up everything else about the 'accident.'"

She hit the last word so hard, his head snapped back. His face twisted first in surprise, then in anger, and he stood, unstable.

Connie needed him to confess, but she couldn't help herself. She relished the upper hand. "Help me out here. I'm guessing an airtight pre-nup, right? You get nothing. Fired, too. Without Jackie defending you, you didn't stand a chance with the Flint Corporation. And this house?" Connie scanned the room. "You and Deirdre, out on your asses."

"Get out! Get outta here!" he roared, speech slurred.

Her fist encircled the canister of pepper spray. "Tell me about the brakes and GPS tracker. The alternator—?"

"That was your fault. All of it was." He narrowed his eyes. Really seeing Connie for the first time tonight. Then softly, "You don't scare easily. My beautiful goddaughter. I had to keep track of you. Couldn't let you out of my sight."

"Why, Charlie? Why did you have to kill her?" Her rage battled despair. Lost ground. Her lips trembling. "I loved you. My Uncle Charlie." Tears flowed, Connie's resolve shaken.

"I loved you too." Charlie smiled, leaning forward, arms propped on the desk. "But Simone didn't know a good thing when she saw it." His face darkened, his mouth a snarl. "Like all you Tuckers. Pathetic."

His hateful accusation galvanized Connie, her spine stiffening. "Mom wanted you out of her life, didn't she?"

"She loved me. Couldn't admit it."

"Loved you?" A brittle laugh escaped her. "Oh yeah, that had to be it. Because who wouldn't love the charming Charlie O'Shaughnessy?"

He gawked at her as if she'd slapped him, his expression almost comical. Shocked by this heresy.

"You had no idea who she really loved." Angela Westerman.

He dropped into his desk chair and poured another shot of scotch. "Get out before I do something I regret."

"You had it all planned. My parents' divorce would open up the playing field and you could step in. Except that you scared her and Mom called off the divorce," Connie cried.

He rose and grasped the edge of the desk to steady himself.

"You didn't know that, did you? Anyway, Jackie was never going to let you go. You were trapped."

His mouth twitched, menacing. He took a step toward Connie, and she backed up, rubbing one thumb on the tip of the pepper spray canister, the other on the trigger of the gun. *End this*, she told herself. Get the hell out of this house.

Not yet. She had to know. "How'd you get her out of the theatre that night?"

His chuckle ended in a sneer. "I used you as bait."

"You son of a bitch—"

"She fought me—"

"Like she did the first time you assaulted her," Connie yelled. "Porter told me all about it."

"Porter! Another loser," he roared.

"Damn you, Charlie!" Connie choked on her words.

"I told her. Either she's with me or she's dead." He lurched, weaving, at Connie, his hands rising to grab her. "Nobody says 'no' to me forever."

Her vision a blur of red, she backed farther away from him, pointed and pressed the pepper spray, covering her face with her hood, hitting Charlie, some of it landing in his eyes.

He screamed, then howled, arms flailing, staggering backwards. "What the hell? Help me! Gimme something...my eyes!"

He stumbled into the desk chair, moaning, searching the expansive surface of the desk without success for the bottle of water.

Connie's chest heaving, her breath ragged, she stared at her Uncle Charlie in pain. She opened the water and poured it over his head. "This is more mercy than you showed my mother."

Footsteps ran down the hallway as Detective Keogh and two Colmar cops entered the study.

Connie whirled to see them, then turned back to Charlie. The four of them watched as he leaned back in his chair, past the tipping point, and the once-charming, Big Irishman toppled backward.

Connie spun away from the sight, collapsing in relief, Detective Keogh grabbing her before she hit the ground.

It was over.

Chapter 43

Now

The wind chimes at The Shack tinkled in the mid-November breeze, the California sun sinking lower, the day ending. In the chill of the early evening, a handful of brave beachgoers on the sand below the bar packed up towels and chairs and coolers, the smell of salt air wafting in from the ocean. A tune bounced from the speaker on the shelf above the bar, the singer chirping on and on about his one true love. Can't live without her. So glad he found her. Grateful. Connie cocked her head as she tallied a check, bobbing to the beat of the tune. Also grateful, these days.

One of her regulars, at the other end of the bar, waggled an empty beer bottle and she raised a hand in acknowledgment, humming as she grabbed a Heineken and snapped off the lid. She delivered the drink and the check and strolled back to the cash register in time to hear the ping of her cell phone.

A text from Gaby: *Do you like sweet potato pie?*

Connie laughed. Her sister was taking the whole Thanksgiving host thing to a new level. She texted back an all-caps *YES* and added a turkey emoji. She would call her later.

The cell towers had been busy since Connie's return from Hallison, the sisters talking almost every other day and texting in between. They'd made plans for the holiday—Gaby cooking up a storm, inviting a few folks to join them and their father including Mrs. Delano, Old Man Porter, since the bar closed on Thanksgiving, and the library security guard, who was quickly becoming a fixture in her life. Finn had also been heating up the ether, making plans for a winter break in the San Diego warmth.

Connie's Thanksgiving visit back east would coincide with the christening of Brigid's baby—a girl, finally, named Maureen Constance. Connie could hardly refuse to serve as godmother when the child had her name. Dack was ecstatic to have a daughter, and Brigid, relieved the infant was healthy, claimed she was swearing off sex unless Dack got snipped. Connie would have paid a lot to be a fly on the wall for that conversation.

It would be a very festive, fun weekend.

Traveling east again would be exciting this time. No foreboding, not wary about facing her past, or her father. Seeing Hallison through a new lens—with affection instead of acrimony, as a liberated adult instead of a hurt child. The town would always trigger painful memories for her, she knew, but the deepest wounds had begun to heal, the scars fading. In their place was room to breathe.

After the horrific encounter with Charlie, Detective Keogh took her to the Colmar police station where, shaking uncontrollably, she described the events at the Flint estate, and turned over her recording of Charlie confessing to the murder of her mother, though it wouldn't hold up in court. The police assured her they would bring him in for questioning. Detective Keogh said he'd contact Tom Rutherford and the cold case unit.

As a courtesy, Rutherford called the next week with news. After several hours at the station, Charlie O'Shaughnessy was arrested, lawyered up, and out on bail. He then disappeared into thin air. They put out an APB on him, but Connie knew it was pointless. As a former cop, Charlie understood how to escape the law. He'd done it for fifteen years, after all.

She read *The Star-Ledger* online, following New Jersey news, especially local events. The Flint Corporation was thriving, the new condominium development on schedule for a ribbon-cutting ceremony a year from now. At the Flint Theatre, Ted and company had planned a second half of the current season beginning in January. Notable was the appointment of a new board, with Angela Westerman as president. Gaby had passed on neighborhood news gleaned from the rumor mill. The O'Shaughnessy family had sunk into oblivion, Deirdre surfacing in Newark with relatives. No mention of Charlie.

Though Gaby grilled her about that last night at the Flint estate, Connie had pleaded the fifth on details, assuring her sister that Charlie had confessed, was guilty for the crime of murdering their mother, and would probably never serve time in prison. Gaby decided to leave well enough alone, with none of them having to see him ever again.

"Hey," her regular called out. "Whatever happened to all of that ABBA music? Haven't heard one of their songs for months."

"I've outgrown them. Time for a change."

Her cell phone rang. Connie glanced at the number. Gaby. She smiled.

Acknowledgments

The seeds of *The First to Die* were planted years ago. On a family vacation, my brother-in-law related a story about a woman he knew and it immediately triggered a thought: what an interesting character she would make, once I found the right story to give her a fictional life. Many drafts later, the plot of the novel twisted and turned, characters arrived and departed, the story morphed again, and the woman who inspired the original idea for the book became a secondary character. Still, some themes and relationships remained pretty much intact. The creative process is, truly, a zigzag affair. So, thank you, John Huffman.

I am grateful to Between the Lines Publishing for the care and support they provided at every step along the way. Thanks to Abby Macenka for believing in the novel, Cherie Macenka for attention to details, Siân Helyg for keeping the project on track, Morgan Bliadd for beautiful artwork, and Amber Soha for her editing eye.

The novel couldn't have been born without the editorial guidance given to various versions of the story by Elaine Ash, Judith Lindbergh at the Writers Circle, Tiffany Yates Martin, and David Downing. Their feedback was invaluable in shaping the words and structure of the story.

My gratitude, as always, to my wonderful sisters—Kate, Patty, Jeanette, Eileen, Denise, and Charlene. And Mom, always. Your love and encouragement through the years have kept me plowing ahead with this writing thing. Many thanks to my growing family of nieces and nephews. You all are a lot of fun! I also appreciate my lifelong friends who have provided great company, a welcome sounding board, and refreshments now and then.

I am grateful to my early readers for taking the time out of their busy lives to supply quotes and reviews, and thanks to Barbara Bos and Women Writers, Women's Books, and Dru Ann Love of Dru's Musings. You are champions to writers everywhere! I am grateful to authors I have read and reread and been inspired by, including Megan Abbott, Louise Penny, Hank Phillippi Ryan, Karen Dionne, S.A. Cosby, Lori Rader-Day, Attica Locke, and David Baldacci, among many others.

And, yes, I am thankful for New Jersey because there are so many potential stories in this fertile Garden State. More to come...

Finally, love and gratitude to Elaine, my first and most significant reader. I owe you.

Suzanne Trauth is a novelist and playwright. Her novels include *What Remains of Love* and the Dodie O'Dell mystery series, as well as plays and non-fiction books. In her previous career, she spent many years as a university professor of theatre. She is a member of the Mystery Writers of America, Sisters in Crime, the Dramatists Guild, and the League of Professional Theatre Women and lives in Woodland Park, New Jersey.

Visit her website: www.suzannetrauth.com or connect on Facebook: https://www.facebook.com/SuzanneTrauth

Praise for *What Remains of Love*

Trauth's novel builds on several subtle layers that beautifully blend to create a profoundly moving story. A phenomenal story of life and everlasting love, What Remains of Love will remain with readers long after the last page. Highly recommended. - **S. Hinrichs, Chanticleer Review**

What Remains of Love is a tenderly wrought novel by author Suzanne Trauth, who is also an award-winning playwright and screenwriter. Clearly, her dialogue-writing expertise is critical to the page-turning flow of this carefully braided story, a heart-centered and brave tale about believable people who struggle with what is most human in themselves. Readers will recognize the truth of their own meaningful experiences, and that of their often fate-bound families. A list of engaging "Questions for Discussion" included in the book, invites readers to consider how their own family secrets, told or untold, might affect familial connection and intimacy across generations. A perfect book for book clubs! **--Susan F. Glassmeyer, author of *Invisible Fish*, and *Four Blue Eggs: American Cinquains***

"Beautifully written and timely, *What Remains of Love* perfectly blends one family's history with today's times. A five-star book by Suzanne Trauth that gives deep insight into two generations and the depth of love and sacrifice made to honor a promise. Beautifully done." **-Books and Pens on Green Gables**

"A wartime love affair between a young French girl and American soldier in the 1940s. The daughter of this American soldier who finds out about her father's long lost love after his passing. Secrets uncovered in an old diary and mementos of precious time spent. What Remains of Love is beautifully written in both past and present tense with descriptions of France in the 1940s and the effect the war had. Heartbreaking, eye-opening, and unputdownable, readers will cherish the words on each page as they follow the story through the eyes of Emilie and Kate." —**Kristi Elizabeth, Manhattan Book Review**

What Remains of Love by Suzanne Trauth is a riveting saga of grand passion during the French Resistance in World War II, and its repercussions, which reverberate through generations on both sides of the Atlantic. This is a beautifully told family story of love, mystery, and forgiveness in the face of necessary secrets and the amends that must be made, even beyond the grave. *Can a child ever really know a parent? Can love transcend loss? Can lifelong sacrifice justify unintentional betrayal? And can the heart expand to include relationships long denied?* Trauth tackles it all and more in this gripping, moving, and deeply satisfying novel. A must read! --**Roselee Blooston, award-winning author of** *Dying in Dubai,* **Trial by Family,** **and** *The Chocolate Jar and Other Stories*

Sifting through the effects of her recently deceased father, a woman uncovers the story of his long-ago wartime affair with a beautiful French woman. WHAT REMAINS OF LOVE begins as a family mystery but opens up into a heartfelt story of loves past but not forgotten, of the burden of being torn between passion and honorable commitment, of living with knowing you can't have what you most want. By turns sweet and bittersweet, a touching read. Keep the Kleenex close by. - **Bill Mesce, Jr., Author** *Median Gray*